Sir Walter Scott, Bart

The Waverley Novels by Sir Walter Scott, Bart

The heart of Mid-Lothian. I VOL. XI

Sir Walter Scott, Bart

The Waverley Novels by Sir Walter Scott, Bart
The heart of Mid-Lothian. I VOL. XI

ISBN/EAN: 9783741194436

Manufactured in Europe, USA, Canada, Australia, Japa

Cover: Foto ©Andreas Hilbeck / pixelio.de

Manufactured and distributed by brebook publishing software
(www.brebook.com)

Sir Walter Scott, Bart

The Waverley Novels by Sir Walter Scott, Bart

WAVERLEY NOVELS

WAVERLEY NOVELS.

VOL. XI.

HEART OF MID-LOTHIAN.

THE

WAVERLEY NOVELS

BY

SIR WALTER SCOTT, BART.

VOL. XI.

THE HEART OF MID-LOTHIAN—I.

EDINBURGH:

ADAM AND CHARLES BLACK.

1860.

LIST OF ILLUSTRATIONS.

* * *

Engravings on Steel.

Engravings on Wood.

vi   LIST OF ILLUSTRATIONS

THE HEART OF MID-LOTHIAN.

INTRODUCTION—(1829.)

THE author has stated in the preface to the Chronicles of the Canongate, 1827, that he received from an anonymous correspondent an account of the incident upon which the following story is founded. He is now at liberty to say, that the information was conveyed to him by a late amiable and ingenious lady, whose wit and power of remarking and judging of character still survive in the memory of her friends. Her maiden name was Miss Helen Lawson, of Girthhead, and she was wife of Thomas Goldie, Esq., of Craigmuie, Commissary of Dumfries.

Her communication was in these words:

"I had taken for summer lodgings a cottage near the old Abbey of Lincluden. It had formerly been inhabited by a lady who had pleasure in embellishing cottages, which she found perhaps homely and even poor enough ; mine therefore possessed many marks of taste and elegance unusual in this species of habitation

in Scotland, where a cottage is literally what its name
declares.

"From my cottage door I had a partial view of the
old Abbey before mentioned; some of the highest
arches were seen over, and some through, the trees
scattered along a lane which led down to the ruin, and
the strange fantastic shapes of almost all those old ashes
accorded wonderfully well with the building they at
once shaded and ornamented.

"The Abbey itself from my door was almost on a
level with the cottage; but on coming to the end of the
lane, it was discovered to be situated on a high per-
pendicular bank, at the foot of which run the clear
waters of the Cluden, where they hasten to join the
sweeping Nith,

Whose distant roaring swells and fa's.

As my kitchen and parlour were not very far distant, I
one day went in to purchase some chickens from a person I heard offering them for sale. It was a little,
rather stout-looking woman, who seemed to be between
seventy and eighty years of age; she was almost covered
with a tartan plaid, and her cap had over it a black silk
hood, tied under the chin, a piece of dress still much in
use among elderly women of that rank of life in Scotland; her eyes were dark, and remarkably lively and
intelligent; I entered into conversation with her, and
began by asking how she maintained herself, etc.

"She said that in winter she footed stockings, that
is, knit feet to country-people's stockings, which bears

about the same relation to stocking-knitting that cobbling does to shoe-making, and is of course both less profitable and less dignified; she likewise taught a few children to read, and in summer she whiles reared a few chickens.

"I said I could venture to guess from her face she had never been married. She laughed heartily at this, and said, 'I maun hae the queerest face that ever was seen, that ye could guess that. Now, do tell me, madam, how ye cam to think sae?' I told her it was from her cheerful disengaged countenance. She said, 'Mem, have ye na far mair reason to be happy than me, wi' a gude husband and a fine family o' bairns, and plenty o' every thing? for me, I'm the puirest o' a' puir bodies, and can hardly contrive to keep mysell alive in a' the wee bits o' ways I hae tell't ye.' After some more conversation, during which I was more and more pleased with the old woman's sensible conversation, and the *naïveté* of her remarks, she rose to go away, when I asked her name. Her countenance suddenly clouded, and she said gravely, rather colouring, 'My name is Helen Walker; but your husband kens weel about me.'

"In the evening I related how much I had been pleased, and inquired what was extraordinary in the history of the poor woman. Mr. —— said, there were perhaps few more remarkable people than Helen Walker. She had been left an orphan, with the charge of a sister considerably younger than herself, and who was educated and maintained by her exertions. Attached to

her by so many ties, therefore, it will not be easy to
conceive her feelings, when she found that this only
sister must be tried by the laws of her country for
child-murder, and upon being called as principal witness
against her. The counsel for the prisoner told Helen,
that if she could declare that her sister had made any
preparations, however slight, or had given her any intimation on the subject, that such a statement would
save her sister's life, as she was the principal witness
against her. Helen said, 'It is impossible for me to
swear to a falsehood; and, whatever may be the consequence, I will give my oath according to my conscience.'

"The trial came on, and the sister was found guilty
and condemned; but, in Scotland, six weeks must elapse
between the sentence and the execution, and Helen
Walker availed herself of it. The very day of her
sister's condemnation, she got a petition drawn stating
the peculiar circumstances of the case, and that very
night set out on foot to London.

"Without introduction or recommendation, with her
simple (perhaps ill-expressed) petition, drawn up by
some inferior clerk of the court, she presented herself,
in her tartan plaid and country attire, to the late Duke
of Argyle, who immediately procured the pardon she
petitioned for, and Helen returned with it, on foot, just
in time to save her sister.

"I was so strongly interested by this narrative, that
I determined immediately to prosecute my acquaintance
with Helen Walker; but as I was to leave the country

next day, I was obliged to defer it till my return in
spring, when the first walk I took was to Helen
Walker's cottage.

"She had died a short time before. My regret was
extreme, and I endeavoured to obtain some account of
Helen from an old woman who inhabited the other end
of her cottage. I inquired if Helen ever spoke of her
past history, her journey to London, etc. 'Na,' the old
woman said, 'Helen was a wily body, and whene'er ony
o' the neebors asked ony thing about it, she aye turned
the conversation.'

"In short, every answer I received only tended to
increase my regret, and raise my opinion of Helen
Walker, who could unite so much prudence with so
much heroic virtue."

This narrative was enclosed in the following letter to
the author, without date or signature:—

"SIR,—The occurrence just related happened to me
twenty-six years ago. Helen Walker lies buried in the
churchyard of Irongray, about six miles from Dumfries.
I once proposed that a small monument should have
been erected to commemorate so remarkable a character,
but I now prefer leaving it to you to perpetuate her
memory in a more durable manner."

The reader is now able to judge how far the author
has improved upon, or fallen short of, the pleasing and
interesting sketch of high principle and steady affection
displayed by Helen Walker, the prototype of the fictitious Jeanie Deans. Mrs. Goldie was unfortunately
dead before the author had given his name to these

volumes, so he lost all opportunity of thanking that lady for her highly valuable communication. But her daughter, Miss Goldie, obliged him with the following additional information :—

"Mrs. Goldie endeavoured to collect further particulars of Helen Walker, particularly concerning her journey to London, but found this nearly impossible; as the natural dignity of her character, and a high sense of family respectability, made her so indissolubly connect her sister's disgrace with her own exertions, that none of her neighbours durst ever question her upon the subject. One old woman, a distant relation of Helen's, and who is still living, says she worked a harvest with her, but that she never ventured to ask her about her sister's trial, or her journey to London; 'Helen,' she added, 'was a lofty body, and used a high style o' language.' The same old woman says, that every year Helen received a cheese from her sister, who lived at Whitehaven, and that she always sent a liberal portion of it to herself or to her father's family. This fact, though trivial in itself, strongly marks the affection subsisting between the two sisters, and the complete conviction on the mind of the criminal, that her sister had acted solely from high principle, not from any want of feeling, which another small but characteristic trait will further illustrate. A gentleman, a relation of Mrs. Goldie's, who happened to be travelling in the North of England, on coming to a small inn, was shown into the parlour by a female servant, who, after cautiously shutting the door, said, 'Sir, I'm Nelly Walker's sister.'

Thus practically showing that she considered her sister as better known by her high conduct, than even herself by a different kind of celebrity.

"Mrs. Goldie was extremely anxious to have a tomb-stone and an inscription upon it, erected in Irongray churchyard; and if Sir Walter Scott will condescend to write the last, a little subscription could be easily raised in the immediate neighbourhood, and Mrs. Goldie's wish be thus fulfilled."

It is scarcely necessary to add, that the request of Miss Goldie will be most willingly complied with, and without the necessity of any tax on the public. Nor is there much occasion to repeat how much the author conceives himself obliged to his unknown correspondent, who thus supplied him with a theme affording such a pleasing view of the moral dignity of virtue, though unaided by birth, beauty, or talent. If the picture has suffered in the execution, it is from the failure of the author's powers to present in detail the same simple and striking portrait, exhibited in Mrs. Goldie's letter.

ABBOTSFORD, *April* 1, 1830.

POSTSCRIPT.

ALTHOUGH it would be impossible to add much to Mrs. Goldie's picturesque and most interesting account of Helen Walker, the prototype of the imaginary Jeanie Deans, the Editor may be pardoned for introducing two or three anecdotes respecting that excellent person, which he has collected from a volume entitled, "Sketches from Nature, by John M'Diarmid," a gentleman who conducts an able provincial paper in the town of Dumfries.

Helen was the daughter of a small farmer in a place called Dalwhairn, in the parish of Irongray; where, after the death of her father, she continued, with the unassuming piety of a Scottish peasant, to support her mother by her own unremitted labour and privations; a case so common, that even yet, I am proud to say, few of my countrywomen would shrink from the duty.

Helen Walker was held among her equals *pensy*, that is, proud or conceited; but the facts brought to prove this accusation seem only to evince a strength of character superior to those around her. Thus it was remarked, that when it thundered, she went with her work and her Bible to the front of the cottage, alleging that the Almighty could smite in the city as well as in the field.

Mr. M'Diarmid mentions more particularly the misfortune of her sister, which he supposes to have taken place previous to 1736. Helen Walker, declining every proposal of saving her relation's life at the expense of truth, borrowed a sum of money sufficient for her journey, walked the whole distance to London barefoot, and made her way to John Duke of Argyle. She was heard to say, that, by the Almighty's strength, she had been enabled to meet the Duke at the most critical moment, which, if lost, would have caused the inevitable forfeiture of her sister's life.

Isabella, or Tibby Walker, saved from the fate which

impended over her, was married by the person who had wronged her (named Waugh), and lived happily for great part of a century, uniformly acknowledging the extraordinary affection to which she owed her preservation.

Helen Walker died about the end of the year 1791, and her remains are interred in the churchyard of her native parish of Irongray, in a romantic cemetery on the banks of the Cairn. That a character so distinguished for her undaunted love of virtue, lived and died in poverty, if not want, serves only to show us how insignificant, in the sight of Heaven, are our principal objects of ambition upon earth.

TO THE BEST OF PATRONS,

A PLEASED AND INDULGENT READER,

JEDEDIAH CLEISHBOTHAM

WISHES HEALTH, AND INCREASE, AND CONTENTMENT.

COURTEOUS READER,

IF ingratitude comprehendeth every vice, surely so foul
a stain worst of all beseemeth him, whose life has been
devoted to instructing youth in virtue and in humane
letters. Therefore have I chosen, in this prolegomenon,
to unload my burden of thanks at thy feet, for the
favour with which thou hast kindly entertained the
Tales of my Landlord. Certes, if thou hast chuckled
over their facetious and festivous descriptions, or hadst
thy mind filled with pleasure at the strange and pleasant
turns of fortune which they record, verily, I have also
simpered when I beheld a second storey with attics, that
has arisen on the basis of my small domicile at Gandercleugh, the walls having been aforehand pronounced by
Deacon Barrow to be capable of enduring such an elevation. Nor has it been without delectation, that I have

endued a new coat (snuff-brown, and with metal buttons),
having all nether garments corresponding thereto.   We
do therefore lie, in respect of each other, under a recipro-
cation of benefits, whereof those received by me being
the most solid (in respect that a new house and a new
coat are better than a new tale and an old song), it is
meet that my gratitude should be expressed with the
louder voice and more preponderating vehemence.   And
how should it be so expressed?—Certainly not in words
only, but in act and deed.   It is with this sole purpose,
and disclaiming all intention of purchasing that pendicle
or poffle of land called the Carlinescroft, lying adjacent
to my garden, and measuring seven acres, three roods,
and four perches, that I have committed to the eyes of
those who thought well of the former tomes, these four
additional volumes of the Tales of my Landlord.   Not
the less, if Peter Prayfort be minded to sell the said
poffle, it is at his own choice to say so ; and, peradventure, he may meet with a purchaser : unless (gentle
reader) the pleasing pourtraictures of Peter Pattieson,
now given unto thee in particular, and unto the public
in general, shall have lost their favour in thine eyes,
whereof I am no way distrustful.   And so much confidence do I repose in thy continued favour, that, should
thy lawful occasions call thee to the town of Gandercleugh, a place frequented by most at one time or other
in their lives, I will enrich thine eyes with a sight of
those precious manuscripts whence thou hast derived so
much delectation, thy nose with a snuff from my mull,
and thy palate with a dram from my bottle of strong

waters, called, by the learned of Ganderclough, the
Dominie's Dribble o' Drink.

It is there, O highly esteemed and beloved Reader,
thou wilt be able to bear testimony, through the medium
of thine own senses, against the children of vanity, who
have sought to identify thy friend and servant with I
know not what inditer of vain fables ; who hath cumbered
the world with his devices, but shrunken from the
responsibility thereof. Truly, this hath been well
termed a generation hard of faith ; since what can a
man do to assert his property in a printed tome, saving
to put his name in the title-page thereof, with his
description, or designation, as the lawyers term it, and
place of abode ?   Of a surety I would have such sceptics
consider how they themselves would brook to have their
works ascribed to others, their names and professions
imputed as forgeries, and their very existence brought
into question ; even although, peradventure, it may be
it is of little consequence to any but themselves, not
only whether they are living or dead, but even whether
they ever lived or no.   Yet have my maligners carried
their uncharitable censures still farther.

These cavillers have not only doubted mine identity,
although thus plainly proved, but they have impeached
my veracity and the authenticity of my historical narratives !   Verily, I can only say in answer, that I have
been cautelous in quoting mine authorities.   It is true,
indeed, that if I had hearkened with only one ear, I
might have rehearsed my tale with more acceptation
from those who love to hear but half the truth.   It is,

it may hap, not altogether to the discredit of our kindly
nation of Scotland, that we are apt to take an interest,
warm, yea partial, in the deeds and sentiments of our
forefathers. He whom his adversaries describe as a
perjured prelatist, is desirous that his predecessors
should be held moderate in their power, and just in
their execution of its privileges, when, truly, the
unimpassioned peruser of the Annals of those times
shall deem them sanguinary, violent, and tyrannical.
Again, the representatives of the suffering nonconform-
ists desire that their ancestors, the Cameronians, shall
be represented not simply as honest enthusiasts,
oppressed for conscience-sake, but persons of fine
breeding, and valiant heroes. Truly, the historian cannot gratify these predilections. He must needs describe
the cavaliers as proud and high-spirited, cruel, remorseless, and vindictive ; the suffering party as honourably
tenacious of their opinions under persecution ; their
own tempers being, however, sullen, fierce, and rude ;
their opinions absurd and extravagant, and their whole
course of conduct that of persons whom hellebore would
better have suited than prosecutions unto death for
high-treason. Natheless, while such and so preposterous were the opinions on either side, there were, it
cannot be doubted, men of virtue and worth on both, to
entitle either party to claim merit from its martyrs. It
has been demanded of me, Jedediah Cleishbotham, by
what right I am entitled to constitute myself an
impartial judge of their discrepancies of opinions, seeing
(as it is stated) that I must necessarily have descended

from one or other of the contending parties, and be, of
course, wedded for better or for worse, according to the
reasonable practice of Scotland, to its dogmata, or
opinions, and bound, as it were, by the tie matrimonial,
or, to speak without metaphor, *ex jure sanguinis*, to
maintain them in preference to all others.

But, nothing denying the rationality of the rule,
which calls on all now living to rule their political and
religious opinions by those of their great-grandfathers,
and inevitable as seems the one or the other horn of the
dilemma betwixt which my adversaries conceive they
have pinned me to the wall, I yet spy some means of
refuge, and claim a privilege to write and speak of both
parties with impartiality. For, O ye powers of logic!
when the Prelatists and Presbyterians of old times went
together by the ears in this unlucky country, my
ancestor (venerated be his memory!) was one of the
people called Quakers, and suffered severe handling
from either side, even to the extenuation of his purse
and the incarceration of his person.

Craving thy pardon, gentle Reader, for these few
words concerning me and mine, I rest, as above expressed, thy sure and obligated friend,*

J. C.

GANDERCLEUGH, *this 1st of April,* 1818.

---

* It is an old proverb, that "many a true word is spoken in
jest." The existence of Walter Scott, third son of Sir William
Scott of Harden, is instructed, as it is called, by a charter under
the great seal, Domino Willielmo Scott de Harden Militi, et

Waltero Scott suo filio legitimo tertio genito, terrarum de Roberton.* The munificent old gentleman left all his four sons considerable estates, and settled those of Eilrig and Raeburn, together with valuable possessions around Lessudden, upon Walter his third son, who is ancestor of the Scotts of Raeburn, and of the Author of Waverley. He appears to have become a convert to the doctrine of the Quakers, or Friends, and a great assertor of their peculiar tenets. This was probably at the time when George Fox, the celebrated apostle of the sect, made an expedition into the south of Scotland about 1657, on which occasion he boasts, that "as he first set his horse's feet upon Scottish ground, he felt the seed of grace to sparkle about him like innumerable sparks of fire." Upon the same occasion, probably, Sir Gideon Scott of Highchester, second son of Sir William, immediate elder brother of Walter, and ancestor of the author's friend and kinsman, the present representative of the family of Harden, also embraced the tenets of Quakerism. This last convert, Gideon, entered into a controversy with the Rev. James Kirkton, author of the Secret and True History of the Church of Scotland, which is noticed by my ingenious friend Mr. Charles Kirkpatrick Sharpe, in his valuable and curious edition of that work, 4to, 1817. Sir William Scott, eldest of the brothers, remained, amid the defection of his two younger brethren, an orthodox member of the Presbyterian Church, and used such means for reclaiming Walter of Raeburn from his heresy, as savoured far more of persecution than persuasion. In this he was assisted by MacDougal of Makerston, brother to Isabella MacDougal, the wife of the said Walter, and who, like her husband, had conformed to the Quaker tenets.

The interest possessed by Sir William Scott and Makerston was powerful enough to procure the two following acts of the Privy Council of Scotland, directed against Walter of Raeburn as an heretic and convert to Quakerism, appointing him to be imprisoned first in Edinburgh jail, and then in that of Jedburgh; and his children to be taken by force from the society and direction of their parents, and educated at a distance from them, besides the assignment of a sum for their maintenance, sufficient in those times to be burdensome to a moderate Scottish estate.

* See Douglas's Baronage, page 215.

" Apud Edin. vigesimo Junil 1665.

" The Lords of his Magesty's Privy Council having receaved
information that Scott of Raeburn, and Isobel Mackdougall, his
wife, being infected with the error of Quakerism, doe endeavour
to breid and traine up William, Walter, and Isobel Scotts, their
children, in the same profession, doe therefore give order and
command to Sir William Scott of Harden, the said Raeburn's
brother, to separat and take away the saids children from the
custody and society of the saids parents, and to cause educat and
bring them up in his owne house, or any other convenient place,
and ordaines letters to be direct at the said Sir William's instance
against Raeburn, for a maintenance to the saids children, and
that the said Sir Wm. give one account of his diligence with all
conveniency."

" Edinburgh, 5th July 1666.

" Anent a petition presented be Sir Wm. Scott of Harden, for
himself and in name and behalf of the three children of Walter
Scott of Raeburn, his brother, showing that the Lords of Councill,
by ane act of the 22d day of Junii 1665, did grant power and
warrand to the petitioner, to separat and take away Raeburn's
children, from his family and education, and to breed them in
some convenient place, where they might be free from all infection
in their younger years, from the principalls of Quakerism, and,
for maintenance of the saids children, did ordain letters to be
direct against Raeburn; and seeing the Petitioner, in obedience
to the said order, did take away the saids children, being two
sonnes and a daughter, and after some paines taken upon them in
his owne family, hes sent them to the city of Glasgow, to be
bread at schooles, and there to be principled with the knowledge
of the true religion, and that it is necessary the Councill determine what shall be the maintenance for which Raeburn's three
children may be charged, as likewise that Raeburn himself, being
now in the Tolbooth of Edinburgh, where he dayley converses
with all the Quakers who are prisoners there, and others who
daily resort to them, whereby he is hardened in his pernitious
opinions and principles, without all hope of recovery, unlesse he
be separat from such pernitious company, humbly therefore,
desyring that the Councell might determine npon the soume of

money to be payed be Raeburn, for the education of his children,
to the petitioner, who will be countable therefor; and that, in
order to his conversion, the place of his imprisonment may be
changed. The Lords of his Maj. Privy Councell having at length
heard and considered the foresaid petition, doe modifie the soume
of two thousand pounds Scots, to be payed yearly at the terme of
Whitsunday be the said Walter Scott of Raeburn, furth of his
estate to the petitioner, for the entertainment and education of
the said children, beginning the first termes payment thereof at
Whitsunday last for the half year preceding, and so furth yearly,
at the said terme of Whitsunday in tym comeing till furder
orders; and ordaines the said Walter Scott of Raeburn to be
transported from the tolbooth of Edinburgh to tho prison of Jedburgh, where his friends and others may have occasion to convert
him. And to the effect he may be secured from the practice of
other Quakers, the said Lords doe hereby discharge the magistrates of Jedburgh to suffer any persons suspect of these principles
to have access to him; and in case any contraveen, that they
secure ther persons till they be therfore puneist; and ordaines
letters to be direct heirupon in form, as efleirs."

Both the sons, thus harshly separated from their father, proved
good scholars. The eldest, William, who carried on the line of
Raeburn, was, like his father, a deep Orientalist; the younger,
Walter, became a good classical scholar, a great friend and
correspondent of the celebrated Dr. Pitcairn, and a Jacobite so
distinguished for zeal that he made a vow never to shave his
beard till the restoration of the exiled family. This last Walter
Scott was the author's great-grandfather.

There is yet another link betwixt the author and the simple-
minded and excellent Society of Friends, through a proselyte of
much more importance than Walter Scott of Raeburn. The
celebrated John Swinton of Swinton, sixth baron in descent of
that ancient and once powerful family, was, with Sir William
Lockhart of Lee, the person whom Cromwell chiefly trusted in
the management of the Scottish affairs during his usurpation.
After tho Restoration, Swinton was devoted as a victim to the
new order of things, and was brought down in the same vessel
which conveyed the Marquis of Argyle to Edinburgh, where that
nobleman was tried and executed. Swinton was destined to the

same fate. He had assumed the habit, and entered into the society of the Quakers, and appeared as one of their number before the Parliament of Scotland. He renounced all legal defence, though several pleas were open to him, and answered, in conformity to the principles of his sect, that at the time these crimes were imputed to him, he was in the gall of bitterness and bond of iniquity; but that God Almighty having since called him to the light, he saw and acknowledged those errors, and did not refuse to pay the forfeit of them, even though, in the judgment of the Parliament, it should extend to life itself.

Respect to fallen greatness, and to the patience and calm resignation with which a man once in high power expressed himself under such a change of fortune, found Swinton friends; family connections, and some interested considerations of Middleton the Commissioner, joined to procure his safety, and he was dismissed, but after a long imprisonment, and much dilapidation of his estates, It is said, that Swinton's admonitions, while confined in the Castle of Edinburgh, had a considerable share in converting to the tenets of the Friends Colonel David Barclay, then lying there in the garrison. This was the father of Robert Barclay, author of the celebrated Apology for the Quakers. It may be observed among the inconsistencies of human nature, that Kirkton, Wodrow, and other Presbyterian authors, who have detailed the sufferings of their own sect for non-conformity with the established church, censure the government of the time for not exerting the civil power against the peaceful enthusiasts we have treated of, and some express particular chagrin at the escape of Swinton. Whatever might be his motives for assuming the tenets of the Friends, the old man retained them faithfully till the close of his life.

Jean Swinton, grand-daughter of Sir John Swinton, son of Judge Swinton, as the Quaker was usually termed, was mother of Anne Rutherford, the author's mother.

And thus, as in the play of the Anti-Jacobin, the ghost of the author's grandmother having arisen to speak the Epilogue, it is full time to conclude, lest the reader should remonstrate that his desire to know the Author of Waverley never included a wish to be acquainted with his whole ancestry.

The

Heart of Mid-Lothian

CHAPTER THE FIRST.

BEING INTRODUCTORY.

So down thy hill, romantic Ashbourn, glides
The Derby dilly, carrying six insides.

FRERE.

THE times have changed in nothing more (we follow as we were wont the manuscript of Peter Pattieson) than in the rapid conveyance of intelligence and communication betwixt one part of Scotland and another. It is not above twenty or thirty years, according to the evidence of many credible witnesses now alive, since a little miserable horse-cart, performing with difficulty a journey of thirty miles *per diem*, carried our mails from the capital of Scotland to its extremity. Nor was Scotland much more deficient in these accommodations, than our rich sister had been

about eighty years before. Fielding, in his Tom Jones,
and Farquhar, in a little farce called the Stage-Coach,
have ridiculed the slowness of these vehicles of public
accommodation. According to the latter authority, the
highest bribe could only induce the coachman to
promise to anticipate by half an hour the usual time of
his arrival at the Bull and Mouth.

But in both countries these ancient, slow, and sure
modes of conveyance, are now alike unknown; mail-
coach races against mail-coach, and high-flyer against
high-flyer, through the most remote districts of Britain.
And in our village alone, three post-coaches, and four
coaches with men armed, and in scarlet cassocks,
thunder through the streets each day, and rival in
brilliancy and noise the invention of the celebrated
tyrant :—

> *Demens, qui nimbos et non imitabile fulmen,*
> *Ære et cornipedum pulsu, simularat, equorum.*

Now and then, to complete the resemblance, and to
correct the presumption of the venturous charioteers, it
does happen that the career of these dashing rivals of
Salmoneus meets with as undesirable and violent a
termination as that of their prototype. It is on such
occasions that the Insides and Outsides, to use the
appropriate vehicular phrases, have reason to rue the
exchange of the slow and safe motion of the ancient Fly-
coaches, which, compared with the chariots of Mr.
Palmer, so ill deserve the name. The ancient vehicle
used to settle quietly down, like a ship scuttled and left

to sink by the gradual influx of the waters, while the
modern is smashed to pieces with the velocity of the same
vessel hurled against breakers, or rather with the fury of a
bomb bursting at the conclusion of its career through the
air.   The late ingenious Mr. Pennant, whose humour
it was to set his face in stern opposition to these speedy
conveyances, had collected, I have heard, a formidable
list of such casualties, which, joined to the imposition
of innkeepers, whose charges the passengers had no time
to dispute, the sauciness of the coachman, and the uncontrolled and despotic authority of the tyrant called the
Guard, held forth a picture of horror, to which murder,
theft, fraud, and peculation, lent all their dark colouring.   But that which gratifies the impatience of the
human disposition will be practised in the teeth of
danger, and in defiance of admonition ; and, in despite
of the Cambrian antiquary, mail-coaches not only roll
their thunders round the base of Penman-Maur and
Cader-Edris, but

> Frighted Skiddaw hears afar
> The rattling of the unscythed car.

And perhaps the echoes of Ben-Nevis may soon be
awakened by the bugle, not of a warlike chieftain, but
of the guard of a mail-coach.

It was a fine summer day, and our little school had
obtained a half holiday, by the intercession of a good-
humoured visitor.*   I expected by the coach a new

* His Honour Gilbert Goslinn of Gandercleugh ; for I love to
be precise in matters of importance.—J. C.

number of an interesting periodical publication, and walked forward on the highway to meet it, with the impatience which Cowper has described as actuating the resident in the country when longing for intelligence from the mart of news :—

> —— The grand debate,
> The popular harangue,—the tart reply,—
> The logic, and the wisdom, and the wit,
> And the loud laugh,—I long to know them all ;—
> I burn to set the imprisoned wranglers free,
> And give them voice and utterance again.

It was with such feelings that I eyed the approach of the new coach, lately established on our road, and known by the name of the Somerset, which, to say truth, possesses some interest for me, even when it conveys no such important information. The distant tremulous sound of its wheels was heard just as I gained the summit of the gentle ascent, called the Goslin-brae, from which you command an extensive view down the valley of the river Gander. The public road, which comes up the side of that stream, and crosses it at a bridge about a quarter of a mile from the place where I was standing, runs partly through enclosures and plantations, and partly through open pasture land. It is a childish amusement perhaps,—but my life has been spent with children, and why should not my pleasures be like theirs ?—childish as it is then, I must own I have had great pleasure in watching the approach of the carriage, where the openings of the road permit it to be seen. The gay glancing of the equipage, its diminished and

toy-like appearance at a distance, contrasted with the
rapidity of its motion, its appearance and disappearance
at intervals, and the progressively increasing sounds
that announce its nearer approach, have all to the idle
and listless spectator, who has nothing more important
to attend to, something of awakening interest.   The
ridicule may attach to me, which is flung upon many
an honest citizen, who watches from the window of his
villa the passage of the stage coach ; but it is a very
natural source of amusement notwithstanding, and
many of those who join in the laugh are perhaps not
unused to resort to it in secret.

On the present occasion, however, fate had decreed
that I should not enjoy the consummation of the amusement by seeing the coach rattle past me as I sat on the
turf, and hearing the hoarse grating voice of the guard
as he skimmed forth for my grasp the expected packet,
without the carriage checking its course for an instant.
I had seen the vehicle thunder down the hill that leads
to the bridge with more than its usual impetuosity,
glittering all the while by flashes from a cloudy taber-
nacle of the dust which it had raised, and leaving a
train behind it on the road resembling a wreath of
summer mist.   But it did not appear on the top of the
nearer bank within the usual space of three minutes,
which frequent observation had enabled me to ascertain
was the medium time for crossing the bridge and
mounting the ascent.   When double that space had
elapsed, I became alarmed, and walked hastily forward.
As I came in sight of the bridge, the cause of delay

was too manifest, for the Somerset had made a summer-
set in good earnest, and overturned so completely, that
it was literally resting upon the ground, with the roof
undermost, and the four wheels in the air. The "exertions of the guard and coachman," both of whom were
gratefully commemorated in the newspapers, having
succeeded in disentangling the horses by cutting the
harness, were now proceeding to extricate the *insides* by
a sort of summary and Cæsarean process of delivery,
forcing the hinges from one of the doors which they
could not open otherwise. In this manner were two
disconsolate damsels set at liberty from the womb of
the leathern conveniency. As they immediately began
to settle their clothes, which were a little deranged, as
may be presumed, I concluded they had received no
injury, and did not venture to obtrude my services at
their toilet, for which, I understand, I have since been
reflected upon by the fair sufferers. The *outsides*, who
must have been discharged from their elevated situation
by a shock resembling the springing of a mine, escaped,
nevertheless, with the usual allowance of scratches and
bruises, excepting three, who, having been pitched into
the river Gander, were dimly seen contending with the
tide, like the relics of Æneas's shipwreck,—

Rari apparent nantes in gurgite vasto.

I applied my poor exertions where they seemed to
be most needed, and with the assistance of one or two
of the company who had escaped unhurt, easily succeeded in fishing out two of the unfortunate passengers,

who were stout active young fellows, and but for the
preposterous length of their great-coats, and the equally
fashionable latitude and longitude of their Wellington
trousers, would have required little assistance from any
one.   The third was sickly and elderly, and might have
perished but for the efforts used to preserve him.

When the two great-coated gentlemen had extricated
themselves from the river, and shaken their ears like
huge water-dogs, a violent altercation ensued betwixt
them and the coachman and guard, concerning the
cause of their overthrow.   In the course of the squabble,
I observed that both my new acquaintances belonged to
the law, and that their professional sharpness was
likely to prove an overmatch for the surly and official
tone of the guardians of the vehicle.   The dispute ended
in the guard assuring the passengers that they should
have seats in a heavy coach which would pass that spot
in less than half an hour, provided it were not full.
Chance seemed to favour this arrangement, for when
the expected vehicle arrived, there were only two places
occupied in a carriage which professed to carry six.
The two ladies who had been disinterred out of the
fallen vehicle were readily admitted, but positive objec-
tions were stated by those previously in possession to
the admittance of the two lawyers, whose wetted
garments being much of the nature of well-soaked
sponges, there was every reason to believe they would
refund a considerable part of the water they had collected, to the inconvenience of their fellow-passengers.
On the other hand, the lawyers rejected a seat on the

roof, alleging that they had only taken that station for pleasure for one stage, but were entitled in all respects to free egress and regress from the interior, to which their contract positively referred. After some altercation, in which something was said upon the edict *Nautæ, caupones stabularii*, the coach went off, leaving the learned gentlemen to abide by their action of damages.

They immediately applied to me to guide them to the next village and the best inn ; and from the account I gave them of the Wallace-Head, declared they were much better pleased to stop there than to go forward upon the terms of that impudent scoundrel the guard of the Somerset. All that they now wanted was a lad to carry their travelling bags, who was easily procured from an adjoining cottage ; and they prepared to walk forward, when they found there was another passenger in the same deserted situation with themselves. This was the elderly and sickly-looking person, who had been precipitated into the river along with the two young lawyers. He, it seems, had been too modest to push his own plea against the coachman when he saw that of his betters rejected, and now remained behind with a look of timid anxiety, plainly intimating that he was deficient in those means of recommendation which are necessary passports to the hospitality of an inn.

I ventured to call the attention of the two dashing young blades, for such they seemed, to the desolate condition of their fellow-traveller. They took the hint with ready good-nature.

"O, true, Mr. Dunover," said one of the youngsters,

" you must not remain on the pavé here ; you must go
and have some dinner with us—Halkit and I must
have a post-chaise to go on, at all events, and we will
set you down wherever suits you best."

The poor man, for such his dress, as well as his
diffidence, bespoke him, made the sort of acknowledging
bow by which says a Scotchman, " It's too much honour
for the like of me ;" and followed humbly behind his
gay patrons, all three besprinkling the dusty road as
they walked along with the moisture of their drenched
garments, and exhibiting the singular and somewhat
ridiculous appearance of three persons suffering from
the opposite extreme of humidity, while the summer
sun was at its height, and every thing else around them
had the expression of heat and drought.   The ridicule
did not escape the young gentlemen themselves, and
they had made what might be received as one or two
tolerable jests on the subject before they had advanced
far on their peregrination.

" We cannot complain, like Cowley," said one of
them, " that Gideon's fleece remains dry, while all
around is moist ; this is the reverse of the miracle."

" We ought to be received with gratitude in this
good town ; we bring a supply of what they seem to
need most," said Halkit.

" And distribute it with unparalleled generosity,"
replied his companion ; " performing the part of three
water-carts for the benefit of their dusty roads."

" We come before them, too," said Halkit, " in full
professional force—counsel and agent"—

"And client," said the young advocate, looking behind him. And then added, lowering his voice, "that looks as if he had kept such dangerous company too long."

It was, indeed, too true, that the humble follower of the gay young men had the threadbare appearance of a worn-out litigant, and I could not but smile at the conceit, though anxious to conceal my mirth from the object of it.

When we arrived at the Wallace Inn, the elder of the Edinburgh gentlemen, and whom I understood to be a barrister, insisted that I should remain and take part of their dinner; and their inquiries and demands speedily put my landlord and his whole family in motion to produce the best cheer which the larder and cellar afforded, and proceed to cook it to the best advantage, a science in which our entertainers seemed to be admirably skilled. In other respects they were lively young men, in the hey-day of youth and good spirits, playing the part which is common to the higher classes of the law at Edinburgh, and which nearly resembles that of the young templars in the days of Steele and Addison. An air of giddy gaiety mingled with the good sense, taste, and information which their conversation exhibited ; and it seemed to be their object to unite the character of men of fashion and lovers of the polite arts. A fine gentleman, bred up in the thorough idleness and inanity of pursuit, which I understand is absolutely necessary to the character in perfection, might in all probability have traced a tinge of professional pedantry which marked the barrister in spite of his efforts, and something of active bustle in his companion, and would certainly have detected more than a fashionable mixture of information and animated interest in the language of both. But to me, who had no pretensions to be so critical, my companions seemed to form a very happy mixture of good-breeding and liberal information, with a disposition to lively rattle, pun, and jest, amusing to a grave man, because it is what he himself can least easily command.

The thin pale-faced man, whom their good-nature had brought into their society, looked out of place, as well as out of spirits; sate on the edge of his seat, and kept the chair at two feet distance from the table; thus incommoding himself considerably in conveying the victuals to his mouth, as if by way of penance for partaking of them in the company of his superiors. A short time after dinner, declining all entreaty to partake of the wine, which circulated freely round, he informed himself of the hour when the chaise had been ordered to attend; and saying he would be in readiness, modestly withdrew from the apartment.

"Jack," said the barrister to his companion, "I remember that poor fellow's face; you spoke more truly than you were aware of; he really is one of my clients, poor man."

"Poor man!" echoed Halkit—"I suppose you mean he is your one and only client?"

"That's not my fault, Jack," replied the other, whose name I discovered was Hardie. "You are to give me

all your business, you know; and if you have none, the
learned gentleman here knows nothing can come of
nothing."

"You seem to have brought something to nothing
though, in the case of that honest man. He looks as
if he were just about to honour with his residence the
HEART OF MID-LOTHIAN."

"You are mistaken—he is just delivered from it.—
Our friend here looks for an explanation. Pray, Mr.
Pattieson, have you been in Edinburgh?"

I answered in the affirmative.

"Then you must have passed, occasionally at least,
though probably not so faithfully as I am doomed to
do, through a narrow intricate passage, leading out of
the north-west corner of the Parliament Square, and
passing by a high and antique building, with turrets
and iron grates,

> Making good the saying odd,
> 'Near the church and far from God '—

Mr. Halkit broke in upon his learned counsel, to
contribute his moiety to the riddle—"Having at the
door the sign of the Red Man"——

"And being on the whole," resumed the counsellor,
interrupting his friend in his turn, "a sort of place
where misfortune is happily confounded with guilt,
where all who are in wish to get out"——

"And where none who have the good luck to be
out, wish to get in," added his companion.

"I conceive you, gentlemen," replied I; "you mean
the prison."

"The prison," added the young lawyer—"You have hit it—the very reverend Tolbooth itself; and let me tell you, you are obliged to us for describing it with so much modesty and brevity; for with whatever amplifications we might have chosen to decorate the subject, you lay entirely at our mercy, since the Fathers Conscript of our city have decreed that the venerable edifice itself shall not remain in existence to confirm or to confute us."

"Then the Tolbooth of Edinburgh is called the Heart of Mid-Lothian?" said I.

"So termed and reputed, I assure you."

"I think," said I, with the bashful diffidence with which a man lets slip a pun in presence of his superiors, "the metropolitan county may, in that case, be said to have a sad heart."

"Right as my glove, Mr. Pattieson," added Mr. Hardie; "and a close heart, and a hard heart—Keep it up, Jack."

"And a wicked heart, and a poor heart," answered Halkit, doing his best.

"And yet it may be called in some sort a strong heart, and a high heart," rejoined the advocate. "You see I can put you both out of heart."

"I have played all my hearts," said the younger gentleman.

"Then we'll have another lead," answered his companion.—"And as to the old and condemned Tolbooth, what pity the same honour cannot be done to it as has been done to many of its inmates. Why should not

the Tolbooth have its 'Last Speech, Confession, and Dying Words?'   The old stones would be just as conscious of the honour as many a poor devil who has dangled like a tassel at the west end of it, while the hawkers were shouting a confession the culprit had never heard of."

"I am afraid," said I, "if I might presume to give my opinion, it would be a tale of unvaried sorrow and guilt."

"Not entirely, my friend," said Hardie; "a prison is a world within itself, and has its own business, griefs, and joys, peculiar to its circle.   Its inmates are sometimes short-lived, but so are soldiers on service; they are poor relatively to the world without, but there are degrees of wealth and poverty among them, and so some are relatively rich also.   They cannot stir abroad, but neither can the garrison of a besieged fort, or the crew of a ship at sea; and they are not under a dispensation quite so desperate as either, for they may have as much food as they have money to buy, and are not obliged to work whether they have food or not."

"But what variety of incident," said I (not without a secret view to my present task), "could possibly be derived from such a work as you are pleased to talk of?"

"Infinite," replied the young advocate.   "Whatever of guilt, crime, imposture, folly, unheard-of misfortunes, and unlooked-for change of fortune, can be found to chequer life, my Last Speech of the Tolbooth should illustrate with examples sufficient to gorge even the public's all-devouring appetite for the wonderful and

horrible. The inventor of fictitious narratives has to
rack his brains for means to diversify his tale, and after
all can hardly hit upon characters or incidents which
have not been used again and again, until they are
familiar to the eye of the reader, so that the develop-
ment, *enlèvement*, the desperate wound of which the
hero never dies, the burning fever from which the
heroine is sure to recover, become a mere matter of
course. I join with my honest friend Crabbe, and have
an unlucky propensity to hope when hope is lost, and
to rely upon the cork-jacket, which carries the heroes
of romance safe through all the billows of affliction."
He then declaimed the following passage, rather with
too much than too little emphasis :—

> " Much have I feared, but am no more afraid,
> When some chaste beauty, by some wretch betrayed,
> Is drawn away with such distracted speed,
> That she anticipates a dreadful deed.
> Not so do I—Let solid walls impound
> The captive fair, and dig a moat around;
> Let there be brazen locks and bars of steel,
> And keepers cruel, such as never feel;
> With not a single note the purse supply,
> And when she begs, let men and maids deny;
> Be windows there from which she dares not fall,
> And help so distant, 'tis in vain to call;
> Still means of freedom will some Power devise,
> And from the baffled ruffian snatch his prize."

"The end of uncertainty," he concluded, "is the
death of interest; and hence it happens that no one now
reads novels."

"Hear him, ye gods!" returned his companion.

" I assure you, Mr. Patticeson, you will hardly visit this learned gentleman, but you are likely to find the new novel most in repute lying on his table,—snugly intrenched, however, beneath Stair's Institutes, or an open volume of Morrison's Decisions."

"Do I deny it?" said the hopeful jurisconsult, "or wherefore should I, since it is well known these Dalilahs seduce my wisers and my betters? May they not be found lurking amidst the multiplied memorials of our most distinguished counsel, and even peeping from under the cushion of a judge's arm-chair? Our seniors at the bar, within the bar, and even on the bench, read novels; and, if not belied, some of them have written novels into the bargain. I only say, that I read from habit and from indolence, not from real interest; that, like Ancient Pistol devouring his leek, I read and swear till I get to the end of the narrative. But not so in the real records of human vagaries—not so in the State Trials, or in the Books of Adjournal, where every now and then you read new pages of the human heart, and turns of fortune far beyond what the boldest novelist ever attempted to produce from the coinage of his brain."

"And for such narratives," I asked, "you suppose the History of the Prison of Edinburgh might afford appropriate materials?"

"In a degree unusually ample, my dear sir," said Hardie—"Fill your glass, however, in the meanwhile. Was it not for many years the place in which the Scottish parliament met? Was it not James's place of refuge, when the mob, inflamed by a seditious preacher, broke forth on him with the cries of 'The sword of the Lord and of Gideon—bring forth the wicked Haman?' Since that time how many hearts have throbbed within these walls, as the tolling of the neighbouring bell announced to them how fast the sands of their life were ebbing; how many must have sunk at the sound —how many were supported by stubborn pride and dogged resolution—how many by the consolations of religion? Have there not been some, who, looking back on the motives of their crimes, were scarce able to understand how they should have had such temptation as to seduce them from virtue; and have there not, perhaps, been others, who, sensible of their innocence, were divided between indignation at the undeserved doom which they were to undergo, consciousness that they had not deserved it, and racking anxiety to discover some way in which they might yet vindicate themselves? Do you suppose any of these deep, powerful, and agitating feelings, can be recorded and perused without exciting a corresponding depth of deep, powerful, and agitating interest?—O! do but wait till I publish the *Causes Célèbres* of Caledonia, and you will find no want of a novel or a tragedy for some time to come. The true thing will triumph over the brightest inventions of the most ardent imagination. *Magna est veritas, et prævalebit.*"

"I have understood," said I, encouraged by the affability of my rattling entertainer, "that less of this interest must attach to Scottish jurisprudence than to

that of any other country. The general morality of
our people, their sober and prudent habits "——

"Secure them," said the barrister, "against any
great increase of professional thieves and depredators,
but not against wild and wayward starts of fancy and
passion, producing crimes of an extraordinary description, which are precisely those to the detail of which
we listen with thrilling interest. England has been
much longer a highly civilized country; her subjects
have been very strictly amenable to laws administered
without fear or favour, a complete division of labour
has taken place among her subjects, and the very
thieves and robbers form a distinct class in society,
subdivided among themselves according to the subject
of the depredations, and the mode in which they carry
them on, acting upon regular habits and principles,
which can be calculated and anticipated at Bow Street,
Hatton Garden, or the Old Bailey. Our sister kingdom
is like a cultivated field,—the farmer expects that, in
spite of all his care, a certain number of weeds will rise
with the corn, and can tell you beforehand their names
and appearance. But Scotland is like one of her own
Highland glens, and the moralist who reads the records
of her criminal jurisprudence, will find as many curious
anomalous facts in the history of mind, as the botanist
will detect rare specimens among her dingles and cliffs."

"And that's all the good you have obtained from
three perusals of the Commentaries on Scottish Criminal
Jurisprudence?" said his companion. "I suppose the
learned author very little thinks that the facts which

his erudition and acuteness have accumulated for the
illustration of legal doctrines, might be so arranged as
to form a sort of appendix to the half-bound and slip-
shod volumes of the circulating library."

"I'll bet you a pint of claret," said the elder lawyer,
"that he will not feel sore at the comparison. But as
we say at the bar, 'I beg I may not be interrupted;' I
have much more to say upon my Scottish collection of
Causes Célèbres. You will please recollect the scope
and motive given for the contrivance and execution of
many extraordinary and daring crimes, by the long
civil dissensions of Scotland—by the hereditary juris-
dictions, which, until 1748, rested the investigation of
crimes in judges, ignorant, partial or interested—by the
habits of the gentry, shut up in their distant and solitary
mansion-houses, nursing their revengeful passions just
to keep their blood from stagnating—not to mention
that amiable national qualification, called the *perfer-
vidum ingenium Scotorum,* which our lawyers join in
alleging as a reason for the severity of some of our
enactments. When I come to treat of matters so
mysterious, deep, and dangerous, as these circumstances
have given rise to, the blood of each reader shall be
curdled, and his epidermis crisped into goose skin.—
But hist!—here comes the landlord, with tidings, I
suppose, that the chaise is ready."

It was no such thing—the tidings bore, that no
chaise could be had that evening, for Sir Peter Plyem
had carried forward my landlord's two pairs of horses
that morning to the ancient royal borough of Bubble-

burgh, to look after his interest there. But as Bubbleburgh is only one of a set of five boroughs which club
their shares for a member of parliament, Sir Peter's
adversary had judiciously watched his departure, in
order to commence a canvass in the no less royal
borough of Bitem, which, as all the world knows, lies
at the very termination of Sir Peter's avenue, and has
been held in leading-strings by him and his ancestors
for time immemorial. Now Sir Peter was thus placed
in the situation of an ambitious monarch, who, after
having commenced a daring inroad into his enemies'
territories, is suddenly recalled by an invasion of his
own hereditary dominions. He was obliged in consequence to return from the half-won borough of Bubbleburgh, to look after the half-lost borough of Bitem, and
the two pairs of horses which had carried him that
morning to Bubbleburgh, were now forcibly detained
to transport him, his agent, his valet, his jester, and
his hard-drinker, across the country to Bitem.   The
cause of this detention, which to me was of as little
consequence as it may be to the reader, was important
enough to my companions to reconcile them to the
delay.   Like eagles, they smelled the battle afar off,
ordered a magnum of claret and beds at the Wallace,
and entered at full career into the Bubbleburgh and
Bitem politics, with all the probable "petitions and
complaints" to which they were likely to give rise.

   In the midst of an anxious, animated, and, to me,
most unintelligible discussion, concerning provosts,
bailies, deacons, sets of boroughs, leets, town-clerks,

burgesses resident and non-resident, all of a sudden the lawyer recollected himself. "Poor Dunover, we must not forget him;" and the landlord was dispatched in quest of the *paurre honteux*, with an earnestly civil invitation to him for the rest of the evening. I could not help asking the young gentlemen if they knew the history of this poor man; and the counsellor applied himself to his pocket to recover the memorial or brief from which he had stated his cause.

"He has been a candidate for our *remedium miserabile*," said Mr. Hardie, "commonly called a *cessio bonorum*. As there are divines who have doubted the eternity of future punishments, so the Scotch lawyers seem to have thought that the crime of poverty might be atoned for by something short of perpetual imprisonment. After a month's confinement, you must know, a prisoner for debt is entitled, on a sufficient statement to our Supreme Court, setting forth the amount of his funds, and the nature of his misfortunes, and surrendering all his effects to his creditors, to claim to be discharged from prison."

"I had heard," I replied, "of such a humane regulation."

"Yes," said Halkit, "and the beauty of it is, as the foreign fellow said, you may get the *cessio* when the *bonorums* are all spent—But what, are you puzzling in your pockets to seek your only memorial among old play-bills, letters requesting a meeting of the Faculty, rules of the Speculative Society, syllabus' of lectures— all the miscellaneous contents of a young advocate's pocket, which contains every thing but briefs and bank notes? Can you not state a case of *cessio* without your memorial? Why it is done every Saturday. The events follow each other as regularly as clock-work, and one form of condescendence might suit every one of them.

"This is very unlike the variety of distress which this gentleman stated to fall under the consideration of your judges," said I.

"True," replied Halkit; "but Hardie spoke of criminal jurisprudence, and this business is purely civil. I could plead a *cessio* myself without the inspiring honours of a gown and three-tailed periwig—Listen.— My client was bred a journeyman weaver—made some little money—took a farm—(for conducting a farm, like driving a gig, comes by nature)—late severe times— induced to sign bills with a friend, for which he received no value—landlord sequestrates—creditors accept a composition—pursuer sets up a public-house—fails a second time—is incarcerated for a debt of ten pounds seven shillings and sixpence—his debts amount to blank—his losses to blank—his funds to blank—leaving a balance of blank in his favour. There is no opposition; your lordships will please grant commission to take his oath."

Hardie now renounced this ineffectual search, in which there was perhaps a little affectation, and told us the tale of poor Dunover's distresses, with a tone in which a degree of feeling, which he seemed ashamed of as unprofessional, mingled with his attempts at wit, and did him more honour. It was one of those tales

which seem to argue a sort of ill-luck or fatality attached
to the hero. A well-informed, industrious, and blame-
less, but poor and bashful man, had in vain essayed all
the usual means by which others acquire independence,
yet had never succeeded beyond the attainment of bare
subsistence. During a brief gleam of hope, rather than
of actual prosperity, he had added a wife and family to
his cares, but the dawn was speedily overcast. Every
thing retrograded with him towards the verge of the
miry Slough of Despond, which yawns for insolvent
debtors; and after catching at each twig, and experienc-
ing the protracted agony of feeling them one by one
elude his grasp, he actually sunk into the miry pit
whence he had been extricated by the professional
exertions of Hardie.

"And, I suppose, now you have dragged this poor
devil ashore, you will leave him half naked on the
beach to provide for himself?" said Halkit. "Hark ye,
—and he whispered something in his ear, of which the
penetrating and insinuating words, "Interest with my
Lord," alone reached mine.

"It is *pessimi exempli*," said Hardie, laughing, "to
provide for a ruined client? but I was thinking of what
you mention, provided it can be managed—But hush !
here he comes."

The recent relation of the poor man's misfortunes
had given him, I was pleased to observe, a claim to the
attention and respect of the young men, who treated
him with great civility, and gradually engaged him in
a conversation, which, much to my satisfaction, again

turned upon the *Causes Célèbres* of Scotland. Emboldened by the kindness with which he was treated, Mr. Dunover began to contribute his share to the amusement of the evening.   Jails, like other places, have their ancient traditions, known only to the inhabitants, and handed down from one set of the melancholy lodgers to the next who occupy their cells. Some of these, which Dunover mentioned, were interesting, and served to illustrate the narratives of remarkable trials, which Hardie had at his finger ends, and which his companion was also well skilled in.   This sort of conversation passed away the evening till the early hour when Mr. Dunover chose to retire to rest, and I also retreated to take down memorandums of what I had learned, in order to add another narrative to those which it had been my chief amusement to collect, and to write out in detail.   The two young men ordered a broiled bone, Madeira negus, and a pack of cards, and commenced a game at picquet.

Next morning the travellers left Gandercleugh.   I afterwards learned from the papers that both have been since engaged in the great political cause of Bubbleburgh and Bitem, a summary case, and entitled to particular despatch; but which, it is thought, nevertheless, may outlast the duration of the parliament to which the contest refers.   Mr. Halkit, as the newspapers informed me, acts as agent or solicitor; and Mr. Hardie opened for Sir Peter Plyem with singular ability, and to such good purpose, that I understand he has since had fewer play-bills and more briefs in his pocket.

And both the young gentlemen deserve their good
fortune; for I learned from Dunover, who called on
me some weeks afterwards, and communicated the
intelligence with tears in his eyes, that their interest
had availed to obtain him a small office for the decent
maintenance of his family; and that, after a train of
constant and uninterrupted misfortune, he could trace
a dawn of prosperity to his having the good fortune to
be flung from the top of a mail-coach into the river
Gander, in company with an advocate and a writer to
the signet.   The reader will not perhaps deem himself
equally obliged to the accident, since it brings upon
him the following narrative, founded upon the conversation of the evening.

CHAPTER THE SECOND.

Whoe'er's been at Paris must needs know the Grève,
The fatal retreat of the unfortunate brave,
Where honour and justice most oddly contribute,
To ease heroes' pains by an halter and gibbet.

There death breaks the shackles which force had put on,
And the hangman completes what the judge but began;
There the squire of the poet, and knight of the post,
Find their pains no more baulked, and their hopes no more
    crossed.   PRIOR.

IN former times, England had her Tyburn, to which
the devoted victims of justice were conducted in solemn
procession up what is now called Oxford Road.   In

Edinburgh, a large open street, or rather oblong square,
surrounded by high houses, called the Grassmarket,
was used for the same melancholy purpose. It was
not ill chosen for such a scene, being of considerable
extent, and therefore fit to accommodate a great number
of spectators, such as are usually assembled by this
melancholy spectacle. On the other hand, few of the
houses which surround it were, even in early times,
inhabited by persons of fashion; so that those likely to
be offended or over deeply affected by such unpleasant
exhibitions were not in the way of having their quiet
disturbed by them. The houses in the Grassmarket
are, generally speaking, of a mean description; yet the
place is not without some features of grandeur, being
overhung by the southern side of the huge rock on
which the castle stands, and by the moss-grown battle-
ments and turreted walls of that ancient fortress.

It was the custom, until within these thirty years,
or thereabouts, to use this esplanade for the scene of
public executions. The fatal day was announced to the
public, by the appearance of a huge black gallows-tree
towards the eastern end of the Grassmarket. This ill-
omened apparition was of great height, with a scaffold
surrounding it, and a double ladder placed against it,
for the ascent of the unhappy criminal and executioner. As this apparatus was always arranged before
dawn, it seemed as if the gallows had grown out of the
earth in the course of one night, like the production of
some foul demon; and I well remember the fright with
which the school-boys, when I was one of their number,

used to regard these ominous signs of deadly preparation. On the night after the execution the gallows
again disappeared, and was conveyed in silence and
darkness to the place where it was usually deposited,
which was one of the vaults under the Parliament-house,
or courts of justice. This mode of execution is now
exchanged for one similar to that in front of Newgate,
—with what beneficial effect is uncertain. The mental
sufferings of the convict are indeed shortened. He no
longer stalks between the attendant clergymen, dressed
in his grave-clothes, through a considerable part of the
city, looking like a moving and walking corpse, while
yet an inhabitant of this world; but, as the ultimate
purpose of punishment has in view the prevention of
crimes, it may at least be doubted, whether, in abridg-
ing the melancholy ceremony, we have not in part
diminished that appalling effect upon the spectators
which is the useful end of all such inflictions, and in
consideration of which alone, unless in very particular
cases, capital sentences can be altogether justified.

On the 7th day of September 1736, these ominous
preparations for execution were descried in the place we
have described, and at an early hour the space around
began to be occupied by several groups, who gazed on
the scaffold and gibbet with a stern and vindictive show
of satisfaction very seldom testified by the populace,
whose good-nature, in most cases, forgets the crime of
the condemned person, and dwells only on his misery.
But the act of which the expected culprit had been
convicted was of a description calculated nearly and

closely to awaken and irritate the resentful feelings of the multitude. The tale is well known; yet it is neces- sary to recapitulate its leading circumstances, for the better understanding what is to follow; and the narra- tive may prove long, but I trust not uninteresting, even to those who have heard its general issue. At any rate, some detail is necessary, in order to render intelligible the subsequent events of our narrative.

Contraband trade, though it strikes at the root of legitimate government, by encroaching on its revenues, —though it injures the fair trader, and debauches the minds of those engaged in it,—is not usually looked upon, either by the vulgar or by their betters, in a very heinous point of view. On the contrary, in those countries where it prevails, the cleverest, boldest, and most intelligent of the peasantry, are uniformly engaged in illicit transactions, and very often with the sanction of the farmers and inferior gentry. Smuggling was almost universal in Scotland in the reigns of George I. and II.; for the people, unaccustomed to imposts, and regarding them as an unjust aggression upon their ancient liberties, made no scruple to elude them when- ever it was possible to do so.

The county of Fife, bounded by two firths on the south and north, and by the sea on the east, and having a number of small seaports, was long famed for main- taining successfully a contraband trade; and, as there were many seafaring men residing there, who had been pirates and buccaneers in their youth, there were not wanting a sufficient number of daring men to carry it on.

Among these, a fellow, called Andrew Wilson, originally
a baker in the village of Pathhead, was particularly
obnoxious to the revenue officers. He was possessed of
great personal strength, courage, and cunning,—was
perfectly acquainted with the coast, and capable of conducting the most desperate enterprises. On several
occasions he succeeded in baffling the pursuit and
researches of the king's officers; but he became so much
the object of their suspicions and watchful attention,
that at length he was totally ruined by repeated seizures.
The man became desperate. He considered himself as
robbed and plundered; and took it into his head, that
he had a right to make reprisals, as he could find opportunity. Where the heart is prepared for evil,
opportunity is seldom long wanting. This Wilson
learned that the Collector of the Customs at Kirkcaldy
had come to Pittenweem, in the course of his official
round of duty, with a considerable sum of public money
in his custody. As the amount was greatly within the
value of the goods which had been seized from him,
Wilson felt no scruple of conscience in resolving to
re-imburse himself for his losses, at the expense of the
Collector and the revenue. He associated with himself
one Robertson, and two other idle young men, whom,
having been concerned in the same illicit trade, he persuaded to view the transaction in the same justifiable
light in which he himself considered it. They watched
the motions of the Collector; they broke forcibly into
the house where he lodged,—Wilson, with two of his
associates, entering the Collector's apartment, while

Robertson, the fourth, kept watch at the door with a
drawn cutlass in his hand. The officer of the customs,
conceiving his life in danger, escaped out of his bedroom
window, and fled in his shirt, so that the plunderers,
with much ease, possessed themselves of about two
hundred pounds of public money. The robbery was committed in a very audacious manner, for several persons
were passing in the street at the time. But Robertson,
representing the noise they heard as a dispute or fray
betwixt the Collector and the people of the house, the
worthy citizens of Pittenweem felt themselves no way
called on to interfere in behalf of the obnoxious revenue
officer; so, satisfying themselves with this very super-
ficial account of the matter, like the Levite in the
parable, they passed on the opposite side of the way.
An alarm was at length given, military were called in,
the depredators were pursued, the booty recovered, and
Wilson and Robertson tried and condemned to death,
chiefly on the evidence of an accomplice.

Many thought, that, in consideration of the men's
erroneous opinion of the nature of the action they had
committed, justice might have been satisfied with a less
forfeiture than that of two lives. On the other hand,
from the audacity of the fact, a severe example was
judged necessary; and such was the opinion of the
government. When it became apparent that the sentence of death was to be executed, files, and other
implements necessary for their escape, were transmitted
secretly to the culprits by a friend from without. By
these means they sawed a bar out of one of the prison-

windows, and might have made their escape, but for the obstinacy of Wilson, who, as he was daringly resolute, was doggedly pertinacious of his opinion. His comrade, Robertson, a young and slender man, proposed to make the experiment of passing the foremost through the gap they had made, and enlarging it from the outside, if necessary, to allow Wilson free passage. Wilson, however, insisted on making the first experiment, and being a robust and lusty man, he not only found it impossible to get through betwixt the bars, but, by his struggles, he jammed himself so fast, that he was unable to draw his body back again. In these circumstances discovery became unavoidable, and sufficient precautions were taken by the jailor to prevent any repetition of the same attempt. Robertson uttered not a word of reflection on his companion for the consequences of his obstinacy; but it appeared from the sequel, that Wilson's mind was deeply impressed with the recollection, that, but for him, his comrade, over whose mind he exercised considerable influence, would not have engaged in the criminal enterprise which had terminated thus fatally; and that now he had become his destroyer a second time, since, but for his obstinacy, Robertson might have effected his escape. Minds like Wilson's, even when exercised in evil practices, sometimes retain the power of thinking and resolving with enthusiastic generosity. His whole thoughts were now bent on the possibility of saving Robertson's life, without the least respect to his own. The resolution which he adopted, and the manner in which he carried it into effect, were striking and unusual.

Adjacent to the tolbooth or city jail of Edinburgh, is one of three churches into which the cathedral of St. Giles is now divided, called, from its vicinity, the Tolbooth Church. It was the custom, that criminals under sentence of death were brought to this church, with a sufficient guard, to hear and join in public worship on the Sabbath before execution. It was supposed that the hearts of these unfortunate persons, however hardened before against feelings of devotion, could not but be accessible to them upon uniting their thoughts and voices, for the last time, along with their fellow-mortals, in addressing their Creator. And to the rest of the congregation, it was thought it could not but be impressive and affecting, to find their devotions mingling with those, who, sent by the doom of an earthly tribunal to appear where the whole earth is judged, might be considered as beings trembling on the verge of eternity. The practice, however edifying, has been discontinued, in consequence of the incident we are about to detail.

The clergyman, whose duty it was to officiate in the Tolbooth Church, had concluded an affecting discourse, part of which was particularly directed to the unfortunate men, Wilson and Robertson, who were in the pew set apart for the persons in their unhappy situation, each secured betwixt two soldiers of the city guard. The clergyman had reminded them, that the next congregation they must join would be that of the just, or of the unjust; that the psalms they now heard must be exchanged, in the space of two brief days, for eternal hallelujahs, or eternal lamentations; and that this fearful

alternative must depend upon the state to which they
might be able to bring their minds before the moment
of awful preparation: that they should not despair on
account of the suddenness of the summons, but rather
to feel this comfort in their misery, that, though all who
now lifted the voice, or bent the knee in conjunction
with them, lay under the same sentence of certain death,
they only had the advantage of knowing the precise
moment at which it should be executed upon them.
"Therefore," urged the good man, his voice trembling
with emotion, "redeem the time, my unhappy brethren,
which is yet left; and remember, that, with the grace
of Him to whom space and time are but as nothing,
salvation may yet be assured, even in the pittance of
delay which the laws of your country afford you."

Robertson was observed to weep at these words; but
Wilson seemed as one whose brain had not entirely
received their meaning, or whose thoughts were deeply
impressed with some different subject;—an expression
so natural to a person in his situation, that it excited
neither suspicion nor surprise.

The benediction was pronounced as usual, and the
congregation was dismissed, many lingering to indulge
their curiosity with a more fixed look at the two
criminals, who now, as well as their guards, rose up, as
if to depart when the crowd should permit them. A
murmur of compassion was heard to pervade the spectators, the more general, perhaps, on account of the
alleviating circumstances of the case; when all at once,
Wilson, who, as we have already noticed, was a very

strong man, seized two of the soldiers, one with each
hand, and calling at the same time to his companion,
"Run, Geordie, run!" threw himself on a third, and
fastened his teeth on the collar of his coat. Robertson
stood for a second as if thunderstruck, and unable to
avail himself of the opportunity of escape; but the cry
of "Run, run!" being echoed from many around, whose
feelings surprised them into a very natural interest in
his behalf, he shook off the grasp of the remaining soldier, threw himself over the pew, mixed with the dispersing congregation, none of whom felt inclined to stop
a poor wretch taking his last chance for his life, gained
the door of the church, and was lost to all pursuit.

The generous intrepidity which Wilson had displayed
on this occasion augmented the feeling of compassion
which attended his fate. The public, where their own
prejudices are not concerned, are easily engaged on the
side of disinterestedness and humanity, admired Wilson's behaviour, and rejoiced in Robertson's escape.
This general feeling was so great, that it excited a vague
report that Wilson would be rescued at the place of
execution, either by the mob or by some of his old
associates, or by some second extraordinary and unexpected exertion of strength and courage on his own
part. The magistrates thought it their duty to provide
against the possibility of disturbance. They ordered
out, for protection of the execution of the sentence, the
greater part of their own City Guard, under the command of Captain Porteous, a man whose name became
too memorable from the melancholy circumstances of

the day, and subsequent events. It may be necessary
to say a word about this person, and the corps which
he commanded. But the subject is of importance sufficient to deserve another chapter.

CHAPTER THE THIRD.

And thou, great god of aqua-vitæ !
Wha sways the empire of this city,
(When fou we 're sometimes capernoity),
        Be thou prepared,
To save us frae that black banditti,
        The City Guard !

                    FERGUSON'S DAFT DAYS.

CAPTAIN JOHN PORTEOUS, a name memorable in the
traditions of Edinburgh, as well as in the records of
criminal jurisprudence, was the son of a citizen of Edinburgh, who endeavoured to breed him up to his own
mechanical trade of a tailor. The youth, however, had
a wild and irreclaimable propensity to dissipation,

which finally sent him to serve in the corps long maintained in the service of the States of Holland, and
called the Scotch Dutch. Here he learned military
discipline; and, returning afterwards, in the course of
an idle and wandering life, to his native city, his services
were required by the magistrates of Edinburgh in the
disturbed year 1715, for disciplining their City Guard,
in which he shortly afterwards received a captain's commission. It was only by his military skill, and an alert
and resolute character as an officer of police, that he
merited this promotion, for he is said to have been a
man of profligate habits, an unnatural son, and a brutal
husband. He was, however, useful in his station, and
his harsh and fierce habits rendered him formidable to
rioters or disturbers of the public peace.

The corps in which he held his command is, or perhaps we should rather say *was*, a body of about one
hundred and twenty soldiers, divided into three com-
panies, and regularly armed, clothed, and embodied.
They were chiefly veterans who enlisted in this corps,
having the benefit of working at their trades when they
were off duty. These men had the charge of preserving
public order, repressing riots and street robberies, acting, in short, as an armed police, and attending on all
public occasions where confusion or popular disturbance
might be expected.* Poor Ferguson, whose irregulari-

* The Lord Provost was ex-officio commander and colonel of
the corps, which might be increased to three hundred men when
the times required it. No other drum but theirs was allowed to
sound on the High Street between the Luckenbooths and the
Netherbow.

ties sometimes led him into unpleasant rencontres with
these military conservators of public order, and who
mentions them so often that he may be termed their
poet laureate, thus admonishes his readers, warned
doubtless by his own experience :

> " Gude folk, as ye come frae the fair,
>   Bide yont frae this black squad ;
>   There 's nae sic savages elsewhere
>   Allowed to wear cockad."

In fact, the soldiers of the City Guard, being, as we
have said, in general discharged veterans, who had
strength enough remaining for this municipal duty, and
being, moreover, for the greater part, Highlanders, were
neither by birth, education, or former habits, trained to
endure with much patience the insults of the rabble, or
the provoking petulance of truant schoolboys, and idle
debauchees of all descriptions, with whom their occupation brought them into contact. On the contrary, the
tempers of the poor old fellows were soured by the indignities with which the mob distinguished them on
many occasions, and frequently might have required
the soothing strains of the poet we have just quoted—

> "O soldiers ! for your ain dear sakes,
>   For Scotland's love, the Land o' Cakes,
>   Gie not her bairns sic deadly paiks,
>   Nor be sae rude,
>   Wi' firelock or Lochaber-axe,
>   As spill their bluid !"

On all occasions when a holiday licensed some riot
and irregularity, a skirmish with these veterans was a

favourite recreation with the rabble of Edinburgh.
These pages may perhaps see the light when many have
in fresh recollection such onsets as we allude to.   But
the venerable corps, with whom the contention was
held, may now be considered as totally extinct.   Of
late the gradual diminution of these civic soldiers,
reminds one of the abatement of King Lear's hundred
knights.   The edicts of each succeeding set of magistrates have, like those of Goneril and Regan, diminished
this venerable band with the similar question, "What
need we five-and twenty?—ten?—or five?"   And it is
now nearly come to, "What need one?"   A spectre may
indeed here and there still be seen, of an old grey-
headed and grey-bearded Highlander, with war-worn
features, but bent double by age; dressed in an old-
fashioned cocked-hat, bound with white tape instead of
silver lace; and in coat, waistcoat, and breeches of a
muddy-coloured red, bearing in his withered hand an
ancient weapon, called a Lochaber-axe; a long pole,
namely, with an axe at the extremity, and a hook at the
back of the hatchet.*   Such a phantom of former days
still creeps, I have been informed, round the statue of
Charles the Second, in the Parliament Square, as if the
image of a Stuart were the last refuge for any memorial
of our ancient manners; and one or two others are
supposed to glide around the door of the guard-house
assigned to them in the Luckenbooths, when their

* This hook was to enable the bearer of the Lochaber-axe to
scale a gateway, by grappling the top of the door, and swinging
himself up by the staff of his weapon.

ancient refuge in the High-Street was laid low.*   But
the fate of manuscripts bequeathed to friends and exe-
cutors is so uncertain, that the narrative containing
these frail memorials of the old Town-Guard of Edinburgh, who, with their grim and valiant corporal, John
Dhu (the fiercest-looking fellow I ever saw), were, in
my boyhood, the alternate terror and derision of the
petulant brood of the High-School, may, perhaps, only
come to light when all memory of the institution has
faded away, and then serve as an illustration of Kay's
caricatures, who has preserved the features of some of
their heroes.   In the preceding generation, when there
was a perpetual alarm for the plots and activity of the
Jacobites, some pains were taken by the magistrates of
Edinburgh to keep this corps, though composed always
of such materials as we have noticed, in a more effective
state than was afterwards judged necessary, when their
most dangerous service was to skirmish with the rabble
on the king's birth-day.   They were, therefore, more
the objects of hatred, and less that of scorn, than they
were afterwards accounted.

To Captain John Porteous, the honour of his command and of his corps seems to have been a matter of

* This ancient corps is now entirely disbanded. Their last
march to do duty at Hallow-fair, had something in it affecting.
Their drums and fifes had been wont on better days to play on
this joyous occasion, the lively tune of

"Jockey to the fair;"

but on this final occasion the afflicted veterans moved slowly to
the dirge of

" The last time I came ower the muir."

high interest and importance. He was exceedingly
incensed against Wilson for the affront which he construed him to have put upon his soldiers, in the effort
he made for the liberation of his companion, and expressed himself most ardently on the subject. He was
no less indignant at the report, that there was an intention to rescue Wilson himself from the gallows, and
uttered many threats and imprecations upon that subject, which were afterwards remembered to his disad-
vantage. In fact, if a good deal of determination and
promptitude rendered Porteous, in one respect, fit to
command guards designed to suppress popular commo-
tion, he seems, on the other, to have been disqualified
for a charge so delicate, by a hot and surly temper,
always too ready to come to blows and violence; a character void of principle; and a disposition to regard the
rabble, who seldom failed to regale him and his soldiers
with some marks of their displeasure, as declared
enemies, upon whom it was natural and justifiable that
he should seek opportunities of vengeance. Being,
however, the most active and trustworthy among the
captains of the City Guard, he was the person to whom
the magistrates confided the command of the soldiers
appointed to keep the peace at the time of Wilson's
execution. He was ordered to guard the gallows and
scaffold, with about eighty men, all the disposable force
that could be spared for that duty.

But the magistrates took farther precautions, which
affected Porteous's pride very deeply. They requested
the assistance of part of a regular infantry regiment,

not to attend upon the execution, but to remain drawn
up on the principal street of the city, during the time
that it went forward, in order to intimidate the multitude, in case they should be disposed to be unruly,
with a display of force which could not be resisted
without desperation. It may sound ridiculous in our
ears, considering the fallen state of this ancient civic
corps, that its officer should have felt punctiliously
jealous of its honour. Yet so it was. Captain Porteous
resented, as an indignity, the introducing the Welsh
Fusileers within the city, and drawing them up in the
street where no drums but his own were allowed to be
sounded, without the special command or permission of
the magistrates. As he could not show his ill-humour
to his patrons the magistrates, it increased his indignation and his desire to be revenged on the unfortunate
criminal Wilson, and all who favoured him. These
internal emotions of jealousy and rage wrought a change
on the man's mien and bearing, visible to all who saw
him on the fatal morning when Wilson was appointed
to suffer. Porteous's ordinary appearance was rather
favourable. He was about the middle size, stout, and
well made, having a military air, and yet rather a gentle
and mild countenance. His complexion was brown, his
face somewhat fretted with the scars of the smallpox,
his eyes rather languid than keen or fierce. On the
present occasion, however, it seemed to those who saw
him as if he were agitated by some evil demon. His
step was irregular, his voice hollow and broken, his
countenance pale, his eyes staring and wild, his speech

imperfect and confused, and his whole appearance so
disordered, that many remarked he seemed to be *fey*, a
Scottish expression, meaning the state of those who are
driven on to their impending fate by the strong impulse
of some irresistible necessity.

One part of his conduct was truly diabolical, if indeed, it has not been exaggerated by the general prejudice entertained against his memory. When Wilson,
the unhappy criminal, was delivered to him by the
keeper of the prison, in order that he might be conducted to the place of execution, Porteous, not satisfied
with the usual precautions to prevent escape, ordered
him to be manacled. This might be justifiable from
the character and bodily strength of the malefactor, as
well as from the apprehensions so generally entertained
of an expected rescue. But the handcuffs which were
produced being found too small for the wrists of a man
so big-boned as Wilson, Porteous proceeded with his
own hands, and by great exertion of strength, to force
them till they clasped together, to the exquisite torture
of the unhappy criminal. Wilson remonstrated against
such barbarous usage, declaring that the pain distracted
his thoughts from the subjects of meditation proper to
his unhappy condition.

"It signifies little," replied Captain Porteous; "your
pain will soon be at an end."

"Your cruelty is great," answered the sufferer.
"You know not how soon you yourself may have occasion to ask the mercy which you are now refusing to a
fellow-creature. May God forgive you!"

These words, long afterwards quoted and remembered, were all that passed between Portcous and his prisoner; but as they took air, and became known to the people, they greatly increased the popular compassion for Wilson, and excited a proportionate degree of indignation against Porteous; against whom, as strict, and even violent in the discharge of his unpopular office, the common people had some real, and many imaginary causes of complaint.

When the painful procession was completed, and Wilson, with the escort, had arrived at the scaffold in the Grassmarket, there appeared no signs of that attempt to rescue him which had occasioned such precautions. The multitude, in general, looked on with deeper interest than at ordinary executions; and there might be seen, on the countenances of many, a stern and indignant expression, like that with which the ancient Cameronians might be supposed to witness the execution of their brethren, who glorified the Covenant on the same occasion, and at the same spot. But there was no attempt at violence. Wilson himself seemed disposed to hasten over the space that divided time from eternity. The devotions proper and usual on such occasions were no sooner finished than he submitted to his fate, and the sentence of the law was fulfilled.

He had been suspended on the gibbet so long as to be totally deprived of life, when at once, as if occasioned by some newly-received impulse, there arose a tumult among the multitude. Many stones were thrown at Porteous and his guards; some mischief was done; and the mob continued to press forward with whoops, shrieks, howls, and exclamations. A young fellow, with a sailor's cap slouched over his face, sprung on the scaffold, and cut the rope by which the criminal was suspended. Others approached to carry off the body, either to secure for it a decent grave, or to try, perhaps, some means of resuscitation. Captain Porteous, was wrought, by this appearance of insurrection against his authority, into a rage so headlong as made him forget, that, the sentence having been fully executed, it was his duty not to engage in hostilities with the misguided multitude, but to draw off his men as fast as possible. He sprung from the scaffold, snatched a musket from one of his soldiers, commanded the party to give fire, and, as several eye-witnesses concurred in swearing, set them the example, by discharging his piece, and shooting a man dead on the spot. Several soldiers obeyed his command or followed his example; six or seven persons were slain, and a great many were hurt and wounded.

After this act of violence, the Captain proceeded to withdraw his men towards their guard-house in the High Street. The mob were not so much intimidated as incensed by what had been done. They pursued the soldiers with execrations, accompanied by volleys of stones. As they pressed on them, the rearmost soldiers turned, and again fired with fatal aim and execution. It is not accurately known whether Porteous commanded this second act of violence; but of course the odium of the whole transactions of the fatal day

attached to him, and to him alone. He arrived at the
guard-house, dismissed his soldiers, and went to make
his report to the magistrates concerning the unfortunate
events of the day.

Apparently by this time Captain Porteous had
begun to doubt the propriety of his own conduct, and
the reception he met with from the magistrates was
such as to make him still more anxious to gloss it over.
He denied that he had given orders to fire; he denied
he had fired with his own hand; he even produced the
fusee which he carried as an officer for examination; it
was found still loaded. Of three cartridges which he
was seen to put in his pouch that morning, two were
still there; a white handkerchief was thrust into the
muzzle of the piece, and returned unsoiled or blackened.
To the defence founded on these circumstances it was
answered, that Porteous had not used his own piece,
but had been seen to take one from a soldier. Among
the many who had been killed and wounded by the
unhappy fire, there were several of better rank; for
even the humanity of such soldiers as fired over the
heads of the mere rabble around the scaffold, proved in
some instances fatal to persons who were stationed in
windows, or observed the melancholy scene from a
distance. The voice of public indignation was loud.
and general; and, ere men's tempers had time to cool,
the trial of Captain Porteous took place before the
High Court of Justiciary. After a long and patient
hearing, the jury had the difficult duty of balancing
the positive evidence of many persons, and those of

respectability, who deposed positively to the prisoner's
commanding his soldiers to fire, and himself firing his
piece, of which some swore that they saw the smoke
and flash, and beheld a man drop at whom it was
pointed, with the negative testimony of others, who,
though well stationed for seeing what had passed,
neither heard Porteous give orders to fire, nor saw him
fire himself; but, on the contrary, averred that the first
shot was fired by a soldier who stood close by him. A
great part of his defence was also founded on the turbu-
lence of the mob, which witnesses, according to their
feelings, their predilections, and their opportunities of
observation, represented differently; some describing
as a formidable riot, what others represented as a trifling
disturbance, such as always used to take place on the
like occasions, when the executioner of the law, and
the men commissioned to protect him in his task, were
generally exposed to some indignities. The verdict of
the jury sufficiently shows how the evidence prepon-
derated in their minds. It declared that John Porteous
fired a gun among the people assembled at the execution; that he gave orders to his soldiers to fire, by
which many persons were killed and wounded; but, at
the same time, that the prisoner and his guard had
been wounded and beaten, by stones thrown at them
by the multitude. Upon this verdict, the Lords of
Justiciary passed sentence of death against Captain
John Porteous, adjudging him, in the common form, to
be hanged on a gibbet at the common place of execution, on Wednesday, 8th September, 1736, and all

his movable property to be forfeited to the king's use, according to the Scottish law in cases of wilful murder.

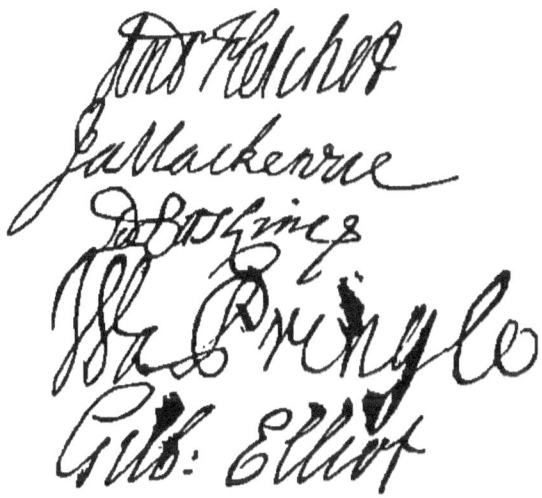

Signatures of the Lords of Justiciary, affixed to the Death-warrant of Captain Porteous.

1. ANDREW FLETCHER, Lord Milton.
2. Sir JAMES MACKENZIE, Lord Royston.
3. DAVID ERSKINE, Lord Dun.
4. Sir WALTER PRINGLE, Lord Newhall.
5. Sir GILBERT ELLIOT, Lord Minto, Lord Justice Clerk.

CHAPTER THE FOURTH.

"The hour's come, but not the man."*

KELPIE.

On the day when the unhappy Porteous was expected to suffer the sentence of the law, the place of execution, extensive as it is, was crowded almost to suffocation. There was not a window in all the lofty tenements around it, or in the steep and crooked street called the Bow, by which the fatal procession was to descend from the High Street, that was not absolutely filled with spectators. The uncommon height and antique appearance of these houses, some of which were formerly the property of the Knights Templars, and the Knights of St. John, and still exhibit on their fronts and gables the iron cross of these orders, gave additional effect to a scene in itself so striking. The area of the Grass-market resembled a huge dark lake or sea of human

---

* There is a tradition, that while a little stream was swollen into a torrent by recent showers, the discontented voice of the Water Spirit was heard to pronounce these words. At the same moment a man, urged on by his fate, or, in Scottish language, *fey*, arrived at a gallop, and prepared to cross the water. No remonstrance from the bystanders was of power to stop him—he plunged into the stream, and perished.

heads, in the centre of which arose the fatal tree, tall,
black, and ominous, from which dangled the deadly
halter.   Every object takes interest from its uses and
associations, and the erect beam and empty noose,
things so simple in themselves, became, on such an
occasion, objects of terror and of solemn interest.

Amid so numerous an assembly there was scarcely
a word spoken, save in whispers.   The thirst of vengeance was in some degree allayed by its supposed
certainty; and even the populace, with deeper feeling
than they are wont to entertain, suppressed all clamorous
exultation, and prepared to enjoy the scene of retalia-
tion in triumph, silent and decent, though stern and
relentless.   It seemed as if the depth of their hatred
to the unfortunate criminal scorned to display itself in
anything resembling the more noisy current of their
ordinary feelings.   Had a stranger consulted only the
evidence of his ears, he might have supposed that so
vast a multitude were assembled for some purpose which
affected them with the deepest sorrow, and stilled those
noises which, on all ordinary occasions, arise from such
a concourse; but if he had gazed upon their faces, he
would have been instantly undeceived.   The compressed
lip, the bent brow, the stern and flashing eye of almost
every one on whom he looked, conveyed the expression
of men come to glut their sight with triumphant
revenge.   It is probable that the appearance of the
criminal might have somewhat changed the temper of
the populace in his favour, and that they might in the
moment of death have forgiven the man against whom

their resentment had been so fiercely heated. It had,
however, been destined, that the mutability of their
sentiments was not to be exposed to this trial.

The usual hour for producing the criminal had been
past for many minutes, yet the spectators observed no
symptom of his appearance. "Would they venture to
defraud public justice?" was the question which men
began anxiously to ask at each other. The first answer
in every case was bold and positive,—"They dare not."
But when the point was further canvassed, other
opinions were entertained, and various causes of doubt
were suggested. Porteous had been a favourite officer
of the magistracy of the city, which, being a numerous
and fluctuating body, requires for its support a degree
of energy in its functionaries, which the individuals
who compose it cannot at all times alike be supposed
to possess in their own persons. It was remembered,
that in the Information for Porteous (the paper, namely,
in which his case was stated to the Judges of the
criminal court), he had been described by his counsel
as the person on whom the magistrates chiefly relied in
all emergencies of uncommon difficulty. It was argued,
too, that his conduct, on the unhappy occasion of
Wilson's execution, was capable of being attributed
to an imprudent excess of zeal in the execution of his
duty, a motive for which those under whose authority
he acted might be supposed to have great sympathy.
And as these considerations might move the magistrates
to make a favourable representation of Porteous's case,
there were not wanting others in the higher depart-

ments of Government, which would make such suggestions favourably listened to.

The mob of Edinburgh, when thoroughly excited,
had been at all times one of the fiercest which could be
found in Europe; and of late years they had risen
repeatedly against the Government, and sometimes not
without temporary success. They were conscious,
therefore, that they were no favourites with the rulers
of the period, and that, if Captain Porteous's violence
was not altogether regarded as good service, it might
certainly be thought, that to visit it with a capital
punishment would render it both delicate and dangerous
for future officers, in the same circumstances, to act
with effect in repressing tumults. There is also a
natural feeling, on the part of all members of Government, for the general maintenance of authority; and it
seemed not unlikely, that what to the relatives of the
sufferers appeared a wanton and unprovoked massacre,
should be otherwise viewed in the cabinet of St. James's.
It might be there supposed, that upon the whole
matter, Captain Porteous was in the exercise of a trust
delegated to him by the lawful civil authority; that he
had been assaulted by the populace, and several of his
men hurt; and that, in finally repelling force by force,
his conduct could be fairly imputed to no other motive
than self-defence in the discharge of his duty.

These considerations, of themselves very powerful,
induced the spectators to apprehend the possibility of a
reprieve; and to the various causes which might interest
the rulers in his favour, the lower part of the rabble

added one which was peculiarly well adapted to their comprehension. It was averred, in order to increase the odium against Porteous, that while he repressed with the utmost severity the slightest excesses of the poor, he not only overlooked the license of the young nobles and gentry, but was very willing to lend them the countenance of his official authority, in execution of such loose pranks as it was chiefly his duty to have restrained. This suspicion, which was perhaps much exaggerated, made a deep impression on the minds of the populace; and when several of the higher rank joined in a petition, recommending Porteous to the mercy of the Crown, it was generally supposed he owed their favour not to any conviction of the hardship of his case, but to the fear of losing a convenient accomplice in their debaucheries. It is scarcely necessary to say how much this suspicion augmented the people's detestation of this obnoxious criminal, as well as their fear of his escaping the sentence pronounced against him.

While these arguments were stated and replied to, and canvassed and supported, the hitherto silent expectation of the people became changed into that deep and agitating murmur, which is sent forth by the ocean before the tempest begins to howl. The crowded populace, as if their motions had corresponded with the unsettled state of their minds, fluctuated to and fro without any visible cause of impulse, like the agitation of the waters, called by sailors the ground-swell. The news, which the magistrates had almost hesitated to communicate to them, were at length announced, and

spread among the spectators with a rapidity like light-
ning. A reprieve from the Secretary of State's office,
under the hand of his Grace the Duke of Newcastle,
had arrived, intimating the pleasure of Queen Caroline,
(regent of the kingdom during the absence of George
II. on the Continent), that the execution of the sentence of death pronounced against John Porteous, late
Captain-Lieutenant of the City-Guard of Edinburgh,
present prisoner in the tolbooth of that city, be respited
for six weeks from the time appointed for his execution.

The assembled spectators of almost all degrees,
whose minds had been wound up to the pitch which we
have described, uttered a groan, or rather a roar of
indignation and disappointed revenge, similar to that of
a tiger from whom his meal has been rent by his keeper
when he was just about to devour it. This fierce
exclamation seemed to forbode some immediate explosion of popular resentment, and, in fact, such had been
expected by the magistrates, and the necessary measures
had been taken to repress it. But the shout was not
repeated, nor did any sudden tumult ensue, such as it
appeared to announce. The populace seemed to be
ashamed of having expressed their disappointment in a
vain clamour, and the sound changed, not into the
silence which had preceded the arrival of these stunning
news, but into stifled mutterings, which each group
maintained among themselves, and which were blended
into one deep and hoarse murmur which floated above
the assembly.

Yet still, though all expectation of the execution

was over, the mob remained assembled, stationary, as it
were, through very resentment, gazing on the preparations for death, which had now been made in vain, and
stimulating their feelings, by recalling the various
claims which Wilson might have had on royal mercy,
from the mistaken motives on which he acted, as well
as from the generosity he had displayed towards his
accomplice. "This man," they said,—"the brave, the
resolute, the generous, was executed to death without
mercy for stealing a purse of gold, which in some sense
he might consider as a fair reprisal; while the profligate
satellite, who took advantage of a trifling tumult,
inseparable from such occasions, to shed the blood of
twenty of his fellow-citizens, is deemed a fitting object
for the exercise of the royal prerogative of mercy. Is
this to be borne?—would our fathers have borne it?
Are not we, like them, Scotsmen and burghers of Edinburgh?"

The officers of justice began now to remove the
scaffold, and other preparations which had been made
for the execution, in hopes, by doing so, to accelerate
the dispersion of the multitude. The measure had the
desired effect; for no sooner had the fatal tree been
unfixed from the large stone pedestal or socket in which
it was secured, and sunk slowly down upon the wain
intended to remove it to the place where it was usually
deposited, than the populace, after giving vent to their
feelings in a second shout of rage and mortification,
began slowly to disperse to their usual abodes and
occupations.

The windows were in like manner gradually deserted, and groups of the more decent class of citizens formed themselves, as if waiting to return homewards when the streets should be cleared of the rabble. Contrary to what is frequently the case, this description of persons agreed in general with the sentiments of their inferiors, and considered the cause as common to all ranks. Indeed, as we have already noticed, it was by no means amongst the lowest class of the spectators, or those most likely to be engaged in the riot at Wilson's execution, that the fatal fire of Porteous's soldiers had taken effect. Several persons were killed who were looking out at windows at the scene, who could not of course belong to the rioters, and were persons of decent rank and condition. The burghers, therefore, resenting the loss which had fallen on their own body, and proud and tenacious of their rights, as the citizens of Edinburgh have at all times been, were greatly exasperated at the unexpected respite of Captain Porteous.

It was noticed at the time, and afterwards more particularly remembered, that, while the mob were in the act of dispersing, several individuals were seen busily passing from one place and one group of people to another, remaining long with none, but whispering for a little time with those who appeared to be declaiming most violently against the conduct of Government. These active agents had the appearance of men from the country, and were generally supposed to be old friends and confederates of Wilson, whose minds were of course highly excited against Porteous.

If, however, it was the intention of those men to stir the multitude to any sudden act of mutiny, it seemed for the time to be fruitless. The rabble, as well as the more docent part of the assembly, dispersed, and went home peaceably; and it was only by observing the moody discontent on their brows, or catching the tenor of the conversation they held with each other, that a stranger could estimate the state of their minds. We will give the reader this advantage, by associating ourselves with one of the numerous groups who were painfully ascending the steep declivity of the West Bow, to return to their dwellings in the Lawnmarket.

"An unco thing this, Mrs. Howden," said old Peter Plumdamas to his neighbour the rouping-wife, or saleswoman, as he offered her his arm to assist her in the toilsome ascent, "to see the grit folk at Lunnon set their face against law and gospel, and let loose sic a reprobate as Porteous upon a peaceable town!"

"And to think o' the weary walk they hae gien us," answered Mrs. Howden, with a groan; "and sic a comfortable window as I had gotten, too, just within a penny-stane-cast of the scaffold—I could hae heard every word the minister said—and to pay twalpennies for my stand, and a' for naething!"

"I am judging," said Mr. Plumdamas, "that this reprieve wadna stand gude in the auld Scots law, when the kingdom *was* a kingdom."

"I dinna ken muckle about the law," answered Mrs. Howden; "but I ken, when we had a king, and a chancellor, and parliament-men o' our ain, we could

aye peeble them wi' stanes when they werena gude
bairns—But naebody's nails can reach the length o'
Lunnon."

"Weary on Lunnon, and a' that e'er came out o't!"
said Miss Grizel Damahoy, an ancient seamstress;
"they hae taen away our parliament, and they hae
oppressed our trade. Our gentles will hardly allow
that a Scots needle can sew ruffles on a sark, or lace on
an owerlay."

"Ye may say that—Miss Damahoy, and I ken o'
them that hae gotten raisins frae Lunnon by forpits at
ance," responded Plumdamas; "and then sic an host
of idle English gaugers and excisemen as hae come
down to vex and torment us, that an honest man canna
fetch sae muckle as a bit anker o' brandy frae Leith
to the Lawnmarket, but he's like to be rubbit o' the
very gudes he's bought and paid for.—Weel, I winna
justify Andrew Wilson for pitting hands on what
wasna his; but if he took nae mair than his ain, there's
an awfu' difference between that and the fact this man
stands for."

"If ye speak about the law," said Mrs. Howden,
"here comes Mr. Saddletree, that can settle it as weel
as ony on the bench."

The party she mentioned, a grave elderly person,
with a superb periwig, dressed in a decent suit of sad-
coloured clothes, came up as she spoke, and courteously
gave his arm to Miss Grizel Damahoy.

It may be necessary to mention, that Mr. Bartoline
Saddletree kept an excellent and highly-esteemed shop

for harness, saddles, etc. etc., at the sign of the Golden
Nag, at the head of Bess Wynd. His genius, however
(as he himself and most of his neighbours conceived),
lay towards the weightier matters of the law, and he
failed not to give frequent attendance upon the pleadings
and arguments of the lawyers and judges in the neighbouring square, where, to say the truth, he was oftener
to be found than would have consisted with his own
emolument; but that his wife, an active painstaking
person, could, in his absence, make an admirable shift
to please the customers and scold the journeymen.
This good lady was in the habit of letting her husband
take his way, and go on improving his stock of legal
knowledge without interruption; but, as if in requital,
she insisted upon having her own will in the domestic
and commercial departments which he abandoned to
her. Now, as Bartoline Saddletree had a considerable
gift of words, which he mistook for eloquence, and
conferred more liberally upon the society in which he
lived than was at all times gracious and acceptable,
there went forth a saying, with which wags used sometimes to interrupt his rhetoric, that, as he had a golden
nag at his door, so he had a grey mare in his shop.
This reproach induced Mr. Saddletree, on all occasions,
to assume rather a haughty and stately tone towards
his good woman, a circumstance by which she seemed
very little affected, unless he attempted to exercise any
real authority, when she never failed to fly into open
rebellion. But such extremes Bartoline seldom provoked; for, like the gentle King Jamie, he was fonder

of talking of authority than really exercising it. This
turn of mind was, on the whole, lucky for him; since
his substance was increased without any trouble on his
part, or any interruption of his favourite studies.

This word in explanation has been thrown in to the
reader, while Saddletree was laying down, with great
precision, the law upon Porteous's case, by which he
arrived at this conclusion, that, if Porteous had fired
five minutes sooner, before Wilson was cut down, he
would have been *versans in licito;* engaged, that is, in
a lawful act, and only liable to be punished *propter
excessum,* or for lack of discretion, which might have
mitigated the punishment to *pæna ordinaria.*

"Discretion!" echoed Mrs. Howden, on whom, it
may well be supposed, the fineness of this distinction
was entirely thrown away,—"whan had Jock Porteous
either grace, discretion, or gude manners?—I mind
when his father"——

"But, Mrs. Howden," said Saddletree——

"And I," said Miss Damahoy, "mind when his
mother"——

"Miss Damahoy," entreated the interrupted orator——

"And I," said Plumdamas, "mind when his wife"——

"Mr. Plumdamas—Mrs. Howden—Miss Damahoy,"
again implored the orator,—"Mind the distinction, as
Counsellor Crossmyloof says—'I,' says he, 'take a
distinction.' Now, the body of the criminal being cut
down, and the execution ended, Porteous was no longer
official; the act which he came to protect and guard,

being done and ended, he was no better than *cuivis ex populo.*"

"*Quivis—quivis*, Mr. Saddletree, craving your pardon," said (with a prolonged emphasis on the first syllable) Mr. Butler, the deputy schoolmaster of a parish near Edinburgh, who at that moment came up behind them as the false Latin was uttered.

"What signifies interrupting me, Mr. Butler?—but I am glad to see ye notwithstanding—I speak after Counsellor Crossmyloof, and he said *cuivis.*"

"If Counsellor Crossmyloof used the dative for the nominative, I would have crossed *his* loof with a tight leathern strap, Mr. Saddletree; there is not a boy on the booby form but should have been scourged for such a solecism in grammar."

"I speak Latin like a lawyer, Mr. Butler, and not like a schoolmaster," retorted Saddletree.

"Scarce like a schoolboy, I think," rejoined Butler.

"It matters little," said Bartoline; "all I mean to say is, that Porteous has become liable to the *pæna extra ordinem*, or capital punishment—which is to say, in plain Scotch, the gallows—simply because he did not fire when he was in office, but waited till the body was cut down, the execution whilk he had in charge to guard implemented, and he himself exonered of the public trust imposed on him."

"But, Mr. Saddletree," said Plumdamas, "do ye really think John Porteous's case wad hae been better if he had begun firing before ony stanes were flung at a'?"

"Indeed do I, neighbour Plumdamas," replied

Bartoline, confidently, "he being then in point of trust
and in point of power, the execution being but inchoat,
or, at least, not implemented, or finally ended; but
after Wilson was cut down, it was a' ower—he was
clean exauctorate, and had nae mair ado but to get awa
wi' his guard up this West Bow as fast as if there had
been a caption after him—And this is law, for I heard
it laid down by Lord Vincovincentem."

"Vincovincentem?—Is he a lord of state, or a lord
of seat?" inquired Mrs. Howden.*

"A lord of seat—a lord of session.—I fash mysell
little wi' lords o' state; they vex me wi' a wheen idle
questions about their saddles, and curpels, and holsters,
and horse-furniture, and what they'll cost, and whan
they'll be ready—a wheen golloping geese.—my wife
may serve the like o' them."

"And so might she, in her day, hae served the best
lord in the land, for as little as ye think o' her, Mr.
Saddletree," said Mrs. Howden, somewhat indignant at
the contemptuous way in which her gossip was mentioned; "when she and I were twa gilpies, we little
thought to hae sitten doun wi' the like o' my auld Davie
Howden, or you either, Mr. Saddletree."

While Saddletree, who was not bright at a reply,
was cudgelling his brains for an answer to this home-
thrust, Miss Damahoy broke in on him.

"And as for the lords of state," said Miss Damahoy,

* A nobleman was called a Lord of State. The Senators of
the College of Justice were termed Lords of Seat, or of the
Session.

"ye suld mind the riding o' the parliament, Mr. Saddle-tree, in the gude auld time before the Union,—a year's rent o' mony a gude estate gaed for horse-graith and harnessing, forby broidered robes and foot-mantles, that wad hae stude by their lane wi' gold brocade, and that were muckle in my ain line."

"Ay, and then the lusty banqueting, with sweet-meats and comfits wet and dry, and dried fruits of divers sorts," said Plumdamas. "But Scotland was Scotland in these days."

"I'll tell ye what it is, neighbours," said Mrs. Howden, "I'll ne'er believe Scotland is Scotland ony mair, if our kindly Scots sit doun with the affront they hae gien us this day. It's not only the blude that is shed, but the blude that might hae been shed, that's required at our hands; there was my daughter's wean, little Eppie Daidle—my oe, ye ken, Miss Grizel—had played the truant frae the school, as bairns will do, ye ken, Mr. Butler"——

"And for which," interjected Mr. Butler, "they should be soundly scourged by their well-wishers."

"And had just cruppen to the gallows' foot to see the hanging, as was natural for a wean; and what for mightna she hae been shot as weel as the rest o' them, and where wad we a' hae been then? I wonder how Queen Carline (if her name be Carline) wad hae liked to hae had ane o' her ain bairns in sic a venture?"

"Report says," answered Butler, "that such a circumstance would not have distressed her majesty beyond endurance."

"Aweel," said Mrs. Howden, "the sum o' the matter is, that, were I a man, I wad hae amends o' Jock Porteous, be the upshot what like o't, if a' the carles and carlines in England had sworn to the nay-say."

"I would claw down the tolbooth door wi' my nails," said Miss Grizel, "but I wad be at him."

"Ye may be very right, ladies," said Butler, "but I would not advise you to speak so loud."

"Speak!" exclaimed both the ladies together, "there will be naething else spoken about frae the Weigh-house to the Water-gate, till this is either ended or mended."

The females now departed to their respective places of abode. Plumdamas joined the other two gentlemen in drinking their *meridian* (a bumper-dram of brandy), as they passed the well-known low-browed shop in the Lawnmarket, where they were wont to take that refreshment. Mr. Plumdamas then departed towards his shop, and Mr. Butler, who happened to have some particular occasion for the rein of an old bridle (the truants of that busy day could have anticipated its application), walked down the Lawnmarket with Mr. Saddletree, each talking as he could get a word thrust in, the one on the laws of Scotland, the other on those of syntax, and neither listening to a word which his companion uttered.

CHAPTER THE FIFTH.

Elswhair he colde right weel lay down the law,
But in his house was meek as is a daw.
                                    DAVIE LINDSAY.

"THERE has been Jock Driver the carrier here, speering about his new graith," said Mrs. Saddletree to her husband, as he crossed his threshold, not with the purpose,

by any means, of consulting him upon his own affairs,
but merely to intimate, by a gentle recapitulation, how
much duty she had gone through in his absence.

"Weel," replied Bartoline, and deigned not a word
more.

"And the Laird of Girdingburst has had his running
footman here, and ca'd himsell (he's a civil pleasant
young gentleman), to see when the broidered saddle-
cloth for his sorrel horse will be ready, for he wants it
agane the Kelso races."

"Weel, aweel," replied Bartoline, as laconically as
before.

"And his lordship, the Earl of Blazonbury, Lord
Flash and Flame, is like to be clean daft, that the harness for the six Flanders mears, wi' the crests, coronets,
housings, and mountings conform, are no sent hame
according to promise gien."

"Weel, weel, weel—weel, weel, gudewife," said
Saddletree, "if he gangs daft, we'll hae him cognosced
—it's a' very weel."

"It's weel that ye think sae, Mr. Saddletree," answered his helpmate, rather nettled at the indifference
with which her report was received; "there's mony
ane wad hae thought themselves affronted, if sae mony
customers had ca'd and naebody to answer them but
women-folk; for a' the lads were aff, as soon as your
back was turned, to see Porteous hanged, that might be
counted upon; and sae, you no being at hame"——

"Houts, Mrs. Saddletree," said Bartoline, with an
air of consequence, "dinna deave me wi' your nonsense;

I was under the necessity of being elsewhere — *non omnia* — as Mr. Crossmyloof said, when he was called by two 'nacers at once — *non omnia possumus — pessimus — possimis* — I ken our law-latin offends Mr. Butler's ears, but it means, Naebody, an it were the Lord President himsell, can do twa turns at ance."

"Very right, Mr. Saddletree," answered his careful helpmate, with a sarcastic smile; "and nae doubt it's a decent thing to leave your wife to look after young gentlemen's saddles and bridles, when ye gang to see a man, that never did ye nae ill, raxing a halter."

"Woman," said Saddletree, assuming an elevated tone, to which the *meridian* had somewhat contributed, "desist, — I say forbear, from intromitting with affairs thou canst not understand. D'ye think I was born to sit here brogging an elshin through bend-leather, when sic men as Duncan Forbes, and that other Arniston chield there, without muckle greater parts, if the close-head speak true, than mysell, maun be presidents and king's advocates, nae doubt, and wha but they? Whereas, were favour equally distribute, as in the days of the wight Wallace"——

"I ken naething we wad hae gotten by the wight Wallace," said Mrs. Saddletree, "unless, as I hae heard the auld folk tell, they fought in thae days wi' bend-leather guns, and then it's a chance but what, if he had bought them, he might have forgot to pay for them. And as for the greatness of your parts, Bartley, the folk in the close-head maun ken mair about them than I do, if they mak sic a report of them."

"I tell ye, woman," said Saddletree, in high dudgeon, "that ye ken naething about these matters. In Sir William Wallace's days, there was nae man pinned down to sic a slavish wark as a saddler's, for they got ony leather gnith that they had use for ready-made out of Holland."

"Well," said Butler, who was, like many of his profession, something of a humorist and dry joker, "if that be the case, Mr. Saddletree, I think we have changed for the better; since we make our own harness, and only import our lawyers from Holland."

"It's ower true, Mr. Butler," answered Bartoline, with a sigh; "if I had had the luck — or rather, if my father had had the sense to send me to Leyden and Utrecht to learn the Substitutes and Pandex "——

"You mean the Institutes — Justinian's Institutes, Mr. Saddletree?" said Butler.

"Institutes and substitutes are synonymous words, Mr. Butler, and used indifferently as such in deeds of tailzie, as you may see in Balfour's Practiques, or Dallas of St. Martin's Styles. I understand these things pretty weel, I thank God; but I own I should have studied in Holland."

"To comfort you, you might not have been farther forward than you are now, Mr. Saddletree," replied Mr. Butler; "for our Scottish advocates are an aristocratic race. Their brass is of the right Corinthian quality, and *Non cuivis contigit adire Corinthum*—Aha, Mr. Saddletree?"

"And aha, Mr. Butler," rejoined Bartoline, upon

whom, as may be well supposed, the jest was lost, and
all but the sound of the words, "ye said a gliff syne it
was *quivis*, and now I heard ye say *cuivis* with my ain
ears, as plain as ever I heard a word at the fore-bar."

"Give me your patience, Mr. Saddletree, and I'll
explain the discrepancy in three words," said Butler, as
pedantic in his own department, though with infinitely
more judgment and learning, as Bartoline was in his
self-assumed profession of the law—"Give me your
patience for a moment—You'll grant that the nominative case is that by which a person or thing is nomina-
ted or designed, and which may be called the primary
case, all others being formed from it by alterations of
the termination in the learned languages, and by pre-
positions in our modern Babylonian jargons—You'll
grant me that, I suppose, Mr. Saddletree?"

"I dinna ken whether I will or no—*ad avisandum*,
ye ken—naebody should be in a hurry to make admis-
sions, either in point of law, or in point of fact," said
Saddletree, looking, or endeavouring to look, as if he
understood what was said.

"And the dative case," continued Butler——

"I ken what a tutor dative is," said Saddletree,
"readily enough."

"The dative case," resumed the grammarian, "is
that in which any thing is given or assigned as properly
belonging to a person, or thing—You cannot deny that,
I am sure."

"I am sure I'll no grant it though," said Saddletree.

"Then, what the *deevil* d'ye take the nominative

and the dative cases to be?" said Butler, hastily, and
surprised at once out of his decency of expression and
accuracy of pronunciation.

"I'll tell you that at leisure, Mr. Butler," said
Saddletree, with a very knowing look ; "I'll take a day
to see and answer every article of your condescendence,
and then I'll hold you to confess or deny, as accords."

"Come, come, Mr. Saddletree," said his wife, "we'll
hae nae confessions and condescendences here; let them
deal in thae sort o' wares that are paid for them—they
suit the like o' us as ill as a demipique saddle would
suit a draught ox."

"Aha!" said Mr. Butler, "*Optat ephippia bos piger*,
nothing new under the sun—But it was a fair hit of
Mrs. Saddletree, however."

"And it wad far better become ye, Mr. Saddletree,"
continued his helpmate, "since ye say ye hae skeel o'
the law, to try if ye can do ony thing for Effie Deans,
puir thing, that's lying up in the tolbooth yonder, cauld,
and hungry, and comfortless—A servant lass of ours,
Mr. Butler, and as innocent a lass, to my thinking, and
as usefu' in the chop—When Mr. Saddletree gangs out,
—and ye're aware he's seldom at hame when there's
ony o' the plea-houses open,—poor Effie used to help
me to tumble the bundles o' barkened leather up and
down, and range out the gudes, and suit a' body's
humours—And troth, she could aye please the customers wi' her answers, for she was aye ceevil, and a bon-
nier lass wasna in Auld Reekie. And when folk were
hasty and unreasonable, she could serve them better

than me, that am no sae young as I hae been, Mr. Butler, and a wee bit short in the temper into the bargain.
For when there's ower mony folks crying on me at anes,
and nane but ae tongue to answer them, folk maun
speak hastily, or they'll ne'er get through their wark—
Sae I miss Effie daily."

"*De die in diem*," added Saddletree.

"I think," said Butler, after a good deal of hesitation, "I have seen the girl in the shop—a modest-look-
ing, fair-haired girl?"

"Ay, ay, that's just puir Effie," said her mistress.
"How she was abandoned to hersell, or whether she was
sackless o' the sinful deed, God in Heaven knows; but if
she's been guilty, she's been sair tempted, and I wad amaist
take my Bible-aith she hasna been hersell at the time."

Butler had by this time become much agitated; he
fidgeted up and down the shop, and showed the greatest
agitation that a person of such strict decorum could be
supposed to give way to. "Was not this girl," he said,
"the daughter of David Deans, that had the parks at
St. Leonard's taken? and has she not a sister?"

"In truth has she—puir Jeanie Deans, ten years
aulder than hersell; she was here greeting a wee while
syne about her tittie. And what could I say to her,
but that she behoved to come and speak to Mr. Saddletree when he was at hame? It wasna that I thought
Mr. Saddletree could do her or ony other body muckle
gude or ill, but it wad aye serve to keep the puir thing's
heart up for a wee while; and let sorrow come when
sorrow maun."

"Ye're mistaen though, gudewife," said Saddletree scornfully, "for I could hae gien her great satisfaction; I could hae proved to her that her sister was indicted upon the statute saxteen hundred and ninety, chapter one—For the mair ready prevention of child-murder—for concealing her pregnancy, and giving no account of the child which she had borne."

"I hope," said Butler,—"I trust in a gracious God, that she can clear herself."

"And sao do I, Mr. Butler," replied Mrs. Saddletree. "I am sure I wad hae answered for her as my ain daughter; but wae's my heart, I had been tender a' the simmer, and scarce ower the door o' my room for twal weeks. And as for Mr. Saddletree, he might be in a lying-in hospital, and ne'er find out what the women cam there for. Sae I could see little or naething o' her, or I wad hae had the truth o' her situation out o' her, I'se warrant ye—But we a' think her sister maun be able to speak something to clear her."

"The haill Parliament House," said Saddletree, "was speaking o' naething else, till this job o' Porteous's put it out o' head—It's a beautiful point of presumptive murder, and there's been nane like it in the Justiciar Court since the case of Luckie Smith the howdie, that suffered in the year saxteen hundred and seventy-nine."

"But what's the matter wi' you, Mr. Butler?" said the good woman; "ye are looking as white as a sheet; will ye tak a dram?"

"By no means," said Butler, compelling himself to

speak. "I walked in from Dumfries yesterday and, this is a warm day."

"Sit down," said Mrs. Saddletree, laying hands on him kindly, "and rest ye—ye'll kill yoursell, man, at that rate.—And are we to wish you joy o' getting the scule, Mr. Butler?"

"Yes—no—I do not know," answered the young man vaguely. But Mrs. Saddletree kept him to the point, partly out of real interest, partly from curiosity.

"Ye dinna ken whether ye are to get the free scule o' Dumfries or no, after hinging on and teaching it a' the simmer?"

"No, Mrs. Saddletree—I am not to have it," replied Butler, more collectedly. "The Laird of Black-at-the-bane had a natural son bred to the kirk, that the presbytery could not be prevailed upon to license; and so"——

"Ay, ye need say nae muir about it; if there was a laird that had a puir kinsman or a bastard that it wad suit, there's enough said.—And ye're e'en come back to Liberton to wait for dead men's shoon?—and, for as frail as Mr. Whackbairn is, he may live as lang as you, that are his assistant and successor."

"Very like," replied Butler with a sigh; "I do not know if I should wish it otherwise."

"Nae doubt it's a very vexing thing," continued the good lady, "to be in that dependent station; and you that has right and title to sae muckle better, I wonder how ye bear these crosses."

"*Quos diligit castigat*," answered Butler; "even the

pagan Seneca could see an advantage in affliction.   The
Heathens had their philosophy, and the Jews their
revelation, Mrs. Saddletree, and they endured their distresses in their day.   Christians have a better dispensation than either—but doubtless "——

He stopped and sighed.

"I ken what ye mean," said Mrs. Saddletree, looking
toward her husband; "there's whiles we lose patience
in spite of baith book and Bible—But ye are no gaun
awa, and looking sae poorly—ye'll stay and tak some
kale wi' us?"

Mr. Saddletree laid aside Balfour's Practiques (his
favourite study, and much good may it do him), to join
in his wife's hospitable importunity.   But the teacher
declined all entreaty, and took his leave upon the spot.

"There's something in a' this," said Mrs. Saddletree,
looking after him as he walked up the street; "I
wonder what makes Mr. Butler sae distressed about
Effie's misfortune—there was nae acquaintance atween
them that ever I saw or heard of; but they were neighbours when David Deans was on the Laird o' Dumbiedikes' land.   Mr. Butler wad ken her father, or some o'
her folk.—Get up, Mr. Saddletree—ye have set yoursell down on the very brecham that wants stitching—
and here's little Willie, the prentice.—Ye little rin-
there-out deil that ye are, what takes you raking through
the gutters to see folk hangit?—how wad ye like when
it comes to be your ain chance, as I winna insure ye, if
ye dinna mend your manners?—And what are ye
maundering and greeting for, as if a word were breaking

your banes ?—Gang in by, and be a better bairn another
time, and tell Peggy to gie ye a bicker o' broth, for
ye'll be as gleg as a gled, I'se warrant ye.—It's a fatherless bairn, Mr. Saddletree, and motherless, whilk in
some cases may be waur, and ane would take care o'
him if they could—it's a Christian duty."

"Very true, gudewife," said Saddletree in reply, " we
are in *loco parentis* to him during his years of pupil-
larity, and I hae had thoughts of applying to the Court
for a commission as factor *loco tutoris*, seeing there is
nae tutor nominate, and the tutor-at-law declines to
act ; but only I fear the expense of the procedure wad
not be in *rem versam*, for I am not aware if Willie has
ony effects whereof to assume the administration."

He concluded' this sentence with a self-important
cough, as one who has laid down the law in an indis·
putable manner.

"Effects !" said Mrs. Saddletree, " what effects has
the puir wean ?—he was in rags when his mother died ;
and the blue polonie that Effie made for him out of an
auld mantle of my ain, was the first decent dress the
bairn ever had on.   Poor Effie ! can ye tell me now
really, wi' a' your law, will her life be in danger, Mr.
Saddletree, when they arena able to prove that ever
there was a bairn ava ?"

"Whoy," said Mr. Saddletree, delighted at having
for once in his life seen his wife's attention arrested by
a topic of legal discussion—" Whoy, there are two sorts
of *murdrum* or *murdragium*, or what you *populariter
et vulgariter* call murther.   I mean there are many

sorts; for there's your *murthrum per vigilias et insidias,* and your *murthrum* under trust."

"I am sure," replied his moiety, "that murther by trust is the way that the gentry murther us merchants, and whiles make us shut the booth up—but that has nuething to do wi' Effie's misfortune."

"The case of Effie (or Euphemia) Deans," resumed Saddletree, "is one of those cases of murder presumptive, that is, a murder of the law's inferring or construction, being derived from certain *indicia* or grounds of suspicion."

"So that," said the good woman, "unless poor Effie has communicated her situation, she'll be hanged by the neck, if the bairn was still-born, or if it be alive at this moment?"

"Assuredly," said Saddletree, "it being a statute made by our sovereign Lord and Lady, to prevent the horrid delict of bringing forth children in secret—The crime is rather a favourite of the law, this species of murther being one of its ain creation."

"Then, if the law makes murders," said Mrs. Saddletree, "the law should be hanged for them; or if they wad hang a lawyer instead, the country wad find nae faut."

A summons to their frugal dinner interrupted the further progress of the conversation, which was otherwise like to take a turn much less favourable to the science of jurisprudence and its professors, than Mr. Bartoline Saddletree, the fond admirer of both, had at its opening anticipated.

CHAPTER THE SIXTH.

But up then raise all Edinburgh,
They all rose up by thousands three.
                    JOHNNIE ARMSTRANG's *Goodnight.*

BUTLER, on his departure from the sign of the Golden
Nag, went in quest of a friend of his connected with the
law, of whom he wished to make particular inquiries
concerning the circumstances in which the unfortunate
young woman mentioned in the last chapter was placed,
having, as the reader has probably already conjectured,
reasons much deeper than those dictated by mere
humanity, for interesting himself in her fate.   He found
the person he sought absent from home, and was equally
unfortunate in one or two other calls which he made
upon acquaintances whom he hoped to interest in her
story.   But every body was, for the moment, stark-mad
on the subject of Porteous, and engaged busily in
attacking or defending the measures of Government in
reprieving him; and the ardour of dispute had excited
such universal thirst, that half the young lawyers and
writers, together with their very clerks, the class whom
Butler was looking after, had adjourned the debate to
some favourite tavern.   It was computed by an experienced arithmetician, that there was as much twopenny

ale consumed on the discussion as would have floated a
first-rate man-of-war.

Butler wandered about until it was dusk, resolving
to take that opportunity of visiting the unfortunate
young woman, when his doing so might be least
observed; for he had his own reasons for avoiding the
remarks of Mrs. Saddletree, whose shop-door opened at
no great distance from that of the jail, though on the
opposite or south side of the street, and a little higher
up.   He passed, therefore, through the narrow and
partly covered passage leading from the north-west end
of the Parliament Square.

He stood now before the Gothic entrance of the
ancient prison, which, as is well-known to all men, rears
its ancient front in the very middle of the High Street,
forming, as it were, the termination to a huge pile of
buildings called the Luckenbooths, which, for some in-
conceivable reason, our ancestors had jammed into the
midst of the principal street of the town, leaving for
passage a narrow street on the north, and on the south,
into which the prison opens, a narrow crooked lane,
winding betwixt the high and sombre walls of the Tolbooth and the adjacent houses on the one side, and the
buttresses and projections of the old Cathedral upon the
other.   To give some gaiety to this sombre passage
(well-known by the name of the Krames), a number of
little booths, or shops, after the fashion of cobblers'
stalls, are plastered, as it were, against the Gothic projections and abutments, so that it seemed as if the
traders had occupied with nests, bearing the same pro-

portion to the building, every buttress and coign of vantage, as the martlett did in Macbeth's Castle.   Of later
years these booths have degenerated into mere toy-shops,
where the little loiterers chiefly interested in such wares
are tempted to linger, enchanted by the rich display of
hobby-horses, babies, and Dutch toys, arranged in artful
and gay confusion ; yet half-scared by the cross-looks of
the withered pantaloon, or spectacled old lady, by whom
these tempting stores are watched and superintended.
But, in the times we write of, the hosiers, the glovers,
the hatters, the mercers, the milliners, and all who dealt
in the miscellaneous wares now termed haberdasher's
goods, were to be found in this narrow alley.

To return from our digression.   Butler found the
outer turnkey, a tall thin old man, with long silver
hair, in the act of locking the outward door of the jail.
He addressed himself to this person, and asked admittance to Effie Deans, confined upon accusation of child-
murder.   The turnkey looked at him earnestly, and,
civilly touching his hat out of respect to Butler's black
coat and clerical appearance, replied, " It was impossible
any one could be admitted at present."

" You shut up earlier than usual, probably on account
of Captain Porteous's affair ?" said Butler.

The turnkey, with the true mystery of a person in
office, gave two grave nods, and withdrawing from the
wards a ponderous key of about two feet in length, he
proceeded to shut a strong plate of steel, which folded
down above the keyhole, and was secured by a steel
spring and catch.   Butler stood still instinctively while

the door was made fast, and then looking at his watch,
walked briskly up the street, muttering to himself
almost unconsciously—

Porta adversa, ingens, solidoque adamante columnæ;
Via ut nulla virûm, non ipsi exscindere ferro
Cœlicolæ valeant—Stat ferrea turris ad auras—etc. *

Having wasted half an hour more in a second fruitless attempt to find his legal friend and adviser, he
thought it time to leave the city and return to his place
of residence, in a small village about two miles and a
half to the southward of Edinburgh. The metropolis
was at this time surrounded by a high wall, with battle-
ments and flanking projections at some intervals, and
the access was through gates, called in the Scottish language *ports*, which were regularly shut at night. A
small fee to the keepers would indeed procure egress and
ingress at any time, through a wicket left for that
purpose in the large gate; but it was of some importance,
to a man so poor as Butler, to avoid even this slight
pecuniary mulct; and fearing the hour of shutting the
gates might be near, he made for that to which he found
himself nearest, although, by doing so, he somewhat
lengthened his walk homewards. Bristo Port was that
by which his direct road lay, but the West Port, which
leads out of the Grassmarket, was the nearest of the

* Wide is the fronting gate, and, raised on high,
With adamantine columns threats the sky;
Vain is the force of man, and Heaven's as vain,
To crush the pillars which the pile sustain;
Sublime on these a tower of steel is reared.
                    DRYDEN'S VIRGIL, book vi.

city gates to the place where he found himself, and to that, therefore, he directed his course. He reached the port in ample time to pass the circuit of the walls, and enter a suburb called Portsburgh, chiefly inhabited by the lower order of citizens and mechanics. Here he was unexpectedly interrupted.

He had not gone far from the gate before he heard the sound of a drum, and, to his great surprise, met a number of persons, sufficient to occupy the whole front of the street, and form a considerable mass behind, moving with great speed towards the gate he had just come from, and having in front of them a drum beating to arms. While he considered how he should escape a party, assembled, as it might be presumed, for no lawful purpose, they came full on him and stopped him.

" Are you a clergyman ?" one questioned him.

Butler replied that " he was in orders, but was not a placed minister."

" It's Mr. Butler from Liberton," said a voice from behind ; " he'll discharge the duty as weel as ony man."

" You must turn back with us, sir," said the first speaker, in a tone civil but peremptory.

" For what purpose, gentlemen ?" said Mr. Butler. " I live at some distance from town—the roads are unsafe by night—you will do me a serious injury by stopping me."

" You shall be sent safely home—no man shall touch a hair of your head—but you must and shall come along with us."

"But to what purpose or end, gentlemen?" said Butler. "I hope you will be so civil as to explain that to me?"

"You shall know that in good time. Come along—for come you must, by force or fair means; and I warn you to look neither to the right hand nor the left, and to take no notice of any man's face, but consider all that is passing before you as a dream."

"I would it were a dream I could awaken from," said Butler to himself; but having no means to oppose the violence with which he was threatened, he was compelled to turn round and march in front of the rioters, two men partly supporting and partly holding him. During this parley the insurgents had made themselves masters of the West Port, rushing upon the Waiters (so the people were called who had the charge of the gates), and possessing themselves of the keys. They bolted and barred the folding doors, and commanded the person, whose duty it usually was, to secure the wicket, of which they did not understand the fastenings. The man, terrified at an incident so totally unexpected, was unable to perform his usual office, and gave the matter up, after several attempts. The rioters, who seemed to have come prepared for every emergency, called for torches, by the light of which they nailed up the wicket with long nails, which, it seemed probable, they had provided on purpose.

While this was going on, Butler could not, even if he had been willing, avoid making remarks on the individuals who seemed to lead this singular mob. The

torch-light, while it fell on their forms and left him in
the shade, gave him an opportunity to do so without
their observing him.   Several of those who seemed
most active were dressed in sailors' jackets, trousers,
and sea caps; others in large loose-bodied great-coats,
and slouched hats; and there were several who, judging
from their dress, should have been called women, whose
rough deep voices, uncommon size, and masculine
deportment and mode of walking, forbade them being
so interpreted.   They moved as if by some well-con-
certed plan of arrangement.   They had signals by
which they knew, and nick-names by which they
distinguished each other.   Butler remarked, that the
name of Wildfire was used among them, to which one
stout Amazon seemed to reply.

    The rioters left a small party to observe the West
Port, and directed the Waiters, as they valued their
lives, to remain within their lodge, and make no attempt
for that night to repossess themselves of the gate.
They then moved with rapidity along the low street
called the Cowgate, the mob of the city everywhere
rising at the sound of their drum, and joining them.
When the multitude arrived at the Cowgate Port, they
secured it with as little opposition as the former, made
it fast, and left a small party to observe it.   It was
afterwards remarked, as a striking instance of prudence
and precaution, singularly combined with audacity, that
the parties left to guard those gates did not remain
stationary on their posts, but flitted to and fro, keeping
so near the gates as to see that no efforts were made to

open them, yet not remaining so long as to have their persons closely observed. The mob, at first only about one hundred strong, now amounted to thousands, and were increasing every moment. They divided themselves so as to ascend with more speed the various narrow lanes which lead up from the Cowgate to the High Street; and still beating to arms as they went, and calling on all true Scotsmen to join them, they now filled the principal street of the city.

The Netherbow Port might be called the Temple-bar of Edinburgh, as, intersecting the High Street at its termination, it divided Edinburgh, properly so called, from the suburb named the Canongate, as Temple-bar separates London from Westminster. It was of the utmost importance to the rioters to possess themselves of this pass, because there was quartered in the Canongate at that time a regiment of infantry, commanded by Colonel Moyle, which might have occupied the city by advancing through this gate, and would possess the power of totally defeating their purpose. The leaders therefore hastened to the Netherbow Port, which they secured in the same manner, and with as little trouble, as the other gates, leaving a party to watch it, strong in proportion to the importance of the post.

The next object of these hardy insurgents was at once to disarm the City Guard, and to procure arms for themselves; for scarce any weapons but staves and bludgeons had been yet seen among them. The Guard-house was a long, low, ugly building (removed in 1787),

which to a fanciful imagination might have suggested
the idea of a long black snail crawling up the middle of
the High Street, and deforming its beautiful esplanade.
This formidable insurrection had been so unexpected,
that there were no more than the ordinary sergeant's
guard of the city-corps upon duty; even these were
without any supply of powder and ball; and sensible
enough what had raised the storm, and which way it
was rolling, could hardly be supposed very desirous to
expose themselves by a valiant defence to the animosity
of so numerous and desperate a mob, to whom they
were on the present occasion much more than usually
obnoxious.

There was a sentinel upon guard, who (that one
town-guard soldier might do his duty on that eventful
evening) presented his piece, and desired the foremost
of the rioters to stand off. The young amazon, whom
Butler had observed particularly active, sprung upon
the soldier, seized his musket, and after a struggle
succeeded in wrenching it from him, and throwing him
down on the causeway. One or two soldiers, who
endeavoured to turn out to the support of their sentinel,
were in the same manner seized and disarmed, and the
mob without difficulty possessed themselves of the
Guard-house, disarming and turning out of doors the
rest of the men on duty. It was remarked, that, notwithstanding the city soldiers had been the instruments
of the slaughter which this riot was designed to revenge,
no ill usage or even insult was offered to them. It
seemed as if the vengeance of the people disdained to

stoop at any head meaner than that which they considered as the source and origin of their injuries.

On possessing themselves of the guard, the first act
of the multitude was to destroy the drums, by which
they supposed an alarm might be conveyed to the
garrison in the castle; for the same reason they now
silenced their own, which was beaten by a young fellow,
son to the drummer of Portsburgh, whom they had
forced upon that service. Their next business was to
distribute among the boldest of the rioters the guns,
bayonets, partisans, halberts, and battle or Lochaber
axes. Until this period the principal rioters had preserved silence on the ultimate object of their rising,
as being that which all knew, but none expressed.
Now, however, having accomplished all the preliminary
parts of their design, they raised a tremendous shout
of " Porteous! Porteous! To the Tolbooth! To the
Tolbooth !"

They proceeded with the same prudence when the
object seemed to be nearly in their grasp, as they had
done hitherto when success was more dubious. A
strong party of the rioters, drawn up in front of the
Luckenbooths, and facing down the street, prevented
all access from the eastward, and the west end of the
defile formed by the Luckenbooths was secured in the
same manner; so that the Tolbooth was completely
surrounded, and those who undertook the task of
breaking it open effectually secured against the risk of
interruption.

The magistrates, in the meanwhile, had taken the

alarm, and assembled in a tavern, with the purpose of
raising some strength to subdue the rioters. The
deacons, or presidents of the trades, were applied to,
but declared there was little chance of their authority
being respected by the craftsmen, where it was the
object to save a man so obnoxious. Mr. Lindsay,
member of parliament for the city, volunteered the
perilous task of carrying a verbal message from the
Lord Provost to Colonel Moyle, the commander of the
regiment lying in the Canongate, requesting him to
force the Netherbow Port, and enter the city to put
down the tumult. But Mr. Lindsay declined to charge
himself with any written order, which, if found on his
person by an enraged mob, might have cost him his
life; and the issue of the application was, that Colonel
Moyle having no written requisition from the civil
authorities, and having the fate of Porteous before his
eyes as an example of the severe construction put by a
jury on the proceedings of military men acting on their
own responsibility, declined to encounter the risk to
which the Provost's verbal communication invited him.

More than one messenger was dispatched by different
ways to the Castle, to require the commanding officer
to march down his troops, to fire a few cannon-shot, or
even to throw a shell among the mob, for the purpose
of clearing the streets. But so strict and watchful
were the various patrols whom the rioters had established in different parts of the streets, that none of the
emissaries of the magistrates could reach the gate of
the Castle. They were, however, turned back without

either injury or insult, and with nothing more of
menace than was necessary to deter them from again
attempting to accomplish their errand.

The same vigilance was used to prevent every body
of the higher, and those which, in this case, might be
deemed the more suspicious orders of society, from
appearing in the street, and observing the movements,
or distinguishing the persons, of the rioters. Every
person in the garb of a gentleman was stopped by small
parties of two or three of the mob, who partly exhorted,
partly required of them, that they should return to
the place from whence they came. Many a quadrille
table was spoilt that memorable evening ; for the sedan
chairs of ladies, even of the highest rank, were interrupted in their passage from one point to another, in
spite of the laced footmen and blazing flambeaux.
This was uniformly done with a deference and attention
to the feelings of the terrified females, which could
hardly have been expected from the videttes of a mob
so desperate. Those who stopped the chair usually
made the excuse, that there was much disturbance on
the streets, and that it was absolutely necessary for the
lady's safety that the chair should turn back. They
offered themselves to escort the vehicles which they
had thus interrupted in their progress, from the apprehension, probably, that some of those who had casually
united themselves to the riot might disgrace their
systematic and determined plan of vengeance, by those
acts of general insult and license which are common on
similar occasions.

Persons are yet living who remember to have heard
from the mouths of ladies thus interrupted on their
journey in the manner we have described, that they
were escorted to their lodgings by the young men who
stopped them, and even handed out of their chairs, with a
polite attention far beyond what was consistent with
their dress, which was apparently that of journeymen
mechanics.*   It seemed as if the conspirators, like those
who assassinated Cardinal Beatoun in former days, had
entertained the opinion, that the work about which they
went was a judgment of Heaven, which, though unsanc-
tioned by the usual authorities, ought to be proceeded
in with order and gravity.

While their outposts continued thus vigilant, and
suffered themselves neither from fear nor curiosity to
neglect that part of the duty assigned to them, and
while the main guards to the east and west secured
them against interruption, a select body of the rioters
thundered at the door of the jail, and demanded instant
admission.   No one answered, for the outer keeper had
prudently made his escape with the keys at the commencement of the riot, and was nowhere to be found.
The door was instantly assailed with sledge-hammers,
iron-crows, and the coulters of ploughs, ready provided
for the purpose, with which they prized, heaved, and

* A near relation of the author's used to tell of having been
stopped by the rioters, and escorted home in the manner described.
On reaching her own home, one of her attendants, in appearance
a *baxter*, i. e., a baker's lad, handed her out of her chair, and took
leave with a bow, which, in the lady's opinion, argued breeding
that could hardly be learned at the oven's mouth.

battered for some time with little effect; for the door, besides being of double oak planks, clenched, both end-long and athwart, with broad-headed nails, was so hung and secured as to yield to no means of forcing, without the expenditure of much time. The rioters, however, appeared determined to gain admittance. Gang after gang relieved each other at the exercise, for, of course, only a few could work at once; but gang after gang retired, exhausted with their violent exertions, without making much progress in forcing the prison-door. Butler had been led up near to this the principal scene of action; so near, indeed, that he was almost deafened by the unceasing clang of the heavy fore-hammers against the iron-bound portal of the prison. He began to enter-tain hopes, as the task seemed protracted, that the populace might give it over in despair, or that some rescue might arrive to disperse them. There was a moment at which the latter seemed probable.

The magistrates, having assembled their officers, and some of the citizens who were willing to hazard them-selves for the public tranquillity, now sallied forth from the tavern where they held their sitting, and approached the point of danger. Their officers went before them with links and torches, with a herald to read the riot act, if necessary. They easily drove before them the outposts and videttes of the rioters; but when they approached the line of guard which the mob, or rather, we should say, the conspirators, had drawn across the street in the front of the Luckenbooths, they were received with an unintermitted volley of stones, and, on

their nearer approach, the pikes, bayonets, and Lochaber-axes, of which the populace had possessed themselves, were presented against them.   One of their
ordinary officers, a strong resolute fellow, went forward,
seized a rioter, and took from him a musket; but, being
unsupported, he was instantly thrown on his back in
the street, and disarmed in his turn.   The officer was
too happy to be permitted to rise and run away without
receiving any farther injury; which afforded another
remarkable instance of the mode in which these men
had united a sort of moderation towards all others, with
the most inflexible inveteracy against the object of their
resentment.   The magistrates, after vain attempts to
make themselves heard and obeyed, possessing no means
of enforcing their authority, were constrained to abandon
the field to the rioters, and retreat in all speed from
the showers of missiles that whistled around their ears.

The passive resistance of the Tolbooth-gate promised
to do more to baffle the purpose of the mob than the
active interference of the magistrates.   The heavy
sledge-hammers continued to din against it without
intermission, and with a noise which, echoed from the
lofty buildings around the spot, seemed enough to have
alarmed the garrison in the Castle.   It was circulated
among the rioters, that the troops would march down
to disperse them, unless they could execute their purpose without loss of time; or that, even without quitting the fortress, the garrison might obtain the same
end by throwing a bomb or two upon the street.

Urged by such motives for apprehension, they

eagerly relieved each other at the labour of assailing the
Tolbooth door: yet such was its strength, that it still
defied their efforts.   At length, a voice was heard to
pronounce the words, "Try it with fire."   The rioters,
with an unanimous shout, called for combustibles, and
as all their wishes seemed to be instantly supplied, they
were soon in possession of two or three empty tar-
barrels.   A huge red glaring bonfire speedily arose close
to the door of the prison, sending up a tall column of
smoke and flame against its antique turrets and strongly-
grated windows, and illuminating the ferocious and
wild gestures of the rioters who surrounded the place,
as well as the pale and anxious groups of those, who,
from windows in the vicinage, watched the progress of
this alarming scene.   The mob fed the fire with what
ever they could find fit for the purpose.   The flames
roared and crackled among the heaps of nourishment
piled on the fire, and a terrible shout soon announced
that the door had kindled, and was in the act of being
destroyed.   The fire was suffered to decay, but, long
ere it was quite extinguished, the most forward of the
rioters rushed, in their impatience, one after another,
over its yet smouldering remains.   Thick showers of
sparkles rose high in the air, as man after man bounded
over the glowing embers, and disturbed them in their
passage.   It was now obvious to Butler, and all others
who were present, that the rioters would be instantly in
possession of their victim, and have it in their power to
work their pleasure upon him, whatever that might be.*

Note A.   The Old Tolbooth.

CHAPTER THE SEVENTH.

The evil you teach us, we will execute; and it shall go hard
but we will better the instruction.
                              MERCHANT OF VENICE.

THE unhappy object of this remarkable disturbance had
been that day delivered from the apprehension of public execution, and his joy was the greater, as he had
some reason to question whether Government would
have run the risk of unpopularity by interfering in
his favour, after he had been legally convicted by the
verdict of a jury, of a crime so very obnoxious. Relieved from this doubtful state of mind, his heart was
merry within him, and he thought, in the emphatic
words of Scripture on a similar occasion, that surely the
bitterness of death was past. Some of his friends,
however, who had watched the manner and behaviour
of the crowd when they were made acquainted with the
reprieve, were of a different opinion. They augured,
from the unusual sternness and silence with which they
bore their disappointment, that the populace nourished
some scheme of sudden and desperate vengeance; and
they advised Porteous to lose no time in petitioning the
proper authorities, that he might be conveyed to the
Castle under a sufficient guard, to remain there in

security until his ultimate fate should be determined.
Habituated, however, by his office, to overawe the
rabble of the city, Porteous could not suspect them of
an attempt so audacious as to storm a strong and defen-
sible prison; and, despising the advice by which he
might have been saved, he spent the afternoon of the
eventful day in giving an entertainment to some friends
who visited him in jail, several of whom, by the indulgence of the Captain of the Tolbooth, with whom he
had an old intimacy, arising from their official connection, were even permitted to remain to supper with him,
though contrary to the rules of the jail.

It was, therefore, in the hour of unalloyed mirth,
when this unfortunate wretch was "full of bread," hot
with wine, and high in mistimed and ill-grounded confidence, and alas! with all his sins full blown, when
the first distant shouts of the rioters mingled with the
song of merriment and intemperance. The hurried call
of the jailor to the guests, requiring them instantly to
depart, and his yet more hasty intimation that a dreadful
and determined mob had possessed themselves of the
city gates and guard-house, were the first explanation
of those fearful clamours.

Porteous might, however, have eluded the fury from
which the force of authority could not protect him, had
he thought of slipping on some disguise, and leaving
the prison along with his guests. It is probable that
the jailor might have connived at his escape, or even
that, in the hurry of this alarming contingency, he
might not have observed it. But Porteous and his

friends alike wanted presence of mind to suggest or
execute such a plan of escape. The former hastily fled
from a place where their own safety seem compromised,
and the latter, in a state resembling stupefaction,
awaited in his apartment the termination of the enterprise of the rioters. The cessation of the clang of the
instruments with which they had at first attempted to
force the door, gave him momentary relief. The flatter-
ing hopes, that the military had marched into the city,
either from the Castle or from the suburbs, and that the
rioters were intimidated and dispersing were soon destroyed by the broad and glaring light of the flames,
which, illuminating through the grated window, every
corner of his apartment, plainly showed that the mob,
determined on their fatal purpose, had adopted a means
of forcing entrance equally desperate and certain.

The sudden glare of light suggested to the stupified
and astonished object of popular hatred the possibility
of concealment or escape. To rush to the chimney, to
ascend it at the risk of suffocation, were the only means
which seemed to have occurred to him ; but his progress
was speedily stopped by one of those iron gratings,
which are, for the sake of security, usually placed across
the vents of buildings designed for imprisonment. The
bars, however, which impeded his farther progress,
served to support him in the situation which he had
gained, and he seized them with the tenacious grasp of
one who esteemed himself clinging to his last hope of
existence. The lurid light which had filled the apartment, lowered and died away ; the sound of shouts was

heard within the walls, and on the narrow and winding
stair, which, cased within one of the turrets, gave access
to the upper apartments of the prison. The huzza of
the rioters was answered by a shout wild and desperate
as their own, the cry, namely, of the imprisoned felons,
who, expecting to be liberated in the general confusion,
welcomed the mob as their deliverers. By some of these
the apartment of Porteous was pointed out to his enemies. The obstacle of the lock and bolts was soon
overcome, and from his hiding place the unfortunate
man heard his enemies search every corner of the apartment, with oaths and maledictions, which would but
shock the reader if we recorded them, but which served
to prove, could it have admitted of doubt, the settled
purpose of soul with which they sought his destruction.

A place of concealment so obvious to suspicion and
scrutiny as that which Porteous had chosen, could not
long screen him from detection. He was dragged from
his lurking-place, with a violence which seemed to
argue an intention to put him to death on the spot.
More than one weapon was directed towards him, when
one of the rioters, the same whose female disguise had
been particularly noticed by Butler, interfered in an
authoritative tone. "Are ye mad?" he said, " or would
ye execute an act of justice as if it were a crime and a
cruelty? This sacrifice will lose half its savour if we
do not offer it at the very horns of the altar. We will
have him die where a murderer should die, on the common gibbet—We will have him die where he spilled
the blood of so many innocents!"

A loud shout of applause followed the proposal, and the cry, "To the gallows with the murderer!—To the Grassmarket with him!" echoed on all hands.

"Let no man hurt him," continued the speaker; "let him make his peace with God, if he can; we will not kill both his soul and body."

"What time did he give better folk for preparing their account?" answered several voices. "Let us mete to him with the same measure he measured to them."

But the opinion of the spokesman better suited the temper of those he addressed, a temper rather stubborn than impetuous, sedate though ferocious, and desirous of colouring their cruel and revengeful action with a show of justice and moderation.

For an instant this man quitted the prisoner, whom he consigned to a selected guard, with instructions to permit him to give his money and property to whomsoever he pleased. A person confined in the jail for debt received this last deposit from the trembling hand of the victim, who was at the same time permitted to make some other brief arrangements to meet his approaching fate. The felons, and all others who wished to leave the jail, were now at full liberty to do so; not that their liberation made any part of the settled purpose of the rioters, but it followed as almost a necessary consequence of forcing the jail doors. With wild cries of jubilee they joined the mob, or disappeared among the narrow lanes to seek out the hidden receptacles of vice and infamy, where they were accustomed to lurk and conceal themselves from justice.

Two persons, a man about fifty years old, and a girl about eighteen, were all who continued within the fatal walls, excepting two or three debtors, who probably saw no advantage in attempting their escape. The persons we have mentioned remained in the strong room of the prison, now deserted by all others. One of their late companions in misfortune called out to the man to make his escape, in the tone of an acquaintance. "Rin for it, Ratcliffe—the road's clear."

"It may be sae, Willie," answered Ratcliffe, composedly, "but I have taen a fancy to leave aff trade, and set up for an honest man."

"Stay there, and be hanged, then, for a donnard auld deevil!" said the other, and ran down the prison-stair.

The person in female attire whom we have distinguished as one of the most active rioters, was about the same time at the car of the young woman. "Flee, Effie, flee!" was all he had time to whisper. She turned towards him an eye of mingled fear, affection, and upbraiding, all contending with a sort of stupified surprise. He again repeated, "Flee, Effie, flee! for the sake of all that's good and dear to you!" Again she gazed on him, but was unable to answer. A loud noise was now heard, and the name of Madge Wildfire was repeatedly called from the bottom of the staircase.

"I am coming,—I am coming," said the person who answered to that appellative; and then reiterating hastily, "For God's sake — for your own sake — for my sake, flee, or they'll take your life!" he left the strong-room.

The girl gazed after him for a moment, and then, faintly muttering, "Better tyne life, since tint is gude fame," she sunk her head upon her hand, and remained, seemingly, unconscious as a statue, of the noise and tumult which passed around her.

That tumult was now transferred from the inside to the outside of the Tolbooth. The mob had brought their destined victim forth, and were about to conduct him to the common place of execution, which they had fixed as the scene of his death. The leader, whom they distinguished by the name of Madge Wildfire, had been summoned to assist at the procession by the impatient shouts of his confederates.

"I will insure you five hundred pounds," said the unhappy man, grasping Wildfire's hand,—"five hundred pounds for to save my life."

The other answered in the same under-tone, and returning his grasp with one equally convulsive, "Five hundred-weight of coined gold should not save you.— Remember Wilson!"

A deep pause of a minute ensued, when Wildfire added, in a more composed tone, "Make your peace with Heaven.—Where is the clergyman?"

Butler, who in great terror and anxiety, had been detained within a few yards of the Tolbooth door, to wait the event of the search after Porteous, was now brought forward, and commanded to walk by the prisoner's side, and to prepare him for immediate death. His answer was a supplication that the rioters would consider what they did. "You are neither judges nor

jury," said he.   "You cannot have, by the laws of God
or man, power to take away the life of a human
creature, however deserving he may be of death.   If it
is murder even in a lawful magistrate to execute an
offender otherwise than in the place, time, and manner
which the judges' sentence prescribes, what must it be
in you, who have no warrant for interference but your
own wills?   In the name of Him who is all mercy, show
mercy to this unhappy man, and do not dip your hands
in his blood, nor rush into the very crime which you
are desirous of avenging!"

"Cut your sermon short—you are not in your
pulpit," answered one of the rioters.

"If we hear more of your clavers," said another,
"we are like to hang you up beside him."

"Peace—hush!" said Wildfire.   "Do the good
man no harm—he discharges his conscience, and I like
him the better."

He then addressed Butler.   "Now, sir, we have
patiently heard you, and we just wish you to understand, in the way of answer, that you may as well argue
to the ashler-work and iron-stanchels of the Tolbooth
as think to change our purpose—Blood must have
blood.   We have sworn to each other by the deepest
oaths ever were pledged, that Porteous shall die the
death he deserves so richly ; therefore, speak no more
to us, but prepare him for death as well as the briefness
of his change will permit."

They had suffered the unfortunate Porteous to put
on his night-gown and slippers, as he had thrown off

his coat and shoes, in order to facilitate his attempted
escape up the chimney. In this garb he was now
mounted on the hands of two of the rioters, clasped
together, so as to form what is called in Scotland, "The
King's Cushion." Butler was placed close to his side,
and repeatedly urged to perform a duty always the most
painful which can be imposed on a clergyman deserving
of the name, and now rendered more so by the peculiar and horrid circumstances of the criminal's case.
Porteous at first uttered some supplications for mercy,
but when he found that there was no chance that these
would be attended to, his military education, and the
natural stubbornness of his disposition, combined to
support his spirits.

"Are you prepared for this dreadful end?" said
Butler, in a faltering voice. "O turn to Him, in
whose eyes time and space have no existence, and to
whom a few minutes are as a lifetime, and a lifetime as
a minute."

"I believe I know what you would say," answered
Porteous sullenly. "I was bred a soldier; if they will
murder me without time, let my sins as well as my
blood lie at their door."

"Who was it," said the stern voice of Wildfire,
"that said to Wilson at this very spot, when he could
not pray, owing to the galling agony of his fetters, that
his pains would soon be over?—I say to you to take
your own tale home; and if you cannot profit by the
good man's lessons, blame not them that are still more
merciful to you than you were to others."

The procession now moved forward with a slow and determined pace. It was enlightened by many blazing links and torches; for the actors of this work were so far from affecting any secrecy on the occasion, that they seemed even to court observation. Their principal leaders kept close to the person of the prisoner, whose pallid yet stubborn features were seen distinctly by the torch-light, as his person was raised considerably above the concourse which thronged around him. Those who bore swords, muskets, and battle-axes, marched on each side, as if forming a regular guard to the procession. The windows, as they went along, were filled with the inhabitants, whose slumbers had been broken by this unusual disturbance. Some of the spectators muttered accents of encouragement; but in general they were so much appalled by a sight so strange and audacious, that they looked on with a sort of stupified astonishment. No one offered, by act or word, the slightest interruption.

The rioters, on their part, continued to act with the same air of deliberate confidence and security which had marked all their proceedings. When the object of their resentment dropped one of his slippers, they stopped, sought for it, and replaced it upon his foot with great deliberation.* As they descended the Bow towards the fatal spot where they designed to complete

---

* This little incident, characteristic of the extreme composure of this extraordinary mob, was witnessed by a lady, who, disturbed, like others, from her slumbers, had gone to the window. It was told to the author by the lady's daughter.

their purpose, it was suggested that there should be a
rope kept in readiness. For this purpose the booth of
a man who dealt in cordage was forced open, a coil of
rope fit for their purpose was selected to serve as a
halter, and the dealer next morning found that a
guinea had been left on his counter in exchange; so
anxious were the perpetrators of this daring action to
show that they meditated not the slightest wrong or
infraction of law, excepting so far as Porteous was
himself concerned.

Leading, or carrying along with them, in this determined and regular manner, the object of their vengeance,
they at length reached the place of common execution,
the scene of his crime, and destined spot of his sufferings. Several of the rioters (if they should not rather
be described as conspirators) endeavoured to remove the
stone which filled up the socket in which the end of
the fatal tree was sunk when it was erected for its fatal
purpose; others sought for the means of constructing a
temporary gibbet, the place in which the gallows itself
was deposited being reported too secure to be forced,
without much loss of time. Butler endeavoured to avail
himself of the delay afforded by these circumstances, to
turn the people from their desperate design. "For God's
sake," he exclaimed, "remember it is the image of your
Creator which you are about to deface in the person of
this unfortunate man! Wretched as he is, and wicked
as he may be, he has a share in every promise of
Scripture, and you cannot destroy him in impenitence
without blotting his name from the Book of Life—

Do not destroy soul and body; give time for preparation."

"What time had they," returned a stern voice, "whom he murdered on this very spot?—The laws both of God and man call for his death."

"But what, my friends," insisted Butler, with a generous disregard to his own safety—"what hath constituted you his judges?"

"We are not his judges," replied the same person; "he has been already judged and condemned by lawful authority. We are those whom Heaven, and our righteous anger, have stirred up to execute judgment, when a corrupt government would have protected a murderer."

"I am none," said the unfortunate Porteous; "that which you charge upon me fell out in self-defence, in the lawful exercise of my duty."

"Away with him—away with him!" was the general cry. "Why do you trifle away time in making a gallows?—that dyester's pole is good enough for the homicide."

The unhappy man was forced to his fate with remorseless rapidity. Butler, separated from him by the press, escaped the last horrors of his struggles. Unnoticed by those who had hitherto detained him as a prisoner, he fled from the fatal spot, without much caring in what direction his course lay. A loud shout proclaimed the stern delight with which the agents of this deed regarded its completion. Butler, then, at the opening into the low street called the Cowgate, cast

back a terrified glance, and, by the red and dusky light
of the torches, he could discern a figure wavering and
struggling as it hung suspended above the heads of the
multitude, and could even observe men striking at it
with their Lochaber-axes and partisans. The sight was
of a nature to double his horror, and to add wings to
his flight.

The street down which the fugitive ran opens to one
of the eastern ports or gates of the city. Butler did
not stop till he reached it, but found it still shut. He
waited nearly an hour, walking up and down in inexpressible perturbation of mind. At length he ventured
to call out, and rouse the attention of the terrified
keepers of the gate, who now found themselves at
liberty to resume their office without interruption.
Butler requested them to open the gate. They hesitated.
He told them his name and occupation.

"He is a preacher," said one; "I have heard him
preach in Haddo's-hole."

"A fine preaching has he been at the night," said
another; "but maybe least said is soonest mended."

Opening then the wicket of the main-gate, the
keepers suffered Butler to depart, who hastened to
carry his horror and fear beyond the walls of Edinburgh. His first purpose was, instantly to take the
road homeward; but other fears and cares, connected
with the news he had learned in that remarkable
day, induced him to linger in the neighbourhood of
Edinburgh until daybreak. More than one group
of persons passed him as he was whiling away the

hours of darkness that yet remained, whom, from the
stifled tones of their discourse, the unwonted hour
when they travelled, and the hasty pace at which they
walked, he conjectured to have been engaged in the late
fatal transaction.

Certain it was, that the sudden and total dispersion
of the rioters, when their vindictive purpose was
accomplished, seemed not the least remarkable feature
of this singular affair. In general, whatever may be
the impelling motive by which a mob is at first raised,
the attainment of their object has usually been only
found to lead the way to farther excesses. But not so
in the present case. They seemed completely satiated
with the vengeance they had prosecuted with such
stanch and sagacious activity. When they were fully
satisfied that life had abandoned their victim, they
dispersed in every direction, throwing down the weapons
which they had only assumed to enable them to carry
through their purpose. At day-break there remained
not the least token of the events of the night, excepting
the corpse of Porteous, which still hung suspended in
the place where he had suffered, and the arms of
various kinds which the rioters had taken from the
city guard-house, which were found scattered about the
streets as they had thrown them from their hands,
when the purpose for which they had seized them was
accomplished.

The ordinary magistrates of the city resumed their
power, not without trembling at the late experience of
the fragility of its tenure. To march troops into the

city, and commence a severe inquiry into the transactions of the preceding night, were the first marks of
returning energy which they displayed.   But these
events had been conducted on so secure and well-
calculated a plan of safety and secrecy, that there was
little or nothing learned to throw light upon the authors
or principal actors in a scheme so audacious.   An
express was dispatched to London with the tidings,
where they excited great indignation and surprise in
the council of regency, and particularly in the bosom
of Queen Caroline, who considered her own authority
as exposed to contempt by the success of this singular
conspiracy.   Nothing was spoke of for some time save
the measure of vengeance which should be taken, not
only on the actors of this tragedy, so soon as they
should be discovered, but upon the magistrates who
had suffered it to take place, and upon the city which
had been the scene where it was exhibited.   On this
occasion, it is still recorded in popular tradition, that
her Majesty, in the height of her displeasure, told the
celebrated John Duke of Argyle, that, sooner than
submit to such an insult, she would make Scotland a
hunting-field.   "In that case, Madam," answered that
high-spirited nobleman, with a profound bow, "I will
take leave of your Majesty, and go down to my own
country to get my hounds ready."

The import of the reply had more than met the
ear; and as most of the Scottish nobility and gentry
seemed actuated by the same national spirit, the royal
displeasure was necessarily checked in mid-volley, and

milder courses were recommended and adopted, to
some of which we may hereafter have occasion to
advert.*

* The following interesting and authentic account of the inquiries made by Crown Counsel into the affair of the Porteous Mob,
seems to have been drawn up by the Solicitor-General. The office
was held in 1737 by Charles Erskine, Esq.

I owe this curious illustration to the kindness of a professional
friend. It throws, indeed, little light on the origin of the tumult;
but shows how profound the darkness must have been, which so
much investigation could not dispel.

"Upon the 7th of September last, when the unhappy wicked
murder of Captain Porteous was committed, his Majesty's Advocate and Solicitor were out of town; the first beyond Inverness,
and the other in Annandale, not far from Carlyle; neither of them
knew any thing of the reprieve, nor did they in the least suspect
that any disorder was to happen.

"When the disorder happened, the magistrates and other
persons concerned in the management of the town, seemed to be
all struck of a heap; and whether, from the great terror that had
seized all the inhabitants, they thought ane immediate inquiry
would be fruitless, or whether, being a direct insult upon the prerogative of the Crown, they did not care rashly to intermeddle;
but no proceedings was had by them. Only, soon after, ane
express was sent to his Majestie's Solicitor, who came to town as
soon as was possible for him; but, in the meantime, the persons
who had been most guilty, had either run off, or, at least, kept
themselves upon the wing until they should see what steps were
taken by the Government.

"When the Solicitor arrived, he perceived the whole inhabitants under a consternation. He had no materials furnished him;
nay, the inhabitants were so much afraid of being reputed
informers, that very few people had so much as the courage to
speak with him on the streets. However, having received her
Majestie's orders, by a letter from the Duke of Newcastle, he
resolved to sett about the matter in earnest, and entered upon ane
inquiry, groping in the dark. He had no assistance from the

magistrates worth mentioning, but called witness after witness in the privatest manner, before himself in his own house, and for six weeks' time, from morning to evening, went on in the inquiry without taking the least diversion, or turning his thoughts to any other business.

"He tried at first what he could do by declarations, by engaging secresy, so that those who told the truth should never be discovered; made use of no clerk, but wrote all the declarations with his own hand, to encourage them to speak out. After all, for some time, he could get nothing but ends of stories, which, when pursued, broke off; and those who appeared and knew any thing of the matter, were under the utmost terror, lest it should take air that they had mentioned any one man as guilty.

"During the course of the inquiry, the run of the town, which was strong for the villanous actors, begun to alter a little, and when they saw the King's servants in earnest to do their best, the generality, who before had spoke very warmly in defence of the wickedness, began to be silent, and at that period more of the criminals begun to abscond.

"At length the inquiry began to open a little, and the Sollicitor was under some difficulty how to proceed. He very well saw that the first warrand that was issued out would start the whole gang; and as he had not come at any of the most notorious offenders, he was unwilling, upon the slight evidence he had, to begin. However, upon notice given him by Generall Moyle, that one King, a butcher in the Canongate, had boasted, in presence of Bridget Knell, a soldier's wife, the morning after Captain Porteus was hanged, that he had a very active hand in the mob, a warrand was issued out, and King was apprehended and imprisoned in the Canongate Tolbooth.

"This obliged the Sollicitor immediately to take up those against whom he had any information. By a signed declaration, William Stirling, apprentice to James Stirling, merchant in Edinburgh, was charged as haveing been at the Nether-Bow, after the gates were shutt, with a Lochaber ax, or halbert in his hand, and haveing begun a huzza, marched upon the head of the mob towards the Guard.

"James Braidwood, son to a candlemaker in town, was, by a signed declaration, charged as haveing been at the Tolbooth

door, giveing directions to the mob about setting fire to the
door, and that the mob named him by his name, and asked his
advice.

"By another declaration, one Stoddart, a journeyman smith,
was charged of haveing boasted publickly, in a smith's shop at
Leith, that he had assisted in breaking open the Tolbooth door.

"Peter Traill, a journeyman wright, by one of the declarations,
was also accused of haveing lockt the Nether-Bow Port when it
was shutt by the mob.

"His Majestie's Sollicitor having these informations, imployed
privately such persons as he could best rely on, and the truth
was, there were very few in whom he could repose confidence.
But he was, indeed, faithfully served by one Webster, a soldier in
the Welsh fuzileers, recommended him by Lieutenant Alshton,
who, with very great address, informed himself, and really run
some risque in getting his information, concerning the places
where the persons informed against used to haunt, and how they
might be seized. In consequence of which, a party of the Guard
from the Canongate was agreed on to march up at a certain hour,
when a message should be sent. The Sollicitor wrote a letter and
gave it to one of the town officers, ordered to attend Captain
Maitland, one of the town Captains, promoted to that command
since the unhappy accident, who, indeed, was extremely diligent
and active throughout the whole; and haveing got Stirling and
Braidwood apprehended, dispatched the officer with the letter to
the military in the Canongate, who immediately begun their
march, and by the time the Sollicitor had half examined the said
two persons in the Burrow-room, where the magistrates were
present, a party of fifty men, drums beating, marched into the
Parliament close, and drew up, which was the first thing that
struck a terror, and from that time forward, the insolence was
succeeded by fear.

"Stirling and Braidwood were immediately sent to the Castle,
and imprisoned. That same night, Stoddart the smith was seized,
and he was committed to the Castle also; as was likewise Traill
the journeyman wright, who were all severally examined, and
denyed the least accession.

"In the meantime, the inquiry was going on, and it haveing
cast up in one of the declarations, that a hump'd-backed creature

marched with a gun as one of the guards to Porteus when he went up to the Lawn Markett, the person who emitted this declaration was employed to walk the streets to see if he could find him out; at last he came to the Sollicitor and told him he had found him, and that he was in a certain house. Whereupon a warrand was issued out against him, and he was apprehended and sent to the Castle, and he proved to be one Dirnie, a helper to the Countess of Weemys's coachman.

"Thereafter, ane information was given in against William M'Lauchlan, ffootman to the said Countess, he haveing been very active in the mob; ffor sometime he kept himself out of the way, but at last he was apprehended and likewise committed to the Castle.

"And these were all the prisoners who were putt under confinement in that place.

"There were other persons imprisoned in the Tolbooth of Edinburgh, and severalls against whom warrands were issued, but could not be apprehended, whose names and cases shall afterwards be more particularly taken notice of.

"The ffriends of Stirling made an application to the Earl of Islay, Lord Justice-Generall, setting furth, that he was seized with a bloody fflux; that his life was in danger; and that upon ane examination of witnesses whose names were given in, it would appear to conviction, that he had not the least access to any of the riotous proceedings of that wicked mob.

"This petition was by his Lordship putt in the hands of his Majestie's Sollicitor, who examined the witnesses; and by their testimonies it appeared that the young man, who was not above eighteen years of age, was that night in company with about half a dozen companions, in a public house in Stephen Law's closs, near the back of the Guard, where they all remained untill the noise came to the house, that the mob had shut the gates and seized the Guard, upon which the company broke up, and he, and one of his companions, went towards his master's house : and, in the course of the after examination, there was a witness who declared, nay, indeed swore (for the Sollicitor, by this time, saw it necessary to put those he examined upon oath), that he met him [Stirling] after he entered into the alley where his master lives, going towards his house; and another witness, fellow-prentice with Stirling, declares, that after the mob had seized the Guard, he went home, where he found Stirling before him; and that his master lockt the door, and kept them both at home till after twelve at night: upon weighing of which testimonies, and upon consideration had, That he was charged by the declaration only of one person, who really did not appear to be a witness of the greatest weight, and that his life was in danger from the imprisonment, he was admitted to baill by the Lord Justice-Generall, by whose warrand he was committed.

"Braidwood's friends applyed in the same manner; but as he stood charged by more than one witness, he was not released—tho', indeed, the witnesses adduced for him say somewhat in his exculpation—that he does not seem to have been upon any original concert; and one of the witnesses says he was along with him at the Tolbooth door, and refuses what is said against him, with regard to his having advised the burning of the Tolbooth door. But he remains still in prison.

"As to Traill, the journeyman wright, he is charged by the same witness who declared against Stirling, and there is none concurrs with him; and to say the truth concerning him, he seemed to be the most ingenuous of any of them whom the Solicitor examined, and pointed out a witness by whom one of the first accomplices was discovered, and who escaped when the warrand was to be putt in execution against them. He positively denys his having shutt the gate, and 'tis thought Traill ought to be admitted to baill.

"As to Birnie, he is charged only by one witness, who had never seen him before, nor knew his name; so, tho' I dare say the witness honestly mentioned him, 'tis possible he may be mistaken; and in the examination of above 200 witnesses, there is no body concurrs with him, and he is ane insignificant little creature.

"With regard to M'Lauchlan, the proof is strong against him by one witness, that he acted as a sergeant or sort of commander, for some time, of a Guard, that stood cross between the upper end of the Luckenbooths and the north side of the street, to stop all but friends from going towards the Tolbooth; and by other witnesses, that he was at the Tolbooth door with a link in his hand, while the operation of beating and burning it was going on;

that he went along with the mob with a halbert in his hand, untill he came to the gallows stone in the Grassmarket, and that he stuck the halbert into the hole of the gallows stone: that afterwards he went in amongst the mob when Captain Portens was carried to the dyer's tree; so that the proof seems very heavy against him.

"To sum up this matter with regard to the prisoners in the Castle, 'tis believed there is strong proof against M'Lauchlan; there is also proof against Braidwood. But as it consists only in emission of words said to have been had by him while at the Tolbooth door, and that he is ane insignificant pitifull creatnro, and will find people to swear heartily in his favours, 'tis at best doubtfull whether a jury will be got to condemn him.

"As to those in the Tolbooth of Edinburgh, John Crawford, who had for some time been employed to ring the bells in the steeple of the new Church of Edinburgh, being in company with a soldier accidentally, the discourse falling in concerning the Captain Portens and his murder, as he appears to be a light-headed fellow, he said, that he knew people that were more guilty than any that were putt in prison. Upon this information, Crawford was seized, and being examined, it appeared, that when the mob began, as he was comeing down from the steeple, the mob took the keys from him; that he was that night in several corners, and did indeed delate severall persons whom he saw there, and immediately warrands wore dispatched, and it was found they had absconded and fled. But there was no evidence against him of any kind. Nay, on the contrary, it appeared, that he had been with the Magistrates in Clerk's, the vintner's, relating to them what he had seen in the streets. Therefore, after haveing detained him in prison ffor a very considerable time, his Majestie's Advocate and Sollicitor signed a warrand for his liberation.

"There was also one James Wilson incarcerated in the said Tolbooth, upon the declaration of one witness, who said he saw him on the streets with a gun; and there he remained for some time, in order to try if a concurring witness could be found, or that he acted any part in the tragedy and wickedness. But nothing further appeared against him; and being seized with a severe sickness, he is, by a warrand signed by his Majestie's Advocate and Sollicitor, liberated upon giveing sufficient baill.

"As to King, inquiry was made, and the fact comes out beyond all exception, that he was in the lodge at the Nether-Bow with Lindsay the waiter, and several other people, not at all concerned in the mob. But after the affair was over, he went up towards the guard, and having met with Sandie the Turk and his wife, who escaped out of prison, they returned to his house at the Abbey, and then 't is very possible he may have thought fitt in his beer to boast of villany, in which he could not possibly have any share for that reason; he was desired to find baill and he should be set at liberty. But he is a stranger and a fellow of very indifferent character, and 't is believed it won't be easy for him to find baill. Wherefore, it 's thought he must be sett at liberty without it. Because he is a burden upon the Government while kept in confinement, not being able to maintain himself.

"What is above is all that relates to persons in custody. But there are warrands out against a great many other persons who had fled, particularly against one William White, a journeyman baxter, who, by the evidence, appears to have been at the beginning of the mob, and to have gone along with the drum, from the West-Port to the Nether-Dow, and is said to have been one of those who attacked the guard, and probably was as deep as any one there.

"Information was given that he was lurking at Falkirk, where he was born. Whereupon directions were sent to the Sheriff of the County, and a warrant from his Excellency Generall Wade, to the commanding officers at Stirling and Linlithgow, to assist, and all possible endeavours were used to catch hold of him, and 't is said he escaped very narrowly, having been concealed in some outhouse; and the misfortune was, that those who were employed in the search did not know him personally. Nor, indeed, was it easy to trust any of the acquaintances of so low obscure a fellow with the secret of the warrand to be putt in execution.

"There was also strong evidence found against Robert Taylor, servant to William and Charles Thomsons, periwig-makers, that he acted as ane officer among the mob, and he was traced from the guard to the well at the head of Forrester's Wynd, where he stood and had the appellation of Captain from the mob, and from that walking down the Bow before Captain Porteus, with his

Lochaber-axe; and by the description given of one who hawl'd the rope by which Captain Porteus was pulled up, 'tis believed Taylor was the person; and 'tis further probable, that the witness who delated Stirling had mistaken Taylor for him, their stature and age (so far as can be gathered from the description) being the same.

"A great deal of pains were taken, and no charge was saved, in order to have catched hold of this Taylor, and warrands were sent to the country where he was born; but it appears he had shipt himself off for Holland, where it is said he now is.

"There is strong evidence also against Thomas Burns, butcher, that he was ane active person from the beginning of the mob to the end of it. He lurkt for some time amongst those of his trade; and artfully enough a train was laid to catch him, under pretence of a message that had come from his father in Ireland, so that he came to a blind alehouse in the Flesh-market close, and a party being ready, was by Webster the soldier, who was upon this exploit, advertised to come down. However, Burns escaped out at a back window, and hid himself in some of the houses which are heaped together upon one another in that place, so that it was not possible to catch him. 'Tis now said he is gone to Ireland to his father, who lives there.

"There is evidence also against one Robert Anderson, journeyman and servant to Colin Alison, wright; and against Thomas Linnen and James Maxwell, both servants also to the said Colin Alison, who all seem to have been deeply concerned in the matter. Anderson is one of those who putt the rope upon Captain Porteus's neck. Linnen seems also to have been very active; and Maxwell (which is pretty remarkable) is proven to have come to a shop upon the Friday before, and charged the journeymen and prentices there to attend in the Parliament close on Tuesday night to assist to hang Captain Porteus. These three did early abscond, and though warrands had been issued out against them, and all endeavours used to apprehend them, could not be found.

"One Waldie, a servant to George Campbell, wright, has also absconded, and many others, and 'tis informed that numbers of them have shipt themselves off ffor the Plantations; and upon an information that a ship was going off from Glasgow, in which severall of the rogues were to transport themselves beyond seas, proper warrands were obtained, and persons dispatched to search the said ship, and seize any that can be found.

"The like warrands had been issued with regard to ships from Leith. But whether they had been scard, or whether the information had been groundless, they had no effect.

"This is a summary of the inquiry, ffrom which it appears there is no prooff on which one can rely, but against M'Lauchlan. There is a prooff also against Draidwood, but more exceptionable. His Majestie's Advocate, since he came to town, has join'd with the Sollicitor, and has done his utmost to gett at the bottom of this matter, but hithorto it stands, as is above represented. They are resolved to have their eyes and their ears open, and to do what they can. But they labour'd exceedingly against the stream; and it may truly be said, that nothing was wanting on their part. Nor have they declined any labour to answer the commands laid upon them to search the matter to the bottom."

THE PORTEOUS MOB.

In the preceding chapters (II. to VII.), the circumstances of that extraordinary riot and conspiracy, called the Porteous Mob, are given with as much accuracy as the author was able to collect them. The order, regularity, and determined resolution with which such a violent action was devised and executed, were only equalled by the secrecy which was observed concerning the principal actors.

Although the fact was performed by torch-light, and in presence of a great multitude, to some of whom, at least, the individual actors must have been known, yet no discovery was ever made concerning any of the perpetrators of the slaughter.

Two men only were brought to trial for an offence which the Government were so anxious to detect and punish. William M'Lauchlan, footman to the Countess of Wemyss, who is mentioned in the report of the Solicitor-General (page 135), against whom strong evidence had been obtained, was brought to trial in March 1737, charged as having been accessory to the riot, armed with a Lochaber-axe. But this man (who was at all times a silly creature) proved that he was in a state of mortal intoxication during the time he was present with the rabble, incapable of

giving them either advice or assistance, or, indeed, of knowing
what he or they were doing. He was also able to prove, that he
was forced into the riot, and upheld while there by two bakers,
who put a Lochaber-axe into his hand. The jury, wisely judging
this poor creature could be no proper subject of punishment, found
the panel Not Guilty. The same verdict was given in the case
of Thomas Linning, also mentioned in the Solicitor's memorial,
who was tried in 1738. In short, neither then, nor for a long
period afterwards, was any thing discovered relating to the organi-
zation of the Porteous Plot.

The imagination of the people of Edinburgh was long irritated,
and their curiosity kept awake, by the mystery attending this
extraordinary conspiracy. It was generally reported of such
natives of Edinburgh as, having left the city in youth, returned
with a fortune amassed in foreign countries, that they had originally fled on account of their share in the Porteous Mob. But
little credit can be attached to these surmises, as in most of the
cases they are contradicted by dates, and in none supported by
any thing but vague rumours, grounded on the ordinary wish of
the vulgar, to impute the success of prosperous men to some
unpleasant source. The secret history of the Porteous Mob has
been till this day unravelled; and it has always been quoted as a
close, daring, and calculated act of violence, of a nature peculiarly
characteristic of the Scottish people.

Nevertheless, the author, for a considerable time, nourished
hopes to have found himself enabled to throw some light on this
mysterious story. An old man, who died about twenty years ago,
at the advanced age of ninety-three, was said to have made a
communication to the clergyman who attended upon his death-
bed, respecting the origin of the Porteous Mob. This person
followed the trade of a carpenter, and had been employed as such
on the estate of a family of opulence and condition. His character, in his line of life and amongst his neighbours, was excellent,
and never underwent the slightest suspicion. His confession was
said to have been to the following purpose: That he was one of
twelve young men belonging to the village of Pathhead, whose
animosity against Porteous, on account of the execution of Wilson,
was so extreme, that they resolved to execute vengeance on him
with their own hands, rather than he should escape punishment.

With this resolution they crossed the Forth at different ferries,
and rendezvoused at the suburb called Portsburgh, where their
appearance in a body soon called numbers around them. The
public mind was in such a state of irritation, that it only wanted
a single spark to create an explosion; and this was afforded by
the exertions of the small and determined band of associates. The
appearance of premeditation and order which distinguished the
riot, according to his account, had its origin, not in any previous
plan or conspiracy, but in the character of those who were engaged
in it. The story also serves to show why nothing of the origin of
the riot has ever been discovered, since, though in itself a great
conflagration, its source, according to this account, was from an
obscure and apparently inadequate cause.

I have been disappointed, however, in obtaining the evidence
on which this story rests. The present proprietor of the estate on
which the old man died (a particular friend of the author), undertook to question the son of the deceased on the subject. This
person follows his father's trade, and holds the employment of
carpenter to the same family. He admits that his father's going
abroad at the time of the Porteous Mob was popularly attributed
to his having been concerned in that affair; but adds, that, so far
as is known to him, the old man had never made any confession
to that effect; and, on the contrary, had uniformly denied being
present. My kind friend, therefore, had recourse to a person
from whom he had formerly heard the story; but who, either
from respect to an old friend's memory, or from failure of his own,
happened to have forgotten that ever such a communication was
made. So my obliging correspondent (who is a fox-hunter)
wrote to me that he was completely *planted;* and all that can be
said with respect to the tradition is, that it certainly once existed,
and was generally believed.

CHAPTER THE EIGHTH.

Arthur's Seat shall be my bed,
 The sheets shall ne'er be pressed by me ;
St. Anton's well shall be my drink,
 Sin' my true-love's forsaken me.
                    OLD SONG.

IF I were to choose a spot from which the rising or setting sun could be seen to the greatest possible advantage,

it would be that wild path winding around the foot of
the high belt of semi-circular rocks, called Salisbury
Crags,* and marking the verge of the steep descent
which slopes down into the glen on the south-eastern
side of the city of Edinburgh. The prospect, in its
general outline, commands a close-built, high-piled city,
stretching itself out beneath in a form, which, to a romantic imagination, may be supposed to represent that of
a dragon ; now, a noble arm of the sea, with its rocks,
isles, distant shores, and boundary of mountains; and
now, a fair and fertile champaign country, varied with
hill, dale, and rock, and skirted by the picturesque
ridge of the Pentland mountains. But as the path
gently circles around the base of the cliffs, the prospect,
composed as it is of these enchanting and sublime
objects, changes at every step, and presents them
blended with, or divided from, each other, in every
possible variety which can gratify the eye and the
imagination. When a piece of scenery so beautiful, yet
so varied,—so exciting by its intricacy, and yet so sublime,—is lighted up by the tints of morning or of evening, and displays all that variety of shadowy depth,
exchanged with partial brilliancy, which gives character
even to the tamest of landscapes, the effect approaches
near to enchantment. This path used to be my favourite
evening and morning resort, when engaged with a

---

* A beautiful and solid pathway has, within a few years, been
formed around these romantic rocks; and the author has the
pleasure to think, that the passage in the text gave rise to the
undertaking.

favourite author, or new subject of study. It is, I am
informed, now become totally impassable ; a circumstance which, if true, reflects little credit on the taste of
the Good Town or its leaders.

It was from this fascinating path—the scene to me
of so much delicious musing, when life was young and
promised to be happy, that I have been unable to pass
it over without an episodical description—it was, I say,
from this romantic path that Butler saw the morning
arise the day after the murder of Porteous. It was
possible for him with ease to have found a much shorter
road to the house to which he was directing his course,
and, in fact, that which he chose was extremely circuitous.   But to compose his own spirits, as well as to
while away the time, until a proper hour for visiting
the family without surprise or disturbance, he was induced to extend his circuit by the foot of the rocks, and
to linger upon his way until the morning should be considerably advanced.   While, now standing with his arms
across, and waiting the slow progress of the sun above
the horizon, now sitting upon one of the numerous
fragments which storms had detached from the rocks
above him, he is meditating, alternately upon the
horrible catastrophe which he had witnessed, and upon
the melancholy, and to him most interesting, news
which he had learned at Saddletree's, we give the
reader to understand who Butler was, and how his fate
was connected with that of Effie Deans, the unfortunate
handmaiden of the careful Mrs. Saddletree.

Reuben Butler was of English extraction, though

born in Scotland. His grandfather was a trooper in
Monk's army, and one of the party of dismounted
dragoons which formed the forlorn hope at the storming
of Dundee in 1651. Stephen Butler (called, from his
talents in reading and expounding, Scripture Stephen,
and Bible Butler) was a stanch Independent, and received
in its fullest comprehension the promise that the saints
should inherit the earth. As hard knocks were what
had chiefly fallen to his share hitherto in the division
of this common property, he lost not the opportunity
which the storm and plunder of a commercial place
afforded him, to appropriate as large a share of the
better things of this world as he could possibly compass.
It would seem that he had succeeded indifferently well,
for his exterior circumstances appeared, in consequence
of this event, to have been much mended.

The troop to which he belonged was quartered at
the village of Dalkeith, as forming the body guard of
Monk, who, in the capacity of general for the Common-
wealth, resided in the neighbouring castle. When, on
the eve of the Restoration, the general commenced his
march from Scotland, a measure pregnant with such
important consequences, he new-modelled his troops,
and more especially those immediately about his person,
in order that they might consist entirely of individuals
devoted to himself. On this occasion Scripture Stephen
was weighed in the balance, and found wanting. It
was supposed he felt no call to any expedition which
might endanger the reign of the military sainthood, and
that he did not consider himself as free in conscience to

join with any party which might be likely ultimately
to acknowledge the interest of Charles Stuart, the son
of "the last man," as Charles I. was familiarly and
irreverently termed by them in their common discourse,
as well as in their more elaborate predications and
harangues. As the time did not admit of cashiering
such dissidents, Stephen Butler was only advised in a
friendly way to give up his horse and accoutrements to
one of Middleton's old troopers, who possessed an
accommodating conscience of a military stamp, and
which squared itself chiefly upon those of the colonel
and paymaster. As this hint came recommended by a
certain sum of arrears presently payable, Stephen had
carnal wisdom enough to embrace the proposal, and
with great indifference saw his old corps depart for
Coldstream, on their route for the south, to establish
the tottering government of England on a new basis.

The *zone* of the ex-trooper, to use Horace's phrase,
was weighty enough to purchase a cottage and two or
three fields (still known by the name of Beersheba),
within about a Scottish mile of Dalkeith ; and there
did Stephen establish himself with a youthful helpmate, chosen out of the said village, whose disposition
to a comfortable settlement on this side of the grave
reconciled her to the gruff manners, serious temper, and
weather-beaten features of the martial enthusiast.
Stephen did not long survive the falling on "evil days
and evil tongues," of which Milton, in the same pre-
dicament, so mournfully complains. At his death, his
consort remained an early widow, with a male child of

three years old, which, in the sobriety wherewith it
demeaned itself, in the old-fashioned and even grim
cast of its features, and in its sententious mode of
expressing itself, would sufficiently have vindicated
the honour of the widow of Beersheba, had any one
thought proper to challenge the babe's descent from
Bible Butler.

Butler's principles had not descended to his family,
or extended themselves among his neighbours.   The
air of Scotland was alien to the growth of independency,
however favourable to fanaticism under other colours.
But, nevertheless, they were not forgotten; and a certain
neighbouring Laird, who piqued himself upon the
loyalty of his principles " in the worst of times " (though
I never heard they exposed him to more peril than
that of a broken head, or a night's lodging in the main
guard, when wine and cavalierism predominated in his
upper storey), had found it a convenient thing to rake
up all matter of accusation against the deceased Stephen.
In this enumeration his religious principles made no
small figure, as, indeed, they must have seemed of the
most exaggerated enormity to one whose own were
so small and so faintly traced, as to be wellnigh imper-
ceptible. . In these circumstances, poor widow Butler
was supplied with her full proportion of fines for non-
conformity, and all the other oppressions of the time,
until Beersheba was fairly wrenched out of her hands,
and became the property of the Laird who had so
wantonly, as it had hitherto appeared, persecuted this
poor forlorn woman.   When his purpose was fairly

achieved, he showed some remorse or moderation, or
whatever the reader may please to term it, in permitting her to occupy her husband's cottage, and cultivate,
on no very heavy terms, a croft of land adjacent. Her
son, Benjamin, in the meanwhile, grew up to man's
estate, and, moved by that impulse which makes men
seek marriage, even when its end can only be the per-
petuation of misery, he wedded and brought a wife,
and, eventually, a son, Reuben, to share the poverty of
Beersheba.

The Laird of Dumbiedikes * had hitherto been
moderate in his exactions, perhaps because he was
ashamed to tax too highly the miserable means of support which remained to the widow Butler. But when
a stout active young fellow appeared as the labourer of
the croft in question, Dumbiedikes began to think so
broad a pair of shoulders might bear an additional
burden. He regulated, indeed, his management of his
dependents (who fortunately were but few in number)
much upon the principle of the carters whom he
observed loading their carts at a neighbouring coal-hill,
and who never failed to clap an additional brace of
hundred-weights on their burden, so soon as by any
means they had compassed a new horse of somewhat
superior strength to that which had broken down the

* Dumbiedikes, selected as descriptive of the taciturn character
of the imaginary owner, is really the name of a house bordering
on the King's Park, so called because the late Mr. Braidwood,
an instructor of the deaf and dumb, resided there with his pupils.
The situation of the real house is different from that assigned to
the ideal mansion.

day before. How reasonable this practice appeared to
the Laird of Dumbiedikes, he ought to have observed,
that it may be overdone, and that it infers, as a matter
of course, the destruction and loss of both horse, and
cart, and loading. Even so it befell when the additional "prestations" came to be demanded of Benjamin
Butler. A man of few words, and few ideas, but
attached to Beersheba with a feeling like that which a
vegetable entertains to the spot in which it chances
to be planted, he neither remonstrated with the Laird,
nor endeavoured to escape from him, but toiling night
and day to accomplish the terms of his task-master, fell
into a burning fever and died. His wife did not long
survive him; and, as if it had been the fate of this family
to be left orphans, our Reuben Butler was about the
year 1704-5, left in the same circumstances in which
his father had been placed, and under the same guardianship, being that of his grandmother, the widow of
Monk's old trooper.

The same prospect of misery hung over the head of
another tenant of this hard-hearted lord of the soil.
This was a tough true-blue Presbyterian, called Deans,
who, though most obnoxious to the Laird on account
of principles in church and state, contrived to maintain
his ground upon the estate by regular payment of mail-
duties, kain, arriage, carriage, dry multure, lock, gowpen,
and knaveship, and all the various exactions now commuted for money, and summed up in the emphatic
word RENT. But the years 1700 and 1701, long
remembered in Scotland for dearth and general dis-

tress, subdued the stout heart of the agricultural whig.
Citations by the ground-officer, decreets of the Baron
Court, sequestrations, poindings of outsight and in-
sight plenishing, flew about his ears as fast as the tory
bullets whistled around those of the Covenanters at
Pentland, Bothwell Brigg, or Airsmoss.   Struggle as
he might, and he struggled gallantly, "Douce David
Deans" was routed horse and foot, and lay at the
mercy of his grasping landlord just at the time that
Benjamin Butler died. The fate of each family was
anticipated; but they who prophesied their expulsion
to beggary and ruin, were disappointed by an accidental
circumstance.

On the very term-day when their ejection should
have taken place, when all their neighbours were prepared to pity, and not one to assist them, the minister
of the parish as well as a doctor from Edinburgh,
received a hasty summons to attend the Laird of Dumbiedikes. Both were surprised, for his contempt for
both faculties had been pretty commonly his theme over
an extra bottle, that is to say, at least once every day.
The leech for the soul, and he for the body, alighted in
the court of the little old manor-house at almost the
same time; and when they had gazed a moment at each
other with some surprise, they in the same breath
expressed their conviction that Dumbiedikes must
needs be very ill indeed, since he summoned them both
to his presence at once.   Ere the servant could usher
them to his apartment the party was augmented by a
man of law, Nichil Novit, writing himself procurator

before the Sheriff-court, for in those days there were
no solicitors. This latter personage was first summoned
to the apartment of the Laird, where, after some short
space, the soul-curer and the body-curer were invited
to join him.

Dumbiedikes had been by this time transported into
the best bedroom, used only upon occasions of death
and marriage, and called, from the former of these
occupations, the Dead-Room. There were in this apartment, besides the sick person himself and Mr. Novit,
the son and heir of the patient, a tall gawky silly-looking
boy of fourteen or fifteen, and a housekeeper, a good
buxom figure of a woman, betwixt forty and fifty, who
had kept the keys and managed matters at Dumbiedikes
since the lady's death. It was to these attendants that
Dumbiedikes addressed himself pretty nearly in the
following words; temporal and spiritual matters, the
care of his health and his affairs, being strangely jumbled
in a head which was never one of the clearest.

"These are sair times wi' me, gentlemen and neighbours! amaist as ill as at the aughty-nine, when I was
rabbled by the collegeaners.*—They mistook me muckle
—they ca'd me a papist, but there was never a papist
bit about me, minister.—Jock, ye'll take warning—it's
a debt we maun a' pay, and there stands Nichil Novit

* Immediately previous to the Revolution, the students at
the Edinburgh College were violent anti-catholics. They were
strongly suspected of burning the house of Priestfield, belonging
to the Lord Provost; and certainly were guilty of creating considerable riots in 1688-9.

that will tell ye I was never gude at paying debts in my
life.—Mr. Novit, ye'll no forget to draw the annual
rent that's due on the yerl's band—if I pay debt to
other folk, I think they suld pay it to me—that equals
aquals.—Jock, when ye has naething else to do, ye may
be aye sticking in a tree; it will be growing, Jock, when
ye're sleeping.*   My father tauld me sae forty years
sin', but I ne'er fand time to mind him—Jock, ne'er
drink brandy in the morning, it files the stamach sair;
gin ye take a morning's draught, let it be aqua mirabilis;
Jenny there makes it weel.—Doctor, my breath is
growing as scant as a broken-winded piper's, when he has
played for four-and-twenty hours at a penny-wedding—
Jenny, pit the cod aneath my head—but it's a' needless!
—Mass John, could ye think o' rattling ower some bit
short prayer, it wad do me gude maybe, and keep some
queer thoughts out o' my head.   Say something, man."

"I cannot use a prayer like a rat-rhyme," answered
the honest clergyman; "and if you would have your
soul redeemed like a prey from the fowler, Laird, you
must needs show me your state of mind."

"And shouldna ye ken that without my telling
you?" answered the patient. "What have I been
paying stipend and teind, parsonage and vicarage, for,
ever sin' the aughty-nine, and I canna get a spell of a

---

* The author has been flattered by the assurance, that this
naive mode of recommending arboriculture (which was actually
delivered in these very words by a Highland laird, while on his
death-bed, to his son) had so much weight with a Scottish earl,
as to lead to his planting a large tract of country.

prayer for't, the only time I ever asked for ane in my
life!—Gang awa wi' your whiggery, if that's a' 'ye
can do; auld Curate Kilstoup wad hae read half the
Prayer-book to me by this time—Awa wi' ye!—Doctor,
let's see if ye can do ony thing better for me."

The Doctor, who had obtained some information in
the meanwhile from the housekeeper on the state of his
complaints, assured him the medical art could not pro-
long his life many hours.

"Then damn Mass John and you baith!" cried the
furious and intractable patient. "Did ye come here for
naething but to tell me that ye canna help me at a
pinch! Out wi' them, Jenny—out o' the house! and,
Jock, my curse, and the curse of Cromwell, go wi' ye,
if ye gie them either fee or bountith, or ase muckle as a
black pair o' cheverons!"*

The clergyman and doctor made a speedy retreat out
of the apartment, while Dumbiedikes fell into one of
those transports of violent and profane language, which
had procured him the surname of Damn-me-dikes.
"Bring me the brandy bottle, Jenny, ye b——," he
cried, with a voice in which passion contended with
pain. "I can die as I have lived, without fashing ony
o' them. But there's ae thing," he said sinking his
voice—"there's ae fearful thing hings about my heart,
and an anker of brandy winna wash it away.—The
Deanses at Woodend!—I sequestrated them in the
dear years, and now they are to flit, they'll starve—
and that Beersheba, and that auld trooper's wife and

* *Cheverons*—gloves.

her oe, they'll starve—they'll starve!—Look out,
Jock; what kind o' night is't?"

"On-ding o' snaw, father," answered Jock, after
having opened the window, and looked out with great
composure.

"They'll perish in the drifts!" said the expiring
sinner—"they'll perish wi' cauld!—but I'll be het
eneugh, gin a' tales be true."

This last observation was made under breath, and in
a tone which made the very attorney shudder. He
tried his hand at ghostly advice, probably for the first
time in his life, and recommended, as an opiate for the
agonized conscience of the Laird, reparation of the injuries he had done to these distressed families, which,
he observed by the way, the civil law called *restitutio
in integrum*. But Mammon was struggling with Remorse for retaining his place in a bosom he had so long
possessed; and he partly succeeded, as an old tyrant
proves often too strong for his insurgent rebels.

"I canna do't," he answered, with a voice of despair.
"It would kill me to do't—how can ye bid me pay
back siller, when ye ken how I want it? or dispone
Beersheba, when it lies sae weel into my ain plaid-
nuik? Nature made Dumbiedikes and Beersheba to
be ae man's land—She did, by ——. Nichil, it wad
kill me to part them."

"But ye maun die whether or no, Laird," said Mr.
Novit; "and maybe ye wad die easier—it's but trying.
I'll scroll the disposition in nae time."

"Dinna speak o't, sir," replied Dumbiedikes, "or

I'll fling the stoup at your head.—But, Jock, lad, ye
see how the warld warstles wi' me on my deathbed—be
kind to the puir creatures the Deanses and the Butlers—
be kind to them, Jock. Dinna let the warld get a grip
o' ye, Jock—but keep the gear thegither! and whate'er
ye do, dispone Beersheba at no rate. Let the creatures
stay at a moderate mailing, and hae bite and soup; it
will maybe be the better wi' your father whare he's
gaun, lad."

After these contradictory instructions, the Laird felt
his mind so much at ease, that he drank three bumpers
of brandy continuously, and "soughed awa," as Jenny
expressed it, in an attempt to sing "Deil stick the
Minister."

His death made a revolution in favour of the distressed families. John Dumbie, now of Dumbiedikes,
in his own right, seemed to be close and selfish enough,
but wanted the grasping spirit and active mind of his
father; and his guardian happened to agree with him
in opinion, that his father's dying recommendation
should be attended to. The tenants, therefore, were
not actually turned out of doors among the snow
wreaths, and were allowed wherewith to procure
butter-milk and peas-bannocks, which they eat under
the full force of the original malediction. The cottage of Deans, called Woodend, was not very distant
from that at Beersheba. Formerly there had been but
little intercourse between the families. Deans was a
sturdy Scotsman, with all sorts of prejudices against the
southern, and the spawn of the southern. Moreover,

Deans was, as we have said, a stanch presbyterian, of
the most rigid and unbending adherence to what he
conceived to be the only possible straight line, as he
was wont to express himself, between right-hand heats
and extremes, and left-hand defections; and, therefore,
he held in high dread and horror all Independents, and
whomsoever he supposed allied to them.

But, notwithstanding these national prejudices and
religious professions, Deans and the widow Butler were
placed in such a situation, as naturally and at length
created some intimacy between the families. They had
shared a common danger and a mutual deliverance.
They needed each other's assistance, like a company,
who, crossing a mountain stream, are compelled to
cling close together, lest the current should be too
powerful for any who are not thus supported.

On nearer acquaintance, too, Deans abated some of
his prejudices. He found old Mrs. Butler, though not
thoroughly grounded in the extent and bearing of the
real testimony against the defections of the times, had
no opinions in favour of the Independent party; neither
was she an Englishwoman.   Therefore, it was to be
hoped, that, though she was the widow of an enthusiastic corporal of Cromwell's dragoons, her grandson
might be neither schismatic nor anti-national, two
qualities concerning which Goodman Deans had as
wholesome a terror as against papists and malignants.
Above all (for Douce Davie Deans had his weak side),
he perceived that widow Butler looked up to him with
reverence, listened to his advice, and compounded for

an occasional fling at the doctrines of her deceased
husband, to which, as we have seen, she was by no
means warmly attached, in consideration of the valuable
counsels which the presbyterian afforded her for the
management of her little farm.   These usually concluded with " they may do otherwise in England,
neighbour Butler, for aught I ken;" or, "it may be
different in foreign parts;" or, "they wha think differently on the great foundation of our covenanted reformation, overturning and mishguggling the government
and discipline of the kirk, and breaking down the
carved work of our Zion, might be for sawing the craft
wi' aits; but I say peace, peace." And as his advice
was shrewd and sensible, though conceitedly given, it
was received with gratitude, and followed with respect.

The intercourse which took place betwixt the families
at Beersheba and Woodend, became strict and intimate, at a very early period, betwixt Reuben Butler,
with whom the reader is already in some degree
acquainted, and Jeanie Deans, the only child of Douce
Davie Deans by his first wife, "that singular Christian
woman," as he was wont to express himself, "whose
name was savoury to all that knew her for a desirable
professor, Christian Menzies in Hochmagirdle." The
manner of which intimacy, and the consequences thereof, we now proceed to relate.

CHAPTER THE NINTH.

Reuben and Rachel, though as fond as doves,
Were yet discreet and cautious in their loves,
Nor would attend to Cupid's wild commands,
Till cool reflection bade them join their hands.
When both were poor, they thought it argued ill
Of hasty love to make them poorer still.

CRABBE's *Parish Register.*

WHILE widow Butler and widower Deans struggled
with poverty, and the hard and sterile soil of those
"parts and portions" of the lands of Dumbiedikes

which it was their lot to occupy, it became gradually
apparent that Deans was to gain the strife, and his ally
in the conflict was to lose it. The former was a man,
and not much past the prime of life—Mrs. Butler a
woman, and declined into the vale of years. This,
indeed, ought in time to have been balanced by the
circumstance, that Reuben was growing up to assist
his grandmother's labours, and that Jeanie Deans, as a
girl, could be only supposed to add to her father's
burdens. But Douce Davie Deans knew better things,
and so schooled and trained the young minion, as he
called her, that from the time she could walk, upwards,
she was daily employed in some task or other, suitable
to her age and capacity; a circumstance which, added
to her father's daily instructions and lectures, tended
to give her mind, even when a child, a grave, serious,
firm, and reflecting cast. An uncommonly strong and
healthy temperament, free from all nervous affection
and every other irregularity, which, attacking the body
in its more noble functions, so often influences the mind,
tended greatly to establish this fortitude, simplicity,
and decision of character.

On the other hand, Reuben was weak in constitution, and, though not timid in temper, might be safely
pronounced anxious, doubtful, and apprehensive. He
partook of the temperament of his mother, who had
died of a consumption in early age. He was a pale,
thin, feeble, sickly boy, and somewhat lame, from an
accident in early youth. He was, besides, the child of
a doting grandmother, whose too solicitous attention to

him soon taught him a sort of diffidence in himself,
with a disposition to overrate his own importance,
which is one of the very worst consequences that
children deduce from over-indulgence.

Still, however, the two children clung to each other's
society, not more from habit than from taste. They
herded together the handful of sheep, with the two or
three cows, which their parents turned out rather to
seek food than actually to feed upon the unenclosed
common of Dumbiedikes. It was there that the two
urchins might be seen seated beneath a blooming bush
of whin, their little faces laid close together under the
shadow of the same plaid drawn over both their heads,
while the landscape around was embrowned by an over-
shadowing cloud, big with the shower which had driven
the children to shelter. On other occasions they went
together to school, the boy receiving that encouragement and example from his companion, in crossing the
little brooks which intersected their path, and encountering cattle, dogs, and other perils, upon their journey,
which the male sex in such cases usually consider it as
their prerogative to extend to the weaker. But when,
seated on the benches of the school-house, they began
to con their lessons together, Reuben, who was as much
superior to Jeanie Deans in acuteness of intellect, as
inferior to her in firmness of constitution, and in that
insensibility to fatigue and danger which depends on
the conformation of the nerves, was able fully to requite
the kindness and countenance with which, in other
circumstances, she used to regard him. He was

decidedly the best scholar at the little parish school;
and so gentle was his temper and disposition, that he
was rather admired than envied by the little mob who
occupied the noisy mansion, although he was the
declared favourite of the master.   Several girls, in
particular (for in Scotland they are taught with the
boys), longed to be kind to, and comfort the sickly lad,
who was so much cleverer than his companions.   The
character of Reuben Butler was so calculated as to offer
scope both for their sympathy and their admiration, the
feelings, perhaps, through which the female sex (the
more deserving part of them at least) is more easily
attached.

But Reuben, naturally reserved and distant, improved
none of these advantages; and only became more
attached to Jeanie Deans, as the enthusiastic approbation of his master assured him of fair prospects in
future life, and awakened his ambition.   In the meantime, every advance that Reuben made in learning
(and, considering his opportunities, they were uncommonly great) rendered him less capable of attending to
the domestic duties of his grandmother's farm.   While
studying the *pons asinorum* in Euclid, he suffered every
cuddie upon the common to trespass upon a large field
of pease belonging to the Laird, and nothing but the
active exertions of Jeanie Deans, with her little dog
Dustiefoot, could have saved great loss and consequent
punishment.   Similar miscarriages marked his progress
in his classical studies.   He read Virgil's Georgics till
he did not know bear from barley; and had nearly

destroyed the crofts of Beersheba, while attempting to cultivate them according to the practice of Columella and Cato the Censor.

These blunders occasioned grief to his grand-dame, and disconcerted the good opinion which her neighbour, Davie Deans, had for some time entertained of Reuben.

"I see naething ye can make of that silly callant, neighbour Butler," said he to the old lady, "unless ye train him to the wark o' the ministry. And ne'er was there mair need of poorfu' preachers than e'en now in these cauld Gallio days, when men's hearts are hardened like the nether mill-stone, till they come to regard none of these things. It's evident this puir callant of yours will never be able to do a usefu' day's wark, unless it be as an ambassador from our Master; and I will make it my business to procure a license when ho is fit for the same, trusting he will be a shaft cleanly polished, and meet to be used in tho body of the kirk; and that he shall not turn again, like the sow, to wallow in the mire of heretical extremes and defections, but shall have the wings of a dove, though he hath lain among the pots."

The poor widow gulped down the affront to her husband's principles, implied in this caution, and hastened to take Butler from the High School, and encourage him in the pursuit of mathematics and divinity, the only physics and ethics that chanced to be in fashion at the time.

Jeanie Deans was now compelled to part from the companion of her labour, her study, and her pastime, and it was with more than childish feeling that both children regarded the separation. But they were young,

and hope was high, and they separated like those who
hope to meet again at a more auspicious hour.

While Reuben Butler was acquiring at the University of St. Andrews the knowledge necessary for a clergyman, and macerating his body with the privations which
were necessary in seeking food for his mind, his grand-
dame became daily less able to struggle with her little
farm, and was at length obliged to throw it up to the
new Laird of Dumbiedikes. That great personage was
no absolute Jew, and did not cheat her in making the
bargain more than was tolerable. He even gave her
permission to tenant the house in which she had lived
with her husband, as long as it should be " tenantable ; "
only he protested against paying for a farthing of
repairs, any benevolence which he possessed being of
the passive, but by no means of the active mood.

In the meanwhile, from superior shrewdness, skill,
and other circumstances, some of them purely accidental,
Davie Deans gained a footing in the world, the possession of some wealth, the reputation of more, and a
growing disposition to preserve and increase his store ;
for which, when he thought upon it seriously, he was
inclined to blame himself. From his knowledge in
agriculture, as it was then practised, he became a sort
of favourite with the Laird, who had no great pleasure
either in active sports or in society, and was wont to end
his daily saunter by calling at the cottage of Woodend.

Being himself a man of slow ideas and confused
utterance, Dumbiedikes used to sit or stand for half an
hour with an old laced hat of his father's upon his

head, and an empty tobacco pipe in his mouth, with his
eyes following Jeanie Deans, or "the lassie," as he
called her, through the course of her daily domestic
labour; while her father, after exhausting the subject
of bestial, of ploughs, and of harrows, often took an
opportunity of going full-sail into controversial subjects,
to which discussions the dignitary listened with much
seeming patience, but without making any reply, or,
indeed, as most people thought, without understanding
a single word of what the orator was saying. Deans,
indeed denied this stoutly, as an insult at once to his
own talents for expounding hidden truths, of which he
was a little vain, and to the Laird's capacity of understanding them. He said, "Dumbiedikes was nane of
those flashy gentles, wi' lace on their skirts and swords
at their tails, that were rather for riding on horseback
to hell than ganging barefooted to heaven. He wasna
like his father—nae profane company-keeper—nae
swearer—nae drinker—nae frequenter of play-house, or
music-house, or dancing-house—nae Sabbath-breaker—
nae imposer of aiths, or bonds, or denier of liberty to
the flock.—He clave to the warld, and the warld's gear,
a wee ower muckle, but then there was some breathing
of a gale upon his spirit," etc. etc. All this honest
Davie said and believed.

It is not to be supposed, that, by a father and a man
of sense and observation, the constant direction of the
Laird's eyes towards Jeanie was altogether unnoticed.
This circumstance, however, made a much greater impression upon another member of his family, a second

helpmate, to wit, whom he had chosen to take to his bosom ten years after the death of his first. Some people were of opinion, that Douce Davie had been rather surprised into this step, for, in general, he was no friend to marriages or giving in marriage, and seemed rather to regard that state of society as a necessary evil, —a thing lawful, and to be tolerated in the imperfect state of our nature, but which clipped the wings with which we ought to soar upwards, and tethered the soul to its mansion of clay, and the creature-comforts of wife and bairns. His own practice, however, had in this material point varied from his principles, since, as we have seen, he twice knitted for himself this dangerous and ensnaring entanglement.

Rebecca, his spouse, had by no means the same horror of matrimony, and as she made marriages in imagination for every neighbour round, she failed not to indicate a match betwixt Dumbiedikes and her step-daughter Jeanie. The goodman used regularly to frown and pshaw whenever this topic was touched upon, but usually ended by taking his bonnet and walking out of the house to conceal a certain gleam of satisfaction, which, at such a suggestion, involuntarily diffused itself over his austere features.

The more youthful part of my readers may naturally ask, whether Jeanie Deans was deserving of this mute attention of the Laird of Dumbiedikes ; and the historian, with due regard to veracity, is compelled to answer, that her personal attractions were of no uncommon description. She was short, and rather too stoutly

made for her size, had grey eyes, light coloured hair, a
round good-humoured face, much tanned with the sun,
and her only peculiar charm was an air of inexpressible
serenity, which a good conscience, kind feelings, contented temper, and the regular discharge of all her
duties, spread over her features.   There was nothing, it
may be supposed, very appalling in the form or manners
of this rustic heroine; yet, whether from sheepish
bashfulness, or from want of decision and imperfect
knowledge of his own mind on the subject, the Laird
of Dumbiedikes, with his old laced hat and empty
tobacco-pipe, came and enjoyed the beatific vision of
Jeanie Deans day after day, week after week, year after
year, without proposing to accomplish any of the pro-
phecies of the step-mother.

   This good lady began to grow doubly impatient
on the subject, when, after having been some years
married, she herself presented Douce Davie with another
daughter, who was named Euphemia, by corruption, Effie.
It was then that Rebecca began to turn impatient with
the slow pace at which the Laird's wooing proceeded,
judiciously arguing, that, as Lady Dumbiedikes would
have but little occasion for tocher, the principal part of
her gudeman's substance would naturally descend to the
child by the second marriage.   Other step-dames have
tried less laudable means for clearing the way to the
succession of their own children; but Rebecca, to do
her justice, only sought little Effie's advantage through
the promotion, or which must have generally been
accounted such, of her elder sister.   She therefore tried

every female art within the compass of her simple skill,
to bring the Laird to a point ; but had the mortification
to perceive that her efforts, like those of an unskilful
angler, only scared the trout she meant to catch.   Upon
one occasion, in particular, when she joked with the
Laird on the propriety of giving a mistress to the house
of Dumbiedikes, he was so effectually startled, that
neither laced hat, tobacco-pipe, nor the intelligent proprietor of these movables, visited Woodend for a fortnight.   Rebecca was therefore compelled to leave the
Laird to proceed at his own snail's pace, convinced, by
experience, of the grave-digger's aphorism, that your
dull ass will not mend his pace for beating.

    Reuben, in the meantime, pursued his studies at the
university, supplying his wants by teaching the younger
lads the knowledge he himself acquired, and thus at
once gaining the means of maintaining himself at the
seat of learning, and fixing in his mind the elements of
what he had already obtained.   In this manner, as is
usual among the poorer students of divinity at Scottish
universities, he contrived not only to maintain himself
according to his simple wants, but even to send considerable assistance to his sole remaining parent, a sacred
duty, of which the Scotch are seldom negligent.   His
progress in knowledge of a general kind, as well as in
the studies proper to his profession, was very considerable, but was little remarked, owing to the retired
modesty of his disposition, which in no respect qualified
him to set off his learning to the best advantage.   And
thus, had Butler been a man given to make complaints,

he had his tale to tell, like others, of unjust preferences, bad luck, and hard usage. On these subjects, however, he was habitually silent, perhaps from modesty, perhaps from a touch of pride, or perhaps from a conjunction of both.

He obtained his license as a preacher of the gospel, with some compliments from the presbytery by whom it was bestowed; but this did not lead to any preferment, and he found it necessary to make the cottage at Beershcba his residence for some months, with no other income than was afforded by the precarious occupation of teaching in one or other of the neighbouring families. After having greeted his aged grandmother, his first visit was to Woodend, where he was received by Jeanie with warm cordiality, arising from recollections which had never been dismissed from her mind, by Rebecca with good-humoured hospitality, and by old Deans in a mode peculiar to himself.

Highly as Douce Davie honoured the clergy, it was not upon each individual of the cloth that he bestowed his approbation; and, a little jealous, perhaps, at seeing his youthful acquaintance erected into the dignity of a teacher and preacher, he instantly attacked him upon various points of controversy, in order to discover whether he might not have fallen into some of the snares, defections, and desertions of the time. Butler was not only a man of stanch presbyterian principles, but was also willing to avoid giving pain to his old friend by disputing upon points of little importance; and therefore he might have hoped to have come like fine gold out

of the furnace of Davie's interrogatories. But the result
on the mind of that strict investigator was not altogether
so favourable as might have been hoped and anticipated.
Old Judith Butler, who had hobbled that evening as
far as Woodend, in order to enjoy the congratulations
of her neighbours upon Reuben's return, and upon his
high attainments, of which she was herself not a little
proud, was somewhat mortified to find that her old
friend Deans did not enter into the subject with the
warmth she expected. At first, indeed, he seemed
rather silent than dissatisfied; and it was not till Judith
had essayed the subject more than once that it led to
the following dialogue.

"Aweel, neibor Deans, I thought ye wad hae been
glad to see Reuben amang us again, poor fallow."

"I *am* glad, Mrs. Butler," was the neighbour's con-
cise answer.

"Since he has lost his grandfather and his father,
(praised be Him that giveth and taketh!) I ken nae
friend he has in the world that's been sae like a father
to him as the sell o' ye, neibor Deans."

"God is the only father of the fatherless," said
Deans, touching his bonnet and looking upwards.
"Give honour where it is due, gudewife, and not to an
unworthy instrument."

"Aweel, that's your way o' turning it, and nae doubt
ye ken best; but I hae ken'd ye, Davie, send a forpit o'
meal to Beersheba when there wasna a bow left in the
meal-ark at Woodend; ay, and I hae ken'd ye"——

"Gudewife," said Davie, interrupting her, "these

are but idle tales to tell me; fit for naething but to puff
up our inward man wi' our ain vain acts. I stude
beside blessed Alexander Peden, when I heard him call
the death and testimony of our happy martyrs but draps
of blude and scarts of ink in respect of fitting discharge
of our duty; and what suld I think of ony thing the
like of me can do?"

"Weel, neibor Deans, ye ken best; but I maun say
that I am sure you are glad to see my bairn again—the
halt's gane now, unless he has to walk ower mony miles
at a stretch; and he has a wee bit colour in his cheek,
that glads my auld een to see it; and he has as decent
a black coat as the minister; and "——

"I am very heartily glad he is weel and thriving,"
said Mr. Deans, with a gravity that seemed intended to
cut short the subject; but a woman who is bent upon
a point is not easily pushed aside from it.

"And," continued Mrs. Butler, "he can wag his
head in a pulpit now, neibor Deans, think but of that
—my ain oe—and a'body maun sit still and listen to
him, as if he were the Paip of Rome."

"The what?—the who?—woman!" said Deans, with
a sternness far beyond his usual gravity, as soon as these
offensive words had struck upon the tympanum of his ear.

"Eh, guide us!" said the poor woman; "I had forgot what an ill will ye had aye at the Paip, and sae had
my puir gudeman, Stephen Butler. Mony an afternoon
he wad sit and take up his testimony again the Paip,
and again baptizing of bairns, and the like."

"Woman!" reiterated Deans, "either speak about

what ye ken something o', or be silent; I say that independency is a foul heresy, and anabaptism a damnable
and deceiving error, whilk suld be rooted out of the
land wi' the fire o' the spiritual, and the sword o' the
civil magistrate."

"Weel, weel, neibor, I'll no say that ye mayna be
right," answered the submissive Judith. "I am sure
ye are right about the sawing and the mowing, the
shearing and the leading, and what for suld ye no be
right about kirkwark, too?—But concerning my oe,
Reuben Butler "——

"Reuben Butler, gudewife," said David with solemnity, "is a lad I wish heartily weel to, even as if he
were mine ain son—but I doubt there will be outs and
ins in the track of his walk. I muckle fear his gifts
will get the heels of his grace. He has ower muckle
human wit and learning, and thinks as muckle about
the form of the bicker as he does about the healsome-
ness of the food—he maun broider the marriage-gar-
ment with lace and passments, or it's no gude eneugh
for him. And it's like he's something proud o' his
human gifts and learning, whilk enables him to dress
up his doctrine in that fine airy dress. But," added he,
at seeing the old woman's uneasiness at his discourse,
"affliction may gie him a jagg, and let the wind out o'
him, as out o' a cow that's eaten wet clover, and the lad
may do weel, and be a burning and a shining light; and
I trust it will be yours to see, and his to feel it, and
that soon."

Widow Butler was obliged to retire, unable to make

any thing more of her neighbour, whose discourse,
though she did not comprehend it, filled her with un-
defined apprehensions on her grandson's account, and
greatly depressed the joy with which she had welcomed
him on his return. And it must not be concealed, in
justice to Mr. Deans's discernment, that Butler, in their
conference, had made a greater display of his learning
than the occasion called for, or than was likely to be
acceptable to the old man, who, accustomed to consider
himself as a person pre-eminently entitled to dictate
upon theological subjects of controversy, felt rather
humbled and mortified when learned authorities were
placed in array against him. In fact, Butler had not
escaped the tinge of pedantry which naturally flowed
from his education, and was apt, on many occasions, to
make parade of his knowledge, when there was no need
of such vanity.

Jeanie Deans, however, found no fault with this
display of learning, but, on the contrary, admired it ;
perhaps on the same score that her sex are said to
admire men of courage, on account of their own defi-
ciency in that qualification. The circumstances of their
families threw the young people constantly together ;
their old intimacy was renewed, though upon a footing
better adapted to their age ; and it became at length
understood betwixt them, that their union should be
deferred no longer than until Butler should obtain some
steady means of support, however humble. This, however, was not a matter speedily to be accomplished.
Plan after plan was formed, and plan after plan failed.

The good-humoured cheek of Jeanie lost the first flush
of juvenile freshness ; Reuben's brow assumed the
gravity of manhood, yet the means of obtaining a settlement seemed remote as ever.   Fortunately for the
lovers, their passion was of no ardent or enthusiastic
cast ; and a sense of duty on both sides induced them
to bear, with patient fortitude, the protracted interval
which divided them from each other.

In the meanwhile, time did not roll on without
effecting his usual changes.   The widow of Stephen
Butler, so long the prop of the family of Beersheba, was
gathered to her fathers ; and Rebecca, the careful spouse
of our friend Davie Deans, was also summoned from
her plans of matrimonial and domestic economy.   The
morning after her death, Reuben Butler went to offer
his mite of consolation to his old friend and benefactor.
He witnessed, on this occasion, a remarkable struggle
betwixt the force of natural affection, and the religious
stoicism, which the sufferer thought it was incumbent
upon him to maintain under each earthly dispensation,
whether of weal or wo.

On his arrival at the cottage, Jeanie, with her eyes
overflowing with tears, pointed to the little orchard,
"in which," she whispered with broken accents, "my
poor father has been since his misfortune."   Somewhat
alarmed at this account, Butler entered the orchard, and
advanced slowly towards his old friend, who, seated in
a small rude arbour, appeared to be sunk in the
extremity of his affliction.   He lifted his eyes somewhat
sternly as Butler approached, as if offended at the inter-

ruption ; but as the young man hesitated whether he ought to retreat or advance, he arose, and came forward to meet him, with a self-possessed, and even dignified air.

"Young man," said the sufferer, "lay it not to heart, though the righteous perish and the merciful are removed, seeing, it may well be said, that they are taken away from the evils to come. Wo to me, were I to shed a tear for the wife of my bosom, when I might weep rivers of water for this afflicted Church, cursed as it is with carnal seekers, and with the dead of heart."

"I am happy," said Butler, "that you can forget your private affliction in your regard for public duty."

"Forget, Reuben?" said poor Deans, putting his handkerchief to his eyes,—"She's not to be forgotten on this side of time; but He that gives the wound can send the ointment. I declare there have been times during this night when my meditation has been so wrapt, that I knew not of my heavy loss. It has been with me as with the worthy John Semple, called Carspharn John,* upon a like trial,—I have been this night on the banks of Ulai, plucking an apple here and there."

Notwithstanding the assumed fortitude of Deans, which he conceived to be the discharge of a great Christian duty, he had too good a heart not to suffer deeply under this heavy loss. Woodend became altogether distasteful to him ; and as he had obtained both substance and experience by his management of that little farm, he resolved to employ them as a dairy-farmer, or cow-feeder, as they are called in Scotland.

* Note B. Carspharn John.

The situation he chose for his new settlement was at a
place called Saint Leonard's Crags, lying betwixt
Edinburgh and the mountain called Arthur's Seat, and
adjoining to the extensive sheep pasture still named the
King's Park, from its having been formerly dedicated
to the preservation of the royal game.   Here he rented
a small lonely house, about half a mile distant from the
nearest point of the city, but the site of which, with all
the adjacent ground, is now occupied by the buildings
which form the south-eastern suburb.   An extensive
pasture-ground adjoining, which Deans rented from the
keeper of the Royal Park, enabled him to feed his
milk-cows ; and the unceasing industry and activity of
Jeanie, his eldest daughter, were exerted in making the
most of their produce.

She had now less frequent opportunities of seeing
Reuben, who had been obliged, after various disappoint-
ments, to accept the subordinate situation of assistant
in a parochial school of some eminence, at three or four
miles' distance from the city.   Here he distinguished
himself, and became acquainted with several respectable
burgesses, who, on account of health, or other reasons,
chose that their children should commence their education in this little village.   His prospects were thus
gradually brightening, and upon each visit which he
paid at Saint Leonard's he had an opportunity of gliding
a hint to this purpose into Jeanie's ear.   These visits
were necessarily very rare, on account of the demands
which the duties of the school made upon Butler's time.
Nor did he dare to make them even altogether so

frequent as these avocations would permit. Deans
received him with civility indeed, and even with kindness; but Reuben, as is usual in such cases, imagined
that he read his purpose in his eyes, and was afraid too
premature an explanation on the subject would draw
down his positive disapproval. Upon the whole,
therefore, he judged it prudent to call at Saint Leonard's
just so frequently as old acquaintance and neighbourhood seemed to authorize, and no oftener. There was
another person who was more regular in his visits.

When Davie Deans intimated to the Laird of Dumbiedikes his purpose of "quitting wi' the land and
house at Woodend," the Laird stared and said nothing.
He made his usual visits at the usual hour without
remark, until the day before the term, when, observing
the bustle of moving furniture already commenced, the
great east-country *awmrie* dragged out of its nook, and
standing with its shoulder to the company, like an
awkward booby about to leave the room, the Laird
again stared mightily, and was heard to ejaculate,
"Hegh, sirs!" Even after the day of departure was
past and gone, the Laird of Dumbiedikes, at his usual
hour, which was that at which David Deans was wont
to "loose the plough," presented himself before the
closed door of the cottage at Woodend, and seemed as
much astonished at finding it shut against his approach
as if it was not exactly what he had to expect. On
this occasion he was heard to ejaculate, "Gude guide
us!" which, by those who knew him, was considered
as a very unusual mark of emotion. From that moment

forward, Dumbiedikes became an altered man, and the
regularity of his movements, hitherto so exemplary,
was as totally disconcerted as those of a boy's watch
when he has broken the main-spring. Like the index
of the said watch, did Dumbiedikes spin round the
whole bounds of his little property, which may be
likened unto the dial of the time-piece, with unwonted
velocity. There was not a cottage into which he did
not enter, nor scarce a maiden on whom he did not
stare. But so it was, that although there were better
farm-houses on the land than Woodend, and certainly
much prettier girls than Jeanie Deans, yet it did some-
how befall that the blank in the Laird's time was not
so pleasantly filled up as it had been. There was no
seat accommodated him so well as the "bunker" at
Woodend, and no face he loved so much to gaze on as
Jeanie Deans's. So, after spinning round and round
his little orbit, and then remaining stationary for a
week, it seems to have occurred to him, that he was
not pinned down to circulate on a pivot, like the hands
of the watch, but possessed the power of shifting his
central point, and extending his circle if he thought
proper. To realize which privilege of change of place,
he bought a pony from a Highland drover, and with its
assistance and company stepped, or rather stumbled, as
far as Saint Leonard's Crags.

Jeanie Deans, though so much accustomed to the
Laird's staring that she was sometimes scarce conscious
of his presence, had nevertheless some occasional fears
lest he should call in the organ of speech to back those

expressions of admiration which he bestowed on her
through his eyes. Should this happen, farewell, she
thought, to all chance of a union with Butler.   For
her father, however stout-hearted and independent in
civil and religious principles, was not without that
respect for the laird of the land, so deeply imprinted
on the Scottish tenantry of the period. Moreover, if
he did not positively dislike Butler, yet his fund of
carnal learning was often the object of sarcasms on
David's part, which were perhaps founded in jealousy,
and which certainly indicated no partiality for the party
against whom they were launched.   And, lastly, the
match with Dumbiedikes would have presented irresistible charms to one who used to complain that he felt
himself apt to take "ower grit an armfu' o' the warld."
So that, upon the whole, the Laird's diurnal visits were
disagreeable to Jeanie from apprehension of future
consequences, and it served much to console her, upon
removing from the spot where she was bred and born,
that she had seen the last of Dumbiedikes, his laced
hat, and tobacco-pipe.   The poor girl no more expected
he could muster courage to follow her to Saint Leonard's
Crags, than that any of her apple-trees or cabbages
which she had left rooted in the "yard" at Woodend,
would spontaneously, and unaided, have undertaken
the same journey.   It was, therefore, with much more
surprise than pleasure that, on the sixth day after their
removal to Saint Leonard's, she beheld Dumbiedikes
arrive, laced hat, tobacco-pipe, and all, and, with the
self-same greeting of " How 's a' wi' ye, Jeanie ?—

Whare's the gudeman?" assume as nearly as he could
the same position in the cottage at Saint Leonard's
which he had so long and so regularly occupied at
Woodend.   He was no sooner, however, seated, than
with an unusual exertion of his powers of conversation,
he added, "Jeanie—I say, Jeanie, woman"—here he
extended his hand towards her shoulder with all the
fingers spread out as if to clutch it, but in so bashful
and awkward a manner, that when she whisked herself
beyond its reach, the paw remained suspended in the
air with the palm open, like the claw of a heraldic
griffin—"Jeanie," continued the swain, in this moment
of inspiration,—"I say, Jeanie, it's a braw day out-by,
and the roads are no that ill for boot-hose."

  "The deil's in the daidling body," muttered Jeanie
between her teeth; "wha wad hae thought o' his
daikering out this length?"   And she afterwards confessed that she threw a little of this ungracious sentiment into her accent and manner; for her father being
abroad, and the "body," as she irreverently termed
the landed proprietor, "looking unco gleg and canty,
she didna ken what he might be coming out wi' next."

  Her frowns, however, acted as a complete sedative,
and the Laird relapsed from that day into his former
taciturn habits, visiting the cow-feeder's cottage three
or four times every week, when the weather permitted,
with apparently no other purpose than to stare at
Jeanie Deans, while Douce Davie poured forth his
eloquence upon the controversies and testimonies of
the day.

CHAPTER THE TENTH.

Her air, her manners, all who saw admired,
Courteous, though coy, and gentle, though retired;
The joy of youth and health her eyes displayed;
And ease of heart her every look conveyed.

                                        CRABBE.

THE visits of the Laird thus again sunk into matters of
ordinary course, from which nothing was to be expected
or apprehended. If a lover could have gained a fair
one as a snake is said to fascinate a bird, by pertina-
ciously gazing on her with great stupid greenish eyes,
which began now to be occasionally aided by spectacles,
unquestionably Dumbiedikes would have been the

person to perform the feat. But the art of fascination seems among the *artes perditæ*, and I cannot learn that this most pertinacious of starers produced any effect by his attentions beyond an occasional yawn.

In the meanwhile, the object of his gaze was gradually attaining the verge of youth, and approaching to what is called in females the middle age, which is impolitely held to begin a few years earlier with their more fragile sex than with men. Many people would have been of opinion, that the Laird would have done better to have transferred his glances to an object possessed of far superior charms to Jeanie's, even when Jeanie's were in their bloom, who began now to be distinguished by all who visited the cottage at St. Leonard's Crags.

Effie Deans, under the tender and affectionate care of her sister, had now shot up into a beautiful and blooming girl. Her Grecian-shaped head was profusely rich in waving ringlets of brown hair, which, confined by a blue snood of silk, and shading a laughing Hebe countenance, seemed the picture of health, pleasure, and contentment. Her brown russet short-gown set off a shape, which time, perhaps, might be expected to render too robust, the frequent objection to Scottish beauty, but which, in her present early age, was slender and taper, with that graceful and easy sweep of outline which at once indicates health and beautiful proportion of parts.

These growing charms, in all their juvenile profusion, had no power to shake the steadfast mind, or divert the fixed gaze, of the constant Laird of Dumbiedikes. But

there was scarce another eye that could behold this
living picture of health and beauty, without pausing on
it with pleasure. The traveller stopped his weary horse
on the eve of entering the city which was the end of his
journey, to gaze at the sylph-like form that tripped by
him, with her milk-pail poised on her head, bearing
herself so erect, and stepping so light and free under
her burden, that it seemed rather an ornament than an
encumbrance. The lads of the neighbouring suburb,
who held their evening rendezvous for putting the
stone, casting the hammer, playing at long bowls, and
other athletic exercises, watched the motions of Effie
Deans, and contended with each other which should
have the good fortune to attract her attention. Even
the rigid presbyterians of her father's persuasion, who
held each indulgence of the eye and sense to be a snare
at least, if not a crime, were surprised into a moment's
delight while gazing on a creature so exquisite,—instantly checked by a sigh, reproaching at once their own
weakness, and mourning that a creature so fair should
share in the common and hereditary guilt and imperfec-
tion of our nature. She was currently entitled the Lily
of St. Leonard's, a name which she deserved as much
by her guileless purity of thought, speech, and action,
as by her uncommon loveliness of face and person.

Yet there were points in Effie's character which
gave rise not only to strange doubt and anxiety on the
part of Douce David Deans, whose ideas were rigid, as
may easily be supposed, upon the subject of youthful
amusements, but even of serious apprehension to her

more indulgent sister. The children of the Scotch of
the inferior classes are usually spoiled by the early
indulgence of their parents; how, wherefore, and to
what degree, the lively and instructive narrative of
the amiable and accomplished authoress of "Glen-
burnie"* has saved me and all future scribblers the
trouble of recording. Effie had had a double share of
this inconsiderate and misjudged kindness. Even the
strictness of her father's principles could not condemn
the sports of infancy and childhood; and to the good
old man, his younger daughter, the child of his old age,
seemed a child for some years after she attained the
years of womanhood, was still called the "bit lassie"
and "little Effie," and was permitted to run up and
down uncontrolled, unless upon the Sabbath, or at the
times of family worship. Her sister, with all the love
and care of a mother, could not be supposed to possess
the same authoritative influence; and that which she had
hitherto exercised became gradually limited and diminished as Effie's advancing years entitled her, in her own
conceit at least, to the right of independence and free
agency. With all the innocence and goodness of disposition, therefore, which we have described, the Lily
of St. Leonard's possessed a little fund of self-conceit
and obstinacy, and some warmth and irritability of
temper, partly natural perhaps, but certainly much
increased by the unrestrained freedom of her childhood.
Her character will be best illustrated by a cottage
evening scene.

* Mrs. Elizabeth Hamilton, now no more.—*Editor.*

The careful father was absent in his well-stocked
byre, foddering those useful and patient animals on
whose produce his living depended, and the summer
evening was beginning to close in, when Jeanie Deans
began to be very anxious for the appearance of her
sister, and to fear that she would not reach home before
her father returned from the labour of the evening,
when it was his custom to have "family exercise," and
when she knew that Effie's absence would give him the
most serious displeasure. These apprehensions hung
heavier upon her mind, because, for several preceding
evenings, Effie had disappeared about the same time,
and her stay, at first so brief as scarce to be noticed, had
been gradually protracted to half an hour, and an hour,
and on the present occasion had considerably exceeded
even this last limit. And now, Jeanie stood at the
door, with her hand before her eyes to avoid the rays
of the level sun, and looked alternately along the
various tracts which led towards their dwelling, to see
if she could discry the nymph-like form of her sister.
There was a wall and a stile which separated the royal
domain, or King's Park, as it is called, from the public
road; to this pass she frequently directed her attention,
when she saw two persons appear there somewhat suddenly, as if they had walked close by the side of the
wall to screen themselves from observation. One of
them, a man, drew back hastily; the other, a female,
crossed the stile, and advanced towards her—It was
Effie. She met her sister with that affected liveliness
of manner, which, in her rank, and sometimes in those

above it, females occasionally assume to hide surprise or
confusion; and she carolled as she came—

> "The elfin knight sate on the brae,
>> The broom grows bonny, the broom grows fair;
>> And by there came lilting a lady so gay,
>> And we daurna gang down to the broom nae mair."

"Whisht, Effie," said her sister; "our father's coming
out o' the byre."—The damsel stinted in her song.—
"Whare hae ye been sae late at e'en?"

"It's no late, lass," answered Effie.

"It's chappit eight on every clock o' the town, and
the sun's gaun down ahint the Corstorphine hills—
Whare can ye hae been sae late?"

"Nae gate," answered Effie.

"And wha was that parted wi' you at the stile?"

"Naebody," replied Effie, once more.

"Nae gate?—Naebody?—I wish it may be a right
gate, and a right body, that keeps folk out sae late at
e'en, Effie."

"What needs ye be aye speering then at folk?"
retorted Effie. "I'm sure, if ye'll ask nae questions,
I'll tell ye nae lees. I never ask what brings the Laird
of Dumbiedikes glowering here like a wull-cat (only
his een's greener, and no sae gleg), day after day, till
we are a' like to gaunt our chafts aff."

"Because ye ken very weel he comes to see our
father," said Jeanie, in answer to this pert remark.

"And Dominie Butler—Does he come to see our
father, that's sae taen wi' his Latin words?" said Effie,
delighted to find that by carrying the war into the

enemy's country, she could divert the threatened attack,
upon herself, and with the petulance of youth she pursued her triumph over her prudent elder sister.   She
looked at her with a sly air, in which there was something like irony, as she chanted, in a low but marked
tone, a scrap of an old Scotch song——

> "Through the kirkyard
> I met wi' the Laird,
> The silly puir body he said me nae harm;
> But just ere 't was dark,
> I met wi' the clerk"——

Here the songstress stopped, looked full at her
sister, and observing the tear gather in her eyes, she
suddenly flung her arms round her neck, and kissed
them away.   Jeanie, though hurt and displeased, was
unable to resist the caresses of this untaught child of
nature, whose good and evil seemed to flow rather from
impulse than from reflection.   But as she returned the
sisterly kiss, in token of perfect reconciliation, she could
not suppress the gentle reproof—"Effie, if ye will learn
fule sangs, ye might make a kinder use of them."

"And so I might, Jeanie," continued the girl, clinging to her sister's neck; "and I wish I had never
learned ane o' them—and I wish we had never come
here—and I wish my tongue had been blistered or I
had vexed ye."

"Never mind that, Effie," replied the affectionate
sister; "I canna be muckle vexed wi' ony thing ye say
to me—but O dinna vex our father!"

"I will not—I will not," replied Effie; "and if

there were as mony dances the morn's night as there
are merry dancers in the north firmament on a frosty
e'en, I winna budge an inch to gang near ane o'
them."

"Dance?" echoed Jeanie Deans in astonishment.
"O, Effie, what could take ye to a dance?"

It is very possible, that, in the communicative mood
into which the Lily of St. Leonard's was now surprised,
she might have given her sister her unreserved confidence, and saved me the pain of telling a melancholy
tale; but at the moment the word dance was uttered, it
reached the ear of old David Deans, who had turned
the corner of the house, and came upon his daughters
ere they were aware of his presence. The word *prelate*,
or even the word *pope*, could hardly have produced so
appalling an effect upon David's ear; for, of all exercises, that of dancing, which he termed a voluntary and
regular fit of distraction, he deemed most destructive of
serious thoughts, and the readiest inlet to all sorts of
licentiousness; and he accounted the encouraging, and
even permitting, assemblies or meetings, whether among
those of high or low degree, for this fantastic and absurd
purpose, or for that of dramatic representations, as one
of the most flagrant proofs of defection and causes of
wrath. The pronouncing of the word *dance* by his
own daughters, and at his own door, now drove him
beyond the verge of patience. "Dance!" he exclaimed,
"Dance!—dance, said ye? I daur ye, limmers that ye
are, to name sic a word at my door-cheek! It's a dis-
solute profane pastime, practised by the Israelites only

at their base and brutal worship of the Golden Calf at
Bethel, and by the unhappy lass wha danced aff the
head of John the Baptist, upon whilk chapter I will
exercise this night for your farther instruction, since ye
need it sae muckle, nothing doubting that she has cause
to rue the day, lang or this time, that e'er she suld hae
shook a limb on sic an errand. Better for her to hae
been born a cripple, and carried frae door to door, like
auld Bessie Bowie, begging bawbees, than to be a king's
daughter, fiddling and flinging the gate she did. I hae
often wondered that ony ane that ever bent a knee for
the right purpose, should ever daur to crook a hough to
fyke and fling at piper's wind and fiddler's squealing.
And I bless God (with that singular worthy, Peter
Walker the packman at Bristo-Port*), that ordered my
lot in my dancing days, so that fear of my head and
throat, dread of bloody rope and swift bullet, and tren-
chant swords and pain of boots and thumkins, cauld
and hunger, wetness and weariness, stopped the lightness of my head, and the wantonness of my feet. And
now, if I hear ye, quean lassies, sae muckle as name
dancing, or think there's sic a thing in this warld as
flinging to fiddler's sounds and piper's spring, as sure as
my father's spirit is with the just, ye shall be no more
either charge or concern of mine! Gang in, then—gang
in, then, hinnies," he added, in a softer tone, for the
tears of both daughters, but especially those of Effie,
began to flow very fast,—"Gang in, dears, and we'll
seek grace to preserve us frae all manner of profane

* Note C. Peter Walker.

folly, whilk causeth to sin, and promoteth the kingdom
of darkness, warring with the kingdom of light."

The objurgation of David Deans, however well
meant, was unhappily timed. It created a division of
feelings in Effie's bosom, and deterred her from her
intended confidence in her sister. "She wad haud me
nae better than the dirt below her feet," said Effie to
herself, "were I to confess I hae danced wi' him four
times on the green down by, and ance at Maggie Mac-
queens's; and she'll maybe hing it ower my head that
she'll tell my father, and then she wad be mistress and
mair. But I'll no gang back there again. I'm resolved
I'll no gang back. I'll lay in a leaf of my Bible,* and
that's very near as if I had made an aith, that I winna
gang back." And she kept her vow for a week, during
which she was unusually cross and fretful, blemishes
which had never before been observed in her temper,
except during a moment of contradiction.

There was something in all this so mysterious as
considerably to alarm the prudent and affectionate
Jeanie, the more so as she judged it unkind to her
sister to mention to their father grounds of anxiety
which might arise from her own imagination. Besides,
her respect for the good old man did not prevent her
from being aware that he was both hot-tempered and
positive, and she sometimes suspected that he carried
his dislike to youthful amusements beyond the verge

---

* This custom, of making a mark by folding a leaf in the
party's Bible when a solemn resolution is formed, is still held to
be, in some sense, an appeal to Heaven for his or her sincerity.

that religion and reason demanded. Jeanie had sense
enough to see that a sudden and severe curb upon her
sister's hitherto unrestrained freedom might be rather
productive of harm than good, and that Effie, in the
headstrong wilfulness of youth, was likely to make
what might be overstrained in her father's precepts an
excuse to herself for neglecting them altogether.   In
the higher classes, a damsel, however giddy, is still
under the dominion of etiquette, and subject to the
surveillance of mammas and chaperons; but the country
girl, who snatches her moment of gaiety during the
intervals of labour, is under no such guardianship or
restraint, and her amusement becomes so much the
more hazardous.   Jeanie saw all this with much distress of mind, when a circumstance occurred which
appeared calculated to relieve her anxiety.

Mrs. Saddletree, with whom our readers have
already been made acquainted, chanced to be a distant
relation of Douce Davie Deans, and as she was a
woman orderly in her life and conversation, and moreover, of good substance, a sort of acquaintance was
formally kept up between the families.   Now, this
careful dame, about a year and a half before our story
commences, chanced to need, in the line of her profession, a better sort of servant, or rather shop-woman.
"Mr. Saddletree," she said, "was never in the shop
when he could get his nose within the Parliament
House, and it was an awkward thing for a woman-body
to be standing among bundles o' barkened leather her
lane, selling saddles and bridles; and she had cast her

eyes upon her far-awa cousin Effie Deans, as just the
very sort of lassie she would want to keep her in countenance on such occasions."

In this proposal there was much that pleased old
David,—there was bed, board, and bountith—it was a
decent situation—the lassie would be under Mrs.
Saddletree's eye, who had an upright walk, and lived
close by the Tolbooth Kirk, in which might still be
heard the comforting doctrines of one of those few
ministers of the Kirk of Scotland who had not bent
the knee unto Baal, according to David's expression,
or become accessory to the course of national defections,
—union, toleration, patronages, and a bundle of prelatical Erastian oaths which had been imposed on the
church since the Revolution, and particularly in the
reign of "the late woman" (as he called Queen Anne),
the last of that unhappy race of Stuarts. In the good
man's security concerning the soundness of the theological doctrine which his daughter was to hear, he was
nothing disturbed on account of the snares of a different
kind, to which a creature so beautiful, young, and
wilful, might be exposed in the centre of a populous
and corrupted city. The fact is, that he thought with
so much horror on all approaches to irregularities of the
nature most to be dreaded in such cases, that he would
as soon have suspected and guarded against Effie's
being induced to become guilty of the crime of murder.
He only regretted that she should live under the same
roof with such a worldly-wise man as Bartoline Saddletree, whom David never suspected of being an ass as

he was, but considered as one really endowed with all
the legal knowledge to which he made pretension, and
only liked him the worse for possessing it. The
lawyers, especially those amongst them who sate as
ruling elders in the General Assembly of the Kirk,
had been forward in promoting the measures of patronage, of the abjuration oath, and others, which, in the
opinion of David Deans, were a breaking down of the
carved work of the sanctuary, and an intrusion upon
the liberties of the kirk. Upon the dangers of listening to the doctrines of a legalized formalist, such as
Saddletree, David gave his daughter many lectures;
so much so, that he had time to touch but slightly
on the dangers of chambering, company-keeping, and
promiscuous dancing, to which, at her time of life,
most people would have thought Effie more exposed,
than to the risk of theoretical error in her religious
faith.

Jeanie parted from her sister, with a mixed feeling
of regret, and apprehension, and hope. She could not
be so confident concerning Effie's prudence as her father,
for she had observed her more narrowly, had more
sympathy with her feelings, and could better estimate
the temptations to which she was exposed. On the
other hand, Mrs. Saddletree was an observing, shrewd,
notable woman, entitled to exercise over Effie the full
authority of a mistress, and likely to do so strictly, yet
with kindness. Her removal to Saddletree's, it was
most probable, would also serve to break off some idle
acquaintances, which Jeanie suspected her sister to

have formed in the neighbouring suburb. Upon the
whole, then, she viewed her departure from Saint
Leonard's with pleasure, and it was not until the very
moment of their parting for the first time in their lives,
that she felt the full force of sisterly sorrow. While
they repeatedly kissed each other's cheeks, and wrung
each other's hands, Jeanie took that moment of affectionate sympathy, to press upon her sister the necessity
of the utmost caution in her conduct while residing in
Edinburgh. Effie listened, without once raising her
large dark eyelashes, from which the drops fell so fast
as almost to resemble a fountain. At the conclusion
she sobbed again, kissed her sister, promised to recollect all the good counsel she had given her, and they
parted.

During the first weeks, Effie was all that her kinswoman expected, and even more. But with time there
came a relaxation of that early zeal which she manifested in Mrs. Saddletree's service. To borrow once
again from the poet, who so correctly and beautifully
describes living manners,—

> Something there was,—what, none presumed to say,—
> Clouds lightly passing on a summer's day;
> Whispers and hints, which went from ear to ear,
> And mixed reports no judge on earth could clear.

During this interval, Mrs. Saddletree was sometimes
displeased by Effie's lingering when she was sent upon
errands about the shop business, and sometimes by a
little degree of impatience which she manifested at
being rebuked on such occasions. But she good-

naturedly allowed, that the first was very natural to a
girl to whom everything in Edinburgh was new, and
the other was only the petulance of a spoiled child,
when subjected to the yoke of domestic discipline for
the first time. Attention and submission could not be
learned at once — Holy-Rood was not built in a day —
use would make perfect.

It seemed as if the considerate old lady had presaged
truly. Ere many months had passed, Effie became
almost wedded to her duties, though she no longer
discharged them with the laughing cheek and light
step, which had at first attracted every customer. Her
mistress sometimes observed her in tears, but they
were signs of secret sorrow, which she concealed as
often as she saw them attract notice. Time wore on,
her cheek grew pale, and her step heavy. The cause
of these changes could not have escaped the matronly
eye of Mrs. Saddletree, but she was chiefly confined by
indisposition to her bedroom for a considerable time
during the latter part of Effie's service. This interval
was marked by symptoms of anguish almost amounting
to despair. The utmost efforts of the poor girl to command her fits of hysterical agony were often totally
unavailing, and the mistakes which she made in the
shop the while were so numerous and so provoking,
that Bartoline Saddletree, who, during his wife's illness,
was obliged to take closer charge of the business than
consisted with his study of the weightier matters of the
law, lost all patience with the girl, who, in his law
Latin, and without much respect to gender, he declared

ought to be cognosced by inquest of a jury, as *fatuus*,
furiosus, and *naturaliter idiota*.   Neighbours, also,
and fellow-servants, remarked, with malicious curiosity
or degrading pity, the disfigured shape, loose dress,
and pale cheeks, of the once beautiful and still interesting girl. But to no one would she grant her confidence, answering all taunts with bitter sarcasm, and all
serious expostulation with sullen denial, or with floods
of tears.

At length, when Mrs. Saddletree's recovery was
likely to permit her wonted attention to the regulation
of her household, Effie Deans, as if unwilling to face
an investigation made by the authority of her mistress,
asked permission of Bartoline to go home for a week or
two, assigning indisposition, and the wish of trying the
benefit of repose and the change of air, as the motives
of her request.   Sharp-eyed as a lynx (or conceiving
himself to be so) in the nice sharp quillits of legal discussion, Bartoline was as dull at drawing inferences from
the occurrences of common life as any Dutch professor
of Mathematics.   He suffered Effie to depart without
much suspicion, and without any inquiry.

It was afterwards found that a period of a week
intervened betwixt her leaving her master's house and
arriving at St. Leonard's. She made her appearance
before her sister in a state rather resembling the spectre
than the living substance of the gay and beautiful girl,
who had left her father's cottage for the first time scarce
seventeen months before. The lingering illness of her
mistress, had, for the last few months, given her a plea

for confining herself entirely to the dusky precincts of
the shop in the Lawnmarket, and Jeanie was so much
occupied, during the same period, with the concerns of
her father's houshold, that she had rarely found leisure
for a walk in the city, and a brief and hurried visit to
her sister.   The young women, therefore, had scarcely
seen each other for several months, nor had a single
scandalous surmise reached the ears of the secluded
inhabitants of the cottage at St. Leonard's.   Jeanie,
therefore, terrified to death at her sister's appearance,
at first overwhelmed her with inquiries, to which the
unfortunate young woman returned for a time incoherent
and rambling answers, and finally fell into a hysterical
fit.   Rendered too certain of her sister's misfortune,
Jeanie had now the dreadful alternative of communicating her ruin to her father, or of endeavouring to
conceal it from him.   To all questions concerning the
name or rank of her seducer, and the fate of the being
to whom her fall had given birth, Effie remained as
mute as the grave, to which she seemed hastening;
and indeed the least allusion to either seemed to drive
her to distraction.   Her sister, in distress and in despair,
was about to repair to Mrs. Saddletree to consult her
experience, and at the same time to obtain what lights
she could upon this most unhappy affair, when she
was saved that trouble by a new stroke of fate, which
seemed to carry misfortune to the uttermost.

David Deans had been alarmed at the state of health
in which his daughter had returned to her paternal
residence; but Jeanie had contrived to divert him from

particular and specific inquiry. It was, therefore, like a clap of thunder to the poor old man, when, just as the hour of noon had brought the visit of the Laird of Dumbiedikes as usual, other and sterner, as well as most unexpected guests, arrived at the cottage of St. Leonard's. These were the officers of justice, with a warrant of justiciary to search for and apprehend Euphemia, or Effie, Deans, accused of the crime of child-murder. The stunning weight of a blow so totally unexpected bore down the old man, who had in his early youth resisted the brow of military and civil tyranny, though backed with swords and guns, tortures and gibbets. He fell extended and senseless upon his own hearth; and the men, happy to escape from the scene of his awakening, raised, with rude humanity, the object of their warrant from her bed, and placed her in a coach, which they had brought with them. The hasty remedies which Jeanie had applied to bring back her father's senses were scarce begun to operate, when the noise of the wheels in motion recalled her attention to her miserable sister. To run shrieking after the carriage was the first vain effort of her distraction, but she was stopped by one or two female neighbours, assembled by the extraordinary appearance of a coach in that sequestered place, who almost forced her back to her father's house. The deep and sympathetic affliction of these poor people, by whom the little family at St. Leonard's were held in high regard, filled the house with lamentation. Even Dumbiedikes was moved from his wonted apathy, and, groping for his purse as he spoke, ejaculated, "Jeanie, woman!—Jeanie, woman! dinna greet—it's sad wark, but siller will help it;" and he drew out his purse as he spoke.

The old man had now raised himself from the ground, and, looking about him as if he missed something, seemed gradually to recover the sense of his wretchedness. "Where," he said, with a voice that made the roof ring, "where is the vile harlot, that has disgraced the blood of an honest man?—Where is she, that has no place among us, but has come foul with her sins, like the Evil One, among the children of God?—Where is she, Jeanie?—Bring her before me, that I may kill her with a word and a look!"

All hastened around him with their appropriate sources of consolation—the Laird with his purse, Jeanie with burnt feathers and strong waters, and the women with their exhortations. "O neighbour—O Mr. Deans, it's a sair trial, doubtless—but think of the Rock of Ages, neighbour—think of the promise!"

"And I do think of it, neighbours—and I bless God that I can think of it, even in the wrack and ruin of a' that's nearest and dearest to me—But to be the father of a cast-away—a profligate—a bloody Zipporah—a mere murderess!—O, how will the wicked exult in the high places of their wickedness!—the prelatists, and the latitudinarians, and the hand-waled murderers, whose hands are hard as horn wi' hauding the slaughter-weapons—they will push out the lip, and say that we are even such as themselves. Sair, sair I am grieved, neighbours, for the poor cast-away—for the child of mine old age—but sairer for the stumbling-block and scandal it will be to all tender and honest souls!"

"Davie—winna siller do't?" insinuated the Laird, still proffering his green purse, which was full of guineas.

"I tell ye, Dumbiedikes," said Deans, "that if telling down my haill substance could hae saved her frae this black snare, I wad hae walked out wi' naething but my bonnet and my staff to beg an awmous for God's sake, and ca'd mysell a happy man—But if a dollar, or a plack, or the nineteenth part of a boddle, wad save her upon guilt and open shame frae open punishment, that purchase wad Davie Deans never make!—Na, na; an eye for an eye, a tooth for a tooth, life for life, blood for blood—it's the law of man, and it's the law of God.—Leave me, sirs—leave me—I maun warstle wi' this trial in privacy and on my knees."

Jeanie, now in some degree restored to the power of thought, joined in the same request. The next day found the father and daughter still in the depth of affliction, but the father sternly supporting his load of ill through a proud sense of religious duty, and the daughter anxiously suppressing her own feelings to avoid again awakening his. Thus was it with the afflicted family until the morning after Porteous's death, a period at which we are now arrived.

CHAPTER THE ELEVENTH.

Is all the counsel that we two have shared,
The sisters' vows, the hours that we have spent
When we have chid the hasty-footed time
For parting us—Oh! and is all forgot?
                              MIDSUMMER NIGHT'S DREAM.

WE have been a long while in conducting Butler to
the door of the cottage at St. Leonard's; yet the space
which we have occupied in the preceding narrative
does not exceed in length that which he actually spent
on Salisbury Crags on the morning which succeeded the
execution done upon Porteous by the* rioters. For
this delay he had his own motives. He wished to
collect his thoughts, strangely agitated as they were,
first by the melancholy news of Effie Deans's situation, and afterwards by the frightful scene which he
had witnessed. In the situation also in which he stood
with respect to Jeanie and her father, some ceremony,
at least some choice of fitting time and season, was necessary to wait upon them. Eight in the morning was
then the ordinary hour for breakfast, and he resolved
that it should arrive before he made his appearance in
their cottage.

Never did hours pass so heavily. Butler shifted his
place and enlarged his circle to while away the time,

and heard the huge bell of St. Giles's toll each successive
hour in swelling tones, which were instantly attested
by those of the other steeples in succession. He had
heard seven struck in this manner, when he began to
think he might venture to approach nearer to St.
Leonard's, from which he was still a mile distant.
Accordingly he descended from his lofty station as low
as the bottom of the valley which divides Salisbury
Crags from those small rocks which take their name
from St. Leonard. It is, as many of my readers may
know, a deep, wild, grassy valley, scattered with huge
rocks and fragments which have descended from the
cliffs and steep ascent to the east.

This sequestered dell, as well as other places of the
open pasturage of the King's Park, was, about this
time, often the resort of the gallants of the time who
had affairs of honour to discuss with the sword. Duels
were then very common in Scotland, for the gentry
were at once idle, haughty, fierce, divided by faction,
and addicted to intemperance, so that there lacked
neither provocation, nor inclination to resent it when
given; and the sword, which was part of every gentleman's dress, was the only weapon used for the decision
of such differences. When, therefore, Butler observed
a young man, skulking, apparently to avoid observation,
among the scattered rocks at some distance from the
foot-path, he was naturally led to suppose that he had
sought this lonely spot upon that evil errand. He was
so strongly impressed with this, that, notwithstanding
his own distress of mind, he could not, according to his

sense of duty as a clergyman, pass this person without
speaking to him.   There are times, thought he to himself, when the slightest interference may avert a great
calamity—when a word spoken in season may do more
for prevention than the eloquence of Tully could do for
remedying evil—And for my own griefs, be they as
they may, I shall feel them the lighter, if they divert
me not from the prosecution of my duty.

Thus thinking and feeling, he quitted the ordinary
path, and advanced nearer the object he had noticed.
The man at first directed his course towards the hill, in
order, as it appeared, to avoid him ; but when he saw
that Butler seemed disposed to follow him, he adjusted
his hat fiercely, turned round, and came forward, as if
to meet and defy scrutiny.

Butler had an opportunity of accurately studying his
features as they advanced slowly to meet each other.
The stranger seemed about twenty-five years old.   His
dress was of a kind which could hardly be said to
indicate his rank with certainty, for it was such as young
gentlemen sometimes wore while on active exercise in
the morning, and which, therefore, was imitated by
those of the inferior ranks, as young clerks and tradesmen, because its cheapness rendered it attainable, while
it approached more nearly to the apparel of youths of
fashion than any other which the manners of the times
permitted them to wear.   If his air and manner could
be trusted, however, this person seemed rather to be
dressed under than above his rank ; for his carriage was
bold and somewhat supercilious, his step easy and free,

his manner daring and unconstrained. His stature was of the middle size, or rather above it, his limbs well proportioned, yet not so strong as to infer the reproach of clumsiness. His features were uncommonly handsome, and all about him would have been interesting and prepossessing, but for that indescribable expression which habitual dissipation gives to the countenance, joined with a certain audacity in look and manner, of that kind which is often assumed as a mask for confusion and apprehension.

Dutler and the stranger met—surveyed each other—when, as the latter, slightly touching his hat, was about to pass by him, Butler, while he returned the salutation, observed, "A fine morning sir—You are on the hill early."

"I have business here," said the young man, in a tone meant to repress farther inquiry.

"I do not doubt it sir," said Butler. "I trust you will forgive my hoping that it is of a lawful kind?"

"Sir," said the other, with marked surprise, "I never forgive impertinence, nor can I conceive what title you have to hope any thing about what no way concerns you."

"I am a soldier, sir," said Butler, "and have a charge to arrest evil-doers in the name of my master."

"A soldier?" said the young man, stepping back, and fiercely laying his hand on his sword—"A soldier, and arrest me! Did you reckon what your life was worth, before you took the commission upon you?"

"You mistake me, sir," said Butler gravely; "neither

my warfare nor my warrant are of this world. I am a
preacher of the gospel, and have power, in my Master's
name, to command the peace upon earth and good-will
towards men, which was proclaimed with the gospel."

"A minister!" said the stranger, carelessly, and
with an expression approaching to scorn. "I know
the gentlemen of your cloth in Scotland claim a strange
right of intermeddling with men's private affairs.
But I have been abroad, and know better than to be
priest-ridden."

"Sir, if it be true that any of my cloth, or, it might
be more decently said, of my calling, interfere with
men's private affairs, for the gratification either of idle
curiosity, or for worse motives, you cannot have learned
a better lesson abroad than to contemn such practices.
But, in my Master's work, I am called to be busy in
season and out of season; and, conscious as I am of a
pure motive, it were better for me to incur your
contempt for speaking, than the correction of my own
conscience for being silent."

"In the name of the devil!" said the young man
impatiently, "say what you have to say, then; though
whom you take me for, or what earthly concern you
have with me, a stranger to you, or with my actions and
motives, of which you can know nothing, I cannot
conjecture for an instant."

"You are about," said Butler, "to violate one of
your country's wisest laws—you are about, which is
much more dreadful, to violate a law, which God himself has implanted within our nature, and written, as it

were, in the table of our hearts, to which every thrill of
our nerves is responsive."

"And what is the law you speak of?" said the
stranger, in a hollow and somewhat disturbed accent.

"Thou shalt do no MURDER," said Butler, with a
deep and solemn voice.

The young man visibly started, and looked considerably appalled. Butler perceived he had made a favourable impression, and resolved to follow it up. "Think,"
he said, "young man," laying his hand kindly upon the
stranger's shoulder, "what an awful alternative you
voluntarily choose for yourself, to kill or be killed.
Think what it is to rush uncalled into the presence of
an offended Deity, your heart fermenting with evil
passions, your hand hot from the steel you had been
urging, with your best skill and malice, against the
breast of a fellow-creature. Or, suppose yourself the
scarce less wretched survivor, with the guilt of Cain,
the first murderer, in your heart, with his stamp upon
your brow—that stamp, which struck all who gazed on
him with unutterable horror, and by which the
murderer is made manifest to all who look upon him.
Think——"

The stranger gradually withdrew himself from under
the hand of his monitor; and, pulling his hat over his
brows, thus interrupted him. "Your meaning, sir, I
daresay, is excellent, but you are throwing your advice
away. I am not in this place with violent intentions
against any one. I may be bad enough—you priests
say all men are so—but I am here for the purpose of

saving life, not of taking it away.   If you wish to spend
your time rather in doing a good action than in talking
about you know not what, I will give you an opportunity.   Do you see yonder crag to the right, over
which appears the chimney of a lone house?   Go
thither, inquire for one Jeanie Deans, the daughter of
the good man ; let her know that he she wots of
remained here from daybreak till this hour, expecting
to see her, and that he can abide no longer.   Tell her,
she *must* meet me at the Hunter's Bog to night, as the
moon rises behind St. Anthony's Hill, or that she will
make a desperate man of me."

   " Who, or what are you," replied Butler, exceedingly
and most unpleasantly surprised, " who charge me with
such an errand ?"

   " I am the devil !"——answered the young man
hastily.

   Butler stepped instinctively back, and commended
himself internally to Heaven ; for, though a wise and
strong-minded man, he was neither wiser nor more
strong-minded than those of his age and education, with
whom, to disbelieve witchcraft or spectres, was held an
undeniable proof of atheism.

   The stranger went on without observing his emotion.
" Yes ! call me Apollyon, Abaddon, whatever name you
shall choose, as a clergyman acquainted with the upper
and lower circles of spiritual denomination, to call me
by, you shall not find an appellation more odious to him
that bears it, than is mine own."

   This sentence was spoken with the bitterness of

self-upbraiding, and a contortion of visage absolutely
demoniacal. Butler, though a man brave by principle,
if not by constitution, was overawed; for intensity of
mental distress has in it a sort of sublimity which repels
and overawes all men, but especially those of kind and
sympathetic dispositions. The stranger turned abruptly
from Butler as he spoke, but instantly returned, and,
coming up to him closely and boldly, said, in a fierce,
determined tone, "I have told you who and what I am
—who, and what are you? What is your name?"

"Butler," answered the person to whom this abrupt
question was addressed, surprised into answering it by
the sudden and fierce manner of the querist—"Reuben
Butler, a preacher of the gospel."

At this answer, the stranger again plucked more deep
over his brows the hat which he had thrown back in
his former agitation. "Butler!" he repeated—"the
assistant of the schoolmaster at Liberton?"

"The same," answered Butler, composedly.

The stranger covered his face with his hand, as if on
sudden reflection, and then turned away, but stopped
when he had walked a few paces; and seeing Butler
follow him with his eyes, called out in a stern yet
suppressed tone, just as if he had exactly calculated
that his accents should not be heard a yard beyond the
spot on which Butler stood. "Go your way, and do
mine errand. Do not look after me. I will neither
descend through the bowels of these rocks, nor vanish
in a flash of fire; and yet the eye that seeks to trace
my motions shall have reason to curse it was ever

shrouded by eyelid or eyelash. Begone, and look not
behind you. Tell Jeanie Deans, that when the moon
rises I shall expect to meet her at Nicol Muschat's Cairn,
beneath Saint Anthony's Chapel."

As he uttered these words, he turned and took the
road against the hill, with a haste that seemed as
peremptory as his tone of authority.

Dreading he knew not what of additional misery to
a lot which seemed little capable of receiving augmen-
tation, and desperate at the idea that any living man
should dare to send so extraordinary a request, couched
in terms so imperious, to the half-betrothed object of
his early and only affection, Butler strode hastily towards the cottage, in order to ascertain how far this
daring and rude gallant was actually entitled to press
on Jeanie Deans a request which no prudent, and scarce
any modest young woman, was likely to comply with.

Butler was by nature neither jealous nor superstitious; yet the feelings which lead to those moods of the
mind were rooted in his heart, as a portion derived
from the common stock of humanity. It was madden-
ing to think that a profligate gallant, such as the manner
and tone of the stranger evinced him to be, should have
it in his power to command forth his future bride and
plighted true love, at a place so improper, and an hour
so unseasonable. Yet the tone in which the stranger
spoke had nothing of the soft half-breathed voice proper
to the seducer who solicits an assignation; it was bold,
fierce, and imperative, and had less of love in it than of
menace and intimidation.

The suggestions of superstition seemed more plausible, had Butler's mind been very accessible to them. Was this indeed the Roaring Lion, who goeth about seeking whom he may devour? This was a question which pressed itself on Butler's mind with an earnestness that cannot be conceived by those who live in the present day. The fiery eye, the abrupt demeanour, the occasionally harsh, yet studiously subdued tone of voice,—the features, handsome, but now clouded with pride, now disturbed by suspicion, now inflamed with passion—those dark hazel eyes which he sometimes shaded with his cap, as if he were averse to have them seen while they were occupied with keenly observing the motions and bearing of others—those eyes that were now turbid with melancholy, now gleaming with scorn, and now sparkling with fury—was it the passions of a mere mortal they expressed, or the emotions of a fiend, who seeks, and seeks in vain, to conceal his fiendish designs under the borrowed mask of manly beauty? The whole partook of the mien, language, and port of the ruined archangel; and, imperfectly as we have been able to describe it, the effect of the interview upon Butler's nerves, shaken as they were at the time by the horrors of the preceding night, were greater than his understanding warranted, or his pride cared to submit to. The very place where he had met this singular person was desecrated, as it were, and unhallowed, owing to many violent deaths, both in duels and by suicide, which had in former times taken place there; and the place which he had named as a rendezvous at so late an hour, was

held in general to be accursed, from a frightful and
cruel murder which had been there committed by the
wretch from whom the place took its name, upon the
person of his own wife.* It was in such places, according to the belief of that period (when the laws against
witchcraft were still in fresh observance, and had even
lately been acted upon), that evil spirits had power to
make themselves visible to human eyes, and to practise
upon the feelings and senses of mankind. Suspicions,
founded on such circumstances, rushed on Butler's mind,
unprepared as it was, by any previous course of reasoning, to deny that which all of his time, country, and
profession, believed; but common sense rejected these
vain ideas as inconsistent, if not with possibility, at
least with the general rules by which the universe is
governed,—a deviation from which, as Butler well
argued with himself, ought not to be admitted as probable, upon any but the plainest and most incontrover-
tible evidence. An earthly lover, however, or a young
man, who, from whatever cause, had the right of exercising such summary and unceremonious authority over the
object of his long-settled, and apparently sincerely returned affection, was an object scarce less appaling to
his mind, than those which superstition suggested.

His limbs exhausted with fatigue, his mind harassed
with anxiety, and with painful doubts and recollections,
Butler dragged himself up the ascent from the valley to
Saint Leonard's Crags, and presented himself at the
door of Deans's habitation, with feelings much akin to
the miserable reflections and fears of its inhabitants.

* Note D. Muschat's Cairn.

CHAPTER THE TWELFTH

Then she stretched out her lily hand,
And for to do her best;
"Hae back thy faith and troth, Willie,
God gie thy soul good rest!"   OLD BALLAD.

"COME in," answered the low and sweet-toned voice he
loved best to hear, as Butler tapped at the door of the

cottage. He lifted the latch, and found himself under
the roof of affliction.   Jeanie was unable to trust herself
with more than one glance towards her lover, whom she .
now met under circumstances so agonizing to her feelings, and at the same time so humbling to her honest
pride.   It is well known, that much, both of what is
good and bad in the Scottish national character, arises
out of the intimacy of their family connections.   " To
be come of honest folk," that is, of people who have
borne a fair and unstained reputation, is an advantage
as highly prized among the lower Scotch, as the emphatic
counterpart, " to be of a good family," is valued among
their gentry.   The worth and respectability of one
member of a peasant's family is always accounted by
themselves and others, not only a matter of honest
pride, but a guarantee for the good conduct of the
whole.   On the contrary, such a melancholy stain as
was now flung on one of the children of Deans, extended
its disgrace to all connected with him, and Jeanie felt
herself lowered at once, in her own eyes, and in those
of her lover.   It was in vain that she repressed this
feeling, as far subordinate and too selfish to be mingled
with her sorrow for her sister's calamity.   Nature prevailed ; and while she shed tears for her sister's distress
and danger, there mingled with them bitter drops of
grief for her own degradation.

As Butler entered, the old man was seated by the
fire with his well-worn pocket Bible in his hands, the
companion of the wanderings and dangers of his youth,
and bequeathed to him on the scaffold by one of those,

who, in the year 1686, sealed their enthusiastic principles with their blood.   The sun sent its rays through
a small window at the old man's back, and, "shining
motty through the reek," to use the expression of a bard
of that time and country, illumined the grey hairs of the
old man, and the sacred page which he studied.   His
features, far from handsome, and rather harsh and
severe, had yet, from their expression of habitual gravity, and contempt for earthly things, an expression of
stoical dignity amidst their sternness.   He boasted, in
no small degree, the attributes which Southey ascribes
to the ancient Scandinavians, whom he terms "firm to
inflict, and stubborn to endure."   The whole formed a
picture, of which the lights might have been given by
Rembrandt, but the outline would have required the
force and vigour of Michael Angelo.

Deans lifted his eye as Butler entered, and instantly
withdrew it, as from an object which gave him at once
surprise and sudden pain.   He had assumed such high
ground with this carnal-witted scholar, as he had in his
pride termed Butler, that to meet him of all men, under
feelings of humiliation, aggravated his misfortune, and
was a consummation like that of the dying chief in the
old ballad—"Earl Percy sees my fall!"

Deans raised the Bible with his left hand, so as partly
to screen his face, and putting back his right as far as he
could, held it towards Butler in that position, at the same
time turning his body from him, as if to prevent his
seeing the working of his countenance.   Butler clasped the
extended hand which had supported his orphan infancy,

wept over it, and in vain endeavoured to say more than the words—"God comfort you—God comfort you!"

"He will—he doth, my friend," said Deans, assuming firmness as he discovered the agitation of his guest; "he doth now, and he will yet more, in his own gude time. I have been ower proud of my sufferings in a gude cause, Reuben, and now I am to be tried with those whilk will turn my pride and glory into a reproach and a hissing. How muckle better I hae thought mysell than them that lay saft, fed sweet, and drank deep, when I was in the moss-haggs and moors, wi' precious Donald Cameron, and worthy Mr. Blackadder, called Guessagain; and how proud I was o' being made a spectacle to men and angels, having stood on their pillory at the Canongate afore I was fifteen years old, for the cause of a National Covenant! To think, Reuben, that I, who hae been sae honoured and exalted in my youth, nay, when I was but a hafflins callant, and that hae borne testimony again the defections o' the times yearly, monthly, daily, hourly, minutely, striving and testifying with uplifted hand and voice, crying aloud, and sparing not, against all great national snares, as the nation-wasting and church-sinking abomination of union, toleration, and patronage, imposed by the last woman of that unhappy race of Stuarts; also against the infringements and invasions of the just powers of eldership, whereanent I uttered my paper, called, a 'Cry of an Howl in the Desert,' printed at the Bow-head, and sold by all flying stationers in town and country—and *now*"——

Here he paused. It may well be supposed that

Butler, though not absolutely coinciding in all the good
old man's ideas about church government, had too much
consideration and humanity to interrupt him, while he
reckoned up with conscious pride his sufferings, and
the constancy of his testimony.   On the contrary, when
he paused under the influence of the bitter recollections
of the moment, Butler instantly threw in his mite of
encouragement.

"You have been well known, my old and revered
friend, a true and tried follower of the Cross; one who,
as Saint Jerome hath it, '*per infamiam et bonam
fumam grassari ad immortalitatem,*' which may be
freely rendered, 'who rusheth on to immortal life,
through bad report and good report.' You have been
one of those to whom the tender and fearful souls cry
during the midnight solitude—'Watchman, what of
the night!—Watchman, what of the night!'—And,
assuredly, this heavy dispensation, as it comes not
without Divine permission, so it comes not without its
special commission and use."

"I do receive it as such," said poor Deans, returning
the grasp of Butler's hand; "and, if I have not been
taught to read the Scripture in any other tongue but
my native Scottish" (even in his distress Butler's Latin
quotation had not escaped his notice), "I have, nevertheless, so learned them, that I trust to bear even this
crook in my lot with submission.   But O! Reuben
Butler, the kirk, of whilk, though unworthy, I have
yet been thought a polished shaft, and meet to be a
pillar, holding, from my youth upward, the place of

ruling elder—what will the lightsome and profane think
of the guide that cannot keep his own family from
stumbling ? How will they take up their song and
their reproach, when they see that the children of
professors are liable to as foul backsliding as the offspring
of Belial ! But I will bear my cross with the comfort,
that whatever showed like goodness in me or mine,
was but like the light that shines frae creeping insects,
on the brae-side, in a dark night—it kythes bright to
the ee, because all is dark around it; but when the
morn comes on the mountains, it is but a puir crawling
kail-worm after a'. And sae it shows, wi' ony rag of
human righteousness, or formal law-work, that we may
pit round us to cover our shame."

As he pronounced these words, the door again
opened, and Mr. Bartoline Saddletree entered, his three-
pointed hat set far back on his head, with a silk
handkerchief beneath it, to keep it in that cool position, his gold-headed cane in his hand, and his whole
deportment that of a wealthy burgher, who might one
day look to have a share in the magistracy, if not
actually to hold the curule chair itself.

Rochefoucault, who has torn the veil from so many
foul gangrenes of the human heart, says, we find something not altogether unpleasant to us in the misfortunes
of our best friends. Mr. Saddletree would have been
very angry had any one told him that he felt pleasure
in the disaster of poor Effie Deans, and the disgrace of
her family; and yet there is great question whether
the gratification of playing the person of importance,

inquiring, investigating, and laying down the law on
the whole affair, did not offer, to say the least, full
consolation for the pain which pure sympathy gave him
on account of his wife's kinswoman.   He had now got
a piece of real judicial business by the end, instead of
being obliged, as was his common case, to intrude his
opinion where it was neither wished nor wanted; and
felt as happy in the exchange as a boy when he gets
his first new watch, which actually goes when wound
up, and has real hands and a true dial-plate.   But
besides this subject for legal disquisition, Bartoline's
brains were also overloaded with the affair of Porteous,
his violent death, and all its probable consequences to
the city and community.   It was what the French call
l'embarras des richesses, the confusion arising from too
much mental wealth.   He walked in with a consciousness of double importance, full fraught with the
superiority of one who possesses more information than
the company into which he enters, and who feels a
right to discharge his learning on them without mercy.
" Good morning, Mr. Deans,—good-morrow to you,
Mr. Butler,—I was not aware that you were acquainted
with Mr. Deans."

Butler made some slight answer; his reasons may
be readily imagined for not making his connection with
the family, which, in his eyes, had something of tender
mystery, a frequent subject of conversation with indifferent persons, such as Saddletree.

The worthy burgher, in the plenitude of self-impor-
tance, now sate down upon a chair, wiped his brow,

collected his breath, and made the first experiment of
the resolved pith of his lungs, in a deep and dignified
sigh, resembling a groan in sound and intonation—
" Awfu' times these, neighbour Deans, awfu' times ! "

" Sinfu', shamefu', heaven-daring times," answered
Deans, in a lower and more subdued tone.

" For my part," continued Saddletree, swelling with
importance, " what between the distress of my friends,
and my poor auld country, ony wit that ever I had may
be said to have abandoned me, sae that I sometimes
think myself as ignorant as if I were *inter rusticos*.
Here when I arise in the morning, wi' my mind just
arranged touching what's to be done in puir Effie's
misfortune, and hae gotten the haill statute at my
finger-ends, the mob maun get up and string Jock
Porteous to a dyester's beam, and ding a' thing out of
my head again."

Deeply as he was distressed with his own domestic
calamity, Deans could not help expressing some interest
in the news.   Saddletree immediately entered on details
of the insurrection and its consequences, while Butler
took the occasion to seek some private conversation
with Jeanie Deans.   She gave him the opportunity he
sought, by leaving the room, as if in prosecution of
some part of her morning labour.   Butler followed her
in a few minutes, leaving Deans so closely engaged by
his busy visitor, that there was little chance of his
observing their absence.

The scene of their interview was an outer apartment,
where Jeanie was used to busy herself in arranging the

productions of her dairy. When Butler found an opportunity of stealing after her into this place, he found her silent, dejected, and ready to burst into tears. Instead of the active industry with which she had been accustomed, even while in the act of speaking, to employ her hands in some useful branch of household business, she was seated listless in a corner, sinking apparently under the weight of her own thoughts. Yet the instant he entered, she dried her eyes, and, with the simplicity and openness of her character, immediately entered on conversation.

"I am glad you have come in, Mr. Butler," said she, "for—for—for I wished to tell ye, that all maun be ended between you and me—it's best for baith our sakes."

"Ended!" said Butler, in surprise; "and for what should it be ended?—I grant this is a heavy dispensation, but it lies neither at your door nor mine—it's an evil of God's sending, and it must be borne; but it cannot break plighted troth, Jeanie, while they that plighted their word wish to keep it."

"But, Reuben," said the young woman, looking at him affectionately, "I ken weel that ye think mair of me than yourself; and, Reuben, I can only in requital think mair of your weal than of my ain. Ye are a man of spotless name, bred to God's ministry, and a' men say that ye will some day rise high in the kirk, though poverty keep ye down e'en now. Poverty is a bad back-friend, Reuben, and that ye ken ower weel; but ill-fame is a waur ane, and that is a truth ye sall never learn through my means."

"What do you mean?" said Butler, eagerly and impatiently; "or how do you connect your sister's guilt, if guilt there be, which, I trust in God, may yet be disproved, with our engagement?—how can that affect you or me?"

"How can you ask me that, Mr. Butler? Will this stain, d'ye think, ever be forgotten, as long as our heads are abune the grund? Will it not stick to us, and to our bairns, and to their very bairns' bairns? To hae been the child of an honest man, might hae been saying something for me and mine; but to be the sister of a——O, my God!"—With this exclamation her resolution failed, and she burst into a passionate fit of tears.

The lover used every effort to induce her to compose herself, and at length succeeded; but she only resumed her composure to express herself with the same positiveness as before. "No, Reuben, I'll bring disgrace hame to nae man's hearth; my ain distresses I can bear, and I maun bear, but there is nae occasion for buckling them on other folk's shouthers. I will bear my load alone—the back is made for the burden."

A lover is by charter wayward and suspicious; and Jeanie's readiness to renounce their engagement, under pretence of zeal for his peace of mind and respectability of character, seemed to poor Butler to form a portentous combination with the commission of the stranger he had met with that morning. His voice faltered as he asked, "Whether nothing but a sense of her sister's present distress occasioned her to talk in that manner?"

"And what else can do sae?" she replied with simplicity. "Is it not ten long years since we spoke together in this way?"

"Ten years?" said Butler. "It's a long time— sufficient perhaps for a woman to weary"——

"To weary of her auld gown," said Jeanie, "and to wish for a new ane, if she likes to be brave, but not long enough to weary of a friend—The eye may wish change, but the heart never."

"Never!" said Reuben,—"that's a bold promise."

"But not more bauld than true," said Jeanie, with the same quiet simplicity which attended her manner in joy and grief, in ordinary affairs, and in those which most interested her feelings.

Butler paused, and looking at her fixedly—"I am charged," he said, "with a message to you, Jeanie."

"Indeed! From whom? Or what can ony ane have to say to me?"

"It is from a stranger," said Butler, affecting to speak with an indifference which his voice belied—"A young man whom I met this morning in the Park."

"Mercy!" said Jeanie, eagerly; "and what did he say?"

"That he did not see you at the hour he expected, but required you should meet him alone at Muschat's Cairn this night, so soon as the moon rises."

"Tell him," said Jeanie, hastily, "I shall certainly come."

"May I ask," said Butler, his suspicions increasing at the ready alacrity of the answer, "who this man is

to whom you are so willing to give the meeting at a
place and hour so uncommon?"

"Folk maun do muckle they have little will to do,
in this world," replied Jeanie.

"Granted," said her lover; "but what compels you
to this?—who is this person? What I saw of him was
not very favourable—who, or what is he?"

"I do not know!" replied Jeanie, composedly.

"You do not know!" said Butler, stepping impatiently through the apartment—"You purpose to
meet a young man whom you do not know, at such a
time, and in a place so lonely—you say you are compelled to do this—and yet you say you do not know
the person who exercises such an influence over you!
—Jeanie, what am I to think of this?"

"Think only, Reuben, that I speak truth, as if I
were to answer at the last day.—I do not ken this man
—I do not even ken that I ever saw him, and yet I
must give him the meeting he asks—there's life and
death upon it."

"Will you not tell your father, or take him with
you?" said Butler.

"I cannot," said Jeanie; "I have no permission."

"Will you let *me* go with you? I will wait in the
Park till nightfall, and join you when you set out."

"It is impossible," said Jeanie; "there maunna be
mortal creature within hearing of our conference."

"Have you considered well the nature of what you
are going to do?—the time—the place—an unknown
and suspicious character?—Why, if he had asked to see

you in this house, your father sitting in the next room, and within call, at such an hour, you should have refused to see him."

"My weird maun be fulfilled, Mr. Butler; my life and my safety are in God's hands, but I'll not spare to risk either of them on the errand I am gaun to do."

"Then, Jeanie," said Butler, much displeased, "we must indeed break short off, and bid farewell. When there can be no confidence betwixt a man and his plighted wife on such a momentous topic, it is a sign that she has no longer the regard for him that makes their engagement safe and suitable."

Jeanie looked at him and sighed. "I thought," she said, "that I had brought myself to bear this parting—but—but—I did not ken that we were to part in unkindness. But I am a woman and you are a man—it may be different wi' you—if your mind is made easier by thinking sae hardly of me, I would not ask you to think otherwise."

"You are," said Butler, "what you have always been—wiser, better, and less selfish in your native feelings, than I can be, with all the helps philosophy can give to a Christian.—But why—why will you persevere in an undertaking so desperate? Why will you not let me be your assistant—your protector, or at least your adviser?"

"Just because I cannot, and I dare not," answered Jeanie.—"But hark, what's that? Surely my father is no weel?"

In fact, the voices in the next room became obstreperously loud of a sudden, the cause of which vociferation it is necessary to explain before we go farther.

When Jeanie and Butler retired, Mr. Saddletree entered upon the business which chiefly interested the family. In the commencement of their conversation he found old Deans, who, in his usual state of mind, was no granter of propositions, so much subdued by a deep sense of his daughter's danger and disgrace, that he heard without replying to, or perhaps without understanding, one or two learned disquisitions on the nature of the crime imputed to her charge, and on the steps which ought to be taken in consequence. His only answer at each pause was, "I am no misdoubting that you wuss us weel—your wife's our far-awa cousin."

Encouraged by these symptoms of acquiescence, Saddletree, who, as an amateur of the law, had a supreme deference for all constituted authorities, again recurred to his other topic of interest, the murder, namely, of Porteous, and pronounced a severe censure on the parties concerned.

"These are kittle times—kittle times, Mr. Deans, when the people take the power of life and death out of the hands of the rightful magistrate into their ain rough grip. I am of opinion, and so I believe will Mr. Crossmyloof and the Privy-Council, that this rising in effeir of war, to take away the life of a reprieved man, will prove little better than perduellion."

"If I hadna that on my mind whilk is ill to bear,

Mr. Saddletree," said Deans, "I wad make bold to dispute that point wi' you."

"How could ye dispute what's plain law, man?" said Saddletree, somewhat contemptuously; "there's no a callant that e'er carried a pock wi' a process in't, but will tell you that perduellion is the warst and maist virulent kind of treason, being an open convocating of the king's lieges against his authority (mair especially in arms, and by touk of drum, to baith whilk acces- sories my een and lugs bore witness), and muckle warse than lese-majesty, or the concealment of a treasonable purpose—It winna bear a dispute, neighbour."

"But it will, though," retorted Douce Davie Deans; "I tell ye it will bear a dispute—I never like your cauld, legal, formal doctrines, neighbour Saddletree. I haud unco little by the Parliament House, since the awfu' downfall of the hopes of honest folk that followed the Revolution."

"But what wad ye hae had, Mr. Deans?" said Saddletree impatiently; "didna ye get baith liberty and conscience made fast, and settled by tailzie on you and your heirs for ever?"

"Mr. Saddletree," retorted Deans, "I ken ye are one of those that are wise after the manner of this world, and that ye haud your part, and cast in your portion, wi' the lang-heads and lang-gowns, and keep with the smart witty-pated lawyers of this our land— Weary on the dark and dolefu' cast that they hae gien this unhappy kingdom, when their black hands of defection were clasped in the red hands of our sworn murtherers: when those who had numbered the towers of our Zion, and marked the bulwarks of Reformation, saw their hope turn into a snare, and their rejoicing into weeping."

"I canna understand this, neighbour," answered Saddletree.   "I am an honest presbyterian of the Kirk of Scotland, and stand by her and the General Assembly, and the due administration of justice by the fifteen Lords o' Session and the five Lords o' Justiciary."

"Out upon ye, Mr. Saddletree!" exclaimed David, who, in an opportunity of giving his testimony on the offences and backslidings of the land, forgot for a moment his own domestic calamity—"out upon your General Assembly, and the back of my hand to your Court o' Session!—What is the tane but a waefu' bunch o' cauldrife professors and ministers, that sate bien and warm when the persecuted remnant were warstling wi' hunger, and cauld, and fear of death, and danger of fire and sword, upon wet brae-sides, peat-haggs, and flow-mosses, and that now creep out of their holes, like blue-bottle flees in a blink of sunshine, to take the pu'pits and places of better folk—of them that witnessed, and testified, and fought, and endured pit, prison-house, and transportation beyond seas?—A bonny bike there's o' them!—And for your Court o' Session ——"

"Ye may say what ye will o' the General Assembly," said Saddletree, interrupting him, "and let them clear them that kens them; but as for the Lords o' Session, forby that they are my next-door neighbours, I would have ye ken, for your ain regulation, that to raise scandal anent them, whilk is termed, to *murmur* again them, is a crime *sui generis—sui generis*, Mr. Deans—ken ye what that amounts to?"

"I ken little o' the language of Antichrist," said Deans; "and I care less than little what carnal courts may call the speeches of honest men. And as to murmur again them, it's what a' the folk that loses their pleas, and nine-tenths o' them that win them, will be gay sure to be guilty in. Sae I wad hae ye ken that I haud a' your gleg-tongued advocates, that sell their knowledge for pieces of silver—and your worldly-wise judges, that will gie three days of hearing in presence to a debate about the peeling of an ingan, and no ae half hour to the gospel testimony—as legalists and formalists, countenancing, by sentences, and quirks, and cunning terms of law, the late begun courses of national defections—union, toleration, patronages, and Yerastian prelatic oaths. As for the soul and body-killing Court o' Justiciary"——

The habit of considering his life as dedicated to bear testimony in behalf of what he deemed the suffering and deserted cause of true religion, had swept honest David along with it thus far; but with the mention of the criminal court, the recollection of the disastrous condition of his daughter rushed at once on his mind; he stopped short in the midst of his triumphant declamation, pressed his hands against his forehead, and remained silent.

Saddletree was somewhat moved, but apparently not
so much so as to induce him to relinquish the privilege
of prosing in his turn, afforded him by David's sudden
silence. "Nae doubt, neighbour," he said, "it's a sair
thing to hae to do wi' courts of law, unless it be to
improve ane's knowledge and practique, by waiting on
as a hearer; and touching this unhappy affair of Effie
—ye'll hae seen the dittay, doubtless?" He dragged
out of his pocket a bundle of papers, and began to turn
them over. "This is no it—this is the information of
Mungo Marsport, of that ilk, against Captain Lackland,
for coming on his lands of Marsport with hawks,
hounds, lying-dogs, nets, guns, cross-bows, hagbuts of
found, or other engines more or less for destruction of
game, sic as red-deer, fallow-deer, cappercailzies, grey-
fowl, moor-fowl, paitricks, herons, and sic like; he, the
said defender not being ane qualified person, in terms
of the statute sixteen hundred and twenty-ane; that is,
not having ane plough-gate of land. Now, the defences
proposed, say, that *non constat* at this present what is
a plough-gate of land, whilk uncertainty is sufficient to
elide the conclusions of the libel. But then the
answers to the defences (they are signed by Mr. Crossmyloof, but Mr. Younglad drew them), they propone,
that it signifies naething, *in hoc statu*, what or how
muckle a plough-gate of land may be, in respect the
defender has nae lands whatsoe'er, less or mair. 'See
grant a plough-gate'" (here Saddletree read from the
paper in his hand) "'to be less than the nineteenth
part of a guse's grass,'—(I trow Mr. Crossmyloof put in

that—I ken his style),—'of a guse's grass, what the
better will the defender be, seeing he hasna a divot-cast
of land in Scotland ?—*Advocatus* for Lackland duplies,
that *nihil interest de possessione*, the pursuer must put
his case under the statute'—(now, this is worth your
notice, neighbour),—'and must show, *formaliter et
specialiter*, as well as *generaliter*, what is the qualification that defender Lackland does *not* possess—let him
tell me what a plough-gate of land is, and I'll tell him
if I have one or no. Surely the pursuer is bound to
understand his own libel, and his own statute that he
founds upon. *Titius* pursues *Mævius* for recovery of
ane *black* horse lent to Mævius—surely he shall have
judgment ; but if Titius pursue Mævius for ane *scarlet* or
crimson horse, doubtless he shall be bound to show
that there is sic ane animal *in rerum natura*. No man
can be bound to plead to nonsense—that is to say, to a
charge which cannot be explained or understood,'—
(he's wrang there—the better the pleadings the fewer
understand them),—'and so the reference unto this un-
defined and unintelligible measure of land is, as if a
penalty was inflicted by statute for any man who suld
hunt or hawk, or use lying-dogs, and wearing a skye-blue
pair of broeches without having'——But I am wearying
you, Mr. Deans,—we'll pass to your ain business,—
though this case of Marsport against Lackland has made
an unco din in the Outer-house. Weel, here's the
dittay against puir Effie : 'Whereas it is humbly meant
and shown to us,' etc. (they are words of mere style),
'that whereas, by the laws of this and every other well-

regulated realm, the murder of any one, more especially
of an infant child, is a crime of ane high nature, and
severely punishable : And whereas, without prejudice
to the foresaid generality, it was, by ane act made in the
second session of the First Parliament of our most High
and Dread Sovereigns William and Mary, especially
enacted, that ane woman who shall have concealed her
condition, and shall not be able to show that she hath
called for help at the birth, in case that the child shall
be found dead or amissing, shall be deemed and held
guilty of the murder thereof ; and the said facts of concealment and pregnancy being found proven or confessed, shall sustain the pains of law accordingly ; yet,
nevertheless, you Effie, or Euphemia Deans'"——

"Read no farther !" said Deans, raising his head up;
"I would rather ye thrust a sword into my heart than
read a word farther !"

"Weel, neighbour," said Saddletree, "I thought it
wad hae comforted ye to ken the best and the warst
o't. But the question is, what's to be dune?"

"Nothing," answered Deans firmly, "but to abide
the dispensation that the Lord sees meet to send us.
O, if it had been his will to take the grey head to rest
before this awful visitation on my house and name!
But His will be done. I can say that yet, though I
can say little mair."

"But neighbour," said Saddletree, "ye'll retain
advocates for the puir lassie? it's a thing maun needs
be thought of."

"If there was ae man of them," answered Deans,

"that held fast his integrity—but I ken them weel,
they are a' carnal, crafty, and warld-hunting self-seekers,
Yerastians, and Arminians, every ane o' them."

"Hout tout, neighbour, ye maunna take the warld
at it's word," said Saddletree; " the very deil is no sae
ill as he's ca'd; and I ken mair than ae advocate that
may be said to hae some integrity as weel as their
neighbours; that is, after a sort o' fashion o' their
ain."

" It is indeed but a fashion of integrity that ye will
find amang them," replied David Deans, "and a fashion
of wisdom, and fashion of carnal learning—gazing,
glancing-glasses they are, fit only to fling the glaiks iu
folk's een, wi' their pawky policy, and earthly ingine,
their flights and refinements, and periods of eloquence,
frae heathen emperors and popish canons.   They canna,
in that daft trash ye were reading to me, sae muckle as
ca' men that are sae ill-starred as to be amang their
hands, by ony name o' the dispensation o' grace, but
maun new baptize them by the names of the accursed
Titus, wha was made the instrument of burning the
holy Temple, and other sic like heathens."

" It's Tishius," interrupted Saddletree, "and no
Titus.   Mr. Crossmyloof cares as little about Titus or the
Latin as ye do.—But it's a case of necessity—she maun
hae counsel.   Now, I could speak to Mr. Crossmyloof—
he's weel kend for a round-spun Presbyterian, and a
ruling elder to boot."

" He's a rank Yerastian," replied Deans; "one of
the public and polititious warldly-wise men that stude

up to prevent ane general owning of the cause in the day of power."

"What say ye to the auld Laird of Cuffabout ?" said Saddletree; "he whiles thumps the dust out of a case gey and weel."

"He ! the fause loon !" answered Deans—"he was in his bandaliers to hae joined the ungracious High-landers in 1715, an they had ever had the luck to cross the Firth."

"Weel, Arniston ! there's a clever chield for ye !" said Bartoline, triumphantly.

"Ay, to bring popish medals in till their very library from that schismatic woman in the north, the Duchess of Gordon."

"Weel, weel, but somebody ye maun hae—What think ye o' Kittlepunt ?"

"He's an Arminian."

"Woodsetter ?"

"He's, I doubt, a Cocceian."

"Auld Whilliewhaw ?"

"He's ony thing ye like."

"Young Nummo ?"

"He's naething at a'."

"Ye're ill to please, neighbour," said Saddletree; "I hae run ower the pick o' them for you, ye maun e'en choose for yoursell; but bethink ye that in the multitude of counsellors there's safety.—What say ye to try young Mackenyie ? he has a' his uncle's Practiques at the tongue's end."

"What, sir, wad ye speak to me," exclaimed the

sturdy presbyterian in excessive wrath, "about a man
that has the blood of the saints at his fingers' ends?
Didna his eme die and gang to his place wi' the name
of the Bluidy Mackenyie? and winna he be kend by
that name sae lang as there's a Scots tongue to speak
the word? If the life of the dear bairn that's under a
suffering dispensation, and Jeanie's, and my ain, and a'
mankind's, depended on my asking sic a slave o' Satan
to speak a word for me or them, they should a' gae
down the water thegither for Davie Deans!"

It was the exalted tone in which he spoke this last
sentence that broke up the conversation between Butler
and Jeanie, and brought them both "ben the house,"
to use the language of the country. Here they found
the poor old man half frantic between grief, and zealous
ire against Saddletree's proposed measures, his cheek
inflamed, his hand clenched, and his voice raised, while
the tear in his eye, and the occasional quiver of his
accents, showed that his utmost efforts were inadequate
to shaking off the consciousness of his misery. Butler,
apprehensive of the consequences of his agitation to an
aged and feeble frame, ventured to utter to him a recommendation to patience.

"I *am* patient," returned the old man, sternly,—
"more patient than any one who is alive to the woful
backslidings of a miserable time can be patient; and in
so much, that I need neither sectarians, nor sons, nor
grandsons of sectarians, to instruct my grey hairs how
to bear my cross."

"But, sir," continued Butler, taking no offence at

the slur cast on his grandfather's faith, "we must use
human means. When you call in a physician, you
would not, I suppose, question him on the nature of
his religious principles!"

"Wad I *no?*" answered David—"But I wad,
though; and if he didna satisfy me that he had a right
sense of the right-hand and left-hand defections of the
day, not a gouttle of his physic should gang through my
father's son."

It is a dangerous thing to trust to an illustration.
Butler had done so and miscarried; but, like a gallant
soldier when his musket misses fire, he stood his ground,
and charged with the bayonet.—"This is too rigid an
interpretation of your duty, sir. The sun shines, and
the rain descends, on the just and unjust, and they are
placed together in life in circumstances which frequently
render intercourse between them indispensable, perhaps
that the evil may have an opportunity of being converted
by the good, and perhaps, also, that the righteous might,
among other trials, be subjected to that of occasional
converse with the profane."

"Ye're a silly callant, Reuben," answered Deans,
"with your bits of argument. Can a man touch pitch
and not be defiled? Or what think ye of the brave
and worthy champions of the Covenant, that wadna sae
muckle as hear a minister speak, be his gifts and graces as
they would, that hadna witnessed against the enormities
of the day? Nae lawyer shall ever speak for me and mine
that hasna concurred in the testimony of the scattered,
yet lovely remnant, which abode in the clifts of the rocks."

So saying, and as if fatigued, both with the arguments and presence of his guests, the old man arose, and seeming to bid them adieu with a motion of his head and hand, went to shut himself up in his sleeping apartment.

"It's throwing his daughter's life awa," said Saddletree to Butler, "to hear him speak in that daft gate. Where will he ever get a Cameronian advocate? Or wha ever heard of a lawyer's suffering either for ae religion or another? The lassie's life is clean flung awa."

During the latter part of this debate, Dumbiedikes had arrived at the door, dismounted, hung the pony's bridle on the usual hook, and sunk down on his ordinary settle. His eyes, with more than their usual animation, followed first one speaker, then another, till he caught the melancholy sense of the whole from Saddletree's last words. He rose from his seat, stumped slowly across the room, and, coming close up to Saddletree's ear, said, in a tremulous, anxious voice, "Will—will siller do naething for them, Mr. Saddletree?"

"Umph!" said Saddletree, looking grave,—"siller will certainly do it in the Parliament House, if ony thing *can* do it; but whare's the siller to come frae? Mr. Deans, yo see, will do naething; and though Mrs. Saddletree's their far-awa friend, and right good weel-wisher, and is weel disposed to assist, yet she wadna like to stand to be bound *singuli in solidum* to such an expensive wark. An ilka friend wad bear a share o' the burden, something might be dune—ilka ane to be

liable for their ain input—I wadna like to see the case
fa' through without being pled—it wadna be creditable,
for a' that daft whig body says."

"I'll—I will—yes" (assuming fortitude), "I will be
answerable," said Dumbiedikes, "for a score of punds
sterling."—And he was silent, staring in astonishment
at finding himself capable of such unwonted resolution
and excessive generosity.

"God Almighty bless ye, Laird!" said Jeanie, in a
transport of gratitude.

"Ye may ca' the twenty punds thretty," said Dumbiedikes, looking bashfully away from her, and towards
Saddletree.

"That will do bravely," said Saddletree, rubbing his
hands; "and ye sall hae a' my skill and knowledge to
gar the siller gang far—I'll tape it out weel—I ken
how to gar the birkies tak short fees, and be glad o'
them too—it's only garring them trow ye hae twa or
three cases of importance coming on, and they'll work
cheap to get custom. Let me alane for whillywhaing
an advocate:—it's nae sin to get as muckle frae them
for our siller as we can—after a', it's but the wind o'
their mouth—it costs them naething; whereas, in my
wretched occupation of a saddler, horse-milliner, and
harness-maker, we are out unconscionable sums just for
barkened hides and leather."

"Can I be of no use?" said Butler. "My means,
alas! are only worth the black coat I wear; but I am
young—I owe much to the family—Can I do nothing?"

"Ye can help to collect evidence, sir," said Saddletree; "if we could but find ony ane to say she had gien the least hint o' her condition, she wad be brought aff wi' a wat finger—Mr. Crossmyloof tell'd me sae. The crown, says he, canna be craved to prove a positive —was't a positive or a negative they couldna be ca'd to prove?—it was the tane or the tither o' them, I am sure, and it maksna muckle matter whilk. Wherefore, says he, the libel maun be redargued by the panel proving her defences. And it canna be done otherwise."

"But the fact, sir," argued Butler, "the fact that this poor girl has borne a child; surely the crown lawyers must prove that?" said Butler.

Saddletree paused a moment, while the visage of Dumbiedikes, which traversed, as if it had been placed on a pivot, from the one spokesmen to the other, assumed a more blithe expression.

"Ye—ye—ye—es," said Saddletree, after some grave hesitation; "unquestionably that is a thing to be proved, as the court will more fully declare by an interlocutor of relevancy in common form; but I fancy that job's done already, for she has confessed her guilt."

"Confessed the murder?" exclaimed Jeanie, with a scream that made them all start.

"No, I didna say that," replied Bartoline. "But she confessed bearing the babe."

"And what became of it, then?" said Jeanie; "for not a word could I get from her but bitter sighs and tears."

"She says it was taken away from her by the woman in whose house it was born, and who assisted her at the time."

"And who was that woman?" said Butler. "Surely by her means the truth might be discovered.—Who was she? I will fly to her directly."

"I wish," said Dumbiedikes, "I were as young and as supple as you, and had the gift of the gab as weel."

"Who is she?" again reiterated Butler impatiently. —"Who could that woman be?"

"Ay, wha kens that but hersell," said Saddletree; "she deponed further, and declined to answer that interrogatory."

"Then to herself will I instantly go," said Butler; "farewell, Jeanie;" then coming close up to her— "Take no *rash steps* till you hear from me. Farewell!" and he immediately left the cottage.

"I wad gang too," said the landed proprietor, in an anxious, jealous, and repining tone, "but my powny winna for the life o' me gang ony other road than just frae Dumbiedikes to this house-end, and sae straight back again."

"Ye'll do better for them," said Saddletree, as they left the house together, "by sending me the throtty punds."

"Thretty punds?" hesitated Dumbiedikes, who was now out of the reach of those eyes which had inflamed his generosity; "I only said *twenty* punds."

"Ay; but," said Saddletree, "that was under pro-

testation to add and eik; and so ye craved leave to
amend your libel, and made it thretty."

"Did I? I dinna mind that I did," answered
Dumbiedikes. "But whatever I said I'll stand to."
Then bestriding his steed with some difficulty, he added,
"Dinna ye think poor Jeanie's een wi' the tears in them
glanced like lamour beads, Mr. Saddletree?"

"I kenna muckle about women's een, Laird," replied
the insensible Bartoline; "and I care just as little. I
wuss I were as weel free o' their tongues; though few
wives," he added, recollecting the necessity of keeping
up his character for domestic rule, "are under better
command than mine, Laird. I allow neither perduellion
nor lese-majesty against my sovereign authority."

The Laird saw nothing so important in this observation as to call for a rejoinder, and when they had
exchanged a mute salutation, they parted in peace upon
their different errands.

CHAPTER THE THIRTEENTH.

I'll warrant that fellow from drowning, were the ship no stronger than a nut-shell.—The Tempest.

Butler felt neither fatigue nor want of refreshment, although, from the mode in which he had spent the night, he might well have been overcome with either. But in the earnestness with which he hastened to the assistance of the sister of Jeanie Deans, he forgot both.

In his first progress he walked with so rapid a pace as almost approached to running, when he was surprised

to hear behind him a call upon his name, contending
with an asthmatic cough, and half-drowned amid the
resounding trot of a Highland pony.   He looked
behind, and saw the Laird of Dumbiedikes making after
him with what speed he might, for it happened
fortunately for the Laird's purpose of conversing with
Butler, that his own road homeward was for about two
hundred yards the same with that which led by the
nearest way to the city.   Butler stopped when he
heard himself thus summoned, internally wishing no
good to the panting equestrian who thus retarded his
journey.   .

   " Uh! uh! uh!" ejaculated Dumbiedikes, as he
checked the hobbling pace of the pony by our friend
Butler.   " Uh! uh! it's a hard-set willyard beast this
o' mine."   He had in fact just overtaken the object of
his chase at the very point beyond which it would have
been absolutely impossible for him to have continued
the pursuit, since there Butler's road parted from that
leading to Dumbiedikes, and no means of influence or
compulsion which the rider could possibly have used
towards his Bucephalus could have induced the Celtic
obstinacy of Rory Bean (such was the pony's name) to
have diverged a yard from the path that conducted him
to his own paddock.

   Even when he had recovered from the shortness of
breath occasioned by a trot much more rapid than Rory
or he were accustomed to, the high purpose of Dumbiedikes seemed to stick as it were in his throat, and
impede his utterance, so that Butler stood for nearly

three minutes ere he could utter a syllable; and when
he did find voice, it was only to say, after one or two
efforts, "Uh! uh! uhm! I say, Mr.—Mr. Butler, it's
a braw day for the har'st."

"Fine day, indeed," said Butler. "I wish you
good morning, sir."

"Stay—stay a bit," rejoined Dumbiedikes; "that
was no what I had gotten to say."

"Then, pray be quick, and let me have your
commands," rejoined Butler; "I crave your pardon,
but I am in haste, and *Tempus nemini*—you know the
proverb."

Dumbiedikes did not know the proverb, nor did he
even take the trouble to endeavour to look as if he did,
as others in his place might have done. He was con-
centrating all his intellects for one grand proposition,
and could not afford any detachment to defend outposts.
"I say, Mr. Butler," said he, "ken ye if Mr. Saddletree's a great lawyer?"

"I have no person's word for it but his own,"
answered Butler, dryly; "but undoubtedly he best
understands his own qualities."

"Umph!" replied the taciturn Dumbiedikes, in a
tone which seemed to say, "Mr. Butler, I take your
meaning." "In that case," he pursued, "I'll employ
my ain man o' business, Nichil Novit (auld Nichil's son
and amaist as gleg as his father), to agent Effie's plea."

And having thus displayed more sagacity than
Butler expected from him, he courteously touched his
gold-laced cocked hat, and by a punch on the ribs,

conveyed to Rory Bean, it was his rider's pleasure that
he should forthwith proceed homewards; a hint which
the quadruped obeyed with that degree of alacrity with
which men and animals interpret and obey suggestions
that entirely correspond with their own inclinations.

Butler resumed his pace, not without a momentary
revival of that jealousy, which the honest Laird's attention to the family of Deans had at different times
excited in his bosom.   But he was too generous long
to nurse any feeling, which was allied to selfishness.
" He is," said Butler to himself, " rich in what I want;
why should I feel vexed that he has the heart to dedi-
cate some of his pelf to render them services, which I
can only form the empty wish of executing ?   In God's
name, let us each do what we can.   May she be but
happy !—saved from the misery and disgrace that
seems impending—Let me but find the means of pre-
venting the fearful experiment of this evening, and
farewell to other thoughts, though my heart-strings
break in parting with them !"

He redoubled his pace, and soon stood before the
door of the Tolbooth, or rather before the entrance
where the door had formerly been placed.   His interview with the mysterious stranger, the message to
Jeanie, his agitating conversation with her on the subject of breaking off their mutual engagements, and the
interesting scene with old Deans, had so entirely
occupied his mind as to drown even recollection of the
tragical event which he had witnessed the preceding
evening.   His attention was not recalled to it by the

groups who stood scattered on the street in conversation,
which they hushed when strangers approached, or by
the bustling search of the agents of the city police,
supported by small parties of the military, or by the
appearance of the Guard-House, before which were
treble sentinels, or, finally, by the subdued and intimidated looks of the lower orders of society, who, conscious that they were liable to suspicion, if they were
not guilty of accession to a riot likely to be strictly
inquired into, glided about with an humble and dis-
mayed aspect, like men whose spirits being exhausted
in the revel and the dangers of a desperate debauch
over night, are nerve-shaken, timorous, and unenter-
prising on the succeeding day.

None of these symptoms of alarm and trepidation
struck Butler, whose mind was occupied with a different,
and to him still more interesting subject, until he stood
before the entrance to the prison, and saw it defended
by a double file of grenadiers, instead of bolts and
bars.   Their "Stand, stand!" the blackened appearance
of the doorless gateway, and the winding staircase and
apartments of the Tolbooth, now open to the public eye,
recalled the whole proceedings of the eventful night.
Upon his requesting to speak with Effie Deans, the
same tall, thin, silver-haired turnkey, whom he had
seen on the preceding evening, made his appearance.

"I think," he replied to Butler's request of admission, with true Scottish indirectness, "ye will be the
same lad that was for in to see her yestreen?"

Butler admitted he was the same person.

"And I am thinking," pursued the turnkey, "that ye speered at me when we locked up, and if we locked up earlier on account of Porteous?"

"Very likely I might make some such observation," said Butler; "but the question now is, can I see Effie Deans?"

"I dinna ken—gang in by, and up the turnpike stair, and turn till the ward on the left hand."

The old man followed close behind him, with his keys in his hand, not forgetting even that huge one which had once opened and shut the outward gate of his dominions, though at present it was but an idle and useless burden. No sooner had Butler entered the room to which he was directed, than the experienced hand of the warder selected the proper key, and locked it on the outside. At first Butler conceived this manœuvre was only an effect of the man's habitual and official caution and jealousy. But when he heard the hoarse command, "Turn out the guard!" and immediately afterwards heard the clash of a sentinel's arms, as he was posted at the door of his apartment, he again called out to the turnkey, "My good friend, I have business of some consequence with Effie Deans, and I beg to see her as soon as possible." No answer was returned. "If it be against your rules to admit me," repeated Butler, in a still louder tone, "to see the prisoner, I beg you will tell me so, and let me go about my business.—*Fugit irrevocabile tempus!*" muttered he to himself.

"If ye had business to do, ye suld hae dune it before

ye cam here," replied the man of keys from the out-side; "ye'll find it's easier wunnin in than wunnin out here—there's ama' likelihood o' another Porteous-mob coming to rabble us again—the law will haud her ain now, neighbour, and that ye'll find to your cost."

"What do you mean by that, sir?" retorted Butler. "You must mistake me for some other person. My name is Reuben Butler, preacher of the gospel."

"I ken that weel eneugh," said the turnkey.

"Well, then, if you know me, I have a right to know from you in return, what warrant you have for detaining me; that, I know, is the right of every British subject."

"Warrant?" said the jailor,—"the warrant's awa to Liberton wi' twa sheriff officers seeking ya. If ye had staid at hame, as honest men should do, ye wad hae seen the warrant; but if ye come to be incarcerated of your ain accord, wha can help it, my jo?"

"So I cannot see Effie Deans, then," said Butler; "and you are determined not to let me out?"

"Troth will I no, neighbour," answered the old man, doggedly; "as for Effie Deans, ye'll hae eneugh ado to mind your ain business, and let her mind hers; and for letting you out, that maun be as the magistrate will determine. And fare ye weel for a bit, for I maun see Deacon Sawyers put on ane or twa o' the doors that your quiet folk broke down yesternight, Mr. Butler."

There was something in this exquisitely provoking, but there was also something darkly alarming. To be imprisoned, even on a false accusation, has something in

it disagreeable and menacing even to men of more con-
stitutional courage than Butler had to boast; for
although he had much of that resolution which arises
from a sense of duty and an honourable desire to discharge it, yet, as his imagination was lively, and his
frame of body delicate, he was far from possessing that
cool insensibility to danger which is the happy portion
of men of stronger health, more firm nerves, and less
acute sensibility.   An indistinct idea of peril, which he
could neither understand nor ward off, seemed to float
before his eyes.   He tried to think over the events of
the preceding night, in hopes of discovering some means
of explaining or vindicating his conduct for appearing
among the mob, since it immediately occurred to him
that his detention must be founded on that circumstance.
And it was with anxiety that he found he could not
recollect to have been under the observation of any
disinterested witness in the attempts that he made from
time to time to expostulate with the rioters, and to
prevail on them to release him.   The distress of Deans's
family, the dangerous rendezvous which Jeanie had
formed, and which he could not now hope to interrupt,
had also their share in his unpleasant reflections.   Yet
impatient as he was to receive an *éclaircissement* upon
the cause of his confinement, and if possible to obtain
his liberty, he was affected with a trepidation which
seemed no good omen; when, after remaining an hour
in this solitary apartment, he received a summons to
attend the sitting magistrate.   He was conducted from
prison strongly guarded by a party of soldiers, with a

parade of precaution, that, however ill-timed and unnecessary, is generally displayed *after* an event, which
such precaution, if used in time, might have prevented.

He was introduced into the Council Chamber, as the
place is called where the magistrates hold their sittings,
and which was then at a little distance from the prison.
One or two of the senators of the city were present, and
seemed about to engage in the examination of an individual who was brought forward to the foot of the long
green-covered table round which the council usually
assembled. "Is that the preacher?" said one of the
magistrates, as the city officer in attendance introduced
Butler. The man answered in the affirmative. "Let
him sit down there for an instant; we will finish this
man's business very briefly."

"Shall we remove Mr. Butler?" queried the assistant.

"It is not necessary—Let him remain where he is."

Butler accordingly sate down on a bench at the
bottom of the apartment, attended by one of his
keepers.

It was a large room, partially and imperfectly
lighted; but by chance, or the skill of the architect,
who might happen to remember the advantage which
might occasionally be derived from such an arrangement,
one window was so placed as to throw a strong light at
the foot of the table at which prisoners were usually
posted for examination, while the upper end, where
the examinants sate, was thrown into shadow. Butler's
eyes were instantly fixed on the person whose examina-

tion was at present proceeding, in the idea that he might recognise some one of the conspirators of the former night. But though the features of this man were sufficiently marked and striking, he could not recollect that he had ever seen them before.

The complexion of this person was dark, and his age somewhat advanced. He wore his own hair, combed smooth down, and cut very short. It was jet black, slightly curled by nature, and already mottled with grey. The man's face expressed rather knavery than vice, and a disposition to sharpness, cunning and roguery, more than the traces of stormy and indulged passions. His sharp, quick black eyes, acute features, ready sardonic smile, promptitude, and effrontery, gave him altogether what is called among the vulgar a *knowing* look, which generally implies a tendency to knavery. At a fair or market, you could not for a moment have doubted that he was a horse-jockey, intimate with all the tricks of his trade; yet had you met him on a moor, you would not have apprehended any violence from him. His dress was also that of a horse-dealer—a close-buttoned jockey-coat, or wrap-rascal, as it was then termed, with huge metal buttons, coarse blue upper stockings, called boot hose, because supplying the place of boots, and a slouched hat. He only wanted a loaded whip under his arm and a spur upon one heel, to complete the dress of the character he seemed to represent.

"Your name is James Ratcliffe?" said the magistrate.

"Ay—always wi' your honour's leave."

"That is to say, you could find me another name if I did not like that one?"

"Twenty to pick and chose upon, always with your honour's leave," resumed the respondent.

"But James Ratcliffe is your present name?—what is your trade?"

"I canna just say, distinctly, that I have what ye wad ca' prececsely a trade."

"But," repeated the magistrate, "what are your means of living—your occupation?"

"Hout tout—your honour, wi' your leave, kens that as weel as I do," replied the examined.

"No matter, I want to hear you describe it," said the examinant.

"Me describe!—and to your honour!—far be it from Jemmie Ratcliffe," responded the prisoner.

"Come, sir, no trifling—I insist on an answer."

"Weel, sir," replied the declarant, "I maun make a clean breast, for ye see, wi' your leave, I am looking for favour—Describe my occupation, quo' ye?—troth it will be ill to do that, in a feasible way in a place like this—but what is't again that the aught command says?"

"Thou shalt not steal," answered the magistrate.

"Are you sure o' that?" replied the accused.— "Troth, then, my occupation, and that command, are sair at odds, for I read it, thou *shall* steal; and that makes an unco difference, though there's but a wee bit word left out."

"To cut the matter short, Ratcliffe, you have been a most notorious thief," said the examinant.

"I believe Highlands and Lowlands ken that, sir, forby England and Holland," replied Ratcliffe, with the greatest composure and effrontery.

"And what d'ye think the end of your calling will be?" said the magistrate.

"I could have gien a braw guess yesterday—but I dinna ken sae weel the day," answered the prisoner.

"And what would you have said would have been your end, had you been asked the question yesterday?"

"Just the gallows," replied Ratcliffe, with the same composure.

"You are a daring rascal, sir," said the magistrate; "and how dare you hope times are mended with you to-day?"

"Dear, your honour," answered Ratcliffe, "there's muckle difference between lying in prison under sentence of death, and staying there of ane's ain proper accord, when it would have cost a man naething to get up and rin awa—what was to hinder me from stepping out quietly, when the rabble walked awa wi' Jock Porteous yestreen?—and does your honour really think I staid on purpose to be hanged?"

"I do not know what you may have proposed to yourself; but I know," said the magistrate, "what the law proposes for you, and that is to hang you next Wednesday eight days."

"Na, na, your honour," said Ratcliffe firmly, "craving your honour's pardon, I'll ne'er believe that till I see it. I have kend the Law this mony a year, and mony a thrawart job I hae had wi' her first and last; but the auld jaud is no sae ill as that comes to—I aye fand her bark waur than her bite."

"And if you do not expect the gallows, to which you are condemned (for the fourth time to my knowledge), may I beg the favour to know," said the magistrate, "what it is you *do* expect, in consideration of your not having taken your flight with the rest of the jail-birds, which I will admit was a line of conduct little to have been expected?"

"I would never have thought for a moment of staying in that auld gousty toom house," answered Ratcliffe, "but that use and wont had just gien me a fancy to the place, and I'm just expecting a bit post in't."

"A post!" exclaimed the magistrate; "a whipping-post, I suppose you mean?"

"Na, na, sir, I had nae thoughts o' a whupping-post. After having been four times doomed to hang by the neck till I was dead, I think I am far beyond being whuppit."

"Then in Heaven's name, what *did* you expect?"

"Just the post of under-turnkey, for I understand there's a vacancy," said the prisoner; "I wadna think of asking the lockman's* place ower his head; it wadna suit me sae weel as ither folk, for I never could put a beast out o' the way, much less deal wi' a man."

"That's something in your favour," said the magistrate, making exactly the inference to which Ratcliffe was desirous to lead him, though he mantled his art

* Note E.   Hangman, or Lockman.

with an affectation of oddity. "But," continued the magistrate, "how do you think you can be trusted with a charge in the prison, when you have broken at your own hand half the jails in Scotland?"

"Wi' your honour's leave," said Ratcliffe, "if I kend sae weel how to wun out mysell, it's like I wad be a' the better a hand to keep other folk in. I think they wad ken their business weel that held me in when I wanted to be out, or wan out when I wanted to haud them in."

The remark seemed to strike the magistrate, but he made no further immediate observation, only desired Ratcliffe to be removed.

When this daring, and yet sly freebooter was out of hearing, the magistrate asked the city-clerk, "what he thought of the fellow's assurance?"

"It's no for me to say, sir," replied the clerk; "but if James Ratcliffe be inclined to turn to good, there is not a man e'er came within the ports of the burgh could be of sae muckle use to the Good Town in the thief and lock-up line of business. I'll speak to Mr. Sharpitlaw about him."

Upon Ratcliffe's retreat, Butler was placed at the table for examination. The magistrate conducted his inquiry civilly, but yet in a manner which gave him to understand that he laboured under strong suspicion. With a frankness which at once became his calling and character, Butler avowed his involuntary presence at the murder of Porteous, and at the request of the magistrate, entered into a minute detail of the circumstances which attended that unhappy affair. All the particulars, such as we have narrated, were taken minutely down by the clerk from Butler's dictation.

When the narrative was concluded, the cross-examination commenced, which it is a painful task even for the most candid witness to undergo, since a story, especially if connected with agitating and alarming incidents, can scarce be so clearly and distinctly told, but that some ambiguity and doubt may be thrown upon it by a string of successive and minute interrogatories.

The magistrate commenced by observing, that Butler had said his object was to return to the village of Liberton, but that he was interrupted by the mob at the West Port. "Is the West Port your usual way of leaving town when you go to Liberton?" said the magistrate with a sneer.

"No, certainly," answered Butler, with the haste of a man anxious to vindicate the accuracy of his evidence; "but I chanced to be nearer that port than any other, and the hour of shutting the gates was on the point of striking."

"That was unlucky," said the magistrate, dryly. "Pray, being, as you say, under coercion and fear of the lawless multitude, and compelled to accompany them through scenes disagreeable to all men of humanity, and more especially irreconcilable to the profession of a minister, did you not attempt to struggle, resist, or escape from their violence?"

Butler replied, "that their numbers prevented him from attempting resistance, and their vigilance from effecting his escape."

"That was unlucky," again repeated the magistrate, in the same dry inacquiescent tone of voice and manner. He proceeded with decency and politeness, but with a stiffness which argued his continued suspicion, to ask many questions concerning the behaviour of the mob, the manners and dress of the ringleaders; and when he conceived that the caution of Butler, if he was deceiving him, must be lulled asleep, the magistrate suddenly and artfully returned to former parts of his declaration, and required a new recapitulation of the circumstances, to the minutest and most trivial point, which attended each part of the melancholy scene. No confusion or contradiction, however, occurred, that could countenance the suspicion which he seemed to have adopted against Butler. At length the train of his interrogatories reached Madge Wildfire, at whose name the magistrate and town-clerk exchanged significant glances. If the fate of the Good Town had depended on her careful magistrate's knowing the features and dress of this personage, his inquiries could not have been more particular. But Butler could say almost nothing of this person's features, which were disguised apparently with red paint and soot, like an Indian going to battle, besides the projecting shade of a curch or coif, which muffled the hair of the supposed female. He declared that he thought he could not know this Madge Wildfire, if placed before him in a different dress, but that he believed he might recognise her voice.

The magistrate requested him again to state by what gate he left the city.

"By the Cowgate Port," replied Butler.

"Was that the nearest road to Liberton?"

"No," answered Butler, with embarrassment; "but it was the nearest way to extricate myself from the mob."

The clerk and magistrate again exchanged glances.

"Is the Cowgate Port a nearer way to Liberton from the Grassmarket than Bristo Port?"

"No," replied Butler; "but I had to visit a friend."

"Indeed!" said the interrogator—"You were in a hurry to tell the sight you had witnessed, I suppose?"

"Indeed I was not," replied Butler; "nor did I speak on the subject the whole time I was at Saint Leonard's Crags."

"Which road did you take to Saint Leonard's Crags?"

"By the foot of Salisbury Crags," was the reply.

"Indeed! you seem partial to circuitous routes," again said the magistrate. "Whom did you see after you left the city?"

One by one he obtained a description of every one of the groups who had passed Butler, as already noticed, their number, demeanour, and appearance; and, at length, came to the circumstance of the mysterious stranger in the King's Park. On this subject Butler would fain have remained silent. But the magistrate had no sooner got a slight hint concerning the incident, than he seemed bent to possess himself of the most minute particulars.

"Look ye, Mr. Butler," said he, "you are a young

man, and bear an excellent character; so much I will myself testify in your favour. But we are aware there has been, at times, a sort of bastard and fiery zeal in some of your order, and those, men irreproachable in other points, which has led them into doing and countenancing great irregularities, by which the peace of the country is liable to be shaken.—I will deal plainly with you. I am not at all satisfied with this story, of your setting out again and again to seek your dwelling by two several roads, which were both circuitous. And, to be frank, no one whom we have examined on this unhappy affair could trace in your appearance any thing like your acting under compulsion. Moreover, the waiters at the Cowgate Port observed something like the trepidation of guilt in your conduct, and declare that you were the first to command them to open the gate, in a tone of authority, as if still presiding over the guards and outposts of the rabble, who had besieged them the whole night."

"God forgive them!" said Butler; "I only asked free passage for myself; they must have much misunderstood, if they did not wilfully misrepresent me."

"Well, Mr. Butler," resumed the magistrate, "I am inclined to judge the best and hope the best, as I am sure I wish the best; but you must be frank with me, if you wish to secure my good opinion, and lessen the risk of inconvenience to yourself. You have allowed you saw another individual in your passage through the King's Park to Saint Leonard's Crags—I must know every word which passed betwixt you."

Thus closely pressed, Butler, who had no reason for concealing what passed at that meeting unless because Jeanie Deans was concerned in it, thought it best to tell the whole truth from beginning to end.

"Do you suppose," said the magistrate pausing, "that the young woman will accept an invitation so mysterious?"

"I fear she will," replied Butler.

"Why do you use the word *fear* it?" said the magistrate.

"Because I am apprehensive for her safety, in meeting, at such a time and place, one who had something of the manner of a desperado, and whose message was of a character so inexplicable."

"Her safety shall be cared for," said the magistrate. "Mr. Butler, I am concerned I cannot immediately discharge you from confinement, but I hope you will not be long detained.—Remove Mr. Butler, and let him be provided with decent accommodation in all respects."

He was conducted back to the prison accordingly; but, in the food offered to him, as well as in the apartment in which he was lodged, the recommendation of the magistrate was strictly attended to.

CHAPTER THE FOURTEENTH.

Dark and eerie was the night,
And lonely was the way,
An Janet, wi' her green mantell,
To Miles' Cross she did gae.
                    OLD BALLAD.

LEAVING Butler to all the uncomfortable thoughts
attached to his new situation, among which, the most
predominant was his feeling that he was, by his confinement, deprived of all possibility of assisting the

family at Saint Leonard's in their greatest need, we
return to Jeanie Deans, who had seen him depart,
without an opportunity of further explanation, in all
that agony of mind with which the female heart bids
adieu to the complicated sensations so well described
by Coleridge,—

> Hopes, and fears that kindle hope,
> An undistinguishable throng;
> And gentle wishes long subdued—
> Subdued and cherished long.

It is not the firmest heart (and Jeanie, under her
russet rokelay, had one that would not have disgraced
Cato's daughter) that can most easily bid adieu to these
soft and mingled emotions. She wept for a few
minutes bitterly, and without attempting to refrain
from this indulgence of passion. But a moment's
recollection induced her to check herself for a grief
selfish and proper to her own affections, while her
father and sister were plunged into such deep and
irretrievable affliction. She drew from her pocket the
letter which had been that morning flung into her
apartment through an open window, and the contents
of which were as singular as the expression was violent
and energetic. "If she would save a human being
from the most damning guilt, and all its desperate
consequences,—if she desired the life and honour of
her sister to be saved from the bloody fangs of an
unjust law,—if she desired not to forfeit peace of mind
here, and happiness hereafter," such was the frantic
style of the conjuration, "she was entreated to give a

sure, secret, and solitary meeting to the writer.   She
alone could rescue him," so ran the letter, "and he
only could rescue her."   He was in such circumstances,
the billet farther informed her, that an attempt to
bring any witness of their conference, or even to
mention to her father, or any other person whatsoever,
the letter which requested it, would inevitably prevent
its taking place, and ensure the destruction of her
sister.   The letter concluded with incoherent but
violent protestations, that in obeying this summons
she had nothing to fear personally.

The message delivered to her by Butler from the
stranger in the Park tallied exactly with the contents
of the letter, but assigned a later hour and a different
place of meeting.   Apparently the writer of the letter
had been compelled to let Butler so far into his confidence, for the sake of announcing this change to
Jeanie.   She was more than once on the point of producing the billet, in vindication of herself from her
lover's half-hinted suspicions.   But there is something
in stooping to justification which the pride of innocence
does not at all times willingly submit to; besides that
the threats contained in the letter, in case of her
betraying the secret, hung heavy on her heart.   It is
probable, however, that, had they remained longer
together, she might have taken the resolution to submit
the whole matter to Butler, and be guided by him as
to the line of conduct which she should adopt.   And
when, by the sudden interruption of their conference,
she lost the opportunity of doing so, she felt as if she

had been unjust to a friend, whose advice might have
been highly useful, and whose attachment deserved her
full and unreserved confidence.

To have recourse to her father upon this occasion,
she considered as highly imprudent. There was no
possibility of conjecturing in what light the matter
might strike old David, whose manner of acting and
thinking in extraordinary circumstances depended upon
feelings and principles peculiar to himself, the operation
of which could not be calculated upon even by those
best acquainted with him.   To have requested some
female friend to have accompanied her to the place of
rendezvous, would perhaps have been the most eligible
expedient; but the threats of the writer, that betraying
his secret would prevent their meeting (on which her
sister's safety was said to depend) from taking place at
all, would have deterred her from making such a confidence, even had she known a person in whom she
thought it could with safety have been reposed.   But
she knew none such.   Their acquaintance with the
cottagers in the vicinity had been very slight, and
limited to trifling acts of good neighbourhood.   Jeanie
knew little of them, and what she knew did not greatly
incline her to trust any of them.   They were of the
order of loquacious good-humoured gossips usually
found in their situation of life; and their conversation
had at all times few charms for a young woman, to whom
nature and the circumstance of a solitary life had given
a depth of thought and force of character superior to the
frivolous part of her sex, whether in high or low degree.

Left alone and separated from all earthly counsel, she had recourse to a friend and adviser, whose ear is open to the cry of the poorest and most afflicted of his people. She knelt, and prayed with fervent sincerity, that God would please to direct her what course to follow in her arduous and distressing situation. It was the belief of the time and sect to which she belonged, that special answers to prayer, differing little in their character from divine inspiration, were, as they expressed it, "borne in upon their minds" in answer to their earnest petitions in a crisis of difficulty. Without entering into an abstruse point of divinity, one thing is plain ;—namely, that the person who lays open his doubts and distresses in prayer, with feeling and sincerity, must necessarily, in the act of doing so, purify his mind from the dross of worldly passions and interests, and bring it into that state, when the resolutions adopted are likely to be selected rather from a sense of duty, than from any inferior motive. Jeanie arose from her devotions, with her heart fortified to endure affliction, and encouraged to face difficulties.

"I will meet this unhappy man," she said to herself —"unhappy he must be, since I doubt he has been the cause of poor Effie's misfortune—but I will meet him, be it for good or ill. My mind shall never cast up to me, that, for fear of what might be said or done to myself I left that undone that might even yet be the rescue of her."

With a mind greatly composed since the adoption of this resolution, she went to attend her father. The old

man, firm in the principles of his youth, did not, in outward appearance at least, permit a thought of his family
distress to interfere with the stoical reserve of his countenance and manners. He even chid his daughter for
having neglected, in the distress of the morning, some
trifling domestic duties which fell under her department.

"Why, what meaneth this, Jeanie?" said the old man
—"The brown four-year-auld's milk is not seiled yet,
nor the bowies put up on the bink. If ye neglect your
warldly duties in the day of affliction, what confidence
have I that ye mind the greater matters that concern
salvation? God knows, our bowies, and our pipkins,
and our draps o' milk, and our bits o' bread, are nearer
and dearer to us than the bread of life."

Jeanie, not unpleased to hear her father's thoughts
thus expand themselves beyond the sphere of his immediate distress, obeyed him, and proceeded to put her
household matters in order; while old David moved
from place to place about his ordinary employments,
scarce showing, unless by a nervous impatience at remaining long stationary, an occasional convulsive sigh,
or twinkle of the eye-lid, that he was labouring under
the yoke of such bitter affliction.

The hour of noon came on, and the father and child
sat down to their homely repast. In his petition for a
blessing on the meal, the poor old man added to his
supplication, a prayer that the bread eaten in sadness of
heart, and the bitter waters of Marah, might be made
as nourishing as those which had been poured forth

from a full cup and a plentiful basket and store; and having concluded his benediction, and resumed the bonnet which he had laid "reverently aside," he proceeded to exhort his daughter to eat, not by example indeed, but at least by precept.

"The man after God's own heart," he said, "washed and anointed himself, and did eat bread, in order to express his submission under a dispensation of suffering, and it did not become a Christian man or woman so to cling to creature-comforts of wife or bairns,"—(here the words became too great, as it were, for his utterance),—"as to forget the first duty—submission to the Divine will."

To add force to his precept, he took a morsel on his plate, but nature proved too strong even for the powerful feelings with which he endeavoured to bridle it. Ashamed of his weakness, he started up, and ran out of the house, with haste very unlike the deliberation of his usual movements. In less than five minutes he returned, having successfully struggled to recover his ordinary composure of mind and countenance, and affected to colour over his late retreat, by muttering that he thought he heard the "young staig loose in the byre."

He did not again trust himself with the subject of his former conversation, and his daughter was glad to see that he seemed to avoid further discourse on that agitating topic. The hours glided on, as on they must and do pass, whether winged with joy or laden with affliction. The sun set beyond the dusky eminence

of the Castle, and the screen of western hills, and
the close of evening summoned David Deans and his
daughter to the family duty of the night. It came
bitterly upon Jeanie's recollection, how often, when the
hour of worship approached, she used to watch the
lengthening shadows, and look out from the door of
the house, to see if she could spy her sister's return
homeward.   Alas! this idle and thoughtless waste of
time, to what evils had it not finally led? and was she
altogether guiltless, who, noticing Effie's turn to idle
and light society, had not called in her father's authority
to restrain her?—But I acted for the best, she again
reflected, and who could have expected such a growth
of evil, from one grain of human leaven, in a disposition
so kind, and candid, and generous?

As they sate down to the "exercise," as it is called,
a chair happened accidentally to stand in the place
which Effie usually occupied. David Deans saw his
daughter's eyes swim in tears as they were directed
towards this object, and pushed it aside, with a gesture
of some impatience, as if desirous to destroy every
memorial of earthly interest when about to address the
Deity.   The portion of Scripture was read, the psalm
was sung, the prayer was made ; and it was remarkable
that, in discharging these duties, the old man avoided
all passages and expressions, of which Scripture affords
so many, that might be considered as applicable to
his own domestic misfortune. In doing so it was
perhaps his intention to spare the feelings of his
daughter, as well as to maintain, in outward show at

least, that stoical appearance of patient endurance of all
the evil which earth could bring, which was, in his
opinion, essential to the character of one who rated all
earthly things at their just estimate of nothingness.
When he had finished the duty of the evening, he came
up to his daughter, wished her good night, and, having
done so, continued to hold her by the hands for half a
minute; then drawing her towards him, kissed her forehead, and ejaculated, "The God of Israel bless you, even
with the blessings of the promise, my dear bairn!"

It was not either in the nature or habits of David
Deans to seem a fond father; nor was he often observed
to experience or at least to evince, that fulness of the
heart which seeks to expand itself in tender expressions
or caresses even to those who were dearest to him.   On
the contrary, he used to censure this as a degree of
weakness in several of his neighbours, and particularly
in poor widow Butler.   It followed, however, from the
rarity of such emotions in this self-denied and reserved
man, that his children attached to occasional marks of
his affection and approbation a degree of high interest
and solemnity; well considering them as evidences of
feelings which were only expressed when they became
too intense for suppression or concealment.

With deep emotion, therefore, did he bestow, and
his daughter receive, this benediction and paternal
caress.   "And you, my dear father," exclaimed Jeanie,
when the door had closed upon the venerable old man,
"may you have purchased and promised blessings
multiplied upon you—upon *you*, who walk in this

world as though you were not of the world, and hold all
that it can give or take away but as the *midges* that the
sun-blink brings out, and the evening wind sweeps away!"

She now made preparation for her night-walk. Her
father slept in another part of the dwelling, and, regular in all his habits, seldom or never left his apartment
when he had betaken himself to it for the evening. It
was therefore easy for her to leave the house unobserved,
so soon as the time approached at which she was to
keep her appointment. But the step she was about to
take had difficulties and terrors in her own eyes, though
she had no reason to apprehend her father's interference. Her life had been spent in the quiet, uniform,
and regular seclusion of their peaceful and monotonous
household. The very hour which some damsels of the
present day, as well of her own as of higher degree,
would consider as the natural period of commencing an
evening of pleasure, brought, in her opinion, awe and
solemnity in it; and the resolution she had taken had
a strange, daring, and adventurous character, to which
she could hardly reconcile herself when the moment
approached for putting it into execution. Her hands
trembled as she snooded her fair hair beneath the
riband, then the only ornament or cover which young
unmarried women wore on their head, and as she
adjusted the scarlet tartan screen or muffler made of
plaid, which the Scottish women wore, much in the
fashion of the black silk veils still a part of female
dress in the Netherlands. A sense of impropriety as
well as of danger pressed upon her, as she lifted the

latch of her paternal mansion to leave it on so wild an
expedition, and at so late an hour, unprotected, and
without the knowledge of her natural guardian.

When she found herself abroad and in the open
fields, additional subjects of apprehension crowded upon
her.   The dim cliffs and scattered rocks, interspersed
with green sward, through which she had to pass to the
place of appointment, as they glimmered before her in
a clear autumn night, recalled to her memory many a
deed of violence, which, according to tradition, had
been done and suffered among them.   In earlier days
they had been the haunt of robbers and assassins, the
memory of whose crimes are preserved in the various
edicts which the council of the city, and even the parliament of Scotland, had passed for dispersing their bands,
and ensuring safety to the lieges, so near the precincts
of the city.   The names of these criminals, and of their
atrocities, were still remembered in traditions of the
scattered cottages and the neighbouring suburb.   In
latter times, as we have already noticed, the sequestered
and broken character of the ground rendered it a fit
theatre for duels and rencontres among the fiery youth
of the period.   Two or three of these incidents, all
sanguinary, and one of them fatal in its termination,
had happened since Deans came to live at Saint Leonard's.   His daughter's recollections, therefore, were of
blood and horror as she pursued the small scarce-tracked
solitary path, every step of which conveyed her to a
greater distance from help, and deeper into the ominous
seclusion of these unhallowed precincts.

As the moon began to peer forth on the scene with a doubtful, flitting, and solemn light, Jeanie's apprehensions took another turn, too peculiar to her rank and country to remain unnoticed. But to trace its origin will require another chapter.

CHAPTER THE FIFTEENTH.

————The spirit I have seen
May be the devil.   And the devil has power
To assume a pleasing shape.
                                        HAMLET.

WITCHCRAFT and demonology, as we have had already
occasion to remark, were at this period believed in by
almost all ranks, but more especially among the stricter
classes of presbyterians, whose government, when their
party were at the head of the state, had been much
sullied by their eagerness to inquire into, and persecute
these imaginary crimes.   Now, in this point of view,

also, Saint Leonard's Crags and the adjacent Chase were a dreaded and ill-reputed district. Not only had witches held their meetings there, but even of very late years the enthusiast, or impostor, mentioned in the Pandæmonium of Richard Bovet, Gentleman,* had, among the recesses of these romantic cliffs, found his way into the hidden retreats where the fairies revel in the bowels of the earth.

With all these legends Jeanie Deans was too well acquainted, to escape that strong impression which they usually make on the imagination. Indeed, relations of this ghostly kind had been familiar to her from her infancy, for they were the only relief which her father's conversation afforded from controversial argument, or the gloomy history of the strivings and testimonies, escapes, captures, tortures, and executions of those martyrs of the Covenant, with whom it was his chiefest, boast to say he had been acquainted. In the recesses of mountains, in caverns, and in morasses, to which these persecuted enthusiasts were so ruthlessly pursued, they conceived they had often to contend with the visible assaults of the Enemy of mankind, as in the cities, and in the cultivated fields, they were exposed to those of the tyrannical government and their soldiery. Such were the terrors which made one of their gifted seers exclaim, when his companion returned to him, after having left him alone in a haunted cavern in Sorn in Galloway, "It is hard living in this world—incarnate devils above the earth, and devils under the earth !

* Note F. The Fairy Boy of Leith.

Satan has been here since ye went away, but I have dismissed him by resistance; we will be no more troubled with him this night." David Deans believed this, and many other such ghostly encounters and victories, on the faith of the Ansars, or auxiliaries of the banished prophets. This event was beyond David's remembrance. But he used to tell with great awe, yet not without a feeling of proud superiority, to his auditors, how he himself had been present at a field-meeting at Crochmade, when the duty of the day was interrupted by the apparition of a tall black man, who, in the act of crossing a ford to join the congregation, lost ground, and was carried down apparently by the force of the stream. All were instantly at work to assist him, but with so little success, that ten or twelve stout men, who had hold of the rope which they had cast in to his aid, were rather in danger to be dragged into the stream, and lose their own lives, than likely to save that of the supposed perishing man. "But famous John Semple of Carspharn," David Deans used to say with exultation, "saw the whaup in the rape.—'Quit the rope,' he cried to us (for I that was but a callant had a haud o' the rape mysell), 'it is the Great Enemy! he will burn, but not drown; his design is to disturb the good wark, by raising wonder and confusion in your minds; to put off from your spirits all that ye hae heard and felt.'—Sae we let go the rape," said David, "and he went adown the water screeching and bullering like a Bull of Bashan, as he's ca'd in Scripture." *

* Note G. Intercourse of the Covenanters with the Invisible World.

Trained in these and similar legends, it was no
wonder that Jeanie began to feel an ill-defined apprehension, not merely of the phantoms which might beset
her way, but of the quality, nature, and purpose of the
being who had thus appointed her a meeting, at a place
and hour of horror, and at a time when her mind must
be necessarily full of those tempting and ensnaring
thoughts of grief and despair, which were supposed to
lay sufferers particularly open to the temptations of the
Evil One.   If such an idea had crossed even Butler's
well-informed mind, it was calculated to make a much
stronger impression upon hers.   Yet firmly believing
the possibility of an encounter so terrible to flesh and
blood, Jeanie, with a degree of resolution of which we
cannot sufficiently estimate the merit, because the
incredulity of the age has rendered us strangers to the
nature and extent of her feelings, persevered in her
determination not to omit an opportunity of doing
something towards saving her sister, although, in the
attempt to avail herself of it, she might be exposed to
dangers so dreadful to her imagination.   So, like
Christiana in the Pilgrim's Progress, when traversing
with a timid yet resolved step the terrors of the Valley
of the Shadow of Death, she glided on by rock and
stone, " now in glimmer and now in gloom," as her path
lay through moonlight or shadow, and endeavoured to
overpower the suggestions of fear, sometimes by fixing
her mind upon the distressed condition of her sister,
and the duty she lay under to afford her aid, should
that be in her power ; and more frequently by recurring

in mental prayer to the protection of that Being to whom night is as noon-day.

Thus drowning at one time her fears by fixing her mind on a subject of overpowering interest, and arguing them down at others by referring herself to the protection of the Deity, she at length approached the place assigned for this mysterious conference.

It was situated in the depth of the valley behind Salisbury Crags, which has for a background the north-western shoulder of the mountain called Arthur's Seat, on whose descent still remain the ruins of what was once a chapel, or hermitage, dedicated to Saint Anthony the Eremite. A better site for such a building could hardly have been selected; for the chapel, situated among the rude and pathless cliffs, lies in a desert, even in the immediate vicinity of a rich, populous, and tumultuous capital: and the hum of the city might mingle with the orisons of the recluses, conveying as little of worldly interest as if it had been the roar of the distant ocean. Beneath the steep ascent on which those ruins are still visible, was, and perhaps is still pointed out, the place where the wretch Nichol Muschat, who has been already mentioned in these pages, had closed a long scene of cruelty towards his unfortunate wife, by murdering her, with circumstances of uncommon barbarity.* The execration in which the man's crime was held extended itself to the place where it was perpetrated, which was marked by a small *cairn*, or heap of stones, composed of those which each chance passenger

* See Note D. Muschat's Cairn.

had thrown there in testimony of abhorrence, and on
the principle it would seem, of the ancient British
malediction, " May you have a cairn for your burial-
place !"

As our heroine approached this ominous and unhallowed spot, she paused and looked to the moon, now
rising broad on the north-west, and shedding a more
distinct light than it had afforded during her walk
thither. Eyeing the planet for a moment, she then
slowly and fearfully turned her head towards the cairn,
from which it was at first averted. She was at first
disappointed. Nothing was visible beside the little
pile of stones, which shone grey in the moonlight. A
multitude of confused suggestions rushed on her mind.
Had her correspondent deceived her, and broken his
appointment ?—was he too tardy at the appointment he
had made ?—or had some strange turn of fate prevented
him from appearing as he proposed ?—or, if he were an
unearthly being, as her secret apprehensions suggested,
was it his object merely to delude her with false hopes,
and put her to unnecessary toil and terror, according to
the nature, as she had heard, of those wandering
demons ?—or did he purpose to blast her with the sudden horrors of his presence when she had come close to
the place of rendezvous ? These anxious reflections did
not prevent her approaching to the cairn with a pace
that, though slow, was determined.

When she was within two yards of the heap of
stones, a figure rose suddenly up from behind it, and
Jeanie scarce forbore to scream aloud at what seemed

the realization of the most frightful of her anticipations. She constrained herself to silence, however, and, making a dead pause, suffered the figure to open the conversation, which he did, by asking, in a voice which agitation rendered tremulous and hollow, "Are you the sister of that ill-fated young woman?"

"I am—I am the sister of Effie Deans!" exclaimed Jeanie. "And as ever you hope God will hear you at your need, tell me, if you can tell, what can be done to save her!"

"I do *not* hope God will hear me at my need," was the singular answer. "I do not deserve—I do not expect he will." This desperate language he uttered in a tone calmer than that with which he had at first spoken, probably because the shock of first addressing her was what he felt most difficult to overcome. Jeanie remained mute with horror to hear language expressed so utterly foreign to all which she had ever been acquainted with, that it sounded in her ears rather like that of a fiend than of a human being. The stranger pursued his address to her without seeming to notice her surprise. "You see before you a wretch, predestined to evil here and hereafter."

"For the sake of Heaven, that hears and sees us," said Jeanie, "dinna speak in this desperate fashion! The gospel is sent to the chief of sinners—to the most miserable among the miserable."

"Then should I have my own share therein," said the stranger, "if you call it sinful to have been the destruction of the mother that bore me—of the friend

that loved me—of the woman that trusted me—of the
innocent child that was born to me. If to have done
all this is to be a sinner, and survive it is to be
miserable, then am I most guilty and most miserable
indeed."

"Then you are the wicked cause of my sister's ruin?"
said Jeanie, with a natural touch of indignation expressed in her tone of voice.

"Curse me for it, if you will," said the stranger; "I
have well deserved it at your hand."

"It is fitter for me," said Jeanie, "to pray to God
to forgive you."

"Do as you will, how you will, or what you will,"
he replied, with vehemence; "only promise to obey my
directions, and save your sister's life."

"I must first know," said Jeanie, "the means you
would have me use in her behalf."

"No!—you must first swear—solemnly swear, that
you will employ them, when I make them known to
you."

"Surely, it is needless to swear that I will do all
that is lawful to a Christian, to save the life of my
sister?"

"I will have no reservation!" thundered the stranger; "lawful or unlawful, Christian or heathen, you
shall swear to do my hest, and act by my counsel, or—
you little know whose wrath you provoke!"

"I will think on what you have said," said Jeanie,
who began to get much alarmed at the frantic vehemence of his manner, and disputed in her own mind,

whether she spoke to a maniac, or an apostate spirit incarnate—"I will think on what you say, and let you ken to-morrow."

"To-morrow!" exclaimed the man, with a laugh of scorn—"And where will I be to-morrow?—or, where will you be to-night, unless you swear to walk by my counsel?—There was one accursed deed done at this spot before now; and there shall be another to match it, unless you yield up to my guidance body and soul."

As he spoke, he offered a pistol at the unfortunate young woman. She neither fled nor fainted, but sunk on her knees, and asked him to spare her life.

"Is that all you have to say?" said the unmoved ruffian.

"Do not dip your hands in the blood of a defenceless creature that has trusted to you," said Jeanie, still on her knees.

"Is that all you can say for your life?—Have you no promise to give?—Will you destroy your sister, and compel me to shed more blood?"

"I can promise nothing," said Jeanie, "which is unlawful for a Christian."

He cocked the weapon, and held it towards her.

"May God forgive you!" she said, pressing her hands forcibly against her eyes.

"D——n!" muttered the man; and, turning aside from her, he uncocked the pistol, and replaced it in his pocket—"I am a villain," he said, "steeped in guilt and wretchedness, but not wicked enough to do you any harm! I only wished to terrify you into my measures—She hears me not—she is gone!—Great God! what a wretch am I become!"

As he spoke, she recovered herself from an agony which partook of the bitterness of death; and, in a minute or two, through the strong exertion of her natural sense and courage, collected herself sufficiently to understand he intended her no personal injury.

"No!" he repeated; "I would not add to the murder of your sister, and of her child, that of any one belonging to her!—Mad, frantic, as I am, and unrestrained by either fear or mercy, given up to the possession of an evil being, and forsaken by all that is good, I would not hurt you, were the world offered me for a bribe! But, for the sake of all that is dear to you, swear you will follow my counsel. Take this weapon, shoot me through the head, and with your own hand revenge your sister's wrong, only follow the course—the only course, by which her life can be saved."

"Alas! is she innocent or guilty?"

"She is guiltless—guiltless of every thing, but of having trusted a villain!—Yet, had it not been for those that were worse than I am—yes, worse than I am, though I am bad indeed—this misery had not befallen."

"And my sister's child—does it live?" said Jeanie.

"No; it was murdered—the new-born infant was barbarously murdered," he uttered in a low, yet stern and sustained voice;—"but," he added hastily, "not by her knowledge or consent."

"Then, why cannot the guilty be brought to justice, and the innocent freed?"

"Torment me not with questions which can serve no purpose," he sternly replied—"The deed was done by those who are far enough from pursuit, and safe enough from discovery!—No one can save Effie but yourself."

"Wo's me! how is it in my power?" asked Jeanie, in despondency.

"Hearken to me!—You have sense—you can apprehend my meaning—I will trust you. Your sister is innocent of the crime charged against her——"

"Thank God for that!" said Jeanie.

"Be still and hearken!—The person who assisted her in her illness murdered the child; but it was without the mother's knowledge or consent.—She is therefore guiltless, as guiltless as the unhappy innocent, that but gasped a few minutes in this unhappy world—the better was its hap to be so soon at rest. She is innocent as that infant, and yet she must die—it is impossible to clear her of the law!"

"Cannot the wretches be discovered, and given up to punishment?" said Jeanie.

"Do you think you will persuade those who are hardened in guilt to die to save another?—Is that the reed you would lean to?"

"But you said there was a remedy," again gasped out the terrified young woman.

"There is," answered the stranger, "and it is in your own hands. The blow which the law aims cannot be broken by directly encountering it, but it may be

turned aside. You saw your sister during the period
preceding the birth of her child—what is so natural as
that she should have mentioned her condition to you?
The doing so would, as their cant goes, take the case
from under the statute, for it removes the quality of
concealment. I know their jargon, and have had sad
cause to know it; and the quality of concealment is
essential to this statutory offence.* Nothing is so
natural as that Effie should have mentioned her condition to you—think—reflect—I am positive that she
did."

"Wo's me!" said Jeanie, "she never spoke to me
on the subject, but grat sorely when I spoke to her
about her altered looks, and the change on her spirits."

"You asked her questions on the subject?" he said
eagerly. "You *must* remember her answer was, a
confession that she had been ruined by a villain—yes,
lay a strong emphasis on that—a cruel false villain call
it—any other name is unnecessary; and that she bore
under her bosom the consequences of his guilt and her
folly; and that he had assured her he would provide
safely for her approaching illness.—Well he kept his
word!" These last words he spoke as if it were to
himself, and with a violent gesture of self-accusation,
and then calmly proceeded, "You will remember all
this?—That is all that is necessary to be said."

"But I cannot remember," answered Jeanie, with
simplicity, "that which Effie never told me."

"Are you so dull—so very dull of apprehension?"

* Note H. Child Murder.

he exclaimed, suddenly grasping her arm, and holding it firm in his hand. "I tell you" (speaking between his teeth, and under his breath, but with great energy), "you *must* remember that she told you all this, whether she ever said a syllable of it or no. You must repeat this tale, in which there is no falsehood, except in so far as it was not told to you, before these Justices— Justiciary—whatever they call their bloodthirsty court, and save your sister from being murdered, and them from becoming murderers. Do not hesitate—I pledge life and salvation, that in saying what I have said, you will only speak the simple truth."

"But," replied Jeanie, whose judgment was too accurate not to see the sophistry of this argument, "I shall be man-sworn in the very thing in which my testimony is wanted, for it is the concealment for which poor Effie is blamed, and you would make me tell a falsehood anent it."

"I see," he said, "my first suspicions of you were right, and that you will let your sister, innocent, fair, and guiltless, except in trusting a villain, die the death of a murderess, rather than bestow the breath of your mouth and the sound of your voice to save her."

"I wad ware the best blood in my body to keep her skaithless," said Jeanie, weeping in bitter agony, "but I canna change right into wrang, or make that true which is false."

"Foolish, hard-hearted girl," said the stranger, "are you afraid of what they may do to you? I tell you, even the retainers of the law, who course life as greyhounds do hares, will rejoice at the escape of a creature so young—so beautiful; that they will not suspect your tale; that, if they did suspect it, they would consider you as deserving, not only of forgiveness, but of praise for your natural affection."

"It is not man I fear," said Jeanie, looking upward; "the God, whose name I must call on to witness the truth of what I say, he will know the falsehood."

"And he will know the motive," said the stranger, eagerly; "he will know that you are doing this—not for lucre of gain, but to save the life of the innocent, and prevent the commission of a worse crime than that which the law seeks to avenge."

"He has given us a law," said Jeanie, "for the lamp of our path; if we stray from it we err against knowledge —I may not do evil, even that good may come out of it. But you—you that ken all this to be true, which I must take on your word—you that, if I understood what you said e'en now, promised her shelter and protection in her travail, why do not *you* step forward, and bear leal and soothfast evidence in her behalf, as ye may with a clear conscience?"

"To whom do you talk of a clear conscience, woman?" said he, with a sudden fierceness which renewed her terrors,—"to *me?*—I have not known one for many a year. Bear witness in her behalf!—a proper witness, that, even to speak these few words to a woman of so little consequence as yourself, must choose such an hour and such a place as this. When you see owls and bats fly abroad, like larks, in the sunshine, you may expect

to see such as I am in the assemblies of men.—Hush—
listen to that."

A voice was heard to sing one of those wild and
monotonous strains so common in Scotland, and to
which the natives of that country chant their old
ballads. The sound ceased—then came nearer, and
was renewed; the stranger listened attentively, still
holding Jeanie by the arm (as she stood by him in
motionless terror), as if to prevent her interrupting the
strain by speaking or stirring. When the sounds were
renewed, the words were distinctly audible :

> When the glede 's in the blue cloud,
>   The lavrock lies still ;
> When the hound 's in the green-wood,
>   The hind keeps the hill.

The person who sung kept a strained and powerful
voice at its highest pitch, so that it could be heard at a
very considerable distance. As the song ceased, they
might hear a stifled sound, as of steps and whispers of
persons approaching them. The song was again raised,
but the tune was changed :

> O sleep ye sound, Sir James, she said,
>   When ye suld rise and ride ;
> There 's twenty men, wi' bow and blade,
>   Are seeking where ye bide.

"I dare stay no longer," said the stranger; "return
home, or remain till they come up—you have nothing
to fear—but do not tell you saw me—your sister's fate
is in your hands." So saying, he turned from her, and
with a swift, yet cautiously noiseless step, plunged into

the darkness on the side most remote from the sounds which they heard approaching, and was soon lost to her sight. Jeanie remained by the cairn terrified beyond expression, and uncertain whether she ought to fly homeward with all the speed she could exert, or wait the approach of those who were advancing towards her. This uncertainty detained her so long, that she now distinctly saw two or three figures already so near to her, that a precipitate flight would have been equally fruitless and impolitic.

CHAPTER THE SIXTEENTH.

————She speaks things in doubt,
That carry but half sense: her speech is nothing,
Yet the unshaped use of it doth move
The hearers to collection; they aim at it,
And botch the words up to fit their own thoughts.

HAMLET.

LIKE the digressive poet Ariosto, I find myself under
the necessity of connecting the branches of my story,
by taking up the adventures of another of the characters,

and bringing them down to the point at which we have
left those of Jeanie Deans.   It is not, perhaps, the most
artificial way of telling a story, but it has the advantage
of sparing the necessity of resuming what a knitter (if
stocking-looms have left such a person in the land)
might call our "dropped stitches;" a labour in which
the author generally toils much, without getting credit
for his pains.

"I could risk a sma' wad," said the clerk to the
magistrate, "that this rascal Ratcliffe, if he were
insured of his neck's safety, could do more than ony
ten of our police-people and constables, to help us to
get out of this scrape of Porteous's.   He is weel acquent
wi' a' the smugglers, thieves, and banditti about Edinburgh; and, indeed, he may be called the father of a'
the misdoers in Scotland, for he has passed amang them
for these twenty years by the name of Daddie Rat."

"A bonny sort of a scoundrel," replied the magistrate, "to expect a place under the city!"

"Begging your honour's pardon," said the city's
procurator-fiscal, upon whom the duties of superinten-
dent of police devolved, "Mr. Fairscrieve is perfectly
in the right.   It is just sic as Ratcliffe that the town
needs in my department; an' if sae be that he's disposed
to turn his knowledge to the city service, ye'll no find
a better man.—Ye'll get nae saints to be searchers for
uncustomed goods, or for thieves and sic like;—and
your decent sort of men, religious professors, and broken
tradesmen, that are put into the like o' sic trust, can do
nae gude ava.   They are feared for this, and they are

scrupulous about that, and they are na free to tell a lie,
though it may be for the benefit of the city ; and they
dinna like to be out at irregular hours, and in a dark
cauld night, and they like a clout ower the croun far
waur ; and ane between the fear o' God, and the fear o'
man, and the fear o' getting a sair throat, or sair banes,
there's a dozen o' our city-folk, baith waiters, and
officers, and constables, that can find out naething but
a wee bit skulduddery for the benefit of the Kirk-
treasurer. Jock Porteous, that's stiff and stark, puir
fallow, was worth a dozen o' them ; for he never had
ony fears, or scruples, or doubts, or conscience, about
ony thing your honours bade him."

"He was a gude servant o' the town," said the
Bailie, "though he was an ower free-living man. But
if you really think this rascal Ratcliffe could do us ony
service in discovering these malefactors, I would insure
him life, reward, and promotion. It's an awsome thing
this mischance for the city, Mr. Fairscrieve. It will
be very ill ta'en wi' abune stairs. Queen Caroline, God
bless her ! is a woman—at least I judge sae, and it 's
nae treason to speak my mind sae far—and ye maybe
ken as weel as I do, for ye hae a housekeeper, though
ye arenn a married man, that women are wilfu', and
downa bide a slight. And it will sound ill in her ears,
that sic a confused mistake suld come to pass, and naebody sae muckle as to be put into the Tolbooth about
it."

"If ye thought that, sir," said the procurator-fiscal,
we could easily clap into prison a few blackguards upon

suspicion. It will have a gude active look, and I hae
aye plenty on my list, that wadna be a hair the waur of
a week or twa's imprisonment; and if ye thought it no
strictly just, ye could be just the easier wi' them the
neist time they did ony thing to deserve it; they arena
the sort to be lang o' geeing ye an opportunity to clear
scores wi' them on that account."

"I doubt that will hardly do in this case, Mr.
Sharpitlaw," returned the town-clerk; "they'll run
their letters,* and be adrift again, before ye ken where
ye are."

"I will speak to the Lord Provost," said the magistrate, "about Ratcliffe's business. Mr. Sharpitlaw, you
will go with me and receive instructions—something
may be made too out of this story of Butler's and his
unknown gentleman—I know no business any man has
to swagger about in the King's Park, and call himself
the devil, to the terror of honest folks, who dinna care
to hear mair about the devil than is said from the pulpit
on the Sabbath. I cannot think the preacher himsell
wad be heading the mob, though the time has been,
they hae been as forward in a bruilzie as their neighbours."

"But these times are lang by," said Mr. Sharpitlaw.
"In my father's time, there was mair search for silenced
ministers about the Bow-head and the Covenant-close,
and all the tents of Kedar, as they ca'd the dwellings
o' the godly in those days, than there's now for thieves

---

* A Scottish form of procedure, answering, in some respects,
to the English Habeas Corpus.

and vagabonds in the Laigh Calton and the back o'
the Canongate.   But that time's weel by, an it bide.
And if the Bailie will get me directions and authority
from the Provost, I'll speak wi' Daddie Rat mysell;
for I'm thinking I'll make mair out o' him than ye'll
do."

Mr. Sharpitlaw, being necessarily a man of high
trust, was accordingly empowered, in the course of the
day, to make such arrangements, as might seem in the
emergency most advantageous for the Good Town.   He
went to the jail accordingly, and saw Ratcliffe in private.

The relative positions of a police-officer and a professed thief bear a different complexion, according to
circumstances.   The most obvious simile of a hawk
pouncing upon his prey is often least applicable.   Sometimes the guardian of justice has the air of a cat watching a mouse, and, while he suspends his purpose of
springing upon the pilferer, takes care so to calculate
his motions that he shall not get beyond his power.
Sometimes, more passive still, he uses the art of fascination ascribed to the rattlesnake, and contents himself
with glaring on the victim, through all his devious
flutterings; certain that his terror, confusion, and disorder of ideas, will bring him into his jaws at last.
The interview between Ratcliffe and Sharpitlaw had an
aspect different from all these.   They sate for five
minutes silent, on opposite sides of a small table, and
looked fixedly at each other, with a sharp, knowing,
and alert cast of countenance, not unmingled with an
inclination to laugh, and resembled more than any

thing else, two dogs, who, preparing for a game at
romps, are seen to couch down, and remain in that
posture for a little time, watching each other's movements, and waiting which shall begin the game.

"So, Mr. Ratcliffe," said the officer, conceiving it
suited his dignity to speak first, "you give up business,
I find?"

"Yes, sir," replied Ratcliffe; "I shall be on that
lay nae mair—and I think that will save your folk
some trouble, Mr. Sharpitlaw?"

"Which Jock Dalgleish" (then finisher of the law
in the Scottish metropolis) "wad save them as easily,"
returned the procurator-fiscal.

"Ay; if I waited in the Tolbooth here to have him
fit my cravat—but that's an idle way o' speaking, Mr.
Sharpitlaw."

"Why, I suppose you know you are under sentence
of death, Mr. Ratcliffe?" replied Mr. Sharpitlaw.

"Ay, so are a', as that worthy minister said in the
Tolbooth Kirk the day Robertson wan off; but naebody
kens when it will be executed. Gude faith, he had
better reason to say sae than he dreamed of, before the
play was played out that morning!"

"This Robertson," said Sharpitlaw, in a lower and
something like a confidential tone, "d'ye ken, Rat—
that is, can ye gie us ony inkling where he is to be
heard tell o'?"

"Troth, Mr. Sharpitlaw, I'll be frank wi' ye;
Robertson is rather a cut abune me—a wild deevil he
was, and mony a daft prank he played; but except the

Collector's job that Wilson led him into, and some tuilzies about run goods wi' the gaugers and the waiters, he never did ony thing that came near our line o' business."

"Umph! that's singular, considering the company he kept."

"Fact, upon my honour and credit," said Ratcliffe, gravely. "He keepit out o' our little bits of affairs, and that's mair than Wilson did; I hae dune business wi' Wilson afore now. But the lad will come on in time; there's nae fear o' him; naebody will live the life he has led, but what he'll come to sooner or later."

"Who or what is he, Ratcliffe? you know, I suppose?" said Sharpitlaw.

"He's better born, I judge, than he cares to let on; he's been a soldier, and he has been a play-actor, and I watna what he has been or hasna been, for as young as he is, sae that it had daffing and nonsense about it."

"Pretty pranks he has played in his time, I suppose?"

"Ye may say that," said Ratcliffe, with a sardonic smile; "and" (touching his nose) "a deevil amang the lasses."

"Like enough," said Sharpitlaw. "Weel, Ratcliffe, I'll no stand niffering wi' ye; ye ken the way that favour's gotten in my office; ye maun be usefu'."

"Certainly, sir, to the best of my power—naething for naething—I ken the rule of the office," said the ex-depredator.

"Now the principal thing in hand e'en now," said

tho official person, "is the job of Porteous's; an ye can
gie us a lift—why, the inner turnkey's office to begin
wi', and the captainship in time—ye understand my
meaning?"

"Ay, troth do I, sir; a wink's as gude as a nod to a
blind horse; but Jock Porteous's job—Lord help ye!—
I was under sentence the haill time. God! but I
couldna help laughing when I heard Jock skirling for
mercy in the lad's hands! Mony a het skin ye hae gien
me, neighbour, thought I, tak ye what's gaun: time
about's fair play; ye'll ken now what hanging's gude for."

"Come, come, this is all nonsense, Rat," said the
procurator. "Ye canna creep out at that hole, lad; you
must speak to the point—you understand me—if you
want favour; gif-gaf makes gude friends, ye ken."

"But how can I speak to the point, as your honour
ca's it," said Ratcliffe, demurely, and with an air of
great simplicity, "when ye ken I was under sentence,
and in the strong-room a' the while the job was going
on?"

"And how can we turn ye loose on the public
again, Daddie Rat, unless ye do or say something to
deserve it?"

"Well, then, d—n it!" answered the criminal,
"since it maun be sae, I saw Geordie Robertson among
the boys that brake the jail; I suppose that will do me
some gude?"

"That's speaking to the purpose, indeed," said the
office-bearer; "and now, Rat, where think ye we'll find
him?"

"Deil haet o' me kens," said Ratcliffe; "he'll no likely gang back to ony o' his auld howffs; he'll be off the country by this time. He has gude friends some gate or other, for a' the life he's led; he's been weel educate."

"He'll grace the gallows the better," said Mr. Sharpitlaw; "a desperate dog, to murder an officer of the city for doing his duty! Wha kens wha's turn it might be next?—But you saw him plainly?"

"As plainly as I see you."

"How was he dressed?" said Sharpitlaw.

"I couldna weel see; something of a woman's bit mutch on his head; but ye never saw sic a ca'-throw. Ane couldna hae cen to a' thing."

"But did he speak to no one?" said Sharpitlaw.

"They were a' speaking and gabbling through other," said Ratcliffe, who was obviously unwilling to carry his evidence farther than he could possibly help.

"This will not do, Ratcliffe," said the procurator; "you must speak *out—out—out*," tapping the table emphatically, as he repeated that impressive monosyllable.

"It's very hard, sir," said the prisoner; "and but for the under-turnkey's place ——"

"And the reversion of the captaincy—the captaincy of the Tolbooth, man—that is, in case of gude behaviour."

"Ay, ay," said Ratcliffe, "gude behaviour!—there's the deevil. And then it's waiting for dead folk's shoon into the bargain."

"But Robertson's head will weigh something," said

Sharpitlaw; "something gay and heavy, Rat; the town maun show cause—that's right and reason—and then ye'll hae freedom to enjoy your gear honestly."

"I dinna ken," said Ratcliffe; "it's a queer way of beginning the trade of honesty—but deil ma care. Weal, then, I heard and saw him speak to the wench Effie Deans, that's up there for child-murder."

"The deil ye did? Rat, this is finding a mare's nest wi' a witness.—And the man that spoke to Butler in the Park, and that was to meet wi' Jeanie Deans at Muschat's Cairn—whew! lay that and that together? As sure as I live he's been the father of the lassie's wean."

"There hae been waur guesses than that, I'm thinking," observed Ratcliffe, turning his quid of tobacco in his cheek, and squirting out the juice. "I heard something a while syne about his drawing up wi' a bonny quean about the Pleasaunts, and that it was a' Wilson could do to keep him frae marrying her."

Here a city officer entered, and told Sharpitlaw that they had the woman in custody whom he had directed them to bring before him.

"It's little matter now," said he, "the thing is taking another turn; however, George, ye may bring her in."

The officer retired, and introduced, upon his return, a tall, strapping wench of eighteen or twenty, dressed fantastically, in a sort of blue riding-jacket, with tarnished lace, her hair clubbed like that of a man, a Highland bonnet, and a bunch of broken feathers, a

riding-skirt (or petticoat) of scarlet camlet, embroidered
with tarnished flowers. Her features were coarse and
masculine, yet at a little distance, by dint of very
bright wild-looking black eyes, an aquiline nose, and a
commanding profile, appeared rather handsome. She
flourished the switch she held in her hand, dropped a
courtesy as low as a lady at a birth-night introduction,
recovered herself seemingly according to Touchstone's
directions to Audrey, and opened the conversation without waiting till any questions were asked.

"God gie your honour gude e'en, and mony o' them,
bonny Mr. Sharpitlaw!—Gude e'en to ye, Daddie
Ratton—they tauld me ye were hanged man; or did
ye get out o' John Dalgleish's hands like half-hangit
Maggie Dickson?"

"Whisht, ye daft jaud," said Ratcliffe, "and hear
what's said to ye."

"Wi' a' my heart, Ratton. Great preferment for
poor Madge to be brought up the street wi' a grand man,
wi' a coat a' passemented wi' worset-lace, to speak wi'
provosts, and bailies, and town-clerks, and prokitors, at
this time o' day—and the haill town looking at me
too—This is honour on earth for anes!"

"Ay, Madge," said Mr. Sharpitlaw, in a coaxing
tone; "and ye're dressed out in your braws, I see;
these are not your every-days' claiths ye have on."

"Deil be in my fingers, then!" said Madge—" Eh,
sirs!" (observing Butler come into the apartment),
"there's a minister in the Toolbooth—wha will ca' it a
graceless place now?—I'se warrant he's in for the gude

auld cause—but it's be nae cause o' mine," and off she
went into a song.

> "Hey for cavaliers, ho for cavaliers,
> Dub a dub, dub a dub,
> Have at old Beelzebub,—
> Oliver's squeaking for fear."

"Did you ever see that mad woman before?" said
Sharpitlaw to Butler.

"Not to my knowledge, sir," replied Butler.

"I thought as much," said the procurator-fiscal,
looking towards Ratcliffe, who answered his glance with
a nod of acquiescence and intelligence.

"But that is Madge Wildfire, as she calls herself,"
said the man of law to Butler.

"Ay, that I am," said Madge, "and that I have been
ever since I was something better—Haigh ho"—(and
something like melancholy dwelt on her features for a
minute)—"But I canna mind when that was—it was
lang syne, at ony rate, and I'll ne'er fash my thumb
about it.—

> I glance like the wildfire through country and town ;
> I'm seen on the causeway—I'm seen on the down ;
> The lightning that flashes so bright and so free,
> Is scarcely so blithe or so bonny as me."

"Haud your tongue, ye skirling limmer!" said the
officer, who had acted as master of the ceremonies to
this extraordinary performer, and who was rather scan-
dalized at the freedom of her demeanour before a person
of Mr. Sharpitlaw's importance—"haud your tongue, or
I'se gie ye something to skirl for!"

"Let her alone, George," said Sharpitlaw, "dinna put her out o' tune; I hae some questions to ask her—But first, Mr. Butler, take another look of her."

"Do sae, minister—do sae," cried Madge; "I am as weel worth looking at as ony book in your aught.—And I can say the single carritch, and the double carritch, and justification, and effectual calling, and the assembly of divines at Westminster, that is" (she added in a low tone), "I could say them anes—but it's lang syne—and ane forgets, ye ken." And poor Madge heaved another deep sigh.

"Weel, sir," said Mr. Sharpitlaw to Butler, "what think ye now?"

"As I did before," said Butler; "that I never saw the poor demented creature in my life before."

"Then she is not the person whom you said the rioters last night described as Madge Wildfire?"

"Certainly not," said Butler. "They may be near the same height, for they are both tall, but I see little other resemblance."

"Their dress, then, is not alike?" said Sharpitlaw.

"Not in the least," said Butler.

"Madge, my bonny woman," said Sharpitlaw, in the same coaxing manner, "what did ye do wi' your ilka-day's claise yesterday?"

"I dinna mind," said Madge.

"Where was ye yesterday at e'en, Madge?"

"I dinna mind onything about yesterday," answered Madge; "ae day is eneugh for ony body to wun ower wi' at a time, and ower muckle sometimes."

"But maybe, Madge, ye wad mind something about it, if I was to give ye this half-crown?" said Sharpitlaw, taking out the piece of money.

"That might gar me laugh, but it culdna gar me mind."

"But Madge," continued Sharpitlaw, "were I to send you to the wark-house in Leith Wynd, and gar Jock Dalgleish lay the tawse on your back ——"

"That wad gar me greet," said Madge, sobbing, "but it couldna gar me mind, ye ken."

"She is ower far past reasonable folk's motives, sir," said Ratcliffe, "to mind siller, or John Dalgleish, or the cat and nine tails either; but I think I could gar her tell us something."

"Try her then, Ratcliffe," said Sharpitlaw, "for I am tired of her crazy pate, and be d——d to her."

"Madge," said Ratcliffe, "hae ye ony joes now?"

"An ony body ask ye, say ye dinna ken.—Set him to be speaking of my joes, auld Daddie Ratton!"

"I dare say, ye hae deil ane?"

"See if I haena then," said Madge, with the toss of the head of affronted beauty—"there's Rob the Ranter, and Will Fleming, and then there's Geordie Robertson, lad—that's Gentleman Geordie—what think ye o' that?"

Ratcliffe laughed, and, winking to the procurator-fiscal, pursued the inquiry in his own way.

"But, Madge, the lads only like ye when ye hae on your braws—they wadna touch you wi' a pair o' tangs when you are in your auld ilka-day rags."

" Ye're a leeing auld sorrow then," replied the fair one; "for Gentle Geordie Robertson put my ilka-day's claise on his ain bonny sell yestreen, and gaed a' through the town wi' them; and gawsie and grand he lookit, like ony queen in the land."

" I dinna believe a word o't," said Ratcliffe, with another wink to the procurator. " Thae duds were a' o' the colour o' moonshine in the water, I'm thinking, Madge—The gown wad be a sky-blue scarlet, I'se warrant ye ?"

" It was nae sic thing," said Madge, whose unretentive memory let out, in the eagerness of contradiction, all that she would have most wished to keep concealed, had her judgment been equal to her inclination. " It was neither scarlet nor sky-blue, but my ain auld brown threshie-coat of a short gown, and my mother's auld mutch, and my red rokelay—and he gaed me a croun and a kiss for the use o' them, blessing on his bonny face—though it's been a dear ane to me."

" And where did he change his clothes again, hinnie ?" said Sharpitlaw, in his most conciliatory manner.

" The procurator's spoiled a'," observed Ratcliffe, dryly.

And it was even so; for the question, put in so direct a shape, immediately awakened Madge to the propriety of being reserved upon those very topics on which Ratcliffe had indirectly seduced her to become communicative.

" What was't ye were speering at us, sir ?" she

resumed, with an appearance of stolidity so speedily
assumed, as showed there was a good deal of knavery
mixed with her folly.

"I asked you" said the procurator, "at what hour,
and to what place, Robertson brought back your clothes."

"Robertson?—Lord haud a care o' us! what Robertson?"

"Why, the fellow we were speaking of, Gentle
Geordie, as you call him."

"Geordie Gentle!" answered Madge, with well-
feigned amazement—"I dinna ken naebody they ca'
Geordie Gentle."

"Come, my jo," said Sharpitlaw, "this will not do;
you must tell us what you did with these clothes of
yours."

Madge Wildfire made no answer, unless the question
may seem connected with the snatch of a song with
which she indulged the embarrassed investigator:—

> "What did ye wi' the bridal ring—bridal ring—bridal ring?
> What did ye wi' your wedding ring, ye little cutty quean, O?
> I gied it till a sodger, a sodger, a sodger,
> I gied it till a sodger, an auld true love o' mine, O."

Of all the madwomen who have sung and said,
since the days of Hamlet the Dane, if Ophelia be the
most affecting, Madge Wildfire was the most provoking.

The procurator-fiscal was in despair. "I'll take
some measures with this d—d Bess of Bedlam," said
he, "that shall make her find her tongue."

"Wi' your favour, sir," said Ratcliffe, "better let

her mind settle a little—Ye have aye made out something."

"True," said the official person; "a brown short-gown, mutch, red rokelay—that agrees with your Madge Wildfire, Mr. Butler?" Butler agreed that it did so. "Yes, there was a sufficient motive for taking this crazy creature's dress and name, while he was about such a job."

"And I am free to say *now*," said Ratcliffe——

"When you see it has come out without you," interrupted Sharpitlaw.

"Just sae, sir," reiterated Ratcliffe. "I am free to say now, since it's come out otherwise, that these were the clothes I saw Robertson wearing last night in the jail, when he was at the head of the rioters."

"That's direct evidence," said Sharpitlaw; "stick to that, Rat—I will report favourably of you to the provost, for I have business for you to-night. It wears late; I must home and get a snack, and I'll be back in the evening. Keep Madge with you, Ratcliffe, and try to get her into a good tune again." So saying, he left the prison.

CHAPTER THE SEVENTEENTH

And some they whistled—and some they sang,
 And some did loudly say,
Whenever Lord Barnard's horn it blew,
 "Away Musgrave, away!"
                    BALLAD OF LITTLE MUSGRAVE.

WHEN the man of office returned to the Heart of Mid-Lothian, he resumed his conference with Ratcliffe, of whose experience and assistance he now held himself secure. "You must speak with this wench, Rat—this Effie Deans—you must sift her a wee bit; for as sure as a tether she will ken Robertson's haunts—till her, Rat—till her, without delay."

"Craving your pardon, Mr. Sharpitlaw," said the turnkey elect, "that's what I am not free to do."

" Free to do, man ? what the deil ails ye now ?— I thought we had settled a' that."

" I dinna ken, sir," said Ratcliffe ; " I hae spoken to this Effie—she's strange to this place and to its ways, and to a' our ways, Mr. Sharpitlaw ; and she greets, the silly tawpie, and she's breaking her heart already about this wild chield ; and were she the means o' taking him, she wad break it outright."

" She wunna hae time, lad," said Sharpitlaw ; " the woodie will hae its ain o' her before that—a woman's heart takes a lang time o' breaking."

" That's according to the stuff they are made o' sir," replied Ratcliffe—" But to make a lang tale short, I canna undertake the job. It gangs against my conscience."

" *Your* conscience, Rat ?" said Sharpitlaw, with a sneer, which the reader will probably think very natural upon the occasion.

" Ou ay, sir," answered Ratcliffe, calmly, " just *my* conscience ; a' body has a conscience, though it may be ill wunnin at it. I think mine's as weel out o' the gate as maist folk's are ; and yet it's just like the noop of my elbow, it whiles gets a bit dirl on a corner."

" Weel, Rat," replied Sharpitlaw, since ye are nice, I'll speak to the hussy mysell."

Sharpitlaw, accordingly, caused himself to be introduced into the little dark apartment tenanted by the unfortunate Effie Deans. The poor girl was seated on her little flock-bed, plunged in a deep reverie. Some food stood on the table, of a quality better than is

usually supplied to prisoners, but it was untouched.
The person under whose care she was more particularly
placed said, " that sometimes she tasted naething from
the tae end of the four-and-twenty hours to the t'other,
except a drink of water."

Sharpitlaw took a chair, and commanding the turnkey to retire, he opened the conversation, endeavouring
to throw into his tone and countenance as much com-
miseration as they were capable of expressing, for the
one was sharp and harsh, the other, sly, acute, and
selfish.

" How's a' wi' ye, Effie?—How d'ye find yoursell,
hinny ?"

A deep sigh was the only answer.

" Are the folk civil to ye, Effie?—it's my duty to
inquire."

" Very civil, sir," said Effie, compelling herself to
answer, yet hardly knowing what she said.

" And your victuals," continued Sharpitlaw, in the
same condoling tone—" do you get what you like?—or
is there ony thing you would particularly fancy, as your
health seems but silly ?"

" It's a' very weel, sir, I thank ye," said the poor
prisoner, in a tone how different from the sportive
vivacity of those of the Lily of St. Leonard's !—" it's
a' very gude—ower gude for me."

" He must have been a great villain, Effie, who
brought you to this pass," said Sharpitlaw.

The remark was dictated partly by a natural feeling,
of which even he could not divest himself, though

accustomed to practise on the passions of others, and
keep a most heedful guard over his own, and partly
by his wish to introduce the sort of conversation which
might best serve his immediate purpose.   Indeed,
upon the present occasion, these mixed motives of
feeling and cunning harmonized together wonderfully ;
for, said Sharpitlaw to himself, the greater rogue
Robertson is, the more will be the merit of bringing
him to justice.   "He must have been a great villain,
indeed," he again reiterated ; "and I wish I had the
skelping o' him."

"I may blame mysell mair than him," said Effie ;
"I was bred up to ken better; but he, poor fellow,"
——(she stopped).

"Was a thorough blackguard a' his life, I dare say,"
said Sharpitlaw.   "A stranger he was in this country,
and a companion of that lawless vagabond, Wilson, I
think, Effie ?"

"It wad hae been dearly telling him that he had
ne'er seen Wilson's face."

"That's very true that you are saying, Effie," said
Sharpitlaw.   "Where was't that Robertson and you
were used to howff thegither ? Somegate about the
Laigh Calton, I am thinking."

The simple and dispirited girl had thus far followed
Mr. Sharpitlaw's lead, because he had artfully adjusted
his observations to the thoughts he was pretty certain
must be passing through her own mind, so that her
answers became a kind of thinking aloud, a mood into
which those who are either constitutionally absent in

mind, or are rendered so by the temporary pressure of
misfortune, may be easily led by a skilful train of
suggestions. But the last observation of the procurator-
fiscal was too much of the nature of a direct interrogatory, and it broke the charm accordingly.

"What was it that I was saying?" said Effie,
starting up from her reclining posture, seating herself
upright, and hastily shading her dishevelled hair back
from her wasted, but still beautiful countenance. She
fixed her eyes boldly and keenly upon Sharpitlaw;—
"You are too much of a gentleman, sir,—too much of
an honest man, to take any notice of what a poor
creature like me says, that can hardly ca' my senses my
ain—God help me !"

"Advantage!—I would be of some advantage to you
if I could," said Sharpitlaw, in a soothing tone; "and
I ken naething sae likely to serve ye, Effie, as gripping
this rascal Robertson."

"O dinna misca' him, sir, that never misca'd you !—
Robertson?—I am sure I had naething to say against
ony man o' the name, and naething will I say."

"But if you do not heed your own misfortune, Effie,
you should mind what distress he has brought on your
family," said the man of law.

"O, Heaven help me !" exclaimed poor Effie—"My
poor father—my dear Jeanie—O, that's sairest to bide
of a'! O, sir, if you hae ony kindness—if ye hae ony
touch of compassion—for a' the folk I see here are as
hard as the wa'-stanes—If ye wad but bid them let my
sister Jeanie in the next time she ca's ! for when I hear

them put her awa frae the door, and canna climb up to
that high window to see sae muckle as her gown-tail,
it's like to pit me out o' my judgment." And she
looked on him with a face of entreaty so earnest, yet so
humble, that she fairly shook the steadfast purpose of
his mind.

"You shall see your sister," he began, "if you'll tell
me,"—then interrupting himself, he added, in a more
hurried tone,—"no, d—n it, you shall see your sister
whether you tell me any thing or no." So saying, he
rose up and left the apartment.

When he had rejoined Ratcliffe, he observed, "You
are right, Ratton; there's no making much of that lassie.
But ae thing I have cleared—that is, that Robertson
has been the father of the bairn, and so I will wager a
bodle it will be he that's to meet wi' Jeanie Deans this
night at Muschat's Cairn, and there we'll nail him, Rat,
or my name is not Gideon Sharpitlaw."

"But," said Ratcliffe, perhaps because he was in no
hurry to see any thing which was like to be connected
with the discovery and apprehension of Robertson, "an
that were the case, Mr. Butler wad hae kend the man
in the King's Park to be the same person wi' him in
Madge Wildfire's claise, that headed the mob."

"That makes nae difference, man," replied Sharpitlaw—"the dress, the light, the confusion, and maybe a
touch o' a blackit cork, or a slake o' paint —hout, Ratton, I have seen ye dress your ainsell, that the deevil ye
belang to durstna hae made oath t'ye."

"And that's true, too," said Ratcliffe.

"And besides, ye dounard carle," continued Sharpit-law, triumphantly, "the minister *did* say, that he thought he knew something of the features of the birkie that spoke to him in the Park, though he could not charge his memory where or when he had seen them."

"It's evident, then, your honour will be right," said Ratcliffe.

"Then, Rat, you and I will go with the party our-sells this night, and see him in grips, or we are done wi' him."

"I seem muckle use I can be o' to your honour," said Ratcliffe, reluctantly.

"Use?" answered Sharpitlaw—"You can guide the party—you ken the ground. Besides, I do not intend to quit sight o' you, my good friend, till I have him in hand."

"Weel, sir," said Ratcliffe, but in no joyful tone of acquiescence; "Ye maun hae it your ain way—but mind he's a desperate man."

"We shall have that with us," answered Sharpitlaw, "that will settle him, if it is necessary."

"But, sir," answered Ratcliffe, "I am sure I couldna undertake to guide you to Muschat's Cairn in the night-time; I ken the place, as mony does, in fair daylight, but how to find it by moonshine, amang sae mony crags and stanes, as like to each other as the collier to the deil, is mair than I can tell. I might as soon seek moonshine in water."

"What's the meaning o' this, Ratcliffe?" said Sharpitlaw, while he fixed his eye on the recusant, with a fatal and ominous expression,—"Have you forgotten that you are still under sentence of death?"

"No, sir," said Ratcliffe, "that's a thing no easily put out o' memory; and if my presence be judged necessary, nae doubt I maun gang wi' your honour. But I was gaun to tell your honour of ane that has mair skeel o' the gate than me, and that's e'en Madge Wildfire."

"The devil she has!—Do you think me as mad as she is, to trust to her guidance on such an occasion?"

"Your honour is the best judge," answered Ratcliffe; "but I ken I can keep her in tune, and garr her haud the straight path—she often sleeps out, or rambles about amang thae hills the haill simmer night, the daft limmer."

"Weel, Ratcliffe," replied the procurator-fiscal, "if you think she can guide us the right way—but take heed to what you are about—your life depends on your behaviour."

"It's a sair judgment on a man," said Ratcliffe, "when he has ance gane sae far wrang as I hae done, that deil a bit he can be honest, try't whilk way he will."

Such was the reflection of Ratcliffe, when he was left for a few minutes to himself, while the retainer of justice went to procure a proper warrant, and give the necessary directions.

The rising moon saw the whole party free from the walls of the city, and entering upon the open ground. Arthur's Seat, like a couchant lion of immense size—

Salisbury Crags, like a huge belt or girdle of granite,
were dimly visible. Holding their path along the
southern side of the Canongate, they gained the Abbey
of Holyroodhouse, and from thence found their way by
step and stile into the King's Park. They were at first
four in number—an officer of justice and Sharpitlaw,
who were well armed with pistols and cutlasses; Ratcliffe, who was not trusted with weapons, lest he might,
peradventure, have used them on the wrong side; and
the female. But at the last stile, when they entered
the Chase, they were joined by other two officers, whom
Sharpitlaw, desirous to secure sufficient force for his
purpose, and at the same time to avoid observation, had
directed to wait for him at this place. Ratcliffe saw this
accession of strength with some disquietude, for he had
hitherto thought it likely that Robertson, who was a
bold, stout, and active young fellow, might have made
his escape from Sharpitlaw and the single officer, by
force or agility, without his being implicated in the
matter. But the present strength of the followers of
justice was overpowering, and the only mode of saving
Robertson (which the old sinner was well disposed to
do, providing always he could accomplish his purpose
without compromising his own safety), must be by con-
triving that he should have some signal of their approach. It was probably with this view that Ratcliffe
had requested the addition of Madge to the party,
having considerable confidence in her propensity to
exert her lungs. Indeed, she had already given them
so many specimens of her clamorous loquacity, that

Sharpitlaw half determined to send her back with one
of the officers, rather than carry forward in his company
a person so extremely ill qualified to be a guide in a
secret expedition. It seemed, too, as if the open air,
the approach to the hills, and the ascent of the moon,
supposed to be so portentous over those whose brain is
infirm, made her spirits rise in a degree tenfold more
loquacious than she had hitherto exhibited. To silence
her by fair means seemed impossible; authoritative commands and coaxing entreaties she set alike at defiance, and
threats only made her sulky, and altogether intractable.

"Is there no one of you," said Sharpitlaw, impatiently, "that knows the way to this accursed place—
this Nichol Muschat's Cairn — excepting this mad
clavering idiot?"

"Deil ane o' them kens it, except mysell," exclaimed
Madge; "how suld they, the poor fule cowards? But
I hae sat on the grave frae bat-fleeing time till cock-
crow, and had mony a fine crack wi' Muschat and Ailie
Muschat, that are lying sleeping below."

"The devil take your crazy brain," said Sharpitlaw;
"will you not allow the men to answer a question?"

The officers obtaining a moment's audience while
Ratcliffe diverted Madge's attention, declared that,
though they had a general knowledge of the spot, they
could not undertake to guide the party to it by the
uncertain light of the moon, with such accuracy as to
ensure success to their expedition.

"What shall we do, Ratcliffe?" said Sharpitlaw;
"if he sees us before we see him,—and that's what he

is certain to do, if we go strolling about, without keeping
the straight road,—we may bid gude day to the job;
and I wad rather lose one hundred pounds, baith for
the credit of the police, and because the Provost says
somebody maun be hanged for this job o' Porteous,
come o't what likes."

"I think," said Ratcliffe, "we maun just try Madge;
and I'll see if I can get her keepit in ony better order.
And at ony rate, if he suld hear her skirling her auld
ends o' sangs, he's no to ken for that that there's ony
body wi' her."

"That's true," said Sharpitlaw; "and if he thinks
her alone he's as like to come towards her as to rin frae
her.   So set forward—we hae lost ower muckle time
already—see to get her to keep the right road."

"And what sort o' house does Nichol Muschat and
his wife keep now?" said Ratcliffe to the mad-woman,
by way of humouring her vein of folly; "they were but
thrawn folk lang syne, an a' tales be true."

"Ou, ay, ay, ay—but a's forgotten now," replied
Madge, in the confidential tone of a gossip giving the
history of her next-door neighbour—"Ye see, I spoke
to them mysell, and tauld them bygancs suld be
bygancs—her throat's sair misguggled and mashackered
though; she wears her corpse-sheet drawn weel up to
hide it, but that canna hinder the bluid seiping through,
ye ken.   I wussed her to wash it in St. Anthony's Well,
and that will cleanse if ony thing can—But they say
bluid never bleaches out o' linen claith — Deacon
Sanders's new cleansing draps winna do't—I tried them

mysell on a bit rug we hae at hame that was mailed wi'
the bluid of a bit skirling wean that was hurt some gate,
but out it winna come—Weel, ye'll say that's queer;
but I will bring it out to St. Anthony's blessed Well
some braw night just like this, and I'll cry up Ailie
Muschat, and she and I will hae a grand bouking-
washing, and bleach our claise in the beams of the
bonny Lady Moon, that's far pleasanter to me than the
sun—the sun's ower het, and ken ye, cummers, my
brains are het enough already.   But the moon, and the
dew, and the night-wind, they are just like a caller
kail-blade laid on my brow; and whiles I think the
moon just shines on purpose to pleasure me, when
naebody sees her but mysell."

This raving discourse she continued with prodigious
volubility, walking on at a great pace, and dragging
Ratcliffe along with her, while he endeavoured, in
appearance at least, if not in reality, to induce her to
moderate her voice.

All at once, she stopped short upon the top of a
little hillock, gazed upward fixedly, and said not one
word for the space of five minutes.   "What the devil
is the matter with her now?" said Sharpitlaw to
Ratcliffe—"Can you not get her forward?"

"Yo maun just take a grain o' patience wi' her, sir,"
said Ratcliffe.   "She'll no gae a foot faster than she
likes hersell."

"D—n her," said Sharpitlaw, "I'll take care she
has her time in Bedlam or Bridewell, or both, for she's
both mad and mischievous."

In the meanwhile, Madge, who had looked very
pensive when she first stopped, suddenly burst into a
vehement fit of laughter, then paused and sighed
bitterly,—then was seized with a second fit of laughter,
—then, fixing her eyes on the moon, lifted up her
voice and sung,—

> Good even, good fair moon, good even to thee;
> I prithee, dear moon, now show to me
> The form and the features, the speech and degree,
> Of the man that true lover of mine shall be.

"But I need not ask that of the bonny Lady Moon—I
ken that weel eneugh mysell—*true*-love though he
wasna—But naebody shall say that I ever tauld a word
about the matter—But whiles I wish the bairn had lived
—Weel, God guide us, there's a heaven aboon us a',"
—(here she sighed bitterly), "and a bonny moon, and
sterns in it forby" (and here she laughed once more).

"Are we to stand here all night?" said Sharpitlaw,
very impatiently. "Drag her forward."

"Ay, sir," said Ratcliffe, "if we kend whilk way to
drag her, that would settle it at ance.—Come, Madge,
hinny," addressing her, "we'll no be in time to see
Nichol and his wife, unless ye show us the road."

"In troth and that I will, Ratton," said she, seizing
him by the arm, and resuming her route with huge
strides, considering it was a female who took them.
"And I'll tell ye, Ratton, blithe will Nichol Muschat
be to see ye, for he says he kens weel there isna sic a
villain out o' hell as ye are, and he wad be ravished to
hae a crack wi' you—like to like, ye ken—it's a proverb

never fails—and ye arc baith a pair o' the deevil's peats,
I trow—hard to ken whilk deserves the hettest corner
o' his ingle side."

Ratcliffe was conscience-struck, and could not forbear
making an involuntary protest against this classification.
" I never shed blood," he replied.

" But ye hae sauld it, Ratton—ye hae sauld blood
mony a time. Folk kill wi' the tongue as weel as wi'
the hand—wi' the word as weel as wi' the gulley !—

> It is the bonny butcher lad,
> That wears the sleeves of blue,
> He sells the flesh on Saturday,
> On Friday that he slew."

" And what is that I am doing now ?" thought
Ratcliffe. " But I 'll hae nae wyte of Robertson's young
bluid, if I can help it;" then speaking apart to Madge,
he asked her, " Whether she did not remember ony o'
her auld sangs ?"

" Mony a dainty ane," said Madge ; " and blithely
can I sing them, for lightsome sangs make merry gate."
And she sang,—

> When the glede 's in the blue cloud,
> The lavrock lies still ;
> When the hound's in the green-wood,
> The hind keeps the hill.

" Silence her cursed noise, if you should throttle
her," said Sharpitlaw; " I see somebody yonder.—Keep
close, my boys, and creep round the shoulder of the
height. George Poinder, stay you with Ratcliffe and
that mad yelling bitch; and you other two, come with
me round under the shadow of the brae."

And he crept forward with the stealthy pace of an Indian savage, who leads his band to surprise an unsuspecting party of some hostile tribe. Ratcliffe saw them glide off, avoiding the moonlight, and keeping as much in the shade as possible. "Robertson's done up," said he to himself; "thae young lads are aye sae thoughtless. What deevil could he hae to say to Jeanie Deans, or to ony woman on earth, that he suld gang awa and get his neck raxed for her? And this mad quean, after cracking like a pen-gun, and skirling like a pea-hen for the haill night, behoves just to hae hadden her tongue when her clavers might have done some gude! But it's aye the way wi' women; if they ever haud their tongues ava', ye may swear it's for mischief. I wish I could set her on again without this blood-sucker kenning what I am doing. But he's as gleg as MacKeachan's elshin, that ran through sax plies of bend-leather and half an inch into the king's heel."

He then began to hum, but in a very low and suppressed tone, the first stanza of a favourite ballad of Wildfire's, the words of which bore some distant analogy with the situation of Robertson, trusting that the power of association would not fail to bring the rest to her mind:

> There's a bloodhound ranging Tinwald wood,
>   There's harness glancing sheen;   ·
> There's a maiden sits on Tinwald brae,
>   And she sings loud between.

Madge had no sooner received the catch-word, than

she vindicated Ratcliffe's sagacity by setting off at score with the song :—

> O sleep ye sound, Sir James, she said,
>   When ye suld rise and ride?
> There 's twenty men, wi' bow and blade,
>   Are seeking where ye hide.

Though Ratcliffe was at a considerable distance from the spot called Muschat's Cairn, yet his eyes, practised like those of a cat to penetrate darkness, could mark that Robertson had caught the alarm. George Poinder, less keen of sight, or less attentive, was not aware of his flight any more than Sharpitlaw and his assistants, whose view, though they were considerably nearer to the cairn, was intercepted by the broken nature of the ground under which they were screening themselves. At length, however, after the interval of five or six minutes, they also perceived that Robertson had fled, and rushed hastily towards the place, while Sharpitlaw called out aloud, in the harshest tones of a voice which resembled a saw-mill at work, "Chase, lads—chase—haud the brae—I see him on the edge of the hill!" Then hollowing back to the rear-guard of his detachment, he issued his farther orders : "Ratcliffe, come here, and detain the woman—George, run and kepp the stile at the Duke's Walk—Ratcliffe, come here directly—but first knock out that mad bitch's brains!"

"Ye had better rin for it, Madge," said Ratcliffe, "far it's ill dealing wi' an angry man."

Madge Wildfire was not so absolutely void of common sense as not to understand this innuendo ; and while Ratcliffe, in seemingly anxious haste of obedience, hastened to the spot where Sharpitlaw waited to deliver up Jeanie Deans to his custody, she fled with all the dispatch she could exert in an opposite direction. Thus the whole party were separated, and in rapid motion of flight or pursuit, excepting Ratcliffe and Jeanie, whom, although making no attempt to escape, he held fast by the cloak, and who remained standing by Muschat's Cairn.

CHAPTER THE EIGHTEENTH.

You have paid the heavens your function, and the prisoner
the very debt of your calling.

MEASURE FOR MEASURE.

JEANIE DEANS,—for here our story unites itself with
that part of the narrative which broke off at the end of
the fifteenth chapter,—while she waited, in terror and
amazement, the hasty advance of three or four men
towards her, was yet more startled at their suddenly
breaking asunder, and giving chase in different directions
to the late object of her terror, who became at that
moment, though she could not well assign a reasonable

cause, rather the cause of her interest. One of the party (it was Sharpitlaw) came straight up to her, and saying, "Your name is Jeanie Deans, and you are my prisoner," immediately added, "but if you will tell me which way he ran I will let you go."

"I dinna ken, sir," was all the poor girl could utter; and, indeed, it is the phrase which rises most readily to the lips of any person in her rank, as the readiest reply to any embarrassing question.

"But," said Sharpitlaw, "ye *ken* wha it was ye were speaking wi', my leddy, on the hill side, and midnight sae near; ye surely ken *that*, my bonny woman ?"

"I dinna ken, sir," again iterated Jeanie, who really did not comprehend in her terror the nature of the questions which were so hastily put to her in this moment of surprise.

"We will try to mend your memory by and by, hinny," said Sharpitlaw, and shouted, as we have already told the reader, to Ratcliffe, to come up and take charge of her, while he himself directed the chase after Robertson, which he still hoped might be successful. As Ratcliffe approached, Sharpitlaw pushed the young woman towards him with some rudeness, and betaking himself to the more important object of his quest, began to scale crags and scramble up steep banks, with an agility of which his profession and his general gravity of demeanour would previously have argued him incapable. In a few minutes there was no one within sight, and only a distant halloo from one of the pursuers to the other, faintly heard on the side of the hill, argued that there was any one within hearing. Jeanie Deans was left in the clear moonlight, standing under the guard of a person of whom she knew nothing, and, what was worse, concerning whom, as the reader is well aware, she could have learned nothing that would not have increased her terror.

When all in the distance was silent, Ratcliffe for the first time addressed her, and it was in that cold sarcastic indifferent tone familiar to habitual depravity, whose crimes are instigated by custom rather than by passion. "This is a braw night for ye, dearie," he said, attempting to pass his arm across her shoulder, "to be on the green hill wi' your jo." Jeanie extricated herself from his grasp, but did not make any reply. "I think lads and lasses," continued the ruffian, "dinna meet at Muschat's Cairn at midnight to crack nuts," and he again attempted to take hold of her.

"If ye are an officer of justice, sir," said Jeanie, again eluding his attempt to seize her, "ye deserve to have your coat stripped from your back."

"Very true, hinny," said he, succeeding forcibly in his attempt to get hold of her, "but suppose I should strip your cloak off first?"

"Ye are more a man, I am sure, than to hurt me, sir," said Jeanie; "for God's sake have pity on a half-distracted creature!"

"Come, come," said Ratcliffe, "you're a good-looking wench, and should not be cross-grained. I was going to be an honest man—but the devil has this very day flung first a lawyer, and then a woman, in my gate.

I 'll tell you what, Jeanie, they are out on the hill-side
—if you 'll be guided by me, I 'll carry you to a wee bit
corner in the Pleasance, that I ken o' in an auld wife's,
that a' the prokitors o' Scotland wot naething o', and
we 'll send Robertson word to meet us in Yorkshire, for
there is a set o' braw lads about the midland counties,
that I hae dune business wi' before now, and sae we 'll
leave Mr. Sharpitlaw to whistle on his thumb."

It was fortunate for Jeanie, in an emergency like the
present, that she possessed presence of mind and courage,
so soon as the first hurry of surprise had enabled her
to rally her recollection. She saw the risk she was in
from a ruffian, who not only was such by profession,
but had that evening been stupifying, by means of
strong liquors, the internal aversion which he felt at
the business on which Sharpitlaw had resolved to
employ him.

"Dinna speak sae loud," said she, in a low voice;
"he's up yonder."

"Who?—Robertson!" said Ratcliffe, eagerly.

"Ay," replied Jeanie; "up yonder;" and she pointed
to the ruins of the hermitage and chapel.

"By G—d, then," said Ratcliffe, "I'll make my ain
of him, either one way or other—wait for me here."

But no sooner had he set off, as fast as he could run,
towards the chapel, than Jeanie started in an opposite
direction, over high and low, on the nearest path homeward. Her juvenile exercise as a herdswoman had put
"life and mettle," in her heels, and never had she followed Dusticfoot, when the cows were in the corn,

with half so much speed as she now cleared the distance
betwixt Muschat's Cairn and her father's cottage at St.
Leonard's.   To lift the latch—to enter—to shut, bolt,
and double bolt the door—to draw against it a heavy
article of furniture (which she could not have moved
in a moment of less energy), so as to make yet farther
provision against violence, was almost the work of a
moment, yet done with such silence as equalled the
celerity.

Her next anxiety was upon her father's account, and
she drew silently to the door of his apartment, in order
to satisfy herself whether he had been disturbed by her
return.   He was awake,—probably had slept but little;
but the constant presence of his own sorrows, the distance of his apartment from the outer-door of the house,
and the precautions which Jeanie had taken to conceal
her departure and return, had prevented him from being
sensible of either.   He was engaged in his devotions,
and Jeanie could distinctly hear him use these words:—
"And for the other child thou hast given me to be a
comfort and stay to my old age, may her days be long
in the land, according to the promise thou hast given
to those who shall honour father and mother; may all
her purchased and promised blessings be multiplied
upon her; keep her in the watches of the night, and
in the uprising of the morning, that all in this land
may know that thou hast not utterly hid thy face from
those that seek thee in truth and in sincerity."   He was
silent, but probably continued his petition in the strong
fervency of mental devotion.

His daughter retired to her apartment, comforted, that while she was exposed to danger, her head had been covered by the prayers of the just as by an helmet, and under the strong confidence, that while she walked worthy of the protection of Heaven, she would experience its countenance. It was in that moment that a vague idea first darted across her mind, that something might yet be achieved for her sister's safety, conscious as she now was of her innocence of the unnatural murder with which she stood charged. It came, as she described it, on her mind, like a sun-blink on a stormy sea; and although it instantly vanished, yet she felt a degree of composure which she had not experienced for many days, and could not help being strongly persuaded that, by some means or other, she would be called upon, and directed, to work out her sister's deliverance. She went to bed, not forgetting her usual devotions, the more fervently made on account of her late deliverance, and she slept soundly in spite of her agitation.

We must return to Ratcliffe, who had started, like a greyhound from the slips when the sportsman cries halloo, as soon as Jeanie had pointed to the ruins. Whether he meant to aid Robertson's escape, or to assist his pursuers, may be very doubtful; perhaps he did not himself know, but had resolved to be guided by circumstances. He had no opportunity, however, of doing either; for he had no sooner surmounted the steep ascent, and entered under the broken arches of the ruins, than a pistol was presented at his head, and

a harsh voice commanded him, in the king's name, to
surrender himself prisoner. "Mr. Sharpitlaw!" said
Ratcliffe, surprised, "is this your honour?"

"Is it only you, and be d—d to you?" answered
the fiscal, still more disappointed—"what made you
leave the woman?"

"She told me she saw Robertson go into the ruins,
so I made what haste I could to cleek the callant."

"It's all over now," said Sharpitlaw; "we shall see
no more of him to-night; but he shall hide himself in
a bean-hool, if he remains on Scottish ground without
my finding him. Call back the people, Ratcliffe."

Ratcliffe hollowed to the dispersed officers, who
willingly obeyed the signal; for probably there was no
individual among them who would have been much
desirous of a rencontre hand to hand, and at a distance
from his comrades, with such an active and desperate
fellow as Robertson.

"And where are the two women?" said Sharpitlaw.

"Both made their heels serve them, I suspect,"
replied Ratcliffe, and he hummed the end of the old
song—

> Then hey play up the rin-awa bride,
> For she has taen the gee.

"One woman," said Sharpitlaw,—for, like all rogues,
he was a great calumniator of the fair sex,*—"one
woman is enough to dark the fairest ploy that was ever
planned; and how could I be such an ass as to expect
to carry through a job that had two in it? But we

* Note I. Calumniator of the Fair Sex.

know how to come by them both, if they are wanted,
that's one good thing."

Accordingly, like a defeated general, sad and sulky,
he led back his discomfited forces to the metropolis,
and dismissed them for the night.

The next morning early, he was under the necessity
of making his report to the sitting magistrate of the
day. The gentleman who occupied the chair of office
on this occasion (for the bailies, *Anglicè*, aldermen, take
it by rotation) chanced to be the same by whom Butler
was committed, a person very generally respected
among his fellow-citizens. Something he was of a
humourist, and rather deficient in general education;
but acute, patient, and upright, possessed of a fortune
acquired by honest industry, which made him perfectly
independent; and, in short, very happily qualified to
support the respectability of the office which he held.

Mr. Middleburgh had just taken his seat, and was
debating in an animated manner, with one of his
colleagues, the doubtful chances of a game at golf
which they had played the day before, when a letter
was delivered to him, addressed "For Bailie Middleburgh ; These : to be forwarded with speed." It contained these words :—

" SIR—I know you to be a sensible and a considerate
magistrate, and one who, as such, will be content to
worship God, though the devil bid you. I therefore
expect that, notwithstanding the signature of this letter
acknowledges my share in an action, which, in a proper

time and place, I would not fear either to avow or to justify, you will not on that account reject what evidence I place before you. The clergyman, Butler, is innocent of all but involuntary presence at an action which he wanted spirit to approve of, and from which he endeavoured, with his best set phrases, to dissuade us. But it was not for him that it is my hint to speak. There is a woman in your jail, fallen under the edge of a law so cruel, that it has hung by the wall, like unscoured armour, for twenty years, and is now brought down and whetted to spill the blood of the most beautiful and most innocent creature whom the walls of a prison ever girdled in. Her sister knows of her innocence, as she communicated to her that she was betrayed by a villain.—O that high Heaven

> Would put in every honest hand a whip,
> To scourge me such a villain through the world !

" I write distractedly—But this girl—this Jeanie Deans, is a peevish puritan, superstitious and scrupulous after the manner of her sect ; and I pray your honour, for so my phrase must go, to press upon her, that her sister's life depends upon her testimony. But though she should remain silent, do not dare to think that the young woman is guilty—far less to permit her execution. Remember the death of Wilson was fearfully avenged ; and those yet live who can compel you to drink the dregs of your poisoned chalice.—I say, remember Porteous,—and say that you had good counsel from

" ONE OF HIS SLAYERS."

The migistrate read over this extraordinary letter twice or thrice. At first he was tempted to throw it aside as the production of a madman, so little did " the scraps from playbooks," as he termed the poetical quotation, resemble the correspondence of a rational being. On a re-perusal, however, he thought that, amid its incoherence, he could discover something like a tone of awakened passion, though expressed in a manner quaint and unusual.

" It is a cruelly severe statute," said the magistrate to his assistant, " and I wish the girl could be taken from under the letter of it. A child may have been born, and it may have been conveyed away while the mother was insensible, or it may have perished for want of that relief which the poor creature herself— helpless, terrified, distracted, despairing, and exhausted —may have been unable to afford to it. And yet it is certain, if the woman is found guilty under the statute, execution will follow. The crime has been too common, and examples are necessary."

" But if this other wench," said the city-clerk, " can speak to her sister communicating her situation, it will take the case from under the statute."

" Very true," replied the Bailie; " and I will walk out one of these days to St. Leonard's, and examine the girl myself. I know something of their father Deans—an old true-blue Cameronian, who would see house and family go to wreck ere he would disgrace his testimony by a sinful complying with the defections of the times; and such he will probably uphold the taking an oath before a civil magistrate. If they are to go on and flourish with their bull-headed obstinacy, the legislature must pass an act to take their affirmations, as in the case of Quakers. But surely neither a father nor a sister will scruple in a case of this kind. As I said before, I will go speak with them myself, when the hurry of this Porteous investigation is somewhat over; their pride and spirit of contradiction will be far less alarmed, than if they were called into a court of justice at once."

"And I suppose Butler is to remain incarcerated?" said the city-clerk.

"For the present, certainly," said the magistrate. "But I hope soon to set him at liberty upon bail."

"Do you rest upon the testimony of that light-headed letter?" asked the clerk.

"Not very much," answered the Bailie; "and yet there is something striking about it too—it seems the letter of a man beside himself, either from great agitation, or some great sense of guilt."

"Yes," said the town-clerk, "it is very like the letter of a mad strolling play-actor, who deserves to be hanged with all the rest of his gang, as your honour justly observes."

"I was not quite so bloodthirsty," continued the magistrate. "But to the point. Butler's private character is excellent; and I am given to understand, by some inquiries I have been making this morning, that he did actually arrive in town only the day before yesterday, so that it was impossible he could have been

concerned in any previous machinations of these unhappy rioters, and it is not likely that he should have
joined them on a suddenty."

"There's no saying anent that—zeal catches fire at
a slight spark as fast as a brunstane match," observed
the secretary.   "I hae kend a minister wad be fair
gude day and fair gude e'en wi' ilka man in the
parochine, and hing just as quiet as a rocket on a stick,
till ye mentioned the word abjuration-oath, or patronage, or siclike, and then, whiz, he was off, and up in
the air an hundred miles beyond common manners,
common sense, and common comprehension."

"I do not understand," answered the burgher-
magistrate, "that the young man Butler's zeal is of so
inflammable a character.   But I will make farther
investigation.   What other business is there before
us?"

And they proceeded to minute investigations concerning the affair of Porteous's death, and other affairs
through which this history has no occasion to trace
them.

In the course of their business they were interrupted
by an old woman of the lower rank, extremely haggard
in look, and wretched in her appearance, who thrust
herself into the council room.

"What do you want, gudewife?—Who are you?"
said Bailie Middleburgh.

"What do I want!" replied she, in a sulky tone—
"I want my bairn, or I want naething frae nane o' ye,
for as grand's ye are."   And she went on muttering to

herself, with the wayward spitefulness of age—"They
maun hae lordships and honours, nae doubt—set them
up, the gutter-bloods! and deil a gentleman amang
them."—Then again, addressing the sitting magistrate,
"Will *your honour* gie me back my puir crazy bairn?—
His honour!—I hae kend the day when less wad ser'd
him, the oe of a Campvere skipper."

"Good woman," said the magistrate to this shrewish
supplicant,—"tell us what it is you want, and do not
interrupt the court."

"That's as muckle as till say, Bark, Bawtie, and be
dune wi't!—I tell ye," raising her termagant voice, "I
want my bairn! is na that braid Scots?"

"Who *are* you?—who is your bairn?" demanded
the magistrate.

"Wha am I?—wha suld I be, but Meg Murdockson,
and wha suld my bairn be but Magdalen Murdockson?
—Your guard soldiers, and your constables, and your
officers, ken us weel enough when they rive the bits o'
duds aff our backs, and take what penny o' siller we
hae, and harle us to the Correction-house in Leith
Wynd, and pettle us up wi' bread and water, and siclike
sunkets."

"Who is she?" said the magistrate, looking round
to some of his people.

"Other than a gude ane, sir," said one of the city-
officers, shrugging his shoulders, and smiling.

"Will ye say sae?" said the termagant, her eye
gleaming with impotent fury; "an I had ye amang the
Frigate-Whins, wadna I set my ten talents in your

wuzzent face for that very word?" and she suited the word to the action, by spreading out a set of claws resembling those of St. George's dragon on a country sign-post.

"What does she want here?" said the impatient magistrate—"Can she not tell her business, or go away?"

"It's my bairn!—it's Magdalen Murdockson I'm wantin'," answered the beldame, screaming at the highest pitch of her cracked and mistuned voice—"havena I been tellin' ye sae this half-hour? And if ye are deaf, what needs ye sit cockit up there, and keep folk scraughin' t'ye this gate?"

"She wants her daughter, sir," said the same officer whose interference had given the hag such offence before—"her daughter, who was taken up last night—Madge Wildfire, as they ca' her."

"Madge HELLFIRE, as they ca' her!" echoed the beldame; "and what business has a blackguard like you to ca' an honest woman's bairn out o' her ain name!"

"An *honest* woman's bairn, Maggie?" answered the peace-officer, smiling and shaking his head with an ironical emphasis on the adjective, and a calmness calculated to provoke to madness the furious old shrew.

"If I am no honest now, I was honest ance," she replied; "and that's mair than ye can say, ye born and bred thief, that never ken'd ither folk's gear frae your ain since the day ye was cleckit. Honest, say ye?—ye pykit your mother's pouch o' twalpennies Scotch when

ye were five years auld, just as she was taking leave o'
your father at the fit o' the gallows."

"She has you there, George," said the assistants,
and there was a general laugh; for the wit was fitted
for the meridian of the place where it was uttered.
This general applause somewhat gratified the passions
of the old hag; the "grim feature" smiled, and even
laughed—but it was a laugh of bitter scorn. She
condescended, however, as if appeased by the success of
her sally, to explain her business more distinctly, when
the magistrate, commanding silence, again desired her
either to speak out her errand, or to leave the place.

"Her bairn," she said, "was her bairn, and she came
to fetch her out of ill haft and waur guiding. If she
wasna sae wise as ither folk, few ither folk had suffered
as muckle as she had done; forby that she could fend
the waur for hersell within the four wa's of a jail. She
could prove by fifty witnesses, and fifty to that, that
her daughter had never seen Jock Porteous, alive or
dead, since he had gien her a loundering wi' his cane,
the neger that he was! for driving a dead cat at the
provost's wig on the Elector of Hanover's birth-day."

Notwithstanding the wretched appearance and violent demeanour of this woman, the magistrate felt the
justice of her argument, that her child might be as dear
to her as to a more fortunate and more amiable mother.
He proceeded to investigate the circumstances which
had led to Madge Murdockson's (or Wildfire's) arrest,
and as it was clearly shown that she had not been
engaged in the riot, he contented himself with directing

that an eye should be kept upon her by the police, but
that for the present she should be allowed to return
home with her mother. During the interval of fetching
Madge from the jail, the magistrate endeavoured to
discover whether her mother had been privy to the
change of dress betwixt that young woman and Robertson. But on this point he could obtain no light. She
persisted in declaring, that she had never seen Robertson since his remarkable escape during service-time;
and that, if her daughter had changed clothes with
him, it must have been during her absence at a hamlet
about two miles out of town, called Duddingstone,
where she could prove that she passed that eventful
night. And, in fact, one of the town-officers, who had
been searching for stolen linen at the cottage of a
washerwoman in that village, gave his evidence, that
he had seen Maggie Murdockson there, whose presence
had considerably increased his suspicion of the house in
which she was a visitor, in respect that he considered
her as a person of no good reputation.

"I tauld ye sae," said the hag; "see now what it is
to hae a character, gude or bad!—Now, maybe after a',
I could tell ye something about Porteous that you
council-chamber bodies never could find out, for as
muckle stir as ye mak."

All eyes were turned towards her—all ears were
alert. "Speak out!" said the magistrate.

"It will be for your ain gude," insinuated the
town-clerk.

"Dinna keep the Bailie waiting," urged the assistants.

She remained doggedly silent for two or three minutes, casting around a malignant and sulky glance, that seemed to enjoy the anxious suspense with which they waited her answer. And then she broke forth at once,—"A' that I ken about him is, that he was neither soldier nor gentleman, but just a thief and a blackguard, like maist o' yoursells, dears—What will ye gie me for that news, now?—He wad hae served the gude town lang or provost or bailie wad hae fund that out, my joe!"

While these matters were in discussion, Madge Wildfire entered, and her first exclamation was "Eh! see if there isna our auld ne'er-do-weel deovil's buckie o' a mither—Heigh, sirs! but we are a hopefu' family, to be twa o' us in the Guard at ance—But there were better days wi' us ance—were there no, mither?"

Old Maggie's eyes had glistened with something like an expression of pleasure when she saw her daughter set at liberty. But either her natural affection, like that of the tigress, could not be displayed without a strain of ferocity, or there was something in the ideas which Madge's speech awakened, that again stirred her cross and savage temper. "What signifies what we were, ye street-raking limmer!" she exclaimed, pushing her daughter before her to the door, with no gentle degree of violence. "I'se tell thee what thou is now— thou's a crazed hellicat Bess o' Bedlam, that sall taste naething but bread and water for a fortnight, to serve ye for the plague ye hae gien me—and ower gude for ye, ye idle taupie!"

Madge, however, escaped from her mother at the door, ran back to the foot of the table, dropped a very low and fantastic courtesy to the judge, and said, with a giggling laugh,—"Our minnie's sair mis-set, after her ordinar, sir—She'll hae had some quarrel wi' her auld gudeman—that's Satan, ye ken, sirs." This explanatory note she gave in a low confidential tone, and the spectators of that credulous generation did not hear it without an involuntary shudder. "The gudeman and her disna aye gree weel, and then I maun pay the piper; but my back's broad eneugh to bear't a'—an' if she hae nae havings, that's nae reason why wiser folk shouldna hae some." Here another deep courtesy, when the ungracious voice of her mother was heard.

"Madge, ye limmer! If I come to fetch ye!"

"Hear till her," said Madge. "But I'll wun out a gliff the night for a' that, to dance in the moonlight, when her and the gudeman will be whirrying through the blue lift on a broom-shank, to see Jean Jap, that they hae putten intill the Kirkcaldy Tolbooth—ay, they will hae a merry sail ower Inchkeith, and ower a' the bits o' bonny waves that are poppling and plashing against the rocks in the gowden glimmer o' the moon, ye ken.—I'm coming, mother—I'm coming," she concluded, on hearing a scuffle at the door betwixt the beldam and the officers, who were endeavouring to prevent her re-entrance. Madge then waved her hand wildly towards the ceiling, and sung, at the topmost pitch of her voice,—

> " Up in the air,
>   On my bonny grey mare,
>   And I see, and I see, and I see her yet;"

And with a hop, skip, and jump, sprung out of the
room, as the witches of Macbeth used, in less refined
days, to seem to fly upwards from the stage.

Some weeks intervened before Mr. Middleburgh,
agreeably to his benevolent resolution, found an opportunity of taking a walk towards St. Leonard's, in order
to discover whether it might be possible to obtain the
evidence hinted at in the anonymous letter respecting
Effie Deans.

In fact, the anxious perquisitions made to discover
the murderers of Porteous occupied the attention of all
concerned with the administration of justice.

In the course of these inquiries, two circumstances
happened material to our story. Butler, after a close
investigation of his conduct, was declared innocent of
accession to the death of Porteous ; but, as having been
present during the whole transaction, was obliged to
find bail not to quit his usual residence at Liberton,
that he might appear as a witness when called upon.
The other incident regarded the disappearance of Madge
Wildfire and her mother from Edinburgh. When they
were sought, with the purpose of subjecting them to
some further interrogatories, it was discovered by Mr.
Sharpitlaw that they had eluded the observation of the
police, and left the city so soon as dismissed from the
council-chamber. No efforts could trace the place of
their retreat.

In the meanwhile the excessive indignation of the Council of Regency, at the slight put upon their authority by the murder of Porteous, had dictated measures, in which their own extreme desire of detecting the actors in that conspiracy were consulted, in preference to the temper of the people, and the character of their churchmen. An act of Parliament was hastily passed, offering two hundred pounds reward to those who should inform against any person concerned in the deed, and the penalty of death, by a very unusual and severe enactment, was denounced against those who should harbour the guilty. But what was chiefly accounted exceptionable, was a clause, appointing the act to be read in churches by the officiating clergyman, on the first Sunday of every month, for a certain period, immediately before the sermon. The ministers who should refuse to comply with this injunction were declared, for the first offence, incapable of sitting or voting in any church judicature, and for the second, incapable of holding any ecclesiastical preferment in Scotland.

This last order united in a common cause those who might privately rejoice in Porteous's death, though they dared not vindicate the manner of it, with the more scrupulous presbyterians, who held that even the pronouncing the name of the "Lords Spiritual" in a Scottish pulpit was, *quodammodo*, an acknowledgment of prelacy, and that the injunction of the legislature was an interference of the civil government with the *jus divinum* of presbytery, since to the General Assembly alone, as representing the invisible head of the kirk, belonged the sole and exclusive right of regulating whatever pertained to public worship.   Very many also, of different political or religious sentiments, and therefore not much moved by these considerations, thought they saw, in so violent an act of parliament, a more vindictive spirit than became the legislature of a great country, and something like an attempt to trample upon the rights and independence of Scotland.   The various steps adopted for punishing the city of Edinburgh, by taking away her charter and liberties, for what a violent and overmastering mob had done within her walls, were resented by many, who thought a pretext was too hastily taken for degrading the ancient metropolis of Scotland.   In short, there was much heart-burning, discontent, and disaffection, occasioned by these ill-considered measures.*

Amidst these heats and dissensions, the trial of Effie Deans, after she had been many weeks imprisoned, was at length about to be brought forward, and Mr. Middleburgh found leisure to inquire into the evidence concerning her.   For this purpose, he chose a fine day for his walk towards her father's house.

* The Magistrates were closely interrogated before the House of Peers concerning the particulars of the Porteous Mob, and the *patois* in which these functionaries made their answers, sounded strange in the ears of the Southern nobles.   The Duke of Newcastle having demanded to know with what kind of shot the guard which Porteous commanded had loaded their muskets, was answered naïvely, "Ow, just sic as ane shoots *dukes and fools* with."   This reply was considered as a contempt of the House of Lords, and the Provost would have suffered accordingly, but that the Duke of Argyle explained, that the expression, properly rendered into English, meant *ducks and water fowl*.

The excursion into the country was somewhat distant, in the opinion of a burgess of those days, although many of the present inhabit suburban villas considerably beyond the spot to which we allude.   Three quarters of an hour's walk, however, even at a pace of magisterial gravity, conducted our benevolent office-bearer to the Crags of St. Leonard's and the humble mansion of David Deans.

The old man was seated on the deas, or turf-seat, at the end of his cottage, busied in mending his cart-harness with his own hands; for in those days any sort of labour which required a little more skill than usual fell to the share of the goodman himself, and that even when he was well to pass in the world.   With stern and austere gravity he persevered in his task, after having just raised his head to notice the advance of the stranger.   It would have been impossible to have discovered, from his countenance and manner, the internal feelings of agony with which he contended. Mr. Middleburgh waited an instant, expecting Deans would in some measure acknowledge his presence, and lead into conversation; but, as he seemed determined to remain silent, he was himself obliged to speak first.

"My name is Middleburgh—Mr. James Middleburgh, one of the present magistrates of the city of Edinburgh."

"It may be sae," answered Deans laconically, and without interrupting his labour.

"You must understand," he continued, "that the duty of a magistrate is sometimes an unpleasant one."

"It may be sae," replied David ; "I hae naething to say in the contrair;" and he was again doggedly silent.

"You must be aware," pursued the magistrate, "that persons in my situation are often obliged to make painful and disagreeable inquiries of individuals, merely because it is their bounden duty."

"It may be sae," again replied Deans ; "I hae naething to say anent it, either the tae way or the t'other. But I do ken there was ance in a day a just and God-fearing magistracy in yon town o' Edinburgh, that did not bear the sword in vain, but were a terror to evil-doers, and a praise to such as kept the path. In the glorious days of auld worthy faithfu' Provost Dick,[*] when there was a true and faithfu' General Assembly of the Kirk, walking hand in hand with the real noble Scottish-hearted barons, and with the magistrates of this and other towns, gentles, burgesses, and commons of all ranks, seeing with one eye, hearing with one ear, and upholding the ark with their united strength — And then folk might see men deliver up their silver to the states' use, as if it had been as muckle sclate stanes. My father saw them toom the sacks of dollars out o' Provost Dick's window intill the carts that carried them to the army at Dunse Law ; and if ye winna believe his testimony, there is the window itsell still standing in the Luckenbooths — I think it's a claith-merchant's booth the day [†] — at the airn stanchells, five doors abune

---

* Note J. Sir William Dick of Braid.

† I think so too—But if the reader be curious, he may consult Mr. Chambers' Traditions of Edinburgh.

Gossford's Close.—But now we haena sic spirit amang us; we think mair about the warst wally-draigle in our ain byre, than about the blessing which the angel of the covenant gave to the Patriarch even at Peniel and Mahanaim, or the binding obligation of our national vows; and we wad rather gie a pund Scots to buy an unguent to clear our auld rannell-trees and our beds o' the English bugs as they ca' them, than we wad gie a plack to rid the land of the swarm of Arminian cater-pillars, Socinian pismires, and deistical Miss Katies, that have ascended out of the bottomless pit, to plague this perverse, insidious, and lukewarm generation."

It happened to Davie Deans on this occasion as it has done to many other habitual orators; when once he became embarked on his favourite subject, the stream of his own enthusiasm carried him forward in spite of his mental distress, while his well exercised memory supplied him amply will all the types and tropes of rhetoric peculiar to his sect and cause.

Mr. Middleburgh contented himself with answering —"All this may be very true, my friend; but, as you said just now, I have nothing to say to it at present either one way or other.—You have two daughters, I think, Mr. Deans?"

The old man winced, as one whose smarting sore is suddenly galled; but instantly composed himself, re-sumed the work which, in the heat of his declamation, he had laid down, and answered with sullen resolution, " Ae daughter, sir—only *ane*."

" I understand you," said Mr. Middleburgh; " you

have only one daughter here at home with you—but this unfortunate girl who is a prisoner—she is, I think, your youngest daughter?"

The presbyterian sternly raised his eyes. "After the world, and according to the flesh, she *is* my daughter; but when she became a child of Belial, and a company-keeper, and a trader in guilt and iniquity, she ceased to be a bairn of mine."

"Alas, Mr. Deans," said Middleburgh, sitting down by him, and endeavouring to take his hand, which the old man proudly withdrew, "we are ourselves all sinners; and the errors of our offspring, as they ought not to surprise us, being the portion which they derive of a common portion of corruption inherited through us, so they do not entitle us to cast them off because they have lost themselves."

"Sir," said Deans, impatiently, "I ken a' that as weel as—I mean to say," he resumed, checking the irritation he felt at being schooled,—a discipline of the mind, which those most ready to bestow it on others, do themselves most reluctantly submit to receive—"I mean to say, that what ye observe may be just and reasonable—But I hae nae freedom to enter into my ain private affairs wi' strangers—And now, in this great national emergency, when there's the Porteous' Act has come doun frae London, that is a deeper blow to this poor sinfu' kingdom and suffering kirk, than ony that has been heard of since the foul and fatal Test—at a time like this——"

"But goodman," interrupted Mr. Middleburgh,

"you must think of your own household first, or else you are worse even than the infidels."

"I tell ye, Bailie Middleburgh," retorted David Deans, "if ye be a bailie, as there is little honour in being one in these evil days—I tell ye, I heard the gracious Saunders Peden—I wotna whan it was; but it was in killing time when the plowers were drawing alang their furrows on the back of the Kirk of Scotland—I heard him tell his hearers, gude and waled Christians they were too, that some o' them wad greet mair for a bit drowned calf or stirk, than for a' the defections and oppressions of the day; and that they were some o' them thinking o' ae thing, some o' anither, and there was Lady Hundleslope thinking o' greeting Jock at the fireside! And the lady confessed in my hearing, that a drow of anxiety had come ower her for her son that she had left at hame weak of a decay*— And what wad he hae said of me, if I had ceased to think of tho gude cause for a cast-away—a—It kills me to think of what she is?"

"But the life of your child, goodman—think of that—if her life could be saved," said Middleburgh.

"Her life!" exclaimed David—"I wadna gie ane o' my grey hairs for her life, if her gude name be gane— And yet," said he, relenting and retracting as he spoke, "I wad make the niffer, Mr. Middleburgh—I wad gie a' these grey hairs that she has brought to shame and sorrow—I wad gie the auld head they grow on for her life, and that she might hae time to amend and return,

* See Life of Peden, p. 111.

for what hae the wicked beyond the breath of their
nosthrils?—But I'll never see her mair.—No!—that—
that I am determined in—I'll never see her mair!"
His lips continued to move for a minute after his voice
ceased to be heard, as if he were repeating the same vow
internally.

"Well, sir," said Mr. Middleburgh, "I speak to you
as a man of sense; if you would save your daughter's
life, you must use human means."

"I understand what you mean; but Mr. Novit, who
is the procurator and doer of an honourable person, the
Laird of Dumbiedikes, is to do what carnal wisdom can
do for her in the circumstances. Mysell am not clear
to trinquet and traffic wi' courts o' justice, as they are
now constituted; I have a tenderness and scruple in my
mind anent them."

"That is to say," said Middleburgh, "that you are a
Cameronian, and do not acknowledge the authority of
our courts of judicature, or present government?"

"Sir, under your favour," replied David, who was
too proud of his own polemical knowledge, to call himself the follower of any one, "ye take me up before I
fall down. I canna see why I suld be termed a Cameronian, especially now that ye hae given the name of
that famous and savoury sufferer, not only until a
regimental band of souldiers, whereof I am told many
can now curse, swear, and use profane language, as fast
as ever Richard Cameron could preach or pray; but also
because ye have, in as far as it is in your power, rendered that martyr's name vain and contemptible, by

pipes, drums, and fifes, playing the vain carnal spring, called the Cameronian Rant, which too many professors of religion dance to—a practice maist unbecoming a professor to dance to any tune whatsoever, more especially promiscuously, that is, with the female sex.* A brutish fashion it is, whilk is the beginning of defection with many, as I may hae as muckle cause as maist folk to testify."

"Well, but, Mr. Deans," replied Mr. Middleburgh, "I only meant to say that you were a Cameronian, or MacMillanite, one of the society people, in short, who think it inconsistent to take oaths under a government where the Covenant is not ratified."

"Sir," replied the controversialist, who forgot even his present distress in such discussions as these, "you cannot fickle me sae easily as you do opine. I am *not* a MacMillanite, or a Russelite, or a Hamiltonian, or a Harleyite, or a Howdenite †—I will be led by the nose by none—I take my name as a Christian from no vessel of clay. I have my own principles and practice to answer for, and am an humble pleader for the gude auld cause in a legal way."

"That is to say, Mr. Deans," said Middleburgh, "that you are a *Deanite*, and have opinions peculiar to yourself."

"It may please you to say sae," said David Deans; "but I have maintained my testimony before as great folk, and in sharper times; and though I will neither

* See Note C. Peter Walker.
† All various species of the great genus Cameronian.

exalt myself nor pull down others, I wish every man
and woman in this land had kept the true testimony,
and the middle and straight path, as it were, on the
ridge of a hill, where wind and water shears, avoiding
right-hand snares ,and extremes, and left-hand way-
slidings, as weel as Johnny Dodds of Farthing's Acre,
and ae man mair that shall be nameless."

"I suppose," replied the magistrate, "that is as
much as to say, that Johnny Dodds of Farthing's Acre,
and David Deans of St. Leonard's, constitute the only
members of the true, real, unsophisticated Kirk of
Scotland ?"

"God forbid that I suld make sic a vain-glorious
speech, when there are sae mony professing Christians !"
answered David ; "but this I maun say, that all men
act according to their gifts and their grace, sae that it is
nae marvel that——"

"This is all very fine," interrupted Mr. Middleburgh ; "but I have no time to spend in hearing it.
The matter in hand is this—I have directed a citation
to be lodged in your daughter's hands—If she appears
on the day of trial and gives evidence, there is reason
to hope she may save her sister's life—if, from any constrained scruples about the legality of her performing
the office of an affectionate sister and a good subject, by
appearing in a court held under the authority of the
law and government, you become the means of deter-
ring her from the discharge of this duty, I must say,
though the truth may sound harsh in your ears, that
you, who gave life to this unhappy girl, will become

the means of her losing it by a premature and violent death."

So saying, Mr. Middleburgh turned to leave him.

"Bide awee—bide awee, Mr. Middleburgh," said Deans, in great perplexity and distress of mind; but the Bailie, who was probably sensible that protracted discussion might diminish the effect of his best and most forcible argument, took a hasty leave, and declined entering farther into the controversy.

Deans sunk down upon his seat, stunned with a variety of conflicting emotions. It had been a great source of controversy among those holding his opinions in religious matters, how far the government which succeeded the Revolution could be, without sin, acknowledged by true presbyterians, seeing that it did not recognise the great national testimony of the Solemn League and Covenant? And latterly, those agreeing in this general doctrine, and assuming the sounding title of the anti-popish, anti-prelatic, anti-erastian, anti-sectarian, true presbyterian remnant, were divided into many petty sects among themselves, even as to the extent of submission to the existing laws and rulers, which constituted such an acknowledgment as amounted to sin.

At a very stormy and tumultuous meeting, held in 1682, to discuss these important and delicate points, the testimonies of the faithful few were found utterly inconsistent with each other.* The place where this conference took place was remarkably well adapted for

* Note K. Meeting at Talla-Linns.

such an assembly. It was a wild and very sequestered
dell in Tweeddale, surrounded by high hills, and far
remote from human habitation. A small river, or
rather a mountain torrent, called the Talla, breaks down
the glen with great fury, dashing successively over a
number of small cascades, which has procured the spot
the name of Talla-Linna. Here the leaders among the
scattered adherents to the Covenant, men who, in their
banishment from human society, and in the recollection
of the soverities to which they had been exposed, had
become at once sullen in their tempers, and fantastic in
their religious opinions, met with arms in their hands,
and by the side of the torrent discussed, with a turbu-
lence which the noise of the stream could not drown,
points of controversy as empty and unsubstantial as its
foam.

It was the fixed judgment of most of the meeting,
that all payment of cess or tribute to the existing
government was utterly unlawful, and a sacrificing to
idols. About other impositions and degrees of submission there were various opinions; and perhaps it is the
best illustration of the spirit of those military fathers
of the church to say, that while all allowed it was
impious to pay the cess employed for maintaining the
standing army and militia, there was a fierce controversy
on the lawfulness of paying the duties levied at ports
and bridges, for maintaining roads and other necessary
purposes; that there were some who, repugnant to
these imposts for turnpikes and pontages, were nevertheless free in conscience to make payment of the usual

freight at public ferries, and that a person of exceeding
and punctilious zeal, James Russel, one of the slayers of
the Archbishop of St. Andrews, had given his testimony
with great warmth even against this last faint shade of
subjection to constituted authority. This ardent and
enlightened person and his followers had also great
scruples about the lawfulness of bestowing the ordinary
names upon the days of the week and the months of
the year, which savoured in their nostrils so strongly of
paganism, that at length they arrived at the conclusion
that they who owned such names as Monday, Tuesday,
January, February, and so forth, " served themselves
heirs to the same, if not greater punishment than had
been denounced against the idolaters of old."

David Deans had been present on this memorable
occasion, although too young to be a speaker among
the polemical combatants. His brain, however, had
been thoroughly heated by the noise, clamour, and
metaphysical ingenuity of the discussion, and it was a
controversy to which his mind had often returned; and
though he carefully disguised his vacillation from others,
and perhaps from himself, he had never been able to
come to any precise line of decision on the subject. In
fact, his natural sense had acted as a counterpoise to his
controversial zeal. He was by no means pleased with
the quiet and indifferent manner in which King
William's government slurred over the errors of the
times, when, far from restoring the presbyterian kirk to
its former supremacy, they passed an act of oblivion
even to those who had been its persecutors, and

bestowed on many of them titles, favours, and employments.   When, in the first General Assembly which
succeeded the Revolution, an overture was made for
the revival of the League and Covenant, it was with
horror that Douce David heard the proposal eluded by
the men of carnal wit and policy, as he called them, as
being inapplicable to the present times, and not falling
under the modern model of the church. The reign of
Queen Anne had increased his conviction, that the
Revolution government was not one of the true presbyterian complexion. But then, more sensible than the
bigots of his sect, he did not confound the moderation
and tolerance of these two reigns with the active
tyranny and oppression exercised in those of Charles
II. and James II. The presbyterian form of religion,
though deprived of the weight formerly attached to its
sentences of excommunication, and compelled to tolerate
the co-existence of episcopacy, and of sects of various
descriptions, was still the National Church; and though
the glory of the second temple was far inferior to that
which had flourished from 1639 till the battle of
Dunbar, still it was a structure that, wanting the
strength and the terrors, retained at least the form and
symmetry, of the original model.   Then came the
insurrection in 1715, and David Deans's horror for the
revival of the popish and prelatical faction reconciled
him greatly to the government of King George, although
he grieved that that monarch might be suspected of a
leaning unto Erastianism.   In short, moved by so many
different considerations, he had shifted his ground at

different times concerning the degree of freedom which
he felt in adopting any act of immediate acknowledgment or submission to the present government, which,
however mild and paternal, was still uncovenanted ;
and now he felt himself called upon by the most
powerful motive conceivable, to authorize his daughter's
giving testimony in a court of justice, which all who
have been since called Cameronians accounted a step of
lamentable and direct defection. The voice of nature,
however, exclaimed loud in his bosom against the
dictates of fanaticism ; and his imagination, fertile
in the solution of polemical difficulties, devised an
expedient for extricating himself from the fearful
dilemma, in which he saw, on the one side, a falling off
from principle, and, on the other, a scene from which
a father's thoughts could not but turn in shuddering
horror.

"I have been constant and unchanged in my testimony," said David Deans ; "but then who has said it
of me, that I have judged my neighbour over closely,·
because he hath had more freedom in his walk than I
have found in mine ? I never was a separatist, nor for
quarrelling with tender souls about mint, cummin, or
other the lesser tithes. My daughter Jean may have a
light in this subject that is hid frae my auld een—it is
laid on her conscience, and not on mine—If she hath
freedom to gang before this judicatory, and hold up her
hand for this poor cast-away, surely I will not say she
steppeth over her bounds ; and if not"——He paused
in his mental argument, while a pang of unutterable

anguish convulsed his features, yet, shaking it off, he firmly resumed the strain of his reasoning—"And IF NOT—God forbid that she should go into defection at bidding of mine! I wunna fret the tender conscience of one bairn—no, not to save the life of the other."

A Roman would have devoted his daughter to death from different feelings and motives, but not upon a more heroic principle of duty.

CHAPTER THE NINETEENTH.

To man, in this his trial state,
    The privilege is given,
When tost by tides of human fate,
    To anchor fast on heaven.
                    WATTS's *Hymns.*

IT was with a firm step that Deans sought his daughter's apartment, determined to leave her to the light of her own conscience in the dubious point of casuistry in which he supposed her to be placed.

The little room had been the sleeping apartment of both sisters, and there still stood there a small occasional bed which had been made for Effie's accommodation, when, complaining of illness, she had declined to share, as in happier times, her sister's pillow. The eyes of Deans rested involuntarily, on entering the room, upon this little couch, with its dark-green coarse curtains, and the ideas connected with it rose so thick upon his soul as almost to incapacitate him from opening his errand to his daughter. Her occupation broke the ice. He found her gazing on a slip of paper, which contained a citation to her to appear as a witness upon her sister's trial in behalf of the accused. For the worthy magistrate, determined to omit no chance of doing Effie

justice, and to leave her sister no apology for not giving
the evidence which she was supposed to possess, had
caused the ordinary citation, or *subpœna*, of the Scottish
criminal court, to be served upon her by an officer
during his conference with David.

This precaution was so far favourable to Deans, that
it saved him the pain of entering upon a formal explanation with his daughter; he only said, with a hollow
and tremulous voice, "I perceive ye are aware of the
matter."

"O father, we are cruelly sted between God's laws
and man's laws—What shall we do?—What can we
do?"

Jeanie, it must be observed, had no hesitation
whatever about the mere act of appearing in a court of
justice. She might have heard the point discussed by
her father more than once; but we have already noticed,
that she was accustomed to listen with reverence to
much which she was incapable of understanding, and
that subtle arguments of casuistry found her a patient,
but unedified hearer. Upon receiving the citation,
therefore, her thoughts did not turn upon the chimerical
scruples which alarmed her father's mind, but to the
language which had been held to her by the stranger
at Muschat's Cairn. In a word, she never doubted
but she was to be dragged forward into the court of
justice, in order to place her in the cruel position of
either sacrificing her sister by telling the truth, or
committing perjury in order to save her life. And so
strongly did her thoughts run in this channel, that she

applied her father's words, " Ye are aware of the matter,"
to his acquaintance with the advice that had been so
fearfully enforced upon her. She looked up with
anxious surprise, not unmingled with a cast of horror,
which his next words, as she interpreted and applied
them, were not qualified to remove.

"Daughter," said David, "it has ever been my
mind, that in things of ane doubtful and controversial
nature, ilk Christian's conscience suld be his ain guide
—Wherefore descend into yourself, try your ain mind
with sufficiency of soul exercise, and as you sall finally
find yourself clear to do in this matter—even so be it."

"But, father," said Jeanie, whose mind revolted
at the construction which she naturally put upon his
language, " can this—THIS be a doubtful or controversial
matter?—Mind, father, the ninth command—' Thou
shalt not bear false witness against thy neighbour.'"

David Deans paused ; for, still applying her speech
to his preconceived difficulties, it seemed to him, as if
she, a woman, and a sister, was scarce entitled to be
scrupulous upon this occasion, where *he*, a man, exercised
in the testimonies of that testifying period, had given
indirect countenance to her following what must have
been the natural dictates of her own feelings. But he
kept firm his purpose, until his eyes involuntarily
rested upon the little settle-bed, and recalled the form
of the child of his old age, as she sate upon it, pale,
emaciated, and broken-hearted. His mind, as the
picture arose before him, involuntarily conceived, and
his tongue involuntarily uttered—but in a tone how

different from his usual dogmatical precision!—arguments for the course of conduct likely to ensure his child's safety.

"Daughter," he said, "I did not say that your path was free from stumbling—and, questionless, this act may be in the opinion of some a transgression, since he who beareth witness unlawfully, and against his conscience, doth in some sort bear false witness against his neighbour. Yet in matters of compliance, the guilt lieth not in the compliance sae muckle, as in the mind and conscience of him that doth comply; and, therefore, although my testimony hath not been spared upon public defections, I haena felt freedom to separate mysell from the communion of many who have been clear to hear those ministers who have taken the fatal indulgence, because they might get good of them, though I could not."

When David had proceeded thus far, his conscience reproved him, that he might be indirectly undermining the purity of his daughter's faith, and smoothing the way for her falling off from strictness of principle. He, therefore, suddenly stopped, and changed his tone:—"Jeanie, I perceive that our vile affections,—so I call them in respect of doing the will of our Father,—cling too heavily to me in this hour of trying sorrow, to permit me to keep sight of my ain duty, or to airt you to yours. I will speak nae mair anent this over-trying matter.—Jeanie, if ye can, wi' God and gude conscience, speak in favour of this puir unhappy"—(here his voice faltered)—"She is your sister in the flesh—worthless

and cast-away as she is, she is the daughter of a saint
in heaven, that was a mother to you, Jeanie, in place
of your ain—but if ye arena free in conscience to speak
for her in the court of judicature, follow your conscience,
Jeanie, and let God's will be done." After this adjuration he left the apartment, and his daughter remained
in a state of great distress and perplexity.

It would have been no small addition to the sorrows
of David Deans, even in this extremity of suffering,
had he known that his daughter was applying the
casuistical arguments which he had been using, not in
the sense of a permission to follow her own opinion on
a dubious and disputed point of controversy, but rather
as an encouragement to transgress one of those divine
commandments which Christians of all sects and de-
nominations unite in holding most sacred.

"Can this be?" said Jeanie, as the door closed on
her father—" Can these be his words that I have heard,
or has the Enemy taken his voice and features to give
weight unto the counsel which causeth to perish?— A
sister's life, and a father pointing out how to save it!—
O God deliver me!—this is a fearfu' temptation."

Roaming from thought to thought she at one time
imagined her father understood the ninth command-
ment literally, as prohibiting false witness *against* our
neighbour, without extending the denunciation against
falsehood uttered *in favour* of the criminal. But her
clear and unsophisticated power of discriminating between good and evil, instantly rejected an interpretation
so limited, and so unworthy of the Author of the law.

She remained in a state of the most agitating terror and uncertainty—afraid to communicate her thoughts freely to her father, lest she should draw forth an opinion with which she could not comply,—wrung with distress on her sister's account, rendered the more acute by reflecting that the means of saving her were in her power, but were such as her conscience prohibited her from using,—tossed, in short, like a vessel in an open roadstead during a storm, and, like that vessel, resting on one only sure cable and anchor,—faith in Providence, and a resolution to discharge her duty.

Butler's affection and strong sense of religion would have been her principal support in these distressing circumstances, but he was still under restraint, which did not permit him to come to St. Leonard's Crags; and her distresses were of a nature, which, with her indifferent habits of scholarship, she found it impossible to express in writing. She was therefore compelled to trust for guidance to her own unassisted sense of what was right or wrong.

It was not the least of Jeanie's distresses, that, although she hoped and believed her sister to be innocent, she had not the means of receiving that assurance from her own mouth.

The double-dealing of Ratcliffe in the matter of Robertson had not prevented his being rewarded, as double-dealers frequently have been, with favour and preferment. Sharpitlaw, who found in him something of a kindred genius, had been intercessor in his behalf with the magistrates, and the circumstance of his having voluntarily remained in the prison, when the doors were forced by the mob, would have made it a hard measure to take the life which he had such easy means of saving. He received a full pardon; and soon afterwards, James Ratcliffe, the greatest thief and housebreaker in Scotland, was, upon the faith, perhaps, of an ancient proverb, selected as a person to be intrusted with the custody of other delinquents.

When Ratcliffe was thus placed in a confidential situation, he was repeatedly applied to by the sapient Saddletree and others, who took some interest in the Deans' family, to procure an interview between the sisters; but the magistrates, who were extremely anxious for the apprehension of Robertson, had given strict orders to the contrary, hoping that, by keeping them separate, they might, from the one or the other, extract some information respecting that fugitive. On this subject Jeanie had nothing to tell them. She informed Mr. Middleburgh, that she knew nothing of Robertson, except having met him that night by appointment to give her some advice respecting her sister's concern, the purport of which, she said, was betwixt God and her conscience. Of his motions, purposes, or plans, past, present, or future, she knew nothing, and so had nothing to communicate.

Effie was equally silent, though from a different cause. It was in vain that they offered a commutation and alleviation of her punishment, and even a free pardon, if she would confess what she knew of her lover. She answered only with tears; unless, when at times driven into pettish sulkiness by the persecution of the interrogators, she made them abrupt and disrespectful answers.

At length, after her trial had been delayed for many weeks, in hopes she might be induced to speak out on a subject infinitely more interesting to the magistracy than her own guilt or innocence, their patience was worn out, and even Mr. Middleburgh finding no ear lent to further intercession in her behalf, the day was fixed for the trial to proceed.

It was now, and not sooner, that Sharpitlaw, recollecting his promise to Effie Deans, or rather being dinned into compliance by the unceasing remonstrances of Mrs. Saddletree, who was his next-door neighbour, and who declared it was heathen cruelty to keep the twa broken-hearted creatures separate, issued the important mandate, permitting them to see each other.

On the evening which preceded the eventful day of trial, Jeanie was permitted to see her sister—an awful interview, and occurring at a most distressing crisis. This, however, formed a part of the bitter cup which she was doomed to drink, to atone for crimes and follies to which she had no accession; and at twelve o'clock noon, being the time appointed for admission to the jail, she went to meet, for the first time for several months, her guilty, erring, and most miserable sister, in that abode of guilt, error, and utter misery.

CHAPTER THE TWENTIETH.

——Sweet sister, let me live !
What sin you do to save a brother's life,
Nature dispenses with the deed so far,
That it becomes a virtue.
                    MEASURE FOR MEASURE.

JEANIE DEANS was admitted into the jail by Ratcliffe.
This fellow, as void of shame as of honesty, as he
opened the now trebly secured door, asked her, with a
leer which made her shudder, "whether she remembered him ?"

A half-pronounced and timid "No," was her
answer.

"What ! not remember moonlight, and Muschat's
Cairn, and Rob and Rat ?" said he, with the same
sneer ;—" Your memory needs redding up, my jo."

If Jeanie's distresses had admitted of aggravation, it
must have been to find her sister under the charge of
such a profligate as this man. He was not, indeed,
without something of good to balance so much that was
evil in his character and habits.   In his misdemeanours
he had never been bloodthirsty or cruel ; and in his
present occupation, he had shown himself, in a certain
degree, accessible to touches of humanity.   But these

good qualities were unknown to Jeanie, who, remember-
ing the scene at Muschat's cairn, could scarce find voice
to acquaint him, that she had an order from Bailie
Middleburgh, permitting her to see her sister.

"I ken that fu' weel, my bonny doo; mair by token,
I have a special charge to stay in the ward wi' you a'
the time ye are thegither."

"Must that be sae?" asked Jeanie, with an imploring voice.

"Hout, ay, hinny," replied the turnkey; "and what
the waur will you and your titty be of Jim Ratcliffe
hearing what ye hae to say to ilk other?—Deil a word
ye'll say that will gar him ken your kittle sex better
than he kens them already; and another thing is, that
if ye dinna speak o' breaking the Tolbooth, deil a word
will I tell ower, either to do ye good or ill."

Thus saying, Ratcliffe marshalled her the way to the
apartment where Effie was confined.

Shame, fear, and grief, had contended for mastery in
the poor prisoner's bosom during the whole morning,
while she had looked forward to this meeting; but
when the door opened, all gave way to a confused and
strange feeling that had a tinge of joy in it, as, throwing
herself on her sister's neck, she ejaculated, "My dear
Jeanie!—my dear Jeanie! it's lang since I hae seen
ye." Jeanie returned the embrace with an earnestness
that partook almost of rapture, but it was only a flitting
emotion, like a sunbeam unexpectedly penetrating
betwixt the clouds of a tempest, and obscured almost
as soon as visible. The sisters walked together to the

side of the pallet bed, and sate down side by side, took
hold of each other's hands, and looked each other in the
face, but without speaking a word. In this posture
they remained for a minute, while the gleam of joy
gradually faded from their features, and gave way to the
most intense expression, first of melancholy, and then
of agony, till, throwing themselves again into each
other's arms, they, to use the language of Scripture,
lifted up their voices and wept bitterly.

Even the hard-hearted turnkey, who had spent his
life in scenes calculated to stifle both conscience and
feeling, could not witness this scene without a touch of
human sympathy. It was shown in a trifling action,
but which had more delicacy in it than seemed to belong
to Ratcliffe's character and station. The unglazed
window of the miserable chamber was open, and the
beams of a bright sun fell right upon the bed where
the sufferers were seated. With a gentleness that had
something of reverence in it, Ratcliffe partly closed the
shutter, and seemed thus to throw a veil over a scene
so sorrowful.

"Ye are ill, Effie," were the first words Jeanie could
utter ; "ye are very ill."

"O, what wad I gie to be ten times waur, Jeanie !"
was the reply—"what wad I gie to be cauld dead afore
the ten o'clock bell the morn ! And our father—but I
am his bairn nae langer now—O, I hae nae friend left
in the warld !—O, that I were lying dead at my mother's
side, in Newbattle kirkyard !"

"Hout, lassie," said Ratcliffe, willing to show the

interest which he absolutely felt, "dinna be sae dooms down-hearted as a' that; there's mony a tod hunted that's no killed. Advocate Langtale has brought folk through waur snappers than a' this, and there's no a cleverer agent than Nichil Novit e'er drew a bill of suspension. Hanged or unhanged, they are weel aff has sic an agent and counsel; ane's sure o' fair play. Ye are a bonny lass, too, an ye wad busk up your cockernonie a bit; and a bonny lass will find favour wi' judge and jury, when they would strap up a grewsome carle like me for the fifteenth part of a flea's hide and tallow, d—n them."

To this homely strain of consolation the mourners returned no answer; indeed, they were so much lost in their own sorrows as to have become insensible of Ratcliffe's presence. "O Effie," said her elder sister, "how could you conceal your situation from me? O woman, had I deserved this at your hand?—had ye spoke but ae word—sorry we might hae been, and shamed we might hae been, but this awfu' dispensation had never come ower us."

"And what gude wad that has dune?" answered the prisoner. "Na, na, Jeanie, a' was ower when ance I forgot what I promised when I faulded down the leaf of my Bible. See," she said, producing the sacred volume, "the book opens aye at the place o' itsell. O see, Jeanie, what a fearfu' scripture!"

Jeanie took her sister's Bible, and found that the fatal mark was made at this impressive text in the book of Job: "He hath stripped me of my glory, and taken the crown from my head. He hath destroyed me on every side, and I am gone. And mine hope hath he removed like a tree."

"Isna that ower true a doctrine?" said the prisoner —"Isna my crown, my honour, removed? And what am I but a poor wasted, wan-thriven tree, dug up by the roots, and flung out to waste in the highway, that man and beast may tread it under foot? I thought o' the bonny bit thorn that our father rooted out o' the yard last May, when it had a' the flush o' blossoms on it; and then it lay in the court till the beasts had trod them a' to pieces wi' their feet. I little thought, when I was wae for the bit silly green bush and its flowers, that I was to gang the same gate mysell."

"O, if ye had spoken ae word," again sobbed Jeanie, —"if I were free to swear that ye had said but ae word of how it stude wi' ye, they couldna hae touched your life this day."

"Could they na?" said Effie, with something like awakened interest—for life is dear even to those who feel it as a burden—"Wha tauld ye that, Jeanie?"

"It was ane that kend what he was saying weel eneugh," replied Jeanie, who had a natural reluctance at mentioning even the name of her sister's seducer.

"Wha was it?—I conjure ye to tell me," said Effie, seating herself upright.—"Wha could tak interest in sic a cast-by as I am now?—Was it—was it *him?*"

"Hout," said Ratcliffe, "what signifies keeping the poor lassie in a swither? I'se uphaud it's been Robertson that learned ye that doctrine when ye saw him at Muschat's Cairn."

"Was it him?" said Effie, catching eagerly at his words—"was it him, Jeanie, indeed?—O, I see it was him—poor lad, and I was thinking his heart was as hard as the nether millstane—and him in sic danger on his ain part—poor George!"

Somewhat indignant at this burst of tender feeling towards the author of her misery, Jeanie could not help exclaiming—"O Effie, how can ye speak that gate of sic a man as that?"

"We maun forgie our enemies, ye ken," said poor Effie, with a timid look and a subdued voice; for her conscience told her what a different character the feelings with which she regarded her seducer bore, compared with the Christian charity under which she attempted to veil it.

"And ye hae suffered a' this for him, and ye can think of loving him still?" said her sister, in a voice betwixt pity and blame.

"Love him!" answered Effie—"If I hadna loved as woman seldom loves, I hadna been within these wa's this day; and trow ye, that love sic as mine is lightly forgotten?—Na, na—ye may hew down the tree, but ye canna change its bend—And O Jeanie, if ye wad do good to me at this moment, tell me every word that he said, and whether he was sorry for poor Effie or no!"

"What needs I tell ye ony thing about it?" said Jeanie. "Ye may be sure he had ower muckle to do to save himsell, to speak lang or muckle about ony body beside."

"That's no true, Jeanie, though a saunt had said it,"

replied Effie, with a sparkle of her former lively and
irritable temper. "But ye dinna ken, though I do, how
far he pat his life in venture to save mine." And looking
at Ratcliffe, she checked herself and was silent.

"I fancy," said Ratcliffe, with one of his familiar
sneers, "the lassie thinks that naebody has cen but
hersell—Didna I see when Gentle Geordie was seeking
to get other folk out of the Tolbooth forby Jock Porteous? but ye are of my mind, hinny—better sit and
rue, than flit and rue—Ye needna look in my face sae
amazed. I ken mair things than that, maybe."

"O my God! my God!" said Effie, springing up and
throwing herself down on her knees before him—
"D'ye ken where they hae putten my bairn?—O my
bairn! my bairn! the poor sackless innocent new-born
wee ane—bone of my bone, and flesh of my flesh!—O
man, if ye wad e'er deserve a portion in heaven, or a
broken-hearted creature's blessing upon earth, tell me
where they hae put my bairn—the sign of my shame,
and the partner of my suffering! tell me wha has taen't
away, or what they hae dune wi't!"

"Hout tout," said the turnkey, endeavouring to
extricate himself from the firm grasp with which she
held him, "that's taking me at my word wi' a witness—
Bairn, quo' she! How the deil suld I ken ony thing of
your bairn, huzzy? Ye maun ask that of auld Meg Murdockson, if ye dinna ken ower muckle about it yoursell."

As his answer destroyed the wild and vague hope
which had suddenly gleamed upon her, the unhappy
prisoner let go her hold of his coat, and fell with her

face on the pavement of the apartment in a strong con-
vulsion fit.

Jeanie Deans possessed, with her excellently clear
understanding, the concomitant advantage of promptitude of spirit, even in the extremity of distress.

She did not suffer herself to be overcome by her own
feelings of exquisite sorrow, but instantly applied herself
to her sister's relief, with the readiest remedies which
circumstances afforded; and which, to do Ratcliffe
justice, he showed himself anxious to suggest, and alert
in procuring. He had even the delicacy to withdraw
to the farthest corner of the room, so as to render his
official attendance upon them as little intrusive as
possible, when Effie was composed enough again to
resume her conference with her sister.

The prisoner once more, in the most earnest and
broken tones, conjured Jeanie to tell her the particulars
of the conference with Robertson, and Jeanie felt it
was impossible to refuse her this gratification.

"Do ye mind," she said, "Effie, when ye were in
the fever before we left Woodend, and how angry your
mother, that's now in a better place, was wi' me for
gieing ye milk and water to drink, because ye grat for
it? Ye were a bairn then, and ye are a woman now,
and should ken better than ask what canna but hurt
you—But come weal or wo, I canna refuse ye ony thing
that ye ask me wi' the tear in your ee."

Again Effie threw herself into her arms, and kissed
her cheek and forehead, murmuring, "O, if ye ken'd
how lang it is since I heard his name mentioned!—if

ye but ken'd how muckle good it does me but to ken ony thing o' him, that's like goodness or kindness, ye wadna wonder that I wish to hear o' him!"

Jeanie sighed, and commenced her narrative of all that had passed betwixt Robertson and her, making it as brief as possible. Effie listened in breathless anxiety, holding her sister's hand in hers, and keeping her eye fixed upon her face, as if devouring every word she uttered. The interjections of "Poor fellow,"—"Poor George," which escaped in whispers, and betwixt sighs, were the only sounds with which she interrupted the story. When it was finished she made a long pause.

"And this was his advice!" were the first words she uttered.

"Just sic as I hae toll'd ye," replied her sister.

"And he wanted you to say something to yon folks, that wad save my young life!"

"He wanted," answered Jeanie, "that I suld be mansworn."

"And you tauld him," said Effie, "that ye wadna hear o' coming between me and the death that I am to die, and me no aughteen year auld yet!"

"I told him," replied Jeanie, who now trembled at the turn which her sister's reflections seemed about to take, "that I daured na swear to an untruth."

"And what d'ye ca' an untruth!" said Effie, again showing a touch of her former spirit—"Ye are muckle to blame, lass, if ye think a mother would, or could, murder her ain bairn—Murder!—I wad hae laid down my life just to see a blink o' its ee!"

"I do believe," said Jeanie, "that ye are as innocent of sic a purpose as the new-born babe itself."

"I am glad ye do me that justice," said Effie, haughtily; "it's whiles the faut of very good folk like you, Jeanie, that they think a' the rest of the warld are as bad as the warst temptations can make them."

"I dinna deserve this frae ye, Effie," said her sister, sobbing, and feeling at once the injustice of the reproach, and compassion for the state of mind which dictated it.

"Maybe no, sister," said Effie. "But ye are angry because I love Robertson—How can I help loving him, that loves me better than body and soul baith?—Here he put his life in a niffer, to break the prison to let me out; and sure am I, had it stood wi' him as it stands wi' you"—Here she paused and was silent.

"O, if it stude wi' me to save ye wi' risk of *my* life!" said Jeanie.

"Ay, lass," said her sister, "that's lightly said, but no sae lightly credited, frae ane that winna ware a word for me; and if it be a wrang word, ye'll hae time eneugh to repent o't."

"But that word is a grievous sin, and it's a deeper offence when it's a sin wilfully and presumptuously committed."

"Weel, weel, Jeanie," said Effie, "I mind a' about the sins o' presumption in the questions—we'll speak nae mair about this matter, and ye may save your breath to say your carritch; and for me, I'll soon hae nae breath to waste on ony body."

"I must needs say," interposed Ratcliffe, "that it's

d—d hard, when three words of your mouth would
give the girl the chance to nick Moll Blood,* that you
make such scrupling about rapping † to them.   D—n me,
if they would take me, if I would not rap to all what
d'ye callum's—Hyssop's Fables, for her life—I am us'd
to 't, b—t me, for less matters.   Why, I have smacked
calf-skin ‡ fifty times in England for a keg of brandy."

"Never speak mair o't," said the prisoner.   "It's
just as weel as it is—and gude day, sister; ye keep Mr.
Ratcliffe waiting on—Ye'll come back and see me, I
reckon, before"——here she stopped, and became deadly
pale.

"And are we to part in this way," said Jeanie, "and
you in sic deadly peril ?   O, Effie, look but up, and say
what ye wad hae me to do, and I could find in my heart
amaist to say that I wad do't."

"No, Jeanie," replied her sister, after an effort, "I
am better minded now.   At my best, I was never half
sae gude as ye were, and what for suld you begin to
mak yoursell waur to save me, now that I am no worth
saving ?   God knows, that in my sober mind, I wadna
wuss ony living creature to do a wrang thing to save
my life.   I might have fled frae this tolbooth on that
awfu' night wi' ane wad hae carried me through the
warld, and friended me, and fended for me.   But I
said to them, let life gang when gude fame is gane
before it.   But this lang imprisonment has broken my
spirit, and I am whiles sair left to mysell, and then I
wad gie the Indian mines of gold and diamonds, just

* The gallows.   † Swearing.   ‡ Kissed the book.

for life and breath—for I think, Jeanie, I have such roving fits as I used to hae in the fever; but, instead of the fiery een, and wolves, and Widow Butler's bullseg, that I used to see spieling upon my bed, I am thinking now about a high, black gibbet, and me standing up, and such seas of faces all looking up at poor Effie Deans, and asking if it be her that George Robertson used to call the Lilly of St. Leonard's. And then they stretch out their faces, and make mouths, and girn at me, and which ever way I look, I see a face laughing like Meg Murdockson, when she tauld me I had seen the last of my wean. God preserve us, Jeanie, that carline has a fearsome face!" She clapped her hands before her eyes as she uttered this exclamation, as if to secure herself against seeing the fearful object she had alluded to.

Jeanie Deans remained with her sister for two hours, during which she endeavoured, if possible, to extract something from her that might be serviceable in her exculpation. But she had nothing to say beyond what she had declared on her first examination, with the purport of which the reader will be made acquainted in proper time and place. "They wadna believe her," she said, "and she had naething mair to tell them."

At length Ratcliffe, though reluctantly, informed the sisters that there was a necessity that they should part. "Mr. Novit," he said, "was to see the prisoner, and maybe Mr. Langtale too. Langtale likes to look at a bonny lass whether in prison or out o' prison."

Reluctantly, therefore, and slowly, after many a
tear and many an embrace, Jeanie retired from the
apartment, and heard its jarring bolts turned upon the
dear being from whom she was separated. Somewhat
familiarized now even with her rude conductor, she
offered him a small present in money, with a request he
would do what he could for her sister's accommodation.
To her surprise, Ratcliffe declined the fee. "I wasna
bloody when I was on the pad," he said, "and I winna
be greedy—that is, beyond what's right and reasonable
—now that I am in the lock.—Keep the siller; and for
civility, your sister sall hae sic as I can bestow; but I
hope you'll think better on it, and rap an oath for her
—deil a hair ill there is in it, if ye are rapping again
the crown. I kend a worthy minister, as gude a man,
bating the deed they deposed him for, as ever ye heard
claver in a pu'pit, that rapped to a hogshead of pigtail
tobacco, just for as muckle as filled his spleuchan.*
But maybe ye are keeping your ain counsel—weel, weel,
there's nae harm in that. As for your sister, I'se see
that she gets her meat clean and warm, and I'll try to
gar her lie down and take a sleep after dinner, for deil
a ee she'll close the night. I hae gude experience of
these matters. The first night is aye the warst o't. I
hae never heard o' ane that sleepit the night afore trial,
but of mony a ane that sleepit as sound as a tap the
night before their necks were straughted. And it's
nae wonder—the worst may be tholed when it's kend
—Better a finger aff as aye wagging."

* Tobacco pouch.

CHAPTER THE TWENTY-FIRST.

Yet though thou mayst be dragged in scorn
   To yonder ignominious tree,
Thou shalt not want one faithful friend
   To share the cruel fates' decree.
                              JEMMY DAWSON.

AFTER spending the greater part of the morning in his
devotions (for his benevolent neighbours had kindly
insisted upon discharging his task of ordinary labour),
David Deans entered the apartment when the breakfast
meal was prepared. His eyes were involuntarily cast
down, for he was afraid to look at Jeanie, uncertain as
he was whether she might feel herself at liberty, with a
good conscience to attend the Court of Justiciary that
day, to give the evidence which he understood that she
possessed, in order to her sister's exculpation. At
length, after a minute of apprehensive hesitation, he
looked at her dress to discover whether it seemed to be
in her contemplation to go abroad that morning. Her
apparel was neat and plain, but such as conveyed no
exact intimation of her intentions to go abroad. She
had exchanged her usual garb for morning labour, for
one something inferior to that with which, as her best,
she was wont to dress herself for church, or any more

rare occasion of going into society. Her sense taught
her, that it was respectful to be decent in her apparel
on such an occasion, while her feelings induced her to
lay aside the use of the very few and simple personal
ornaments, which, on other occasions, she permitted
herself to wear.   So that there occurred nothing in her
external appearance which could mark out to her father,
with any thing like certainty, her intentions on this
occasion.

The preparations for their humble meal were that
morning made in vain.   The father and daughter sat,
each assuming the appearance of eating, when the
other's eyes were turned to them, and desisting from
the effort with disgust, when the affectionate imposture
seemed no longer necessary.

At length these moments of constraint were removed.
The sound of St. Giles's heavy toll announced the hour
previous to the commencement of the trial; Jeanie
arose, and, with a degree of composure for which she
herself could not account, assumed her plaid, and made
her other preparations for a distant walking.   It was a
strange contrast between the firmness of her demeanour,
and the vacillation and cruel uncertainty of purpose
indicated in all her father's motions; and one un-
acquainted with both could scarcely have supposed that
the former was, in her ordinary habits of life, a docile,
quiet, gentle, and even timid country-maiden, while her
father, with a mind naturally proud and strong, and
supported by religious opinions, of a stern, stoical, and
unyielding character, had in his time undergone and

withstood the most severe hardships and the most
imminent peril, without depression of spirit, or subju-
gation of his constancy. The secret of this difference
was, that Jeanie's mind had already anticipated the
line of conduct which she must adopt, with all its
natural and necessary consequences; while her father,
ignorant of every other circumstance, tormented himself
with imagining what the one sister might say or swear,
or what effect her testimony might have upon the awful
event of the trial.

He watched his daughter with a faltering and inde-
cisive look, until she looked back upon him, with a
look of unutterable anguish, as she was about to leave
the apartment.

"My dear lassie," said he, "I will"—His action,
hastily and confusedly searching for his worsted
mittans* and staff, showed his purpose of accompanying
her, though his tongue failed distinctly to announce it.

"Father," said Jeanie, replying rather to his action
than his words, "ye had better not."

"In the strength of my God," answered Deans,
assuming firmness, "I will go forth."

And, taking his daughter's arm under his, he began
to walk from the door with a step so hasty, that she
was almost unable to keep up with him. A trifling
circumstance, but which marked the perturbed state of
his mind, checked his course.—"Your bonnet, father?"
said Jeanie, who observed he had come out with his
grey hairs uncovered. He turned back with a slight

* A kind of worsted gloves used by the lower orders.

blush on his cheek, being ashamed to have been detected
in an omission which indicated so much mental confusion, assumed his large blue Scottish bonnet, and with
a step slower, but more composed, as if the circumstance
had obliged him to summon up his resolution, and
collect his scattered ideas, again placed his daughter's
arm under his, and resumed the way to Edinburgh.

The courts of justice were then, and are still held
in what is called the Parliament Close, or, according
to modern phrase, Parliament Square, and occupied
the buildings intended for the accommodation of the
Scottish Estates.   This edifice, though in an imperfect
and corrupted style of architecture, had then a grave,
decent, and, as it were, a judicial aspect, which was at
least entitled to respect from its antiquity.   For which
venerable front, I observed, on my last occasional visit
to the metropolis, that modern taste had substituted, at
great apparent expense, a pile so utterly inconsistent
with every monument of antiquity around, and in itself
so clumsy at the same time and fantastic, that it may
be likened to the decorations of Tom Errand the porter,
in the Trip to the Jubilee, when he appears bedizened
with the tawdry finery of Beau Clincher.   *Sed transeat
cum cæteris erroribus.*

The small quadrangle, or Close, if we may presume
still to give it that appropriate, though antiquated title,
which at Lichfield, Salisbury, and elsewhere, is properly
applied to designate the enclosure adjacent to a cathedral, already evinced tokens of the fatal scene which
was that day to be acted.   The soldiers of the City

Guard were on their posts, now enduring, and now
rudely repelling with the buts of their muskets, the
motley crew who thrust each other forward, to catch a
glance at the unfortunate object of trial, as she should
pass from the adjacent prison to the Court in which
her fate was to be determined. All must have occasionally observed, with disgust, the apathy with which the
vulgar gaze on scenes of this nature, and how seldom,
unless when their sympathies are called forth by some
striking and extraordinary circumstance, the crowd
evince any interest deeper than that of callous, unthink-
ing bustle, and brutal curiosity. They laugh, jest,
quarrel, and push each other to and fro, with the same
unfeeling indifference as if they were assembled for
some holiday sport, or to see an idle procession. Occasionally, however, this demeanour, so natural to the
degraded populace of a large town, is exchanged for a
temporary touch of human affections; and so it chanced
on the present occasion.

When Deans and his daughter presented themselves
in the Close, and endeavoured to make their way
forward to the door of the Court-house, they became
involved in the mob, and subject, of course, to their
insolence. As Deans repelled with some force the rude
pushes which he received on all sides, his figure and
antiquated dress caught the attention of the rabble,
who often show an intuitive sharpness in ascribing the
proper character from external appearance,—

> " Ye 're welcome, whigs,
>   Frae Bothwell briggs,"

sung one fellow (for the mob of Edinburgh were at that time jacobitically disposed, probably because that was the line of sentiment most diametrically opposite to existing authority).

> "Mess David Williamson,
> Chosen of twenty,
> Ran up the pu'pit stair,
> And sang Killiecrankie,"

chanted a siren, whose profession might be guessed by her appearance. A tattered cadie, or errand porter, whom David Deans had jostled in his attempt to extricate himself from the vicinity of these scorners, exclaimed in a strong north-country tone, " Ta deil ding out her Cameronian een—what gies her titles to dunch gentlemans about?"

" Make room for the ruling elder," said yet another; " he comes to see a precious sister glorify God in the Grassmarket !"

" Whisht; shame's in ye, sirs," said the voice of a man very loudly, which, as quickly sinking, said in a low but distinct tone, " It's her father and sister."

All fell back to make way for the sufferers; and all, even the very rudest and most profligate, were struck with shame and silence.   In the space thus abandoned to them by the mob, Deans stood, holding his daughter by the hand, and said to her, with a countenance strongly and sternly expressive of his internal emotion, " Ye hear with your ears, and ye see with your eyes, where and to whom the backslidings and defections of professors are ascribed by the scoffers.   Not to them-

selves alone, but to the kirk of which they are members, and to its blessed and invisible Head.   Then,
weal may we take wi' patience our share and portion
of this out-spreading reproach."

The man who had spoken, no other than our old
friend Dumbiedikes, whose mouth, like that of the
prophet's ass, had been opened by the emergency of the
case, now joined them, and, with his usual taciturnity,
escorted them into the Court-house.   No opposition
was offered to their entrance, either by the guards or
door-keepers ; and it is even said, that one of the latter
refused a shilling of civility-money, tendered him by
the Laird of Dumbiedikes, who was of opinion that
· " siller wad make a' easy."   But this last incident wants
confirmation.

Admitted within the precincts of the Court-house,
they found the usual number of busy office-bearers, and
idle loiterers, who attend on these scenes by choice, or
from duty.   Burghers gaped and stared ; young lawyers
sauntered, sneered, and laughed, as in the pit of the
theatre ; while others apart sat on a bench retired, and
reasoned highly, *inter apices juris*, on the doctrines of
constructive crime, and the true import of the statute.
The bench was prepared for the arrival of the judges :
The jurors were in attendance.   The crown-counsel,
employed in looking over their briefs and notes of
evidence, looked grave, and whispered with each other.
They occupied one side of a large table placed beneath
the bench ; on the other sat the advocates, whom the
humanity of the Scottish law (in this particular more

liberal than that of the sister country) not only permits, but enjoins, to appear and assist with their advice and skill all persons under trial. Mr. Nichil Novit was seen actively instructing the counsel for the panel (so the prisoner is called in Scottish law phraseology), busy, bustling, and important. When they entered the Court-room, Deans asked the Laird, in a tremulous whisper, " Where will *she* sit ? "

Dumbiedikes whispered Novit, who pointed to a vacant space at the bar, fronting the judges, and was about to conduct Deans towards it.

" No ! " he said ; " I cannot sit by her—I cannot own her—not as yet, at least—I will keep out of her sight, and turn mine own eyes elsewhere—better for us baith."

Saddletree, whose repeated interference with the counsel had procured him one or two rebuffs, and a special request that he would concern himself with his own matters, now saw with pleasure an opportunity of playing the person of importance. He bustled up to the poor old man, and proceeded to exhibit his consequence, by securing, through his interest with the barkeepers and macers, a seat for Deans, in a situation where he was hidden from the general eye by the projecting corner of the bench.

" It's gude to have a friend at court," he said, continuing his heartless harangues to the passive auditor, who neither heard nor replied to them ; " few folk but mysell could hae sorted ye out a seat like this—the Lords will be here incontinent, and proceed *instanter* to

trial. They wunna fence the court as they do at the
Circuit—The High Court of Justiciary is aye fenced.—
But, Lord's sake, what's this o't?—Jeanie, ye are a
cited witness—Macer, this lass is a witness—she maun
be enclosed—she maun on nae account be at large.—
Mr. Novit, suldna Jeanie Deans be enclosed?"

Novit answered in the affirmative, and offered to
conduct Jeanie to the apartment, where, according to
the scrupulous practice of the Scottish Court, the
witnesses remain in readiness to be called into court to
give evidence; and separated, at the same time, from
all who might influence their testimony, or give them
information concerning that which was passing upon
the trial.

"Is this necessary?" said Jeanie, still reluctant to
quit her father's hand.

"A matter of absolute necdcessity," said Saddletree;
"wha ever heard of witnesses no being enclosed?"

"It is really a matter of necessity," said the younger
counsellor, retained for her sister; and Jeanie reluctantly followed the macer of the court to the place
appointed.

"This, Mr. Deans," said Saddletree, "is ca'd
sequestering a witness; but it's clean different (whilk
maybe ye wadna fund out o' yoursell) frae sequestering
ane's estate or effects, as in cases of bankruptcy. I hae
aften been sequestered as a witness, for the Sheriff is in
the use whiles to cry me in to witness the declarations
at precognitions, and so is Mr. Sharpitlaw; but I was
ne'er like to be sequestered o' land and gudes but ance,

and that was lang syne, afore I was married.   But
whisht, whisht I here's the Court coming."

As he spoke, the five Lords of Justiciary, in their
long robes of scarlet, faced with white, and preceded by
their mace-bearer, entered with the usual formalities,
and took their places upon the bench of judgment.

The audience rose to receive them ; and the bustle
occasioned by their entrance was hardly composed when
a great noise and confusion of persons struggling, and
forcibly endeavouring to enter at the doors of the Court-
room and of the galleries, announced that the prisoner
was about to be placed at the bar.   This tumult takes
place when the doors, at first only opened to those
either having right to be present, or to the better and
more qualified ranks, are at length laid open to all
whose curiosity induces them to be present on the occasion.   With inflamed countenances and dishevelled
dresses, struggling with, and sometimes tumbling over
each other, in rushed the rude multitude, while a few
soldiers, forming, as it were, the centre of the tide, could
scarce, with all their efforts, clear a passage for the
prisoner to the place which she was to occupy.   By the
authority of the Court, and the exertions of its officers,
the tumult among the spectators was at length appeased,
and the unhappy girl brought forward, and placed
betwixt two sentinels with drawn bayonets, as a prisoner
at the bar, where she was to abide her deliverance for
good or evil, according to the issue of her trial.

CHAPTER THE TWENTY-SECOND.

We have strict statutes, and most biting laws—
The needful bits, and curbs for headstrong steeds—
Which, for these fourteen years, we have let sleep,
Like to an o'ergrown lion in a cave,
That goes not out to prey.

MEASURE FOR MEASURE.

"EUPHEMIA DEANS," said the presiding Judge, in an accent in which pity was blended with dignity, "stand up, and listen to the criminal indictment now to be preferred against you."

The unhappy girl, who had been stupified by the confusion through which the guards had forced a passage, cast a bewildered look on the multitude of faces around her, which seemed to tapestry, as it were, the walls, in one broad slope from the ceiling to the floor, with human countenances, and instinctively obeyed a command, which rung in her ears like the trumpet of the judgment-day.

"Put back your hair, Effie," said one of the macers. For her beautiful and abundant tresses of long fair hair, which, according to the costume of the country, un-married women were not allowed to cover with any sort of cap, and which, alas! Effie dared no longer confine with the snood or ribband, which implied purity of maiden-fame, now hung unbound and dishevelled over her face, and almost concealed her features. On receiv-ing this hint from the attendant, the unfortunate young woman, with a hasty, trembling, and apparently me-chanical compliance, shaded back from her face her luxuriant locks, and showed to the whole court, except-ing one individual, a countenance, which, though pale and emaciated, was so lovely amid its agony, that it called forth a universal murmur of compassion and sympathy. Apparently the expressive sound of human feeling recalled the poor girl from the stupor of fear, which predominated at first over every other sensation, and awakened her to the no less painful sense of shame and exposure attached to her present situation. Her eye, which had at first glanced wildly around, was turned on the ground; her cheek, at first so deadly

pale, began gradually to be overspread with a faint
blush, which increased so fast, that, when in agony of
shame she strove to conceal her face, her temples, her
brow, her neck, and all that her slender fingers and small
palms could not cover, became of the deepest crimson.

All marked and were moved by these changes, excepting one. It was old Deans, who, motionless in his
seat, and concealed, as we have said, by the corner of
the bench, from seeing or being seen, did nevertheless
keep his eyes firmly fixed on the ground, as if determined that, by no possibility whatever, would he be an
ocular witness of the shame of his house.

"Ichabod !" he said to himself—"Ichabod ! my
glory is departed !"

While these reflections were passing through his
mind, the indictment, which set forth in technical form
the crime of which the panel stood accused, was read as
usual, and the prisoner was asked if she was Guilty, or
Not Guilty.

"Not guilty of my poor bairn's death," said Effie
Deans, in an accent corresponding in plaintive softness
of tone to the beauty of her features, and which was
not heard by the audience without emotion.

The presiding Judge next directed the counsel to
plead to the relevancy; that is, to state on either part
the arguments in point of law, and evidence in point of
fact, against and in favour of the criminal; after which
it is the form of the Court to pronounce a preliminary
judgment, sending the cause to the cognizance of the
jury or assize.

The counsel for the crown briefly stated the frequency of the crime of infanticide, which had given rise to the special statute under which the panel stood indicted. He mentioned the various instances, many of them marked with circumstances of atrocity, which had at length induced the King's Advocate, though with great reluctance, to make the experiment, whether by strictly enforcing the Act of Parliament which had been made to prevent such enormities, their occurrence might be prevented. "He expected," he said, "to be able to establish by witnesses, as well as by the declaration of the panel herself, that she was in the state described by the statute. According to his information, the panel had communicated her pregnancy to no one, nor did she allege in her own declaration that she had done so. This secrecy was the first requisite in support of the indictment. The same declaration admitted, that she had borne a male child, in circumstances which gave but too much reason to believe it had died by the hands, or at least with the knowledge or consent, of the unhappy mother. It was not, however, necessary for him to bring positive proof that the panel was accessory to the murder, nay, nor even to prove that the child was murdered at all. It was sufficient to support the indictment, that it could not be found. According to the stern, but necessary severity of this statute, she who should conceal her pregnancy, who should omit to call that assistance which is most necessary on such occasions, was held already to have meditated the death of her offspring, as an event most likely to be the consequence of her culpable and cruel concealment. And if, under such circumstances, she could not alternatively show by proof that the infant had died a natural death, or produce it still in life, she must, under the construction of the law, be held to have murdered it, and suffer death accordingly."

The counsel for the prisoner, Mr. Fairbrother, a man of considerable fame in his profession, did not pretend directly to combat the arguments of the King's Advocate. He began by lamenting that his senior at the bar, Mr. Langtale, had been suddenly called to the county of which he was Sheriff, and that he had been applied to, on short warning, to give the panel his assistance in this interesting case. He had had little time, he said, to make up for his inferiority to his learned brother by long and minute research; and he was afraid he might give a specimen of his incapacity, by being compelled to admit the accuracy of the indictment under the statute. "It was enough for their Lordships," he observed, "to know, that such was the law, and he admitted the Advocate had a right to call for the usual interlocutor of relevancy." But he stated, "that when he came to establish his case by proof, he trusted to make out circumstances which would satisfactorily elide the charge in the libel. His client's story was a short, but most melancholy one. She was bred up in the strictest tenets of religion and virtue, the daughter of a worthy and conscientious person, who, in evil times, had established a character for courage and religion, by becoming a sufferer for conscience' sake."

David Deans gave a convulsive start at hearing himself thus mentioned, and then resumed the situation, in
which, with his face stooped against his hands, and
both resting against the corner of the elevated bench on
which the Judges sate, he had hitherto listened to the
procedure in the trial.   The whig lawyers seemed to be
interested; the tories put up their lip.

"Whatever may be our difference of opinion," resumed the lawyer, whose business it was to carry his
whole audience with him if possible, "concerning the
peculiar tenets of these people" (here Deans groaned
deeply), "it is impossible to deny them the praise of
sound, and even rigid morals, or the merit of training
up their children in the fear of God; and yet it was the
daughter of such a person whom a jury would shortly
be called upon, in the absence of evidence, and upon
mere presumptions, to convict of a crime, more properly belonging to a heathen, or a savage, than to a
Christian and civilized country.   It was true," he
admitted, "that the excellent nurture and early instruction which the poor girl had received, had not been
sufficient to preserve her from guilt and error.   She had
fallen a sacrifice to an inconsiderate affection for a young
man of prepossessing manners, as he had been informed,
but of a very dangerous and desperate character.   She
was seduced under promise of marriage—a promise,
which the fellow might have, perhaps, done her justice
by keeping, had he not at that time been called upon
by the law to atone for a crime, violent and desperate
in itself, but which became the preface to another

eventful history, every step of which was marked by
blood and guilt, and the final termination of which had
not even yet arrived. He believed that no one would
hear him without surprise, when he stated that the
father of this infant now amissing, and said by the
learned Advocate to have been murdered, was no other
than the notorious George Robertson, the accomplice of
Wilson, the hero of the memorable escape from the
Tolbooth Church, and, as no one knew better than his
learned friend the Advocate, the principal actor in the
Porteous conspiracy."—

" I am sorry to interrupt a counsel in such a case as
the present," said the presiding Judge; "but I must
remind the learned gentleman, that he is travelling out
of the case before us."

The counsel bowed, and resumed. " He only judged
it necessary," he said, " to mention the name and situation of Robertson, because the circumstance in which
that character was placed, went a great way in accounting for the silence on which his Majesty's counsel had
laid so much weight, as affording proof that his client
proposed to allow no fair play for its life, to the helpless
being whom she was about to bring into the world.
She had not announced to her friends that she had been
seduced from the path of honour—and why had she
not done so ?—Because she expected daily to be restored
to character, by her seducer doing her that justice
which she knew to be in his power, and believed to be
in his inclination. Was it natural—was it reasonable
—was it fair, to expect that she should, in the interim,

become *felo de se* of her own character, and proclaim
her frailty to the world, when she had every reason to
expect, that, by concealing it for a season, it might be
veiled for ever 1   Was it not, on the contrary, pardon-
able, that, in such an emergency, a young woman, in
such a situation, should be found far from disposed to
make a confidant of every prying gossip, who, with
sharp eyes, and eager ears, pressed upon her for an explanation of suspicious circumstances, which females in
the lower—he might say which females of all ranks are
so alert in noticing, that they sometimes discover them
where they do not exist ?   Was it strange, or was it
criminal, that she should have repelled their inquisitive
impertinence, with petulant denials ?   The sense and
feeling of all who heard him would answer directly in
the negative.   But although his client had thus remained silent towards those to whom she was not called
upon to communicate her situation,—to whom," said the
learned gentleman, " I will add, it would have been un-
advised and improper in her to have done so ; yet, I trust,
I shall remove this case most triumphantly from under
the statute, and obtain the unfortunate young woman
an honourable dismission from your Lordship's bar, by
showing that she did, in due time and place, and to a
person most fit for such confidence, mention the cala-
mitous circumstances in which she found herself.   This
occurred after Robertson's conviction, and when he was
lying in prison in expectation of the fate which his
comrade Wilson afterwards suffered, and from which he
himself so strangely escaped.   It was then, when all

hopes of having her honour repaired by wedlock vanished from her eyes,—when a union with one in Robertson's situation, if still practicable, might, perhaps, have been regarded rather as an addition to her disgrace, —it was *then*, that I trust to be able to prove that the prisoner communicated and consulted with her sister, a young woman several years older than herself, the daughter of her father, if I mistake not, by a former marriage, upon the perils and distress of her unhappy situation."

"If, indeed, you are able to instruct *that* point, Mr. Fairbrother," said the presiding Judge——

"If I am indeed able to instruct that point, my Lord," resumed Mr. Fairbrother, "I trust not only to serve my client, but to relieve your Lordships from that which I know you feel the most painful duty of your high office; and to give all who now hear me the exquisite pleasure of beholding a creature so young, so ingenuous, and so beautiful, as she that is now at the bar of your Lordships' Court, dismissed from thence in safety and in honour."

This address seemed to affect many of the audience, and was followed by a slight murmur of applause. Deans, as he heard his daughter's beauty and innocent appearance appealed to, was involuntarily about to turn his eyes towards her; but recollecting himself, he bent them again on the ground with stubborn resolution.

"Will not my learned brother, on the other side of the bar," continued the advocate, after a short pause, "share in this general joy, since I know, while he discharges his duty in bringing an accused person here, no one rejoices more in their being freely and honourably sent hence? My learned brother shakes his head doubtfully, and lays his hand on the panel's declaration. I understand him perfectly—he would insinuate that the facts now stated to your Lordships are inconsistent with the confession of Euphemia Deans herself. I need not remind your Lordships, that her present defence is no whit to be narrowed within the bounds of her former confession ; and that it is not by any account which she may formerly have given of herself, but by what is now to be proved for or against her, that she must ultimately stand or fall. I am not under the necessity of accounting for her choosing to drop out of her declaration the circumstances of her confession to her sister. She might not be aware of its importance ; she might be afraid of implicating her sister ; she might even have forgotten the circumstance entirely, in the terror and distress of mind incidental to the arrest of so young a creature on a charge so heinous. Any of these reasons are sufficient to account for her having suppressed the truth in this instance, at whatever risk to herself ; and I incline most to her erroneous fear of criminating her sister, because I observe she has had a similar tenderness towards her lover (however undeserved on his part), and has never once mentioned Robertson's name from beginning to end of her declaration.

"But, my Lords," continued Fairbrother, "I am aware the King's Advocate will expect me to show, that the proof I offer is consistent with other circumstances

of the case, which I do not and cannot deny. He will
demand of me how Effie Deans's confession to her sister,
previous to her delivery, is reconcilable with the
mystery of the birth,—with the disappearance, perhaps
the murder (for I will not deny a possibility which I
cannot disprove) of the infant. My Lords, the explanation of this is to be found in the placability, perchance,
I may say, in the facility and pliability, of the female
sex. The *dulcis Amaryllidis iræ*, as your Lordships
well know, are easily appeased ; nor is it possible to
conceive a woman so atrociously offended by the man
whom she has loved, but that she will retain a fund of
forgiveness, upon which his penitence, whether real or
affected, may draw largely, with a certainty that his bills
will be answered. We can prove, by a letter produced
in evidence, that this villain Robertson, from the bottom
of the dungeon whence he already probably meditated
the escape, which he afterwards accomplished by the
assistance of his comrade, contrived to exercise authority
over the mind, and to direct the motions, of this
unhappy girl. It was in compliance with his in-
junctions, expressed in that letter, that the panel was
prevailed upon to alter the line of conduct which her
own better thoughts had suggested ; and, instead of
resorting, when her time of travail approached, to the
protection of her own family, was induced to confide
herself to the charge of some vile agent of this nefarious
seducer, and by her conducted to one of those solitary
and secret purlieus of villany, which, to the shame of our
police, still are suffered to exist in the suburbs of this

city, where, with the assistance, and under the charge, of
a person of her own sex, she bore a male-child, under
circumstances which added treble bitterness to the wo
denounced against our original mother. What purpose
Robertson had in all this, it is hard to tell or even to
guess. He may have meant to marry the girl, for her
father is a man of substance. But, for the termination
of the story, and the conduct of the woman whom he
had placed about the person of Euphemia Deans, it is
still more difficult to account. The unfortunate young
woman was visited by the fever incidental to her situation. In this fever she appears to have been deceived
by the person that waited on her, and, on recovering
her senses, she found that she was childless in that
abode of misery. Her infant had been carried off, perhaps for the worst purposes, by the wretch that waited
on her. It may have been murdered for what I can
tell."

He was here interrupted by a piercing shriek,
uttered by the unfortunate prisoner. She was with
difficulty brought to compose herself. Her counsel
availed himself of the tragical interruption, to close his
pleading with effect.

"My Lords," said he, "in that piteous cry you
heard the eloquence of maternal affection, far surpassing
the force of my poor words—Rachel weeping for her
children! Nature herself bears testimony in favour of
the tenderness and acuteness of the prisoner's parental
feelings. I will not dishonour her plea by adding a
word more."

" Heard ye ever the like o' that, Laird ?" said Saddle-tree to Dumbiedikes, when the counsel had ended his speech. " There's a chield can spin a muckle pirn out of a wee tait of tow ! Deil haet he kens mair about it than what's in the declaration, and a surmise that Jeanie Deans suld hae been able to say something about her sister's situation, whilk surmise, Mr. Crossmyloof says, rests on sma' authority. And he's cleckit this great muckle bird out o' this wee egg ! He could wile the very flounders out o' the Firth. — What garr'd my father no send me to Utrecht ?—But whisht, the Court is gaun to pronounce the interlocutor of relevancy."

And accordingly the Judges, after a few words, recorded their judgment, which bore, that the indict-ment, if proved, was relevant to infer the pains of law : And that the defence, that the panel had communicated her situation to her sister, was a relevant defence : And, finally, appointed the said indictment and defence to be submitted to the judgment of an assize.

CHAPTER THE TWENTY-THIRD.

Most righteous judge! a sentence.—Come, prepare.
MERCHANT OF VENICE.

IT is by no means my intention to describe minutely
the forms of a Scottish criminal trial, nor am I sure
that I could draw up an account so intelligible and
accurate as to abide the criticism of the gentlemen of
the long robe. It is enough to say that the jury was
impanelled, and the case proceeded. The prisoner was
again required to plead to the charge, and she again
replied, "Not Guilty," in the same heart-thrilling tone
as before.

The crown counsel then called two or three female
witnesses, by whose testimony it was established, that
Effie's situation had been remarked by them, that they
had taxed her with the fact, and that her answers
had amounted to an angry and petulant denial of
what they charged her with. But, as very frequently
happens, the declaration of the panel or accused party
herself was the evidence which bore hardest upon her
case.

In the event of these Tales ever finding their way
across the Border, it may be proper to apprise the
southern reader that it is the practice in Scotland, on

apprehending a suspected person, to subject him to a
judicial examination before a magistrate. He is not
compelled to answer any of the questions asked of him,
but may remain silent if he sees it his interest to do so.
But whatever answers he chooses to give are formally
written down, and being subscribed by himself and
the magistrate, are produced against the accused in case
of his being brought to trial. It is true, that these
declarations are not produced as being in themselves
evidence properly so called, but only as *adminicles* of
testimony, tending to corroborate what is considered as
legal and proper evidence. Notwithstanding this nice
distinction, however, introduced by lawyers to reconcile
this procedure to their own general rule, that a man
cannot be required to bear witness against himself, it
nevertheless usually happens that these declarations
become the means of condemning the accused, as it
ware, out of their own mouths. The prisoner, upon
these previous examinations, has indeed the privilege
of remaining silent if he pleases; but every man necessarily feels that a refusal to answer natural and pertinent
interrogatories, put by judicial authority, is in itself a
strong proof of guilt, and will certainly lead to his being
committed to prison; and few can renounce the hope
of obtaining liberty, by giving some specious account of
themselves, and showing apparent frankness in explaining their motives and accounting for their conduct.
It, therefore, seldom happens that the prisoner refuses
to give a judicial declaration, in which, nevertheless,
either by letting out too much of the truth, or by

endeavouring to substitute a fictitious story, he almost always exposes himself to suspicion and to contradictions, which weigh heavily in the minds of the jury.

The declaration of Effie Deans was uttered on other principles, and the following is a sketch of its contents, given in the judicial form, in which they may still be found in the Books of Adjournal.

The declarant admitted a criminal intrigue with an individual whose name she desired to conceal. " Being interrogated, what her reason was for secrecy on this point ? She declared, that she had no right to blame that person's conduct more than she did her own, and that she was willing to confess her own faults, but not to say any thing which might criminate the absent. Interrogated, if she confessed her situation to any one, or made any preparation for her confinement ? Declares, she did not. And being interrogated, why she forbore to take steps which her situation so peremptorily required ? Declares, she was ashamed to tell her friends, and she trusted the person she has mentioned would provide for her and the infant. Interrogated, if he did so ? Declares, that he did not do so personally ; but that it was not his fault, for that the declarant is convinced he would have laid down his life sooner than the bairn or she had come to harm. Interrogated, what prevented him from keeping his promise ? Declares, that it was impossible for him to do so, he being under trouble at the time, and declines farther answer to this question. Interrogated, where she was from the period she left her master, Mr. Saddletree's family,

until her appearance at her father's, at St. Leonard's
the day before she was apprehended? Declares, she
does not remember. And, on the interrogatory being
repeated, declares, she does not mind muckle about it,
for she was very ill. On the question being again
repeated, she declares, she will tell the truth, if it
should be the undoing of her, so long as she is not
asked to tell on other folk; and admits, that she passed
that interval of time in the lodging of a woman, an
acquaintance of that person who had wished her to
that place to be delivered, and that she was there
delivered accordingly of a male child. Interrogated,
what was the name of that person? Declares and
refuses to answer this question. Interrogated, where
she lives? Declares she has no certainty, for that she
was taken to the lodging aforesaid under cloud of night.
Interrogated, if the lodging was in the city or suburbs?
Declares and refuses to answer that question. Interrogated, whether, when she left the house of Mr.
Saddletree, she went up or down the street? Declares
and refuses to answer the question. Interrogated,
whether she had ever seen the woman before she was
wished to her, as she termed it, by the person whose
name she refuses to answer? Declares and replies, not
to her knowledge. Interrogated, whether this woman
was introduced to her by the said person verbally, or
by word of mouth? Declares, she has no freedom to
answer this question. Interrogated, if the child was
alive when it was born? Declares, that—God help
her and it!—it certainly was alive. Interrogated, if it

died a natural death after birth? Declares, not to her knowledge. Interrogated, where it now is? Declares, she would give her right hand to ken, but that she never hopes to see mair than the banes of it. And being interrogated, why she supposes it is now dead? the declarant wept bitterly, and made no answer. Interrogated, if the woman, in whose lodging she was, seemed to be a fit person to be with her in that situation? Declares, she might be fit enough for skill, but that she was a hard-hearted bad woman. Interrogated, if there was any other person in the lodging excepting themselves two? Declares, that she thinks there was another woman; but her head was so carried with pain of body and trouble of mind, that she minded her very little. Interrogated, when the child was taken away from her? Declared, that she fell in a fever, and was light-headed, and when she came to her own mind, the woman told her the bairn was dead; and that the declarant answered, if it was dead it had had foul play. That, thereupon, the woman was very sair on her, and gave her much ill-language; and that the deponent was frightened, and crawled out of the house when her back was turned, and went home to Saint Leonard's Crags, as well as a woman in her condition dought.* Interrogated, why she did not tell her story to her sister and father, and get force to search the house for her child, dead or alive? Declares, it was her purpose to do so, but she had not time. Interrogated, why she now conceals the name of the woman,

* i. e. was able to do.

and the place of her abode? The declarant remained
silent for a time, and then said, that to do so could not
repair the skaith that was done, but might be the occasion of more.   Interrogated, whether she had herself, at
any time, had any purpose of putting away the child by
violence? Declares, never; so might God be merciful
to her—and then again declares, never, when she was
in her perfect senses; but what bad thoughts the Enemy
might put into her brain when she was out of herself,
she cannot answer.   And again solemnly interrogated,
declares, that she would have been drawn with wild
horses, rather than have touched the bairn with an un-
motherly hand.   Interrogated, declares, that among the
ill-language the woman gave her, she did say sure enough
that the declarant had hurt the bairn when she was in
the brain-fever; but that the declarant does not believe
that she said this from any other cause than to frighten
her, and make her be silent.   Interrogated, what else
the woman said to her?   Declares, that when the
declarant cried loud for her bairn, and was like to raise
the neighbours, the woman threatened her, that they
that could stop the wean's skirling would stop hers,
if she did not keep a' the lounder.*   And that this
threat, with the manner of the woman, made the declarant conclude, that the bairn's life was gone, and her
own in danger, for that the woman was a desperate
bad woman, as the declarant judged, from the language
she used.   Interrogated, declares, that the fever and
delirium were brought on her by hearing bad news,

* i. e. the quieter.

suddenly told to her, but refuses to say what the said news related to. Interrogated, why she does not now communicate these particulars, which might, perhaps, enable the magistrate to ascertain whether the child is living or dead; and requested to observe, that her refusing to do so exposes her own life, and leaves the child in bad hands; as also, that her present refusal to answer on such points, is inconsistent with her alleged intention to make a clean breast to her sister? Declares, that she kens the bairn is now dead, or, if living, there is one that will look after it; that for her own living or dying, she is in God's hands, who knows her innocence of harming her bairn with her will or knowledge; and that she has altered her resolution of speaking out, which she entertained when she left the woman's lodging, on account of a matter which she has since learned. And declares, in general, that she is wearied, and will answer no more questions at this time."

Upon a subsequent examination, Euphemia Deans adhered to the declaration she had formerly made, with this addition, that a paper found in her trunk being shown to her, she admitted that it contained the credentials, in consequence of which she resigned herself to the conduct of the woman at whose lodgings she was delivered of the child.   Its tenor ran thus :—

"DEAREST EFFIE,—I have gotten the means to send to you by a woman who is well qualified to assist you in your approaching streight; she is not what I could wish her but I cannot do better for you in my present condition. I am obliged to trust to her in this present calamity, for myself and you too. I hope for the best, though I am now in a sore pinch; yet thought is free—I think Handie Dandie and I may queer the stifler* for all that is come and gone. You will be angry for me writing this, to my little Cameronian Lily; but if I can but live to be a comfort to you, and a father to your babie, you will have plenty of time to scold.—Once more let none know your counsel—my life depends on this hag, d—n her—she is both deep and dangerous, but she has more wiles and wit than ever were in a beldam's head, and has cause to be true to me. Farewell, my Lily—Do not droop on my account—in a week I will be yours, or no more my own."

Then followed a postscript. " If they must truss me, I will repent of nothing so much, even at the last hard pinch, as of the injury I have done my Lily."

Effie refused to say from whom she had received this letter, but enough of the story was now known, to ascertain that it came from Robertson; and from the date, it appeared to have been written about the time when Andrew Wilson (called for a nickname Handie Dandie) and he were meditating their first abortive attempt to escape, which miscarried in the manner mentioned in the beginning of this history.

The evidence of the Crown being concluded, the counsel for the prisoner began to lead a proof in her defence. The first witnesses were examined upon the

* Avoid the gallows.

girl's character. All gave her an excellent one, but none with more feeling than worthy Mrs. Saddletree, who, with the tears on her cheeks, declared, that she could not have had a higher opinion of Effie Deans, nor a more sincere regard for her, if she had been her own daughter. All present gave the honest woman credit for her goodness of heart, excepting her husband, who whispered to Dumbiedikes, "That Nichil Novit of yours is but a raw hand at leading evidence, I'm thinking. What signified his bringing a woman here to snotter and snivel, and bather their Lordships? He should hae cooted me, sir, and I should hae gien them sic a screed o' testimony, they shouldna hae touched a hair o' her head."

"Hadna ye better get up and try't yet?" said the Laird. "I'll mak a sign to Novit."

"Na, na," said Saddletree, "thank ye for naething, neighbour—that would be ultroneous evidence, and I ken what belangs to that; but Nichil Novit suld hae had me cooted *debito tempore.*" And wiping his mouth with his silk handkerchief with great importance, he resumed the port and manner of an edified and intelligent auditor.

Mr. Fairbrother now premised in a few words, "That he meant to bring forward his most important witness, upon whose evidence the cause must in a great measure depend. What his client was, they had learned from the preceding witnesses; and so far as general character, given in the most forcible terms, and even with tears, could interest every one in her fate, she had

already gained that advantage. It was necessary, he
admitted, that he should produce more positive testimony of her innocence than what arose out of general
character, and this he undertook to do by the mouth of
the person to whom she had communicated her situation
—by the mouth of her natural counsellor and guardian
—her sister.—Macer, call into court, Jean, or Jeanie
Deans, daughter of David Deans, cow-feeder, at Saint
Leonard's Crags."

When he uttered these words, the poor prisoner
instantly started up, and stretched herself half-way
over the bar, towards the side at which her sister was
to enter. And when, slowly following the officer, the
witness advanced to the foot of the table, Effie, with
the whole expression of her countenance altered, from
that of confused shame and dismay, to an eager,
imploring, and almost ecstatic earnestness of entreaty,
with outstretched hands, hair streaming back, eyes
raised eagerly to her sister's face, and glistening through
tears, exclaimed, in a tone which went through the
heart of all who heard her—"O Jeanie, Jeanie, save
me, save me!"

With a different feeling, yet equally appropriated to
his proud and self-dependent character, old Deans drew
himself back still farther under the cover of the bench ;
so that when Jeanie, as she entered the court, cast a
timid glance towards the place at which she had left
him seated, his venerable figure was no longer visible.
He sate down on the other side of Dumbiedikes,
wrung his hand hard, and whispered, "Ah, Laird, this

is warst of a'—if I can but win ower this part—I feel
my head unco dizzy; but my Master is strong in his
servant's weakness." After a moment's mental prayer,
he again started up, as if impatient of continuing in any
one posture, and gradually edged himself forward
towards the place he had just quitted.

Jeanie in the meantime had advanced to the bottom
of the table, when, unable to resist the impulse of
affection, she suddenly extended her hand to her sister.
Effie was just within the distance that she could seize
it with both hers, press it to her mouth, cover it with
kisses, and bathe it in tears, with the fond devotion
that a Catholic would pay to a guardian saint descended
for his safety ; while Jeanie, hiding her own face with
her other hand, wept bitterly. The sight would have
moved a heart of stone, much more of flesh and blood.
Many of the spectators shed tears, and it was some time
before the presiding Judge himself could so far subdue
his emotion, as to request the witness to compose
herself, and the prisoner to forbear those marks of
eager affection, which, however natural, could not be
permitted at that time, and in that presence.

The solemn oath,—" the truth to tell, and no truth
to conceal, as far as she knew or should be asked," was
then administered by the Judge "in the name of God,
and as the witness should answer to God at the great
day of judgment ;" an awful adjuration, which seldom
fails to make impression even on the most hardened characters, and to strike with fear even the most upright.
Jeanie, educated in deep and devout reverence for the

name and attributes of the Deity, was, by the solemnity
of a direct appeal to his person and justice, awed, but
at the same time elevated above all considerations,
save those which she could, with a clear conscience
call him to witness. She repeated the form in a low
and reverent, but distinct tone of voice, after the
Judge, to whom, and not to any inferior officer of the
court, the task is assigned in Scotland of directing the
witness in that solemn appeal, which is the sanction of
his testimony.

When the Judge had finished the established form,
he added in a feeling, but yet a monitory tone, an
advice, which the circumstances appeared to him to call
for.

"Young woman," these were his words, "you come
before this Court in circumstances, which it would be
worse than cruel not to pity and to sympathize with.
Yet it is my duty to tell you, that the truth, whatever
its consequences may be, the truth is what you owe to
your country, and to that God whose word is truth,
and whose name you have now invoked. Use your
own time in answering the questions that gentleman"
(pointing to the counsel) "shall put to you—But
remember, that what you may be tempted to say
beyond what is the actual truth, you must answer both
here and hereafter."

The usual questions were then put to her :—Whether
any one had instructed her what evidence she had to
deliver ? Whether any one had given or promised her
any good deed, hire, or reward, for her testimony ?

Whether she had any malice or ill-will at his Majesty's
Advocate, being the party against whom she was cited
as a witness? To which questions she successively
answered by a quiet negative. But their tenor gave
great scandal and offence to her father, who was not
aware that they are put to every witness as a matter of
form.

"Na, na," he exclaimed, loud enough to be heard,
"my bairn is no like the widow of Tekoah—nae man
has putten words into her mouth."

One of the Judges, better acquainted, perhaps, with
the Books of Adjournal than with the Book of Samuel,
was disposed to make some instant inquiry after this
Widow of Tekoah, who, as he construed the matter,
had been tampering with the evidence. But the
presiding Judge, better versed in Scripture history,
whispered to his learned brother the necessary explanation; and the pause occasioned by this mistake, had
the good effect of giving Jeanie Deans time to collect
her spirits for the painful task she had to perform.

Fairbrother, whose practice and intelligence were
considerable, saw the necessity of letting the witness
compose herself. In his heart he suspected that she
came to bear false witness in her sister's cause.

"But that is her own affair," thought Fairbrother;
"and it is my business to see that she has plenty of
time to regain composure, and to deliver her evidence,
be it true, or be it false—*valeat quantum.*"

Accordingly, he commenced his interrogatories with
uninteresting questions, which admitted of instant reply.

" You are, I think, the sister of the prisoner?"

" Yes, sir."

" Not the full sister, however?"

" No, sir—we are by different mothers."

"True; and you are, I think, several years older than your sister?"

" Yes, sir," etc.

After the advocate had conceived that, by these preliminary and unimportant questions, he had familiarized the witness with the situation in which she stood, he asked, "whether she had not remarked her sister's state of health to be altered, during the latter part of the term when she had lived with Mrs. Saddletree?"

Jeanie answered in the affirmative.

"And she told you the cause of it, my dear, I suppose?" said Fairbrother, in an easy, and, as one may say, an inductive sort of tone.

"I am sorry to interrupt my brother," said the Crown Counsel; rising, "but I am in your Lordships' judgment, whether this be not a leading question?"

"If this point is to be debated," said the presiding Judge, "the witness must be removed."

For the Scottish lawyers regard with a sacred and scrupulous horror, every question so shaped by the counsel examining, as to convey to a witness the least intimation of the nature of the answer which is desired from him. These scruples, though founded on an excellent principle, are sometimes carried to an absurd pitch of nicety, especially as it is generally easy for a

lawyer who has his wits about him to elude the objection. Fairbrother did so in the present case.

"It is not necessary to waste the time of the Court,
my Lord; since the King's Counsel thinks it worth
while to object to the form of my question, I will shape
it otherwise.—I'ray, young woman, did you ask your
sister any question when you observed her looking
unwell?—take courage—speak out."

"I asked her," replied Jeanie, "what ailed her."

"Very well—take your own time—and what was
the answer she made?" continued Mr. Fairbrother.

Jeanie was silent, and looked deadly pale. It was
not that she at any one instant entertained an idea of
the possibility of prevarication—it was the natural
hesitation to extinguish the last spark of hope that
remained for her sister.

"Take courage, young woman," said Fairbrother.—
"I asked what your sister said ailed her when you
inquired?"

"Nothing," answered Jeanie, with a faint voice,
which was yet heard distinctly in the most distant
corner of the Court-room,—such an awful and profound
silence had been preserved during the anxious interval
which had interposed betwixt the lawyer's question and
the answer of the witness.

Fairbrother's countenance fell; but with that ready
presence of mind, which is as useful in civil as in
military emergencies, he immediately rallied.—"Nothing? True; you mean nothing at *first*—but when you
asked her again, did she not tell you what ailed her?"

The question was put in a tone meant to make her comprehend the importance of her answer, had she not been already aware of it. The ice was broken, however, and, with less pause than at first, she now replied,— "Alack! alack! she never breathed a word to me about it."

A deep groan passed through the Court. It was echoed by one deeper and more agonized from the unfortunate father. The hope, to which unconsciously, and in spite of himself, he had still secretly clung, had now dissolved, and the venerable old man fell forward senseless on the floor of the Court-house, with his head at the foot of his terrified daughter. The unfortunate prisoner, with impotent passion, strove with the guards, betwixt whom she was placed. "Let me gang to my father!—I *will* gang to him—I *will* gang to him—he is dead—he is killed—I hae killed him!"—she repeated in frenzied tones of grief, which those who heard them did not speedily forget.

Even in this moment of agony and general confusion, Jeanie did not lose that superiority, which a deep and firm mind assures to its possessor, under the most trying circumstances.

"He is my father—he is our father," she mildly repeated to those who endeavoured to separate them, as she stooped,—shaded aside his grey hairs, and began assiduously to chafe his temples.

The Judge, after repeatedly wiping his eyes, gave directions that they should be conducted into a neighbouring apartment, and carefully attended. The prisoner, as her father was borne from the Court, and her sister slowly followed, pursued them with her eyes so earnestly fixed, as if they would have started from their sockets. But when they were no longer visible, she seemed to find, in her despairing and deserted state, a courage which she had not yet exhibited.

"The bitterness of it is now past," she said, and then boldly addressed the Court. "My Lords, if it is your pleasure to gang on wi' this matter, the weariest day will hae its end at last.

The Judge, who, much to his honour, had shared deeply in the general sympathy, was surprised at being recalled to his duty by the prisoner. He collected himself, and requested to know if the panel's counsel had more evidence to produce. Fairbrother replied, with an air of dejection, that his proof was concluded.

The King's Counsel addressed the jury for the crown. He said in a few words, that no one could be more concerned than he was for the distressing scene which they had just witnessed. But it was the necessary consequence of great crimes to bring distress and ruin upon all connected with the perpetrators. He briefly reviewed the proof, in which he showed that all the circumstances of the case concurred with those required by the act under which the unfortunate prisoner was tried: That the counsel for the panel had totally failed in proving, that Euphemia Deans had communicated her situation to her sister: That, respecting her previous good character, he was sorry to observe, that it was females who possessed the world's good report, and to whom it was justly valuable, who were most strongly tempted, by shame and fear of the world's censure, to the crime of infanticide: That the child was murdered, he professed to entertain no doubt. The vacillating and inconsistent declaration of the prisoner herself, marked as it was by numerous refusals to speak the truth on subjects, when, according to her own story, it would have been natural, as well as advantageous, to have been candid; even this imperfect declaration left no doubt in his mind as to the fate of the unhappy infant. Neither could he doubt that the panel was a partner in this guilt. Who else had an interest in a deed so inhuman? Surely neither Robertson, nor Robertson's agent, in whose house she was delivered, had the least temptation to commit such a crime, unless upon her account, with her connivance, and for the sake of saving her reputation. But it was not required of him, by the law, that he should bring precise proof of the murder, or of the prisoner's accession to it. It was the very purpose of the statute to substitute a certain chain of presumptive evidence in place of a probation, which, in such cases, it was peculiarly difficult to obtain. The jury might peruse the statute itself, and they had also the libel and interlocutor of relevancy to direct them in point of law. He put it to the conscience of the jury, that under both he was entitled to a verdict of Guilty.

The charge of Fairbrother was much cramped by his having failed in the proof which he expected to lead. But he fought his losing cause with courage and con-

stancy. He ventured to arraign the severity of the
statute under which the young woman was tried. "In
all other cases," he said, "the first thing required of the
criminal prosecutor was, to prove unequivocally that the
crime libelled had actually been committed, which
lawyers called proving the *corpus delicti*. But this
statute, made doubtless with the best intentions, and
under the impulse of a just horror for the unnatural
crime of infanticide, ran the risk of itself occasioning
the worst of murders, the death of an innocent person,
to atone for a supposed crime which may never have
been committed by any one. He was so far from
acknowledging the alleged probability of the child's
violent death, that he could not even allow that there
was evidence of its having ever lived."

The King's Counsel pointed to the woman's declaration; to which the counsel replied—"A production
concocted in a moment of terror and agony, and which
approached to insanity," he said, "his learned brother
well knew was no sound evidence against the party who
emitted it. It was true, that a judicial confession, in
presence of the Justices themselves, was the strongest
of all proof, in so much that it is said in law, that '*in
confitentem nullæ sunt partes judicis.*' But this was
true of judicial confession only, by which law meant
that which is made in presence of the justices, and the
sworn inquest. Of extrajudicial confession, all authorities held with the illustrious Farinaceus, and Matheus,
'*confessio extrajudicialis in se nulla est; et quod nullum
est, non potest adminiculari.*' It was totally inept, and

void of all strength and effect from the beginning; incapable, therefore, of being bolstered up or supported, or, according to the law-phrase, adminiculated, by other presumptive circumstances. In the present case, therefore, letting the extrajudicial confession go, as it ought to go, for nothing," he contended, "the prosecutor had not made out the second quality of the statute, that a live child had been born; and *that*, at least, ought to be established before presumptions were received that it had been murdered. If any of the assize," he said, "should be of opinion that this was dealing rather narrowly with the statute, they ought to consider that it was in its nature highly penal, and therefore entitled to no favourable construction."

He concluded a learned speech, with an eloquent peroration on the scene they had just witnessed, during which Saddletree fell fast asleep.

It was now the presiding Judge's turn to address the jury. He did so briefly and distinctly.

"It was for the jury," he said, "to consider whether the prosecutor had made out his plea. For himself, he sincerely grieved to say, that a shadow of doubt remained not upon his mind concerning the verdict which the inquest had to bring in. He would not follow the prisoner's counsel through the impeachment which he had brought against the statute of King William and Queen Mary. He and the jury were sworn to judge according to the laws as they stood, not to criticise, or evade, or even to justify them. In no civil case would a counsel have been permitted to plead his

client's case in the teeth of the law ; but in the hard
situation in which counsel were often placed in the
Criminal Court, as well as out of favour to all presumptions of innocence, he had not inclined to interrupt the·
learned gentleman, or narrow his plea.   The present
law, as it now stood, had been instituted by the wisdom
of their fathers, to check the alarming progress of a
dreadful crime ; when it was found too severe for its
purpose, it would doubtless be altered by the wisdom
of the legislature ; at present it was the law · of the
land, the rule of the court, and according to the oath
which they had taken, it must be that of the jury.
This unhappy girl's situation could not be doubted ;
that she had borne a child, and that the child had disappeared, were certain facts.   The learned counsel had
failed to show that she had communicated her situation.   All the requisites of the case required by the
statute were therefore before the jury.   The learned
gentleman had, indeed, desired them to throw out of
consideration the panel's own confession, which was the
plea usually urged, in penury of all others, by counsel
in his situation, who usually felt that the declarations of
their clients bore hard on them.   But that the Scottish
law designed that a certain weight should be layed on
these declarations, which, he admitted, were *quodammodo* extrajudicial, was evident from the universal
practice by which they were always produced and read,
as part of the prosecutor's probation.   In the present
case, no person, who had heard the witnesses describe the
appearance of the young woman before she left Saddle-

tree's house, and contrasted it with that of her state and
condition at her return to her father's, could have any
doubt that the fact of delivery had taken place, as set
forth in her own declaration, which was, therefore, not
a solitary piece of testimony, but adminiculated and
supported by the strongest circumstantial proof.

"He did not," he said, "state the impression upon
his own mind with the purpose of biassing theirs. He
had felt no less than they had done from the scene of
domestic misery which had been exhibited before them;
and if they, having God and a good conscience, the
sanctity of their oath, and the regard due to the law of
the country, before their eyes, could come to a conclusion
favourable to this unhappy prisoner, he should rejoice
as much as any one in Court; for never had he found
his duty more distressing than in discharging it that
day, and glad he would be to be relieved from the still
more painful task, which would otherwise remain for
him."

The jury, having heard the Judge's address, bowed
and retired, preceded by a macer of Court, to the apartment destined for their deliberation.

CHAPTER THE TWENTY-FOURTH.

Law, take thy victim—May she find the mercy
In yon mild heaven, which this hard world denies her!

IT was an hour ere the jurors returned, and as they
traversed the crowd with slow steps, as men about to

discharge themselves of a heavy and painful responsibility, the audience was hushed into profound, earnest,
and awful silence.

"Have you agreed on your chancellor, gentlemen?"
was the first question of the Judge.

The foreman, called in Scotland the chancellor of
the jury, usually the man of best rank and estimation
among the assizers, stepped forward, and, with a low
reverence, delivered to the Court a sealed paper, containing the verdict, which, until of late years, that
verbal returns are in some instances permitted, was
always couched in writing. The jury remained standing
while the Judge broke the seals, and, having perused
the paper, handed it, with an air of mournful gravity,
down to the Clerk of Court, who proceeded to engross
in the record the yet unknown verdict, of which, however, all omened the tragical contents. A form still
remained, trifling and unimportant in itself, but to
which imagination adds a sort of solemnity, from the
awful occasion upon which it is used. A lighted candle
was placed on the table, the original paper containing
the verdict was enclosed in a sheet of paper, and, sealed
with the Judge's own signet, was transmitted to the
Crown Office, to be preserved among other records of
the same kind. As all this is transacted in profound
silence, the producing and extinguishing the candle
seems a type of the human spark which is shortly
afterwards doomed to be quenched, and excites in the
spectators something of the same effect which in England
is obtained by the Judge assuming the fatal cap of

judgment. When these preliminary forms had been gone through, the Judge required Euphemia Deans to attend to the verdict to be read.

After the usual words of style, the verdict set forth, that the Jury having made choice of John Kirk, Esq., to be their chancellor, and Thomas Moore, merchant, to be their clerk, did, by a plurality of voices, find the said Euphemia Deans GUILTY of the crime libelled; but, in consideration of her extreme youth, and the cruel circumstances of her case did, earnestly entreat that the Judge would recommend her to the mercy of the Crown.

"Gentlemen," said the Judge, "you have done your duty—and a painful one it must have been to men of humanity like you. I will, undoubtedly, transmit your recommendation to the throne. But it is my duty to tell all who now hear me, but especially to inform that unhappy young woman, in order that her mind may be settled accordingly, that I have not the least hope of a pardon being granted in the present case. You know the crime has been increasing in this land, and I know further, that this has been ascribed to the lenity in which the laws have been exercised, and that there is therefore no hope whatever of obtaining a remission for this offence." The jury bowed again, and, released from their painful office, dispersed themselves among the mass of bystanders.

The Court then asked Mr. Fairbrother, whether he had any thing to say, why judgment should not follow on the verdict? The counsel had spent some time in

perusing, and reperusing the verdict, counting the
letters in each juror's name, and weighing every phrase,
nay every syllable, in the nicest scales of legal criticism.
But the clerk of the jury had understood his business
too well. No flaw was to be found, and Fairbrother
mournfully intimated, that he had nothing to say in
arrest of judgment.

The presiding Judge then addressed the unhappy
prisoner :—" Euphemia Deans, attend to the sentence
of the Court now to be pronounced against you."

She rose from her seat, and, with a composure far
greater than could have been augured from her demeanour during some parts of the trial, abode the conclusion
of the awful scene. So nearly does the mental portion
of our feelings resemble those which are corporeal, that
the first severe blows which we receive bring with them
a stunning apathy, which renders us indifferent to those
that follow them. Thus said Mandrin, when he was
undergoing the punishment of the wheel ; and so have
all felt, upon whom successive inflictions have descended
with continuous and reiterated violence.

" Young woman," said the Judge, " it is my painful
duty to tell you, that your life is forfeited under a law,
which, if it may seem in some degree severe, is yet
wisely so, to render those of your unhappy situation
aware what risk they run, by concealing, out of pride or
false shame, their lapse from virtue, and making no
preparation to save the lives of the unfortunate infants
whom they are to bring into the world. When you
concealed your situation from your mistress, your sister,

and other worthy and compassionate persons of your own sex, in whose favour your former conduct had given you a fair place, you seem to me to have had in your contemplation, at least, the death of the helpless creature, for whose life you neglected to provide. How the child was disposed of—whether it was dealt upon by another, or by yourself—whether the extraordinary story you have told is partly false, or altogether so, is between God and your own conscience. I will not aggravate your distress by pressing on that topic, but I do most solemnly adjure you to employ the remaining space of your time in making your peace with God, for which purpose such reverend clergymen, as you yourself may name, shall have access to you. Notwithstanding the humane recommendation of the jury, I cannot afford to you, in the present circumstances of the country, the slightest hope that your life will be prolonged beyond the period assigned for the execution of your sentence. Forsaking, therefore, the thoughts of this world, let your mind be prepared by repentance for those of more awful moments—for death, judgment, and eternity.—Doomster, read the sentence." *

When the Doomster showed himself, a tall haggard figure, arrayed in a fantastic garment of black and grey, passmented with silver lace, all fell back with a sort of instinctive horror, and made wide way for him to approach the foot of the table. As this office was held by the common executioner, men shouldered each other backward to avoid even the touch of his garment, and

Note L. Doomster, or Dempster, of Court.

some were seen to brush their own clothes, which had
accidentally become subject to such contamination.   A
sound went through the court, produced by each person
drawing in their breath hard, as men do when they
expect or witness what is frightful, and at the same
time affecting.   The caitiff villain yet seemed, amid his
hardened brutality, to have some sense of his being the
object of public detestation, which made him impatient
of being in public, as birds of evil omen are anxious to
escape from daylight, and from pure air.

Repeating after the Clerk of Court, he gabbled over
the words of the sentence, which condemned Euphemia
Deans to be conducted back to the Tolbooth of Edinburgh, and detained there until Wednesday the ——
day of ——; and upon that day, betwixt the hours of
two and four o'clock afternoon, to be conveyed to the
common place of execution, and there hanged by the
neck upon a gibbet.   "And this," said the Doomster,
aggravating his harsh voice, "I pronounce for *doom.*"

He vanished when he had spoken the last emphatic
word, like a foul fiend after the purpose of his visitation
has been accomplished ; but the impression of horror,
excited by his presence and his errand, remained upon
the crowd of spectators.

The unfortunate criminal,—for so she must now be
termed,—with more susceptibility, and more irritable
feelings than her father and sister, was found, in this
emergence, to possess a considerable share of their
courage.   She had remained standing motionless at
the bar while the sentence was pronounced, and was

observed to shut her eyes when the Doomster appeared.
But she was the first to break silence when that evil
form had left his place.

"God forgive ye, my Lords," she said, " and dinna
be angry wi' me for wishing it—we a' need forgiveness.
—As for myself I canna blame ye, for ye act up to
your lights ; and if I havena killed my poor infant, ye
may witness a' that hae seen it this day, that I hae
been the means of killing my grey-headed father—I
deserve the warst frae man, and frae God too—But
God is mair mercifu' to us than we are to each other."

With these words, the trial concluded. The crowd
rushed, bearing forward and shouldering each other out
of the court, in the same tumultuary mode in which
they had entered ; and, in excitation of animal motion
and animal spirits, soon forgot whatever they had felt
as impressive in the scene which they had witnessed.
The professional spectators, whom habit and theory had
rendered as callous to the distress of the scene as medical men are to those of a surgical operation, walked
homeward in groups, discussing the general principle of
the statute under which the young woman was condemned, the nature of the evidence, and the arguments
of the counsel, without considering even that of the
Judge as exempt from their criticism.

The female spectators, more compassionate, were
loud in exclamation against that part of the Judge's
speech which seemed to cut off the hope of pardon.

"Set him up, indeed," said Mrs. Howden, "to tell
us that the poor lassie behoved to die, when Mr. John

Kirk, as civil a gentleman as is within the ports of the
town, took the pains to prigg for her himsell."

" Ay, but, neighbour," said Miss Damahoy, drawing
up her thin maidenly form to its full height of prim
dignity—" I really think this unnatural business of
having bastard-bairns should be putten a stop to.—
There isna a hussy now on this side of thirty that you
can bring within your doors but there will be chields
—writer-lads, prentice-lads, and what not—coming
traiking after them for their destruction, and discredit-
ing ane's honest house into the bargain—I hae nae
patience wi' them."

" Hout, neighbour," said Mrs. Howden, "we suld
live and let live—we hae been young oursells, and we
are no aye to judge the warst when lads and lasses
forgather."

"Young oursells! and judge the warst!" said Miss
Damahoy. "I am no ane auld as that comes to, Mrs.
Howden; and as for what ye ca' the warst, I ken
neither good nor bad about the matter, I thank my
stars!"

"Ye are thankfu' for sma' mercies, then," said Mrs.
Howden, with a toss of her head; "and as for *you* and
young—I trow ye were doing for yoursell at the last
riding of the Scots Parliament, and that was in the
gracious year seven, sae ye can be nae sic chicken at
ony rate."

Plumdamas, who acted as squire of the body to the
two contending dames, instantly saw the hazard of
entering into such delicate points of chronology, and

being a lover of peace and good neighbourhood, lost no time in bringing back the conversation to its original subject.

"The Judge didna tell us a' he could hae tell'd us, if he had liked, about the application for pardon, neighbours," said he; "there is aye a whimple in a lawyer's clew; but it's a wee bit of a secret."

"And what is't?—what is't, neighbour Plumdamas?" said Mrs. Howden and Miss Damahoy at once, the acid fermentation of their dispute being at once neutralized by the powerful alkali implied in the word secret.

"Here's Mr. Saddletree can tell ye that better than me, for it was him that tauld me," said Plumdamas as Saddletree came up, with his wife hanging on his arm, and looking very disconsolate.

When the question was put to Saddletree, he looked very scornful.   "They speak about stopping the frequency of child-murder," said he, in a contemptuous tone; "do ye think our auld enemies of England, as Glendook aye ca's them in his printed Statute-book, care a boddle whether we didna kill ane anither, skin and birn, horse and foot, man, woman, and bairns, all and sindry, *omnes et singulos*, as Mr. Crossmyloof says? Na, na, it's no *that* hinders them frae pardoning the bit lassie. But here is the pinch of the plea. The king and queen are sae ill pleased wi' that mistak about Porteous, that deil a kindly Scot will they pardon again, either by reprieve or remission, if the hail town o' Edinburgh should be a' hanged on ae tow."

"Deil that they were back at their German kale

yard then, as my neighbour MacCroskie ca's it," said Mrs.
Howden, "an that's the way they're gaun to guide us!"

"They say for certain," said Miss Damahoy, "that
King George flang his periwig in the fire when he
heard o' the Porteous mob."

"He has done that, they say," replied Saddletree,
"for less thing."

"Aweel," said Miss Damahoy, "he might keep mair
wit in his anger—but it's a' the better for his wig-
maker, I'se warrant."

"The queen tore her biggonets for perfect anger,—
ye'll hae heard o' that too?" said Plumdamas. "And
the king, they say, kickit Sir Robert Walpole for no
keeping down the mob of Edinburgh; but I dinna
believe he wad behave sae ungenteel."

"It's dooms truth, though," said Saddletree, "and
he was for kickin the Duke of Argyle* too."

"Kickin the Duke of Argyle!" exclaimed the
hearers at once, in all the various combined keys of
utter astonishment.

"Ay, but MacCallummore's blood wadna sit down
wi' that; there was risk of Andro Ferrara coming in
thirdsman."

"The duke is a real Scotsman—a true friend to the
country," answered Saddletree's hearers.

"Ay, troth is he, to king and country baith, as ye
sall hear," continued the orator, "if ye will come in bye
to our house, for it's safest speaking of sic things *inter
parietes*."

* Note M.   John Duke of Argyle and Greenwich.

When they entered his shop he thrust his prentice boy out of it, and, unlocking his desk, took out, with an air of grave and complacent importance, a dirty and crumpled piece of printed paper; he observed, "This is new corn—it's no every body could show ye the like o' this. It's the duke's speech about the Porteous mob, just promulgated by the hawkers. Ye shall hear what Ian Roy Cean* says for himself. My correspondent bought it in the Palace-yard, that's like just under the king's nose—I think he claws up their mittans !—It came in a letter about a foolish bill of exchange that the man wanted me to renew for him. I wish ye wad see about it, Mrs. Saddletree."

Honest Mrs. Saddletree had hitherto been so sincerely distressed about the situation of her unfortunate protégée, that she had suffered her husband to proceed in his own way, without attending to what he was saying. The words *bills* and *renew* had, however, an awakening sound in them; and she snatched the letter which her husband held towards her, and wiping her eyes, and putting on her spectacles, endeavoured, as fast as the dew which collected on her glasses would permit, to get at the meaning of the needful part of the epistle; while her husband, with pompous elevation, read an extract from the speech.

"I am no minister, I never was a minister, and I never will be one"——

* Red John the Warrior, a name personal and proper in the Highlands to John Duke of Argyle and Greenwich, as MacCummin was that of his race or dignity.

"I didna ken his grace was ever designed for the ministry," interrupted Mrs. Howden.

"He disna mean a minister of the gospel, Mrs. Howden, but a minister of state," said Saddletree, with condescending goodness, and then proceeded : "The time was when I might have been a piece of a minister, but I was too sensible of my own incapacity to engage in any state affair.   And I thank God that I had always too great a value for those few abilities which nature has given me, to employ them in doing any drudgery, or any job of what kind soever.   I have, ever since I set out in the world (and I believe few have set out more early), served my prince with my tongue; I have served him with any little interest I had, and I have served him with my sword, and in my profession of arms.   I have held employments which I have lost, and were I to be to-morrow deprived of those which still remain to me, and which I have endeavoured honestly to deserve, I would still serve him to the last acre of my inheritance, and to the last drop of my blood.——"

Mrs. Saddletree here broke in upon the orator :—
"Mr. Saddletree, what *is* the meaning of a' this? Here are ye clavering about the Duke of Argyle, and this man Martingale gaun to break on our hands, and lose us gude sixty pounds—I wonder what duke will pay that, quotha—I wish the Duke of Argyle would pay his ain accounts—He is in a thousand punds Scots on thae very books when he was last at Roystoun— I'm no saying but he's a just nobleman, and that it's

gude siller—but it wad drive ane daft to be confused wi' doukes and drakes, and thae distressed folk up stairs, that's Joanie Deans and her father. And then, putting the very callant that was sewing the curpel, out o' the shop, to play wi' blackguards in the close— Sit still, neighbours, it's no that I mean to disturb *you;* but what between courts o' law and courts o' state, and upper and under parliaments, and parliament-houses, here and in London, the gudeman's gane clean gyte, I think."

The gossips understood civility, and the rule of doing as they would be done by, too well, to tarry upon the slight invitation implied in the conclusion of this speech, and therefore made their farewells and departure as fast as possible, Saddletree whispering to Plumdamas that he would " meet him at MacCroskie's " (the low-browed shop in the Luckenbooths, already mentioned), " in the hour of cause, and put MacCallummore's speech in his pocket, for a' the gudewife's din."

When Mrs. Saddletree saw the house freed of her importunate visitors, and the little boy reclaimed from the pastimes of the wynd to the exercise of the awl, she went to visit her unhappy relative, David Deans, and his elder daughter, who had found in her house the nearest place of friendly refuge.

CHAPTER THE TWENTY-FIFTH

Isab. Alas! what poor ability's in me
  To do him good?
Lucio. Assay the power you have.
                    MEASURE FOR MEASURE.

WHEN Mrs. Saddletree entered the apartment in which
her guests had shrouded their misery, she found the
window darkened. The feebleness which followed his

long swoon had rendered it necessary to lay the old man in bed. The curtains were drawn around him, and Jeanie sate motionless by the side of the bed. Mrs. Saddletree was a woman of kindness, nay, of feeling, but not of delicacy. She opened the half-shut window, drew aside the curtain, and taking her kinsman by the hand, exhorted him to sit up, and bear his sorrow like a good man, and a Christian man, as he was. But when she quitted his hand, it fell powerless by his side, nor did he attempt the least reply.

"Is all over?" asked Jeanie, with lips and cheeks as pale as ashes,—"And is there nae hope for her?"

"Nane, or next to nane," said Mrs. Saddletree; "I heard the Judge-carle say it with my ain ears—It was a burning shame to see sae mony o' them set up yonder in their red gowns and black gowns, and to take the life o' a bit senseless lassie. I had never muckle broo o' my gudeman's gossips, and now I like them waur than ever. The only wiselike thing I heard ony body say, was decent Mr. John Kirk of Kirk-knowe, and he wussed them just to get the king's mercy, and nae mair about it. But he spake to unreasonable folk—he might just hae keepit his breath to hae blawn on his porridge."

"But *can* the king gie her mercy?" said Jeanie, earnestly. "Some folk tell me he canna gie mercy in cases of muur—— in cases like hers."

"*Can* he gie mercy, hinny?—I weel I wot he *can*, when he likes. There was young Singlesword, that stickit the Laird of Ballencleuch, and Captain Hackum, the Englishman, that killed Lady Colgrain's gudeman,

and the master of Saint Clair, that shot the twa Shaws,
and mony mair in my time—to be sure they were gentle
blood, and had their kin to speak for them—And there
was Jock Porteous the other day—I'se warrant there's
mercy, an folk could win at it."

"Porteous?" said Jeanie; "very true—I forget
a' that I suld maist mind.—Fare ye weel, Mrs. Saddletree; and may ye never want a friend in the hour o'
distress !"

"Will ye no stay wi' your father, Jeanie, bairn ?—
Ye had better," said Mrs. Saddletree.

"I will be wanted ower yonder," indicating the
Tolbooth with her hand, "and I maun leave him now,
or I will never be able to leave him. I fearna for his
life—I ken how strong-hearted he is—I ken it," she
said, laying her hand on her bosom, "by my ain heart
at this minute."

"Weel, hinny, if ye think it's for the best, better
he stay here and rest him, than gang back to St.
Leonard's."

"Muckle better—muckle better—God bless you !—
God bless you !—At no rate let him gang till ye hear
frae me," said Jeanie.

"But ye'll be back belive ?" said Mrs. Saddletree,
detaining her; "they wunna let ye stay yonder, hinny."

"But I maun gang to St. Leonard's—there's muckle
to be dune, and little time to do it in—And I have
friends to speak to—God bless you—take care of my
father."

She had reached the door of the apartment, when,

suddenly turning, she came back, and knelt down by
the bedside.—"O father, gie me your blessing—I dare
not go till ye bless me. Say but God bless ye, and
prosper ye, Jeanie—try but to say that !"

Instinctively, rather than by an exertion of intellect,
the old man murmured a prayer, that "purchased and
promised blessings might be multiplied upon her."

"He has blessed mine errand," said his daughter,
rising from her knees, "and it is borne in upon my
mind that I shall prosper."

So saying, she left the room.

Mrs. Saddletree looked after her, and shook her
head. "I wish she binna roving, poor thing—There's
something queer about a' thae Deanses. I dinna like
folk to be sae muckle better than other folk—seldom
comes gude o't. But if she's gaun to look after the
kye at St. Leonard's, that's another story ; to be sure
they maun be sorted.—Grizzie, come up here, and tak
tent to the honest auld man, and see he wants naething.
—Ye silly tawpie" (addressing the maid servant as she
entered), "what garr'd ye busk up your cockernony
that gate ?—I think there's been enough the day to gie
an awfu' warning about your cockups and your fallal
duds—see what they a' come to," etc. etc. etc.

Leaving the good lady to her lecture upon worldly
vanities, we must transport our reader to the cell in
which the unfortunate Effie Deans was now immured,
being restricted of several liberties which she had enjoyed before the sentence was pronounced.

When she had remained about an hour in the state

of stupified horror so natural in her situation, she was disturbed by the opening of the jarring bolts of her place of confinement, and Ratcliffe showed himself. "It's your sister," he said, "wants to speak t'ye, Effie."

"I canna see naebody," said Effie, with the hasty irritability which misery had rendered more acute—"I canna see naebody, and least of a' her—Bid her take care o' the auld man—I am naething to ony o' them now, nor them to me."

"She says she maun see ye, though," said Ratcliffe; and Jeanie, rushing into the apartment, threw her arms round her sister's neck, who writhed to extricate herself from her embrace.

"What signifies coming to greet ower me," said poor Effie, "when you have killed me?—killed me, when a word of your mouth would have saved me—killed me, when I am an innocent creature—innocent of that guilt at least—and me that wad hae wared body and soul to save your finger from being hurt!"

"You shall not die," said Jeanie, with enthusiastic firmness; "say what ye like o' me—think what ye like o' me—only promise—for I doubt your proud heart—that ye wunna harm yourself, and you shall not die this shameful death."

"A *shameful* death I will not die, Jeanie, lass. I have that in my heart—though it has been ower kind a ane—that wunna bide shame. Gae hame to our father, and think nae mair on me—I have eat my last earthly meal." .

"O, this was what I feared!" said Jeanie.

"Hout, tont, hinnie," said Ratcliffe; "it's but little ye ken o' thae things. Ane aye thinks at the first dinnle o' the sentence, they hae heart eneugh to die rather than bide out the sax weeks; but they aye bide the sax weeks out for a' that. I ken the gate o't weel; I hae fronted the doomster three times, and here I stand, Jim Ratcliffe, for a' that. Had I tied my napkin strait the first time, as I had a great mind till't—and it was a' about a bit grey cowt, wasna worth ten punds sterling—where would I have been now?"

"And how *did* you escape?" said Jeanie, the fates of this man, at first so odious to her, having acquired a sudden interest in her eyes from their correspondence with those of her sister.

"*How* did I escape?" said Ratcliffe, with a knowing wink,—"I tell ye I 'scapit in a way that naebody will escape from this Tolbooth while I keep the keys."

"My sister shall come out in the face of the sun," said Jeanie; "I will go to London, and beg her pardon from the king and queen. If they pardoned Porteous, they may pardon her; if a sister asks a sister's life on her bended knees, they *will* pardon her—they *shall* pardon her—and they will win a thousand hearts by it."

Effie listened in bewildered astonishment, and so earnest was her sister's enthusiastic assurance, that she almost involuntarily caught a gleam of hope; but it instantly faded away.

"Ah, Jeanie! the king and queen live in London, a thousand miles from this—far ayont the saut sea; I'll be gane before ye win there."

"You are mistaen," said Jeanie; "it is no sae far, and they go to it by land; I learned something about thae things from Reuben Butler."

"Ah, Jeanie! ye never learned ony thing but what was gude frae the folk ye keepit company wi'; but I— but I"—she wrung her hands, and wept bitterly.

"Dinna think on that now," said Jeanie; "there will be time for that if the present space be redeemed. Fare ye weel. Unless I die by the road, I will see the king's face that gies grace— O, sir" (to Ratcliffe), "be kind to her—She ne'er ken'd what it was to need a stranger's kindness till now.—Fareweel—fareweel, Effie! —Dinna speak to me—I maunna greet now—my head's ower dizzy already!"

She tore herself from her sister's arms, and left the cell. Ratcliffe followed her, and beckoned her into a small room. She obeyed his signal, but not without trembling.

"What's the fule thing shaking for?" said he; "I mean nothing but civility to you. D—n me, I respect you, and I can't help it. You have so much spunk, that, d—n me, but I think there's some chance of your carrying the day. But you must not go to the king till you have made some friend; try the Duke—try MacCallummore; he's Scotland's friend—I ken that the great folks dinna muckle like him—but they fear him, and that will serve your purpose as weel. D'ye ken naebody wad gie ye a letter to him?"

"Duke of Argyle!" said Jeanie, recollecting herself suddenly—"What was he to that Argyle that suffered in my father's time—in the persecution?"

"His son or grandson, I'm thinking," said Ratcliffe; "but what o' that?"

"Thank God!" said Jeanie, devoutly clasping her hands.

"You whigs are aye thanking God for something," said the ruffian. "But hark ye, hinny, I'll tell ye a secret. Ye may meet wi' rough customers on the Border, or in the Midland, afore ye get to Lunnon. Now, deil ane o' them will touch an acquaintance o' Daddie Ratton's; for though I am retired frae public practice, yet they ken I can do a gude or an ill turn yet— and deil a gude fellow that has been but a twelvemonth on the lay, be he ruffler or padder, but he knows my gybe * as well as the jark † of e'er a queer cuffin ‡ in England—and there's rogues latin for you."

It was, indeed, totally unintelligible to Jeanie Deans, who was only impatient to escape from him. He hastily scrawled a line or two on a dirty piece of paper, and said to her, as she drew back when he offered it, "Hey!—what the deil—it wunna bite you, my lass—if it does nae gude, it can do nae ill. But I wish you to show it, if you have ony fasherie wi' ony o' St. Nicholas's clerks.

"Alas!" said she, "I do not understand what you mean?"

"I mean if ye fall among thieves, my precious,— that is a Scripture phrase, if ye will hae ane—the bauldest of them will ken a scart o' my guse feather. And now awa wi' ye—and stick to Argyle; if ony body can do the job, it maun be him."

* Pass.   † Seal.   ‡ Justice of Peace.

After casting an anxious look at the grated windows and blackened walls of the old Tolbooth, and another scarce less anxious at the hospitable lodging of Mrs. Saddletree, Jeanie turned her back on that quarter, and soon after on the city itself. She reached Saint Leonard's Crags without meeting any one whom she knew, which, in the state of her mind, she considered as a great blessing. I must do naething, she thought, as she went along, that can soften or weaken my heart —it's ower weak already, for what I hae to do. I will think and act as firmly as I can, and speak as little.

There was an ancient servant, or rather cottar, of her father's, who had lived under him for many years, and whose fidelity was worthy of full confidence. She sent for this woman, and explaining to her that the circumstances of her family required that she should undertake a journey, which would detain her for some weeks from home, she gave her full instructions concerning the management of the domestic concerns in her absence. With a precision, which, upon reflection, she herself could not help wondering at, she described and detailed the most minute steps which were to be taken, and especially such as were necessary for her father's comfort. "It was probable," she said, "that he would return to St. Leonard's to-morrow; certain that he would return very soon—all must be in order for him. He had enough to distress him, without being fashed about warldly matters."

In the meanwhile she toiled busily, along with May Hettly, to leave nothing unarranged.

It was deep in the night when all these matters
were settled; and when they had partaken of some
food, the first which Jeanie had tasted on that eventful
day, May Hettly, whose usual residence was a cottage
at a little distance from Deans's house, asked her young
mistress, whether she would not permit her to remain
in the house all night? "Ye hae had an awfu' day,"
she said, "and sorrow and fear are but bad companions
in the watches of the night, as I hae heard the gudeman say himsell."

"They are ill companions indeed," said Jeanie;
"but I maun learn to abide their presence, and better
begin in the house than in the field."

She dismissed her aged assistant accordingly,—for
so slight was the gradation in their rank of life that we
can hardly term May a servant,—and proceeded to make
a few preparations for her journey.

The simplicity of her education and country made
these preparations very brief and easy. Her tartan
screen served all the purposes of a riding-habit, and of
an umbrella; a small bundle contained such changes of
linen as were absolutely necessary. Barefooted, as
Sancho says, she had come into the world, and barefooted she proposed to perform her pilgrimage; and her
clean shoes and change of snow-white thread stockings
were to be reserved for special occasions of ceremony.
She was not aware that the English habits of *comfort*
attach an idea of abject misery to the idea of a barefooted traveller; and if the objection of cleanliness had
been made to the practice, she would have been apt to

vindicate herself upon the very frequent ablutions to
which, with Mahometan scrupulosity, a Scottish damsel
of some condition usually subjects herself. Thus far,
therefore, all was well.

From an oaken press or cabinet, in which her father
kept a few old books, and two or three bundles of
papers, besides his ordinary accounts and receipts, she
sought out and extracted from a parcel of notes of ser-
mons, calculations of interest, records of dying speeches
of the martyrs, and the like, one or two documents
which she thought might be of some use to her upon her
mission. But the most important difficulty remained
behind, and it had not occurred to her until that very
evening. It was the want of money; without which it
was impossible she could undertake so distant a journey
as she now meditated.

David Deans, as we have said, was easy, and even
opulent in his circumstances. But his wealth, like that
of the patriarchs of old, consisted in his kine and herds,
and in two or three sums lent out at interest to neighbours or relatives, who, far from being in circumstances
to pay any thing to account of the principal sums,
thought they did all that was incumbent on them
when, with considerable difficulty, they discharged
"the annual rent." To these debtors it would be in
vain, therefore, to apply, even with her father's con-
currence; nor could she hope to obtain such concur-
rence, or assistance in any mode, without such a series
of explanations and debates as she felt might deprive
her totally of the power of taking the step, which,

however daring and hazardous, she felt was absolutely necessary for trying the last chance in favour of her sister. Without departing from filial reverence, Jeanie had an inward conviction that the feelings of her father, however just, and upright, and honourable, were too little in unison with the spirit of the time to admit of his being a good judge of the measures to be adopted in this crisis. Herself more flexible in manner, though no less upright in principle, she felt that to ask his consent to her pilgrimage would be to encounter the risk of drawing down his positive prohibition, and under that she believed her journey could not be blessed in its progress and event. Accordingly, she had determined upon the means by which she might communicate to him her undertaking and its purpose, shortly after her actual departure. But it was impossible to apply to him for money without altering this arrangement, and discussing fully the propriety of her journey; pecuniary assistance from that quarter, therefore, was laid out of the question.

It now occurred to Jeanie that she should have consulted with Mrs. Saddletree on this subject. But, besides the time that must now necessarily be lost in recurring to her assistance, Jeanie internally revolted from it. Her heart acknowledged the goodness of Mrs. Saddletree's general character, and the kind interest she took in their family misfortunes; but still she felt that Mrs. Saddletree was a woman of an ordinary and worldly way of thinking, incapable, from habit and

temperament, of taking a keen or enthusiastic view of
such a resolution as she had formed; and to debate the
point with her, and to rely upon her conviction of its
propriety for the means of carrying it into execution,
would have been gall and wormwood.

Butler, whose assistance she might have been assured
of, was greatly poorer than herself. In these circumstances, she formed a singular resolution for the purpose
of surmounting this difficulty, the execution of which
will form the subject of the next chapter.

NOTES TO VOLUME XI.

———◆———

NOTE A, p. 115. THE OLD TOLBOOTH OF EDINBURGH.

The ancient Tolbooth of Edinburgh, situated as described in chapter VI., was built by the citizens in 1561, and destined for the accommodation of Parliament, as well as of the High Courts of Justice; and at the same time for the confinement of prisoners for debt, or on criminal charges. Since the year 1640, when the present Parliament House was erected, the Tolbooth was occupied as a prison only. Gloomy and dismal as it was, the situation in the centre of the High Street rendered it so particularly well-aired, that when the plague laid waste the city in 1645, it affected none within these melancholy precincts. The Tolbooth was removed, with the mass of buildings in which it was incorporated, in the autumn of the year 1817. At that time the kindness of his old schoolfellow and friend, Robert Johnstone, Esquire, then Dean of Guild of the city, with the liberal acquiescence of the persons who had contracted for the work, procured for the Author of Waverley the stones which composed the gateway, together with the door, and its ponderous fastenings, which he employed in decorating the entrance of his kitchen-court at Abbotsford. "To such base offices may we return." The application of these relics of the Heart of Mid-Lothian to serve as the postern gate to a court of modern offices, may be justly ridiculed as whimsical; but yet it is not without interest that we see the gateway through which so much of the stormy politics of a rude age, and the vice and misery of later times, had found their passage, now occupied in the service of rural economy. Last year, to complete the change, a tom-tit was pleased to build her nest within the lock of the Tolbooth,—a strong temptation to have committed a sonnet, had the author, like Tony Lumpkin, been in a concatenation accordingly.

It is worth mentioning, that an act of beneficence celebrated the demolition of the Heart of Mid-Lothian. A subscription, raised and applied by the worthy Magistrate above-mentioned, procured the manumission of most of the unfortunate debtors confined in the old jail, so that there were few or none transferred to the new place of confinement.

NOTE B, p. 175. CARSPHARN JOHN.

John Semple, called Carspharn John, because minister of the parish in Galloway so called, was a presbyterian clergyman of singular piety and great zeal, of whom Patrick Walker records the following passage : "That night after his wife died, he spent the whole ensuing night in prayer and meditation in his garden. The next morning, one of his elders coming to see him, and lamenting his great loss and want of rest, he replied,—'I declare I have not all night, had one thought of the death of my wife, I have been so taken up in meditating on heavenly things. I have been this night on the banks of Ulai, plucking an apple here and there."— *Walker's Remarkable Passages of the Life and Death of Mr. John Semple.*

NOTE C, p. 189. PETER WALKER.

This personage, whom it would be base ingratitude in the author to pass over without some notice, was by far the most zealous and faithful collector and recorder of the actions and opinions of the Cameronians. He resided, while stationary, at the Bristo Port of Edinburgh, but was by trade an itinerant merchant or pedlar, which profession he seems to have exercised in Ireland as well as Britain. He composed biographical notices of Alexander Peden, John Semple, John Welwood, and Richard Cameron, all ministers of the Cameronian persuasion, to which the last-mentioned member gave the name.

It is from such tracts as these, written in the sense, feeling, and spirit of the sect, and not from the sophisticated narratives of a later period, that the real character of the persecuted class is

to be gathered. Walker writes with a simplicity which sometimes slides into the burlesque, and sometimes attains a tone of
simple pathos, but always expressing the most daring confidence
in his own correctness of creed and sentiments, sometimes with
narrow-minded and disgusting bigotry. His turn for the mar-
vellous was that of his time and sect; but there is little room to
doubt his veracity concerning whatever he quotes on his own
knowledge.   His small tracts now bring a very high price,
especially the earlier and authentic editions.

The tirade against dancing, pronounced by David Deans, is,
as intimated in the text, partly borrowed from Peter Walker.
He notices, as a foul reproach upon the name of Richard Cameron,
that his memory was vituperated "by pipers and fiddlers playing
the Cameronian march—carnal vain springs, which too many
professors of religion dance to; a practice unbecoming the professors of Christianity to dance to any spring, but somewhat
more to this. Whatever," he proceeds, "be the many foul blots
recorded of the saints in Scripture, none of them is charged with
this regular fit of distraction. We find it has been practised by
the wicked and profane, as the dancing at that brutish, base
action of the calf-making; and it had been good for that unhappy
lass, who danced off the head of John the Baptist, that she had
been born a cripple, and never drawn a limb to her. Historians
say, that her sin was written upon her judgment, who some time
thereafter was dancing upon the ice, and it broke, and snapt the
head off her; her head danced above, and her feet beneath.
There is ground to think and conclude, that when the world's
wickedness was great, dancing at their marriages was practised;
but when the heavens above, and the earth beneath, were let
loose upon them with that overflowing flood, their mirth was
soon staid; and when the Lord in holy justice rained fire and
brimstone from heaven upon that wicked people and city Sodom,
enjoying fulness of bread and idleness, their fiddle-strings and
hands went all in a flame; and the whole people in thirty miles
of length, and ten of breadth, as historians say, were all made to
fry in their skins; and at the end, whoever are giving in marriages and dancing when all will go in a flame, they will quickly
change their note.

"I have often wondered thorow my life, how any that ever

know what it was to bow a knee in earnest to pray, durst crook a
hough to fyke and fling at a piper's and fiddler's springs. I bless
the Lord that ordered my lot so in my dancing days, that made
the fear of the bloody rope and bullets to my neck and head, the
pain of boots, thumikens, and irons, cold and hunger, wetness and
weariness, to stop the lightness of my head, and the wantonness
of my feet. What the never-to-be forgotten Man of God, John
Knox, said to Queen Mary, when she gave him that sharp
challenge, which would strike our mean-spirited, tongue-tacked
ministers dumb, for his giving public faithful warning of the
danger of the church and nation, through her marrying the
Dauphine of France, when he left her bubbling and greeting, and
came to an outer court, where her Lady Maries were fyking and
dancing, he said, 'O brave ladies, a brave world, if it would last,
and heaven at the hinder end! But fye upon the knave Death,
that will seize upon those bodies of yours; and where will all your
fiddling and flinging be then?' Dancing being such a common
evil, especially amongst young professors, that all the lovers of
the Lord should hate, has caused me to insist the more upon it,
especially that foolish spring the Cameronian march!"—*Life
and Death of three Famous Worthies, etc., by Peter Walker*,
12mo, p. 59.

It may be here observed, that some of the milder class of
Cameronians made a distinction between the two sexes dancing
separately, and allowed of it as a healthy and not unlawful exercise; but when men and women mingled in sport, it was then
called *promiscuous dancing*, and considered as a scandalous
enormity.

NOTE D, p. 212. MUSCHAT'S CAIRN.

Nichol Muschat, a debauched and profligate wretch, having
conceived a hatred against his wife, entered into a conspiracy with
another brutal libertine and gambler, named Campbell of Burnbank
(repeatedly mentioned in Pennycuick's satirical poems of the
time), by which Campbell undertook to destroy the woman's
character, so as to enable Muschat, on false pretences, to obtain
a divorce from her. The brutal devices to which these worthy
accomplices resorted for that purpose having failed, they endea-

voared to destroy her by administering medicine of a dangerous kind, and in extraordinary quantities.

This purpose also failing, Nichol Muschat, or Muschet, did finally, on the 17th October, 1720, carry his wife under cloud of night to the King's Park, adjacent to what is called the Duke's Walk, near Holyrood Palace, and there took her life by cutting her throat almost quite through, and inflicting other wounds. He pleaded guilty to the indictment, for which he suffered death. His associate, Campbell, was sentenced to transportation for his share in the previous conspiracy. See MacLaurin's Criminal Cases, pages 64 and 738.

In memory, and at the same time execration, of the deed, a *cairn*, or pile of stones long marked the spot. It is now almost totally removed, in consequence of an alteration on the road in that place.

Note E, p. 254. Hangman, or Lockman.

Lockman, so called from the small quantity of meal (Scottice, *lock*) which he was entitled to take out of every boll exposed to market in the city. In Edinburgh the duty has been very long commuted; but in Dumfries the finisher of the law still exercises, or did lately exercise, his privilege, the quantity taken being regulated by a small iron ladle, which he uses as the measure of his perquisite. The expression *lock*, for a small quantity of any readily divisible dry substance, as corn, meal, flax, or the like, is still preserved, not only popularly, but in a legal description, as the *lock* and *gowpen*, or small quantity and handful, payable in thirlage cases, as in-town multure.

Note F, p. 274. The Fairy Boy of Leith.

This legend was in former editions inaccurately said to exist in Baxter's " World of Spirits;" but is, in fact, to be found in " Pandemonium, or the Devil's Cloyster; being a further blow to Modern Sadduceism," by Richard Bovet, Gentleman, 12mo, 1684. The work is inscribed to Dr. Henry More. The story is entitled, " A remarkable passage of one named the Fairy Boy of Leith, in Scotland, given me by my worthy friend Captain George Burton, and attested under his hand;" and is as follows :—

"About fifteen years since, having business that detained me
for some time in Leith, which is near Edenborough, in the kingdom of Scotland, I often met some of my acquaintance at a certain
house there, where we used to drink a glass of wine for our refec-
tion. The woman which kept the honse was of honest reputation
amongst the neighbours, which made me give the more attention
to what she told me one day about a Fairy Boy (as they called
him) who lived about that town. She had given me so strange an
account of him, that I desired her I might see him the first opportunity, which she promised; and not long after, passing that way,
she told me there was the Fairy Boy but a little before I came
by; and casting her eye into the street, said, 'Look you, sir, yonder
he is at play with those other boys,' and designing him to me, I
went, and by smooth words, and a piece of money, got him to
come into the house with me; where, in the presence of divers
people, I demanded of him several astrological questions, which
he answered with great subtility, and through all his discourse
carried it with a cunning much beyond his years, which seemed
not to exceed ten or eleven. He seemed to make a motion like
drumming upon the table with his fingers, upon which I asked
him, whether he could beat a drum, to which he replied, 'Yes,
sir, as well as any man in Scotland; for every Thursday night I
beat all points to a sort of people that use to meet under yon
hill' (pointing to the great hill between Edenborough and Leith).
'How, boy,' quoth I; 'what company have you there?'—'There
are, sir,' said he, 'a great company both of men and women, and
they are entertained with many sorts of music besides my drum;
they have, besides, plenty variety of meats and wine; and many
times we are carried into France or Holland in a night, and return
again; and whilst we are there, we enjoy all the pleasures the
country doth afford.' I demanded of him, how they got under
that hill? To which he replied, 'that there were a great pair of
gates that opened to them, though they were invisible to others,
and that within there were brave large rooms, as well accommodated
as most in Scotland.' I then asked him, how I should know what
he said to be true? upon which he told me he would read my fortune, saying I should have two wives, and that he saw the forms
of them sitting on my shoulders; that both would be very handsome women.

"As he was thus speaking, a woman of the neighbourhood, coming into the room, demanded of him what her fortune should be? He told her that she had two bastards before she was married; which put her in such a rage, that she desired not to hear the rest. The woman of the house told me that all the people in Scotland could not keep him from the rendezvous on Thursday night; upon which, by promising him some more money, I got a promise of him to meet me at the same place, in the afternoon of the Thursday following, and so dismissed him at that time. The boy came again at the place and time appointed, and I had prevailed with some friends to continue with me, if possible, to prevent his moving that night; he was placed between us, and answered many questions, without offering to go from us, until about eleven of the clock, he was got away unperceived of the company; but I suddenly missing him, hasted to the door, and took hold of him, and so returned him into the same room: we all watched him, and on a sudden he was again got out of the doors. I followed him close, and he made a noise in the street as if he had been set upon; but from that time I could never see him.

"GEORGE BURTON."

NOTE G, p. 275.   INTERCOURSE OF THE COVENANTERS WITH THE INVISIBLE WORLD.

The gloomy, dangerous, and constant wanderings of the persecuted sect of Cameronians, naturally led to their entertaining with peculiar credulity the belief, that they were sometimes persecuted, not only by the wrath of men, but by the secret wiles and open terrors of Satan. In fact, a flood could not happen, a horse cast a shoe, or any other the most ordinary interruption thwart a minister's wish to perform service at a particular spot, than the accident was imputed to the immediate agency of fiends. The encounter of Alexander Peden with the Devil in the cave, and that of John Semple with the demon in the ford, are given by Peter Walker, almost in the language of the text.

NOTE H, p. 284.   CHILD MURDER.

The Scottish Statute Book, anno 1690, chapter 21, in consequence of the great increase of the crime of child murder, both

from the temptations to commit the offence and the difficulty of
discovery, enacted a certain set of presumptions, which, in the
absence of direct proof, the jury were directed to receive as evidence of the crime having actually been committed. The circumstances selected for this purpose were, that the woman should
have concealed her situation during the whole period of pregnancy;
that she should not have called for help at her delivery; and
that, combined with these grounds of suspicion, the child should
be either found dead or be altogether missing. Many persons
suffered death during the last century under this severe act.
But during the author's memory a more lenient course was followed, and the female accused under the act, and conscious of no
competent defence, usually lodged a petition to the Court of Justiciary, denying, for form's sake, the tenor of the indictment, but
stating, that as her good name had been destroyed by the charge,
she was willing to submit to sentence of banishment, to which the
crown counsel usually consented. This lenity in practice, and
the comparative infrequency of the crime since the doom of public
ecclesiastical penance has been generally dispensed with, have
led to the abolition of the statute of William and Mary, which is
now replaced by another, imposing banishment in those circumstances in which the crime was formerly capital. This alteration
took place in 1803.

NOTE I, p. 331. CALUMNIATOR OF THE FAIR SEX.

The journal of Graves, a Bow street officer, dispatched to Holland to obtain the surrender of the unfortunate William Brodie,
bears a reflection on the ladies somewhat like that put in the
mouth of the police-officer Sharpitlaw. It had been found difficult
to identify the unhappy criminal; and, when a Scotch gentleman
of respectability had seemed disposed to give evidence on the
point required, his son-in-law, a clergyman in Amsterdam, and
his daughter, were suspected by Graves to have used arguments
with the witness to dissuade him from giving his testimony. On
which subject the journal of the Bow-street officer proceeds thus :
    "Saw then a manifest reluctance in Mr. ——, and had no
doubt the daughter and parson would endeavour to persuade him
to decline troubling himself in the matter, but judged he could

not go back from what he had said to Mr. Rich.—NOTA BENE. *No mischief but a woman or a priest in it*—here both."

NOTE J, p. 347. SIR WILLIAM DICK OF BRAID.

This gentleman formed a striking example of the instability of human prosperity. He was once the wealthiest man of his time in Scotland, a merchant in an extensive line of commerce, and a farmer of the public revenue; insomuch that, about 1640, he estimated his fortun at two hundred thousand pounds sterling. Sir William Dick was a zealous Covenanter; and in the memorable year 1641, he lent the Scottish Convention of Estates one hundred thousand merks at once, and thereby enabled them to support and pay their army, which must otherwise have broken to pieces. He afterwards advanced £20,000 for the service of King Charles during the usurpation; and having, by owning the royal cause, provoked the displeasure of the ruling party, he was fleeced of more money, amounting in all to £65,000 sterling.

Being in this manner reduced to indigence, he went to London to try to recover some part of the sums which had been lent on government security. Instead of receiving any satisfaction, the Scottish Crœsus was thrown into prison, in which he died, 19th December, 1655. It is said his death was hastened by the want of common necessaries. But this statement is somewhat exaggerated, if it be true, as is commonly said, that though he was not supplied with bread, he had plenty of pie-crust, thence called, "Sir William Dick's necessity."

The changes of fortune are commemorated in a folio pamphlet entitled, "The lamentable state of the deceased Sir William Dick." It contains several copper-plates, one representing Sir William on horseback, and attended with guards as Lord Provost of Edinburgh, superintending the unloading of one of his rich argosies. A second exhibiting him as arrested, and in the hands of the bailiffs. A third presents him dead in prison. The tract is esteemed highly valuable by collectors of prints. The only copy I ever saw upon sale was rated at £30.

NOTE K, p. 354. MEETING AT TALLA-LINNS.

This remarkable convocation took place upon 15th June, 1682, and an account of its confused and divisive proceedings may be found in Michael Shield's Faithful Contendings Displayed, Glasgow, 1780, p. 21. It affords a singular and melancholy example how much a metaphysical and polemical spirit had crept in amongst these unhappy sufferers, since, amid so many real injuries which they had to sustain, they were disposed to add disagreement and disunion concerning the character and extent of such as were only imaginary.

Note L, p. 431.   Doomster, or Dempster, of Court.

The name of this officer is equivalent to the pronouncer of doom or sentence. In this comprehensive sense, the Judges of the Isle of Man were called Dempsters. But in Scotland the word was long restricted to the designation of an official person, whose duty it was to recite the sentence after it had been pronounced by the Court, and recorded by the clerk; on which occasion the Dempster legalized it by the words of form, "*And this I pronounce for doom.*" For a length of years, the office, as mentioned in the text, was held *in commendam* with that of the executioner; for when this odious but necessary officer of justice received his appointment, he petitioned the Court of Justiciary to be received as their Dempster, which was granted as a matter of course.

The production of the executioner in open court, and in presence of the wretched criminal, had something in it hideous and disgusting to the more refined feelings of later times. But if an old tradition of the Parliament House of Edinburgh may be trusted, it was the following anecdote which occasioned the disuse of the Dempster's office.

It chanced at one time that the office of public executioner was vacant. There was occasion for some one to act as Dempster, and, considering the party who generally held the office, it is not wonderful that a *locum tenens* was hard to be found. At length, one Hume, who had been sentenced to transportation, for an attempt to burn his own house, was induced to consent that he would pronounce the doom on this occasion. But when brought forth to officiate, instead of repeating the doom to the criminal, Mr. Hume addressed himself to their lordships in a bitter complaint of the injustice of his own sentence. It was in vain that he was interrupted, and reminded of the purpose for which he had come hither. "I ken what ye want of me weel eneugh," said the fellow, "ye want me to be your Dempster; but I am come to be none of your Dempster, I am come to summon you, Lord T—, and you, Lord E—, to answer at the bar of another world for the injustice you have done me in this." In short, Hume had only made a pretext of complying with the proposal, in order to have an opportunity of reviling the Judges to their faces, or giving them, in the phrase of his country, "a sloan." He was hurried off amid the laughter of the audience, but the indecorous scene which had taken place contributed to the abolition of the office of Dempster. The sentence is now read over by the clerk of court, and the formality of pronouncing doom is altogether omitted.

NOTE M, p. 436.   JOHN DUKE OF ARGYLE AND GREENWICH.

This nobleman was very dear to his countrymen, who were justly proud of his military and political talents, and grateful for the ready zeal with which he asserted the rights of his native country. This was never more conspicuous than in the matter of the Porteous Mob, when the Ministers brought in a violent and vindictive bill, for declaring the Lord Provost of Edinburgh incapable of bearing any public office in future, for not foreseeing a disorder which no one foresaw, or interrupting the course of a riot too formidable to endure opposition. The same bill made provision for pulling down the city gates, and abolishing the city guard, —rather a Hibernian mode of enabling them better to keep the peace within burgh in future.

The Duke of Argyle opposed this bill as a cruel, unjust, and fanatical proceeding, and an encroachment upon the privileges of the royal burghs of Scotland, secured to them by the treaty of Union. "In all the proceedings of that time," said his Grace, "the nation of Scotland treated with the English as a free and independent people; and as that treaty, my Lords, had no other guarantee for the due performance of its articles, but the faith and honour of a British Parliament, it would be both unjust and ungenerous, should this House agree to any proceedings that have a tendency to injure it."

Lord Hardwicke, in reply to the Duke of Argyle, seemed to insinuate, that his Grace had taken up the affair in a party point of view, to which the nobleman replied in the spirited language quoted in the text—Lord Hardwicke apologized.   The bill was much modified, and the clauses concerning the dismantling the city, and disbanding the Guard, were departed from.   A fine of £2000 was imposed on the city for the benefit of Porteous's widow. She was contented to accept three-fourths of the sum, the payment of which closed the transaction.   It is remarkable, that, in our day, the Magistrates of Edinburgh have had recourse to both those measures, held in such horror by their predecessors, as necessary steps for the improvement of the city.

It may be here noticed, in explanation of another circumstance mentioned in the text, that there is a tradition in Scotland, that George II., whose irascible temper is said sometimes to have hurried him into expressing his displeasure *par voie du fait*, offered to the Duke of Argyle, in angry audience, some menace of this nature, on which he left the presence in high disdain, and with little ceremony.   Sir Robert Walpole, having met the Duke as he retired, and learning the cause of his resentment and discomposure, endeavoured to reconcile him to what had happened by saying, "Such was his Majesty's way, and that he often took such liberties with himself without meaning any harm."   This did not mend matters in MacCallummore's eyes, who replied, in great disdain, "You will please to remember, Sir Robert, the infinite distance there is betwixt you and me."   Another frequent expression of passion on the part of the same monarch, is alluded to in the old Jacobite song—

> The fire shall get both hat and wig,
>   As oft times they've got a' that.